I0565551

Siblings-Revelations

Other Novels by:

Julie C. Lombard

"Siblings" (2016)

"Siblings-Revival" (2018)

ISBN: 978-0-9971771-3-8

Editor: Brandi Perry-Johnson

Contributing editors: Nancy Erickson & Mary Lombard

Cover credits: Jesse Vaughan & Julie Lombard

Note: An index of character names is listed on the website
JCLProductionarts.com

Dedication To:

**Mom, without your help,
I never would have finished
one novel, much less three.**

Chapter one

Austria: May 5th – 2022

Victoria tucked a strand of red hair back behind her ear and continued to tune the strings of her violin. She looked up, annoyed, as the stage door opened again, and she saw that it was only more loaders there to remove backdrops. She couldn't wait much longer. Soon, it would all be gone and then so would she.

She had waited years for this chance, and this morning she finally received the message that they could meet tonight. He was to send the details.

She looked up again as a man, she didn't recognize, entered. He walked toward her, and her heartbeat quickened.

"Are you Ms. Victoria H?" he asked, looking at her expectantly and then around at the otherwise empty concert hall.

"I am," She answered, noting the package he held out.

"Please sign here," he continued, holding out a pen and wiping the sweat from his brow. "Hot evening. Isn't it?"

He seemed nervous, and that was making Victoria nervous. She took the package, gaging its weight and feel. Papers, she concluded, as she handed back the pen with a curt nod of her head.

"Thanks. Have a good night," he said and turned, but then paused and turned back. She looked up. "I wish I'd been able to make the concert. I've heard the rehearsals passing by. You play beautifully," he said, with a sudden awkwardness.

"Thank you," she replied, wondering why he was still there. "Was there something else?" she asked.

"Actually, I... This is going to sound weird, but the man

who gave me that package to deliver called back and wanted me to ask you a question. I think it must be some kind of joke though, and you look busy, so…"

"Who gave you this?" Victoria asked, indicating the package. "Do you know where they are now?"

"I'm not sure. It sounded like a man. He dropped it at our drive-up window about an hour ago."

"And you said he wanted you to ask me a question?"

"Yah, he said he'd add another fifty to my tip, but he must have been joking. I mean, how would he know if I asked or not? Right?"

"What is the question?"

"Uhm… I really don't think I can."

She watched as his cheeks turned red, then arched an eyebrow at him and asked him to just write it down.

He sighed in relief and handed her a crumpled piece of paper from his pocket.

"Here, I wrote it down when he called, but…"

Her eyebrow arched again as she read the paper.

"Are you sure this is from the same man who dropped off the package?"

"That's who he said he was. Anyway, I'll be going now. He didn't ask for the answer, and I wouldn't know how to get it to him if he had. So, um… Well, goodnight," he finished, turning toward the door.

"Wait!" she called after him. "Just one minute."

"Okay," he said, nervously picking at the skin around his nails, as the loading crew rolled past with a grand piano.

A minute later, Victoria returned and handed him an envelope.

He met her eyes, questioningly. They were an intense green and unreadable.

"This is to thank you for not actually *saying* the words on that paper. I need to leave now," she said, placing her violin in its case and walking away.

He watched her disappear behind the curtains before he left. Back in his car, he opened the envelope to find a hundred Euro note.

Though the night was warm, Victoria couldn't stop shivering. She had to find somewhere safe. She stared at the package on her lap. It terrified her. She was confused too. Could it be the same person? But why? Why send her this package and ask the courier to ask her that question? Did she dare to open the package? There could be instructions for their meeting inside. Yet, she was leery. It didn't make sense. The man she had been in contact with would not have sent that question. Whoever did though, was aware of this package delivery.

She turned to look out the back window of her taxi. Was she being followed? To be certain, she asked the driver to take a detour as she carefully studied traffic behind them.

The car she felt was following them fell back, but just before they reached the flat she was borrowing from her friend Janine, she spotted either it or the same make and model behind them again.

Telling the driver to continue to a nearby coffee shop, just a few buildings down, she exited the taxi. For the next hour she sat sipping coffee and watching through the window.

The vehicle in question seemed to have disappeared, but she was still relieved when she saw Leo, one of the flutists, and his girlfriend Fierrina arrive. She invited them over and sat until closing, pretending to be interested in Fierrina's new line of cosmetics and their search for an apartment in the nearby city of Salzburg.

In the end, she asked the name of their hotel and checked to see if there was another room available. There was. So, instead of chancing being seen going into her friend's apartment, she asked if they would mind giving her a lift to the hotel.

"Don't you need to get some clothes first?" Fierrina asked.

"No, everything in the apartment is soaked and laid out to dry until a plumber can get there in the morning. And then it will all need rewashing," she lied. "I have one change and most of what I need in the bag from my dressing room," she concluded, patting the brown leather bag at her side, which did in fact contain a change of clothing, along with the envelope she had received, her passport, and laptop. She had all she needed to get to the performance scheduled in Vienna on the 13th.

Picking up her bag and her violin, she followed them out to where Leo's car was parked. She scanned the area and kept one eye on the rearview mirror all the way to the hotel but spotted nothing more suspicious.

When she finally checked into the room, she fell across the bed, exhausted. She lay there, staring at the bag for several minutes before she retrieved the package and located her nail file, which she used to carefully slit it open.

On the first page was a note, apologizing that they would be unable to meet. Then there was a list of phone numbers with a note instructing her to use each one only once and only in case of an emergency. Under this page was a thick file with her name.

By dawn, she had read through the entire file. It included a mix of genealogy and genetic biology, x-rays, and diagrams. It also came with a warning. She didn't need to be warned though. She was always looking over her shoulder, biting her tongue, in case the wrong person overheard and cautious of new contacts, lest they activate her trigger before she could detect and somehow deactivate it. At least now she knew, in part, what one of the verbal triggers entailed.

Seattle

Edgar Morgan transferred the tokens to the institute in Paris and slid the crypto wallet back into a keychain. It was the one account the police couldn't track, and even his wife, Suzanna didn't know existed.

It had been over three years since Alice disappeared, he and Suzanna kidnapped, and the discovery of the true goals Meschner pursued. The experiments they had kept hidden for decades could now begin to see the light. Restrictions on genetic engineering in humans had been loosened under the guise of healing terminal disease and preventing another pandemic. In truth, it was more about the vanity of those in power, who wanted to both stay young and in power for as long as medical progress could allow.

The idea of designer children was even public. People could legally decide the gender of their children, and though not to the same extent of the project, influence the growth of certain traits.

They had worked hard, convincing multiple governments to allow broader, less restricted research. Abortions had been legal for a half century already. And despite some diehard pro-life groups, it was often even encouraged in the name of further research to sustain the lives of those deemed more worthy, also known as those with money and political power.

Soon, these would be the only people even allowed to produce offspring. The world needed intelligent, healthy men and women and would be a much better place as soon as the inferiors were bred out.

Eugenics had it right from the beginning, but the time of its acceptance had yet to be realized. The Nazis had given it a bad name, so much so that many believed they had started it. In truth the idea was propagated even before Christ, and it was the good ole USA that started the wheels turning in the late 1800's with forced sterilization of the mentally ill and certain immigrant populations.

Edgar frowned. The current project goals had not been his original intent, but he was convinced, it was now, not only the best, but the only way for the world to progress. The bad genes, including his own, must be annihilated. For this reason, he would allow them to take him.

He looked at Suzanna practicing her serve on the tennis courts beyond the back yard. He wanted to take her with him, but she had grown distant, and he was certain that she would refuse to go.

Southern France

The children took their daily injection from their father and left with their mother back to the schoolroom. Mel beamed with pride as they easily answered questions on the screens in front of them in French, English, Chinese, Russian and Arabic. These were considered the most important for their fluency. Next, would be German, Greek, Korean, Italian and Hindi. Then Japanese, Hebrew, Spanish, Latin, and Vietnamese. They discovered training the brain with five distinct languages at once was most efficient, and so far, they were on track for fluency in all of the above by age five. Followed by the language skills would be math and science, along with defensive training in martial arts. At puberty, the next stage would begin, then the next generation, a fully highbred generation would be born.

Istanbul, Turkey

Walking through the alleyways of the bazaar, Leona watched as two young girls chased each other, ducking in and out from behind the curtains of a shop where a woman, she supposed was their mother, sat sewing colorful cushions.

She wondered about her own sister. What had really happened to Cora? Leona shook her head. She couldn't think about that now. Her whole life, her very existence was part of the plan. She had been stupid though and made many mistakes. The biggest being Nadier. The man was insane, but was she any less insane? She felt like two different people at times. One was the woman, the soldier, she had been trained as. The other was a woman who had let herself fall in love and have a baby. Sebastian wasn't part of the plan. He should have been gotten rid of, but she was too weak. Too weak, both to give him up, or to let herself love him. Instead, she tried to train him, to bring him into the plan, but he had betrayed her.

To Leona the soldier, the strong her, both her sister and son were dead. But to this other entity that lurked inside of her, the weak side of her, the one who had let herself love once, their memory refused to let her go.

It had been three years since she had last seen Sebastian. And in those three years she had fought, and she was winning. She had extracted herself from Nadier and developed her own plan, one that used many of the same resources as the Paris project. Yet, it would take humanity in a vastly different direction.

As she read the ancient texts and talked with the advisors of wisdom, as they were known, she had come to new revelations about the projects. She became aware of the faults and dangerous realities they would create.

Her travels had taken her through Egypt, Israel, Jordan, Iraq, and into Turkey. Soon she would leave to meet with the man she hoped would help her put the final pieces of her plan in place. He would be her resource to the Paris Project, but she would go nowhere near Paris herself, not until she had her own project safely underway.

The Paris2Project lacked balance, and balance was needed to maintain power. Without the balance of powerful and weak, there could only be war with the powerful fighting amongst themselves. No, not all could achieve the power or intelligence that the projects intended, nor could all be allowed to survive. This made it all the more important that she strengthen her resolve and not let emotions have any say. She had no family, and soon she would have no rivals.

Nadier, if not dead already, would soon enough waste away in the cell where she left him. As for his son, well, she knew how to handle Adam. After all, she had known him his whole life. She even knew his triggers. In fact, it was the main reason she had come to the bazaar today. There was a certain spice vendor she heard about, who would finally fulfill her list. There were just two more that she needed to complete the recipe.

Leona smiled at the simplicity of it, the way that each one of the human senses connected and reacted. Meschner had used all the senses to his advantage, manipulating not only the genes to cause increased sensitivity, but he had been utilizing implants since the nineteen sixties. It was possible that she had one. Her last surgical upgrade was just before Ana's arrival.

Leona would have no more. Based on what she had learned over the past three years, surgery would no longer be needed to upgrade. She had discovered more powerful sources, far more powerful, within herself.

Brazil: November 1951

The three men, all in surgical gowns clapped each other on the back as the infant let out her first wail. It was shortly followed by a second wailing infant and then a third. They had succeeded.

Each man took an infant and placed them in an incubator, then affixed the electrodes to their heads, before taking them to the nursery.

Shortly after, they returned to clean up the blood and remnants. There would be no trace left behind.

Switzerland: November- 1990

The leaves blew like tiny ghosts across the field. The field of time. That was all life had become to her since they placed her here. Some days she didn't even know where here was. Those were the good days. The days her memories didn't haunt her. She looked away from the window, startled by her own reflection. When had she started to look old? She wasn't supposed to age, at least not as others. If she had cooperated, she wouldn't have. The wail erupted in her head, like the scream of a poltergeist. She grabbed her head, and someone came from behind and handed her pills with a glass of water. Ten minutes later, she was asleep, with the shadows of leaves dancing like children in her dreams. They danced and then they crumbled.

Austria: May 11ᵗʰ –2022

The sun was casting its final hour of light across the vase of pink and yellow tulips as Claire laid the place settings and looked at the time. She jumped when she heard a crash come from the kitchen, but breathed a sigh of relief when, Rubix, the three-legged spaniel, her daughter Rosie had insisted on adopting, made his way to her and looked up with eyes that said, "I'm sorry."

Claire looked in the kitchen and watched in dismay as, Trek, their Husky, a retired sled dog, chewed on the leg of lamb that had fallen to the floor.

It was too late to save dinner, so she just rolled her eyes, took the bone from Trek and gave some to each dog. Then she wrapped the rest and put it in the refrigerator with a label "For dogs".

She pulled out a frozen lasagna and turned almost tripping over the dogs who lay sprawled on the floor. They didn't move.

"Trek? Rubix?" she said, nudging them with her foot as a sense of panic ensued. She grabbed a knife from the counter and looked at the clock. Rosie should have been back by now.

"Put the knife down Claire. No one wants to hurt you," she heard the voice behind her say, as she felt the needle prick her shoulder.

How had they found her? "What do you want?" she whispered, as she was gently lowered into a chair.

Rosie hid on the floor of the truck's cab as she listened to footsteps crunching over the gravel drive. They sounded heavier. She thought she knew why but didn't dare to look.

She had taken an earlier bus and then the path through the woods at the back of the house, enjoying the spring sun and almost not seeing the large, white, battery powered cargo van slowly and silently pull off the road at the end of their drive. Ducking behind some bushes, Rosie watched two figures, clad in ski masks and hoodies, enter the house.

She wanted to call out and warn her mother, but she knew better. While she could now walk normally, she couldn't yet run, much less out run or overpower two people, who quite likely possessed strength far superior to the average. No, her only hope was to use her head.

Due to a curve in the road, the van was parked so that it had a clear view of the bus stop, but it would not be seen until the passenger was almost across the road. She knew they would wait to see if she got off the next bus. So, she lay still for over an hour, until she heard the bus come and go.

She had heard footsteps going to and from the house again, and someone had even tried the door of the truck where she hid, but it was locked and she was well hidden under the front bench seat, with a blanket on the seat hanging down in front of her. It was one of the hiding places they had arranged for exactly this possibility, and the truck was stocked with bottled waters, non-perishable foods, thermal sleeping bags, money, and a cell phone with one number programmed in; Magdeline Anglistan.

Claire refused to trust anyone else, and Magdeline's number was not to her phone but to the number on the SIM of her tablet, where a text only message could be sent.

Austria

Magdeline and Soren strolled through the park as their boys played tag, running in and out among the oak trees. The day was perfect. They had taken the boys on their first camping trip and Soren had taught them how to fish. To all appearances they were a happy, normal young family and they would do everything in their power to keep it that way for the boys.

Both Magdeline and Soren had given up their jobs in Switzerland. Magdeline now ran a private lab in Vienna and Soren took a position he had been offered at the (IMP) Institute of Molecular Pathology.

Spencer came flying around and crashed into a pile of leaves, his brothers following to fall on top of him. Soren picked up the two, carrying one in each arm and spinning them around as Spencer ran in circles around them, laughing as they all stumbled around dizzily.

Magdeline looked on smiling. She was checking an alert on the tablet she carried in her purse.

Soren watched, as her smile turn to concern. Kneeling down, so that one boy could ride on his shoulders, he took

the other two by the hand, and they made their way over to
Magdeline.

"Mommy!"

"Mommy!"

"Mommy!"

The boys all chorused.

"I think it's time for dinner. When we get back you can all
go play on the playground while daddy and I fix the food."

After dinner, when the boys were down for the night,
Soren and Magdeline discussed how they would get to
Rosie. They were only an hour away from where Claire and
Rosie had been placed. It was supposed to be a safe house,
not an official one, but Shane made payments to an agent
for it through monies that, Suzanna Morgan, Claire's sister
agreed to give him. For three years all had been quiet.

"I knew she was always worried, but what reason could
they possibly have to go after them? All they wanted was to
be left in peace," Magdeline said.

"Yes, but, remember Jonathan's letter. I think that they
may simply know too much to be left alone. And if they
know how far Rosie has come in her recovery..."

"They'll want her as a lab rat to study. Yet, they leave us
alone, thank God, but for how long?" Magdeline wondered,
"Until they think we're a threat, or they see the boys as
potential?"

"They won't. Our boys are normal," Soren tried to
reassure her.

"No, they're not, because I'm not. I feel like we're being
watched sometimes."

"We probably are," Soren admitted, "but by who? I've
checked everyone, and I can't see a connection to anyone at
the institute, and your lab is independent. Your assistants
are all students you handpicked. I think the only way we

are being watched is from a distance. I think, as long as we don't do anything to set off alarms, they'll leave us alone."

"And how do you propose we help Rosie without setting off those alarms? We can't just leave her."

"Can she drive the truck?"

"I'll ask," Magdeline said, typing in a message to Rosie.

A minute later, Rosie replied.

"She said yes," Magdeline read.

"Is the tank full?" asked Soren.

"Yes. What are you thinking? Soren?"

"I'm thinking a lot of things, but mostly how to keep you and our boys safe. I know we have to help Rosie. A part of me was just hoping, that after three years of peace, maybe it really was over."

"You know as well as I do that it's too big for that."

"She'll need to get to somewhere highly populated, where she'd be hard to follow."

"It also has to be somewhere we can get her out of without anything looking suspicious."

"Ask her if she can manage in the truck until Friday afternoon? I need to make a call."

Magdeline sent the text, trying to reassure Rosie, while Soren was on his phone. Magdeline looked up, as he hung up.

"Have her meet us at the concert hall tomorrow. The doors open at 18:00. Here's the address. She'll need to go into the underground garage. Then she can just follow the crowd up to the lobby. There will be a ticket waiting for her under Jenkins, that's Allister's niece."

"The one you got the tickets through at work?"

"Exactly. I told him we had a family member who was in town unexpectedly and asked if there was a way to get another ticket. It's been sold out for weeks, so once she gets in, it won't be easy for anyone to follow. We should get there by 18:30."

"If someone else sees her though? I mean, she looks so much like me," Magdeline said, concerned. "And what is she supposed to wear? I doubt she has a nice dress in the truck."

"Okay. So, tell her that if she has a hat, to put her hair up and wear it. She must have a bag of some sort that she can say she has her dress in. Then she can ask where the restrooms are and immediately go there to wait in a stall until we arrive, and you can meet her with a dress and a disguise."

"Have I told you lately that I love the way your mind works?" Magdeline asked Soren, as she typed to Rosie.

Chapter 2

Greece: May 11- 12th

Alice, now known as Sandra, looked in the mirror. It had started last week, the odd feelings of fatigue, and now there were visible dark circles under her eyes. And her eyes, oh her eyes, they had been so sensitive lately. It was almost as it had been right after her escape back in Canada, over three years before.

She had not had any need of medication or suffered any physical problems since the operation in Paris. But that also had been three years ago. Now she looked at the scratch she received the day before, when her vision blurred, and she bumped a Myrrh tree while leading a tour group up the trail to St. Stephen's Nunnery at Meteora. It was still clearly visible.

She needed to talk to Jonathan, or Sherman, as he was now called. She was scared, though no longer of him, but of what would happen if he were unable to help her on his own. She couldn't go to a regular doctor because she wasn't a regular human. At times she still doubted her humanity at all. That was the one plus. At least now she felt more human.

She lay down, closed her eyes, and fell, almost immediately into a deep sleep.

***

Nick and Sophie had arrived in Athens three days before. Their actual anniversary had been in March. However, they had needed to wait and make reservations for May, in part due to seasonal closures of March in that region and the Easter holidays of April, which, in the Greek Orthodox church, were celebrated a week later and had left everything in the area fully booked.

They celebrated with a candlelight dinner on the balcony of their hotel, in the Plaka, under the shadow of the Acropolis.

Today was the last day before their tour of Meteora and discovering the identity of the guides they had seen in the photos. The more Sophie looked at the one photo, the more certain she felt it must be Alice.

What would they say? What could they say after three years? And who was the man? Was it one of the brothers that had been on the island with Alice's parents or was it another look-alike?

She had spotted them in photos of Nick's parents' vacation as they discussed what to do for their anniversary, and now here they were, about to learn something that could disrupt their whole lives again, just as it had three years before.

Sophie smiled at Nick, still sleeping soundly, and remembered that it was those same circumstances, which had brought them together. As horrible and chaotic as it had been, she wouldn't trade her husband and beautiful son for anything. She couldn't let go of the hope though, that somehow, she could have her whole family back together again.

She wasn't even certain where her parents were anymore. She knew that they had gone to France to protect her and with the help of her cousins, Amber and Pollina, one who was a teenage mirror image of herself, she had discovered a lot about both her parents and aunt Josephine's involvement.

For three years, Sophie and Nick had enjoyed a nearly normal life, but the questions were always just under the surface, and now she prayed that at least the question of what had become of Alice would be answered.

The train to Meteora, or rather Kalampaka, which hosted the nearest station, left at 8:20 in the morning. Once Nick and Sophie arrived, they would have lunch while they waited to meet their guide, who they hoped would prove to be Alice, for the nunnery tour at 15:00.

They sipped retsina and nibbled on a plate of local cheese and olives while the other tourists explored the nearby shops.

"What if she runs?" Sophie asked.

"What if it's not even her?" Nick answered with another question.

"You mean if she's another one," Sophie clarified.

"We've been over all this before Soph. All we can do is wait and see. You can't know how she'll react. You never could."

"I should have dyed my hair. It will be too obvious, to everyone. Why didn't I at least dye my hair?"

"Here," Nick said, handing Sophie her hat and sunglasses from their day pack.

"Thank you. I don't know why I'm suddenly so nervous. I know we've been over all of this before, but..." Sophie stopped and turned to look toward the tall natural outcroppings of stone upon which the nunnery and monasteries had been built half a millennia before. "I can feel her. I know it's her Nick," Sophie said, standing and looking around.

"What is it? What's wrong Soph?" Nick asked, suddenly concerned.

"It's the same feeling I had in New York. Something's wrong. Last time I felt like this, Jack and I found her passed out in Central Park."

"Come sit down and finish your drink. There are only a few minutes until the guide should be here. Until then, come sit with me," Nick said, putting his arm around her shoulder and steering her gently back to the table. "You look white as a sheet Soph."

"I'm fine. Alice isn't. We have to find her."

"She may find us in a few minutes."

Sophie shook her head.

"Here," Nick said, handing her the rest of her wine, as he looked toward the others of the group, who were starting to gather around the shuttle they had taken from the train. He looked at his watch. "We should probably rejoin the rest of the group."

Sophie nodded and stood. At least she looked a little steadier and some color was back in her cheeks, Nick thought. Holding hands, they walked toward the group. That was when Sophie spotted him and squeezed Nick's hand so hard, he had to shake free. He followed her gaze as it landed on the man wearing a guide jacket and coming towards their group. Sophie pulled her hat down and moved behind Nick.

It was hard for Nick to tell at first, and if not for Sophie, he may not have known. The guide wore a thick beard and his hair had grown enough for a ponytail. The look on Sophie's face left no doubt. It was one of the brothers, but which one? Could he even be a fifth?

The guide introduced himself as Sherman and apologized that his partner would not be able to join him today. "Sandra is the real pro, especially when it comes to the nunnery. Unfortunately, she is under the weather today, so I hope you will forgive any fumbles I may make," he continued.

Sophie whispered in Nick's ear. "I knew there was something wrong. Sandra must be Alice."

Sweden

Carl looked through the microscope and then over to the two hospital beds where two, very opposite men, his mother's husband, Oscar, and Carl's brother, Richter, were connected by a menagerie of colored tubing and drips. A machine between them rotated, separating out and transferring elements of blood from one to the other, while another measured the levels of bacterium, separating out the beneficial from the deadly. A third machine was all but invisible, and it was currently at work generating new stem cells, developed through those extracted from Oscar's son, Ivan's, children.

Carl stared at his brother. He could hardly believe all that had transpired over the past three years. He thought of the files again that he had discovered in Malmo. Once he had learned the full genetic codes of all his siblings, everything about his life had become so much clearer. The donor DNA, gene manipulations and psychological programming. He understood himself so much better, and that understanding increased his control, but not in the way daddy Meschner had intended.

He had learned much from his birth mother and brother Ivan. They taught him that there was a power far greater than anything within the projects or anything that they could ever hope to accomplish. Love.

It reminded him of the Morgans, though he doubted that even their original goals had much to do with love. If they did, why had Edgar Morgan so quickly seemed to give up on finding Alice? No, Edgar Morgan may not have originally agreed with Meschner's intents and techniques, but the more Carl had learned about his other father, the less he wanted to be like either one of them.

Neither had ever been happy in their power. In fact, Carl was hard pressed to even imagine either face with a smile. Carl, on the other hand, considered himself relatively happy. The one thing he still wished for in life, was someone to share it with.

An image of his last day at the chateau in France, as he painted Laura, entered his mind. He wished he could go back in time and have the control he now had. He felt it was

too late, but he wanted to apologize to her. It was
something that he had discussed recently with both his
mother and Ivan. They told him that he had shown them it
was never too late. If they could have the hope of Oscar's
recovery, then he should have the hope of Laura's
forgiveness.

It was agreed that it would not be safe for him to return
to France and that his presence was also still critical to
supervise Oscar's recovery. Sending a letter would not be
wise either, as they wanted to be careful to prevent anyone
related to the project possibly tracing him to Sweden,
much less discovering his impersonation of Jonathan and
the whereabouts of Richter. The only ones who knew that
he was not Jonathan were family. None of the other
medical technicians, lab assistants or other workers could
know, except Chantel, who had been a necessary exception.

They had come up with a way for Carl to reach Laura
through Chantel, the nurse whose family Carl had brought
from Paris. The painting he was working on, next to his
desk, was what kept that last day with Laura close in his
mind. And Chantel would deliver it personally. Having a
photographic memory could be a curse in some ways, but a
blessing in others, he thought, as he looked at the nearly
completed painting.

Right now, he needed to focus on other things. He would
come back to the painting this evening. Now, he needed to
take the chopper and visit the University in Uppsala, where
a professor of genetics was speaking. This particular
professor was tied to the projects in China, which Carl
knew little about, and he was curious to hear what
Madame Ling had to say.

***

Richter's senses felt numbed and hypersensitive at the
same time. Images, sights, sounds and smells seemed to be

assaulting him, yet he could not even open his eyes or reach out to push any of it away from him. He wanted to kill his brother. How could Carl betray him, betray the family like this? There had to be some way to stop him.

Switzerland

Ana stared toward the church in the town below, as the toll of bells echoed. She had lost him. Sebastian was entering seminary next week. She wiped angrily at her eyes to prevent the tears, took a deep breath and turned to go back into the dining hall.

She was helping in the restaurant and working as a part time tennis instructor at a local lodge, where she also took skiing lessons from the owner's daughter, Aida.

Unlike most people she met, Ana liked Aida immediately and even with the fifteen-year age difference, they found themselves connecting.

"It will be okay, eventually," Aida said, as Ana entered the dining hall, and they began to prepare the tables.

Ana tried to smile as they laid the blue and white checkered table clothes and she asked, "Which one of us are you trying to convince?"

Seattle

Shane sat across from Edgar Morgan. They were discussing the latest genetic test of the twins.

The past three years had been so up and down for Shane and his wife Patricia that there were times he wished... He didn't really know. Was there a solution? He had to believe there was, or he would lose Patty again.

He adored Daniel, who had experienced the same initial growth spurt as his brother, Kenneth, but Daniel's growth seemed to taper off after their second birthday. Daniel always seemed to have a smile for Shane, giggling at the faces Shane made, and on the playground, he made quick friends. It was awkward, as at only three years, he was the size of a kindergartener. Fortunately, his intelligence matched or even surpassed this age. So, not knowing what else to do, Shane passed Daniel off as a five-year old.

Daniel had fit in wonderfully, and just last week they attended a birthday party filled with five and six-year-old children. Shane was proud of the little boy he called his son.

Kenneth on the other hand was another problem, in more ways than one. And this was what was putting a strain on not just their marriage, but on Shane's sanity.

Not only was Kenneth still growing at an alarming rate, he had nearly two inches on Daniel, but he was also extremely aggressive. He was never aggressive in front of Patty though. To her, he was the angel of the two. She felt bad because of the muscle aches and pains he frequently broke into tears over. She doted on him, and he seemed to almost worship her. Kenneth would listen in rapt attention as Patty talked about anything, and he was always trying to impress her with how well he could read already. Sometimes he would even take over the bedtime story reading. She would smile in awe, tuck him in with a kiss to his forehead, and he would feign sleep.

She would never believe that he was like a devil in disguise every time she turned away. Instead of believing that he was faking sleep, and even how much pain he claimed to be in, Patty believed that Daniel, or Shane was to blame for waking Kenneth nearly every night. She thought Shane was unsympathetic. After all, despite appearances, he was only an innocent three-year old.

Shane had tried putting cameras in the room to catch Kenneth in action, but for three nights Kenneth had behaved, and after that, Patty had removed them.

There were times when she had become nearly irate in defending Kenneth against both Shane and Daniel's accusations. Even when another parent accused Kenneth of biting her son, Patty had refused to believe it.

Most recently, she had taken to letting Kenneth sleep in bed with her. The boy had, Shane believed purposely, kicked him several times in the groin, and one night, Shane had woken to find Kenneth raised on his arms glaring down at him. Shane had rolled away, and Kenneth let out a wail, accusing Shane of scratching him. When Patty saw the marks, Shane was sure were self-inflicted on Kenneth's arm, she had been the one glaring at Shane.

Since then, Kenneth had slept with Patty, and Shane was relegated to a cot in the boy's room with Daniel.

Shane had thought about discussing the aggression with Magdeline, but she and Patty had become close, and he didn't want to risk further strain on his marriage. So, instead, he was talking to one of the founding foes of this whole madness, Edgar Morgan.

Edgar smiled as he read the reports, and it was all Shane could do not to lunge across the coffee table and backhand the smile off his face. He could do it now. Shane had left the Seattle police to work as a private investigator.

"Well?" Shane asked, and Edgar took on a more serious expression.

"I may be able to help slow his growth."

"Is it legal?" Shane asked.

"Not in this country. The FDA here is only fast to approve things that are financially beneficial to it. This particular substance is... Well, I prefer to keep its origin to myself."

"What about his aggression? Daniel's not aggressive."

"You must realize, they have very different genetic codes," Edgar paused. "You also know that Dr. Meschener's goals for the project were far from altruistic. He always was a power monger." Edgar grinned. "I digress. I was thinking of our younger days. Getting old is tough sometimes, especially when it is one of the things we planned to cure."

"Cure? Cure old age by developing children who age in double time?"

"The acceleration is only until cellular maturity. I would assume that they are programmed to only age unto a certain genetically desirable point, and then the aging all but stops. Alice was never meant to grow old, well, at least not as we do."

"And what exactly does that mean?"

"Call it the Methuselah concept. With Alice, we managed to slow the deterioration of mature cells and speed the repair of damage. At least that was the idea. Now that she's vanished and has no, how should I say, access to regular maintenance? God only knows what will happen to her."

"You make your daughter sound like a car engine, in need of regular tune ups."

"We all need regular tune ups, Mr. McDougle. But we've digressed again. You are here to find out about your son. Is there anything I can do to stop Kenneth's aggression? Well, is there anything you think you could have done to stop the aggressive behavior of any of the violent criminals you've dealt with over the years?"

Shane thought for a moment. "Some of them," he answered, not liking where he felt this going.

"Only some?" Edgar asked. "Why not all?"

"Because some of them just seem to be bad seeds, which is what you think Kenneth is."

"That depends on your definition of bad. Some would call him simply the stronger. Without knowing his full genetic code, though, I have no way of really saying. Perhaps…"

"Perhaps he was programmed to be evil. That is what you were about to say, isn't it?"

"Now we're into the nature verses nurture question, and perhaps that was part of Meschener's whole experiment with Patricia, to have twins programmed as opposites in nature. You might call it a Cain and Able experiment. What you also have to remember, is that they were intended to be raised in a controlled environment, and not by you."

"Thanks for your input," Shane said, rising to leave.

"If only I had access to Meschener's files, to know whose DNA and which genes he chose, perhaps I could be of more help," Edgar said, rising and walking to the door with Shane. "Is it true, you're moving soon?"

"How did you know about that?"

"I overheard. I was going into the kitchen for a coffee," he continued at the look on Shane's face. "Detective Yarnok was here for her regular check in, thinly disguised I may add, as playing tennis with Suzanna."

"Yarnok likes tennis, besides, we agreed, none of us wanted to air this publicly. Continue, you were saying you overheard, Lidia, I mean detective Yarnok."

"Yes, she was on the phone, with you I assumed. Don't worry. She didn't say the address. I was simply curious if I understood correctly that you were moving. Not too far away, I hope. Too drastic of a change could make things more stressful on the boys."

"No. I won't be far. Seattle, as I'm sure you know, isn't what it used to be."

"Yes, it's a shame. I'm considering moving Morgan's offices as well. Charice said there was a homeless man camped out in the vestibule last week. Not exactly the image we want for our clients."

"I'm sure. How is Charice?" Shane asked, as they walked to his car. Charice, Mr. Morgan's secretary, had been very helpful in the original investigation when the Morgans had been kidnapped and Alice originally disappeared three years before, and Shane wanted to leave on friendlier terms than he felt. Animosity could hardly help and could be, God forbid, dangerous for Lidia's future visits.

"She's doing well. Marriage seems to agree with her," Edgar replied, with a smile that Shane couldn't quite define on his face.

"That's good. I guess I should give her a call myself. I haven't seen her or Max since the wedding. Tell Suzanna I said hello," Shane concluded.

"I will," Edgar replied, and waved as Shane pulled out of the drive.

Edgar looked across at the tennis court, where Suzanna was just saying goodbye to a friend. He went to the kitchen and took a bottle of Pinot Grigio from the cooler, along with two glasses and some cheese and crackers. It was a nice day for a picnic. A good day to say goodbye.

Chapter 3

Greece: May 13ᵗʰ

During the tour, the day before, Nick left Sophie to look at some of the handmade lace products sold at the nunnery's gift shop, while he went to find Sherman. He found the guide sitting in the garden, enjoying a coffee with a friar and several cats.

He stood, observing them for a while. Nick could hardly garner an image of this man as some evil entity. Perhaps he wasn't to be feared. He wondered how best to approach a conversation that could help them find Alice.

"You are welcome to join us," Sherman said, turning with a smile. He had known this would happen at some point and had been all too aware of Sophie's presence. No matter what she did to hide her identity, Sherman would always recognize any of... his sisters? He had never been quite certain what to call them. The fact was all offspring of the projects were siblings to some varying degree. His father, at least the one who raised him, had often referred to the *'family'*, which now felt more cult-like than anything.

He had hoped to permanently remove himself from them all, some for his own safety and others for theirs. Then Alice appeared, and he knew that wasn't possible. The past three years had been a kind of vacation for them both, but like all vacations, this one too would come to an end. He knew Alice was ill, so in a way, he was relieved. He knew who Nick was from photos Alice had shown him online, and he hoped that somehow, together, they could help Alice and protect her at the same time.

The friar rose and went to get another coffee. Sherman nodded and thanked him as Nick approached.

"I hope you like strong coffee. Please, come sit. We need to talk, Nick, about Alice."

"You know who I am."

"She's shown me pictures. And Sophie, I'd recognize anywhere. I don't really know where to start," Sherman said, as the friar returned with more coffee.

Nick looked at the friar and thanked him. The friar nodded in reply and sat to finish his own coffee.

"He doesn't speak English. You can speak freely," Sherman continued.

"Where is Alice?"

"I'll take you both to her after the tour," he said, and turned to say a few words in Greek to the friar. "Brother Archibald will be coming as well."

"Why?" asked Nick, as he took a sip of the coffee.

"The friar is also a doctor. And Sandra, Alice, hasn't been well. For obvious reasons, a regular doctor is out of the question."

"What's happened to her?"

"I don't know, but I believe it has to do with the operations she underwent in Paris. Alice had, what would have been considered, an upgrade. She escaped before it was complete, and she never had any follow up."

"Who are you?" Sophie asked, as she came up behind them.

Sherman took a deep breath. "I worked hard to make a new life here. I have no desire to have anything to do with my father's projects. That includes my brothers, who I would prefer to think me dead. Alice will explain more. She knows me well and I think it's better if she explains who I am. Please," he said, looking at his watch, "It's time to meet at the shuttle."

They had followed Sherman and the friar to Alice's apartment and found her barely conscious. The room was dark, but when they turned on the light, she moaned and clenched her eyes shut.

"She's been having sensitivity to light as well as blurred

vision. She told me that it was your father, Sophie, who helped her escape in Paris."

Sophie eyed Sherman, suspiciously, as she placed a cool cloth on Alice's forehead.

"Sherman," Alice moaned.

"I'm here. Brother Archibald is in the kitchen. And Sandra, Sophie and Nick are here too."

Alice tensed. She had thought she was hallucinating, but Sophie was here, and Nick. She couldn't help but wonder about Jack. "Jack?"

Sophie glanced at Nick, then spoke to Alice. "Jack's not with us, Alice, but I'm here and Nick. We'll take care of you."

Alice didn't realize she had said his name out loud, and she didn't expect to feel the twinge in her heart when she heard he wasn't there. She told herself she should be glad. Part of the reason she had vanished was to protect him, to protect Sophie and Nick as well, but now Sophie was here, and she could barely stand to open her eyes. She knew the numbers were back. She could feel it, see it even when she squeezed her eyes tightly. And she had a fever. They could track her now.

"Ice. On my head, I need ice." Alice stammered. "The tracker. They'll find us."

"What is she talking about?" Nick asked, as Brother Archibald returned with a mixture of herbs.

"Ice," Alice said again, as Sophie applied more cool water and looked at Sherman.

"The herbs will help bring the fever down and relax her," Sherman said, and Sophie helped raise Alice into a sitting position while Brother Archibald administered the herbs. "As for the ice," Sherman continued, "They implanted a tracker in her forehead. She escaped Paris by disabling it with ice. There's no way for me to know if it's reactivated."

"Why didn't you help her and remove it!" Sophie snapped.

"Because it's neurologically woven into her. From what I recall of the new trackers at the time, they have two main sensors. One is imbedded into the brainstem, the other into the frontal lobe. The one in the frontal lobe is the tracker and is connected to the optic nerve, which connects to the occipital lobe, controlling visual processing. There are also micro motes implanted in her corneas."

"Micro what?" Sophie asked.

"Minicomputers," Nick said. "They're smaller than a grain of sand. They were created in Michigan, I believe, back in 2018."

"Very good, Nick," Sherman answered. "Everything they implanted was what they called an upgrade. They intended her to be a hybrid of human and artificial intelligence."

"I just want to be human," Alice whispered.

"You are human," Sophie tried to soothe, as Brother Archibald returned from the kitchen again with ice packs.

The friar looked concerned as he spoke to Sherman.

"He's concerned that she's worse," Sherman said. "It's obvious that the implanted systems are malfunctioning. To try and put it simply, like any computer, regular upgrades are needed. Even though the one in Alice had been effectively turned off, it's still connected and active to a degree via her body's own electrical impulses and it isn't only affecting her vision anymore.

Brother Archibald pushed Alice's sleeve up to reveal several dark bruises.

"It's started to affect her vital functions, blood flow, her immune system. Her body can't even perform the normal self-repair. Before she would have been on a stringent formula of..."

"I know," Sophie stated. "Anti-rejection drugs and vitamins. What do we do now? How do we help her now? Will the same pills work again?"

"They may help, but no. The only place that I know of that could help her is somewhere in France. I'm assuming they went underground after her escape, but if your father is working with them, then he could..."

"I don't know how to reach my father. Both my parents disappeared, even my aunt is gone because of this, and now," Sophie looked down at Alice and Nick put his arm around her, but she brushed him off and moved to confront Sherman.

"You are responsible for this. If you've really changed, prove it!"

"Have you really never located any of my brothers?"

"No. I just have to keep looking over my shoulder, hoping one of you don't try to take me again."

"Take you?"

"I know I was inferior to Alice, but yes, I was kidnapped and taken to Paris too. I don't know which one of you it was. We don't even know which one you are yet," Sophie almost spit at him.

"Jonathan. I'm, I was, Jonathan." He closed his eyes, sighed, but he knew there was no other choice. "We can take her to Sweden."

"What?" Nick and Sophie asked at once.

"There is another project in Sweden. I don't know who might be there, but it should have the needed facilities. I'll come with you, of course. It will be dangerous."

"Dangerous, for who? Alice is already in danger but it's not really her you're concerned about, it's you. *You*, are who you are worried about," Sophie said.

"Her passport is in the top drawer in the closet." Jonathan continued. "The best way is to get the next train to Athens and catch a flight into Kiruna, Sweden."

Nick was already looking up flights while Sherman, or Jonathan, spoke with Brother Archibald and Sophie tended to Alice.

"The earliest one we can make with the train schedule is tomorrow at 13:45. There are only three seats left though."

Sophie and Nick stared at each other.

"You think I should stay behind, don't you?" Sophie said.

"I think you should take another flight home and, and..."

He didn't need to finish. She knew he was right. There was no need to tell Jonathan about their son, and she knew that no matter how much Alice may need her, Jeremy needed her more, and it would be safer if Nick were the one to go on to Sweden. She didn't want him to go. She couldn't bear the thought of something happening to him.

For now, she would go home to their son, but then... Well, she wasn't exactly certain. She wished she knew how to get in touch with her parents or even her aunt Josephine or her cousins, but even Amber and Pollina had gone silent. She knew it was because of Uncle Simon. It wouldn't have been safe for any of them if he discovered they had been in contact. Sophie had tried their friend's phone that she had contacted them through before, but even that number was disconnected.

Austria

Magdeline dug out the blond wig she had worn to a masquerade and gave it a more stylish trim. Then she added hairpins, makeup, a dress, and a pair of ballet style slippers to her purse, as she knew Rosie would not be able to deal with heals. She could barely close her bag and would have to carry her own pocketbook in her coat pocket.

Soren also picked up a pair of reading glasses at the local drug store on the way back, to complete the look.

The boys hated having to leave the campground, but it had been a good week, and they were excited about being able to stay up late and make popcorn with the babysitter and even more excited when they learned that their mother's cousin would be coming to visit.

Magdeline took a deep breath. This would work. It had to. No one could suspect that Rosie was anyone other than a visiting family member. She prayed as she watched the boys playing in the yard. She wanted them to always be able to play like that, safely.

She had just put on a pot of tea, when her computer dinged that she had a message from Patricia.

Patricia McDougle was, in many ways, much like her. She was a part of the project more from the side, brought in by her father's half- brother, who had been one of the major founders. Patricia had been kidnapped and impregnated via their experiments and had two sons the same age as Magdeline's boys, only Patricia's boys were far from the normal three-year old boys that Magdeline was blessed with.

Patricia had been calling nearly every day, as the boys seemed to be putting a huge strain on her marriage to her husband, Shane, who had been a lead investigator into a case of another woman, whose father was a founder and who had now been missing for over three years, Alice Morgan.

It was Shane that Magdeline really needed to speak with now. Not only was she concerned about things Patricia had told her regarding his relationship with their boys, but he needed to know what had happened with Rosie and Claire.

Magdeline went to her computer. She would tell Patricia that she needed to keep it short, due to preparing to go out, though, she did feel bad, having been away camping for the week. Technically they still could have face timed, but Magdeline had wanted it to just be her, Soren, and their boys, so had claimed they would have no reception. She did a quick calculation of the time difference and decided to call Shane after Rosie was safely home with them, and the boys were asleep.

Things had only deteriorated more between Patricia and Shane, and Magdeline wished that she had better advice. The problem was that she tended to think Patricia was wrong. She understood her desire to defend Kenneth, but not at the expense of Daniel and Shane. She had to be objective, or Patricia would only get more defensive. She had thought of a suggestion but decided to wait and suggest it to Shane when she called him later. Patricia was too emotional right now. So, Magdeline played the role of a sympathetic ear and simply listened for the next hour until it was time to get the boys inside for a nap.

***

Rosie was nervous as she started up the truck. She had only ever practiced on the rural roads and feared the drive into Vienna. She had no license of her own. In fact, she had no identity cards of her own at all. Instead, she had a copy of Magdeline's license to show when needed.

All the way there, she kept one eye on her speed and another in the rearview mirror. Her knuckles were white when she finally found the entrance and pulled into the parking garage. Though she had not noted anyone following her, she didn't like how quiet the garage was. Granted, she was early, having given herself extra time.

Fifteen minutes later, another car entered the garage. Rosie ducked and held her breath until she heard the couple chatting and heard them go through the doors to the elevators. She checked the time and followed them up. She knew she must look a mess. She was thankful to see a lady's room off the lobby. She ducked in and sent a text to Magdeline, who told her to just stay put and promised that she was bringing a wig, so the hair would not matter, and she was also bringing some items to help her clean up.

Rosie took a deep breath and splashed cool water on her face and took some large gulps as well. When she heard another woman enter, she ducked into a stall where she would stay until Magdeline arrived.

They were running late, due to traffic, and pulled into the garage at 18:41. Magdeline hurried into the lady's room.

Unfortunately, it was packed, but she could tell which stall Rosie was in by her shoes and excused herself past the others in line, saying that she was bringing her niece clothes to change into, and they were running late.

"I'm sorry, I'm late. Traffic was terrible," Magdeline said, as Rosie threw her arms around her. "Everything will be okay, Soren is collecting our tickets, but we have to hurry."

Magdeline pulled out the dress and wig, as Rosie undressed and put on the deodorant Magdeline handed her. They didn't have time to bother with pantyhose, and they only had time to dust on some foundation and give quick swipe of lipstick after pinning the wig in place.

They were making the last call for seating, as they hurried out of the restroom and over to Soren, who had waited by the auditorium doors, tickets in hand.

Rosie was moving, as in a trance, letting Magdeline lead. She had only seen Soren once before, briefly when she was in the hospital, and would not have time to be officially introduced until later. What distracted all three of them from the start was the solo violinist, Victoria Hunt, who began the concert. Rosie gripped Magdeline's hand and Magdeline gripped Soren's. Magdeline squeezed Rosie's hand, in attempt to reassure her, and Soren did the same to Magdeline.

***

Victoria had felt off all evening, but she couldn't place why. She had received no further messages and was positive that she had not been followed. She had looked over every name on the reservations for the evening, no one was there alone, and this wasn't an event where strangers walked up and simply purchased tickets at the box office. It had been sold out well in advance. That didn't mean that someone wasn't lurking outside, but she had no intention of giving anyone a chance to catch her alone.

As she finished her solo, Victoria scanned the crowd as they applauded. She could feel their eyes on her, and her breath caught as her eyes locked with those of Magdeline Anglistan.

Forcing herself to smile, she took a bow and turned to walk as calmly as possible, filing in with the others now entering the stage, to her seat in the orchestra. She trembled, trying to focus on the music in front of her. She had known there were others, and surely, she had nothing to fear from this woman, whose face had looked as stunned as she felt. Perhaps this was a good thing. She may even be able to get more answers to the many questions she had been asking herself ever since that day, back in Australia, when life as she'd known it, changed forever.

Finally, she felt herself reconnecting with the music, focusing on the positive possibilities. Focus on the music, she told herself as the tempo increased. She closed her eyes, allowing herself to become one with the music. She knew it so well that she could have easily played blindfolded.

She opened her eyes again only after the set was over. She gazed up to the seats, midway back of the auditorium, on the right, where three now stood empty.

Somewhere

Claire stared, dazedly, as they injected her again.

"We don't want to hurt you, Claire. Just tell us where Rosie is," the man said.

"I don't know."

"Who are her friends?"

"All we have is each other. Please, let me go."

"I'm afraid we can't do that."

The next thing Claire knew, she was being wheeled into a small room with two beds, squeezed into it. She noted a window, at least three floors up and a bath. They lifted her onto one of the beds.

"Try to think Claire. Where could she be?" the man prodded, as he gave her a wink that made her think of a one-eyed demon she'd seen in a painting once. "We'll give it another try soon," he said, and left.

She noted that he hadn't locked the door, but then again, the shots they'd been giving her left her numb below the waist. Even if she knew where she was and which way was out, she wouldn't be able to get very far, dragging herself along with her arms. That was if she could first figure a way out of the straitjacket they'd put her in.

At least she knew that they hadn't found Rosie yet, and Claire prayed that she had managed to reach Magdeline.

Claire looked up as the door opened and another woman was wheeled into the room.

"You have a roommate now, Cora," said a pretty, blond nurse of around twenty-five, as she helped the woman from the wheelchair onto the other bed. "Someone will be back to take you to dinner."

The woman only nodded, and the nurse left. This time Claire both saw and heard the computerized lock.

"Where are we?" Claire asked.

Cora blinked and turned to look out the window. "Who are you?" she asked, staring out at the night sky.

"My name is Claire. Do you know where we are?"

"It doesn't matter. I've tried to escape, and that was long before they had the fancy locks and security cameras."

There was a long pause before Claire asked, "Why are you here?"

"I wouldn't cooperate. They let me live. If you can call it that."

"I have to get out of here," Claire said.

"Not yet," Cora replied, eying Claire with a mix of fear and compassion. They had never put anyone else with her, at least not that she remembered, but there had been so many drugs. What if this woman was being used to spy on her? She shouldn't have said anything. If this woman was a spy... There was one way to know. "What year is it?" Cora asked.

"2022," Claire replied, thinking that this woman was in worse shape than she had ever been in, even when she had been dying of cancer. Cora's hair was a tangled nest, her eyes drooped. Her limbs were held at awkward angles, and as Claire looked closer, she could make out multiple pail scars on her face and arms, some, where it appeared, she had tried to slit her wrists.

A smile slowly spread over Cora's face and suddenly Claire wondered if the woman was demented.

"Why are you here?" Cora asked.

Claire wasn't sure for a moment if she should answer, but when she looked back up at Cora, she noted that instead of derangement, she saw intelligent eyes that were suddenly wide open and probing her own.

"You've noticed the change?" Cora smiled again. "It's taken me a long time to develop, and as soon as the lock beeps I go back to this," Cora said, as her eyes again took on a droopy appearance and she contorted her body back into a slump with her arms and legs stiffly angled. "It's magic," Cora said, as she again straightened her posture and opened her eyes. "If they could see my eyes, they'd know. They still think that I believe it's the nineteen sixties.

That's why I asked for the year. I needed to know that you weren't one of them."

"Nineteen Sixties? Surely you can't have been here that long," Claire said.

"I'm older than I look and look older than I should. Now tell me why you're here and maybe we can help each other."

Austria

"She saw us," Rosie said, as she clung onto Magdeline's arm.

"We knew there were likely more," Magdeline said.

"What do you want to do?" asked Soren.

"You take Rosie back to the house and..."

"I'm not leaving you here alone," Soren said.

"Surely Allister and his family must be questioning why we disappeared."

"I'm sure he is, but he has only seen you briefly in the dark of the auditorium. He may not have noted the resemblance, which would be one less thing to try and explain. I think a better idea is for me to text Allister that our guest felt unwell, and we all go home together."

"But..."

"Let's find out more about her first. The only thing confronting her right now would do is scare her. She's a featured violinist. She can't be that hard to find out more about."

Magdeline started to protest, but Rosie cut her off.

"He's right. Meeting us could put her in danger. We can't do that."

"And I can't argue with both of you," Magdeline replied, as she got in their SUV and Soren drove toward the garage exit. "I'm just wondering what she must be thinking. We know from Jonathan's letter that the projects were meant to be kept secret and that the children were dispersed all over the world, with the intention that they would be under enough control to never meet. I was a loose end, who wasn't supposed to have lived. That's why I grew up with the freedom I did, but her, she travels the world with an orchestra. She's in the public eye more than I ever was, even with my research. How could she not be known to the projects?"

"You're right. They have to know about her and soon we'll find out more about her too, but for tonight, can we deal with one crisis at a time?" Soren asked.

"I'm sorry. You're right, Soren. Rosie, everything will be okay," Magdeline said, squeezing her hand, as Soren merged onto the main avenue.

"Thank you," Rosie replied, returning the squeeze.

When they arrived home, the boys were already in bed. Magdeline motioned to Rosie, who followed her around the back, through the French doors, to their bedroom, while Soren took care of the babysitter.

After the sitter left, Magdeline and Rosie went to check in on the boys. Rosie smiled.

"They've really grown," Rosie said, as they made their way back to the living room. "I'd like to have children."

Magdeline smiled, "It can happen. If you believe, anything is possible."

"I know. Just that fact that I can walk and talk taught me that. I just hope my mom will be with us. She'd love to have grandchildren," Rosie said, as she sat on the sofa, and Soren brought in a tray with coffee and biscuits.

"Are you okay to talk now, or would you rather get some sleep?" Magdeline asked.

"I can't sleep," Rosie replied, taking a chocolate Hob-Nob from the platter. "Why couldn't they just leave us alone?"

"I don't know," Magdeline answered, and she couldn't help but feel a sense of foreboding.

Chapter 4

Austria: May 14th

It took Rosie awhile to orient herself when she woke up. She had been exhausted the night before, and soon after she began to go over all the events of the past days, she had started to yawn. The sofa was incredibly comfortable after the truck, and even though her mind was racing, her body gave into sleep. After the third time she dozed off mid conversation, Magdeline insisted on taking her to the guest room, where she now lay, stretching under the down comforter.

From the light through the windows, she guessed it to be around 8:00 in the morning. She snuggled down under the covers and closed her eyes, not wanting to leave what she thought had to be the most comfortable bed in the world and face the real world.

Her mind kept flipping back and forth between concern for her mother and wondering about the violinist. She couldn't think where they would even start to look for her mother, and even if they found her, how would they get her out and keep her safe?

Rosie had never felt truly safe. Even as a child at the children's home in Canada, she had always felt scrutinized. Strange men had come to examine her, and she had cringed at their touch. She always had a fear that one of them would simply snap her neck over disapproval of her existence. She wasn't supposed to be alive. That had always been made clear.

She could still remember their faces, their looks of contempt when they saw her deformed face. The other children hadn't been much better. Her mother was all she had ever really had, the only person she trusted. She only allowed herself to trust Magdeline because her mother had. Everyone else felt threatening.

Shaking the tangled web of thoughts from her mind, she forced herself out of bed and went into the on-suite bath, where she showered and changed into clean jeans and a sweater, Magdeline had left for her.

The day was over-cast, and she could smell a tempting aroma coming from the kitchen as she made her way down the hall. She also heard giggles. The boys, she realized as she peered around the corner. They were all dressed in different super- hero pajamas, watching cartoons while Soren made crepes.

"It smells delicious," Rosie said.

"Thank you," Soren replied, and the boys turned from the television.

"Aunt Rosie!" came three shouts at once, as they hurried over to greet her.

"Take it easy guys," Soren said.

"Why?" asked Spencer, looking from his dad to Rosie "Will you break?"

"No," she smiled, "I won't break," she said and knelt down.

All three boys hugged her at once.

"Do you like cartoons?" Thadeus asked.

"I think so."

"Come on," Hamilton, who was already back in front of the television, called.

Rosie gave Soren a reassuring smile and allowed herself to be pulled onto the sofa.

"Magdeline will be right back. She's in the garden," Soren said. "Would you like some coffee?"

"I'll wait. Thank you," Rosie said, and tried to listen as Thadeus and Spencer gave dual running dialogs about what had happened and was happening in the cartoon, and

Hamilton, eyes still glued to the screen, made his way onto her lap.

A couple minutes later, the sliding door to the garden opened and Magdeline came in carrying a basket of freshly picked apples.

"Okay, you three, time for breakfast," she said to the boys.

"Wait. The dingo is about to catch super skunk!" Spencer said.

"And the opossum isn't really dead. He's just playing and…" Thadeus added, and then they all broke into laughter as Mr. Opossum tripped the Dingo and Super Skunk raised his tail with a wink. Then suddenly all the boys hurried to the kitchen table and Magdeline handed them each a small apple, which they eagerly bit into.

"That will hold them for about a minute," Magdeline said to Rosie. "How did you sleep?"

"Too good. I didn't want to get up."

"Who's hungry?" Soren asked the boys, seeing they were near to finishing the apples. All three raised their arms in the air and he served them each a crepe, buying Magdeline and Rosie a couple more minutes.

"They're really adorable," Rosie said.

"And they wake up energized," Magdeline added, "Would you like some coffee?"

Rosie smiled. "Please."

Magdeline poured two mugs. Soren already had his at the table with the boys.

"Aunt Rosie! Come have breakfast with us!" Thadeus called.

"Mommy and Aunt Rosie need some time alone. You can play together later," Soren said, and added a crepe to every plate, two to his own. He had also made up two plates and left them on the counter next to condiments for Rosie and Magdeline.

Magdeline motioned at Rosie to the plates, and after adding berries and cream, both women took their crepes and coffee to a small table in Magdeline's office.

"I think we need to talk with Larry Marquet and Shane McDougle," Magdeline said.

"Are you sure we can trust them? Supposedly they were the only ones who knew where my mother and I were."

"I've spent a lot of time talking with Shane and his wife over the past three years. Our children are the same age, and yes, I trust him, and I know that he trusts Marquet."

Rosie was quiet. She took a bite of the crepes and drank some coffee. Magdeline did the same and waited.

"I guess we will need some help. I don't want to put you and your family in danger, but I feel safe knowing that no one else knows where I am." Rosie paused, twisting her fingers. "I just want my mother back," Rosie said, wiping at a tear and taking a long swallow of coffee before she continued. "Shane is on the other side of the planet, so I don't see how he can help. Marquet works with INTERPOL, in France, right?"

"He used to be a liaison officer to them, but he's since gone private and so has Shane, but they still maintain the connections, minus the protocols, which means they can help with less likelihood of anyone else being involved. Shane did tell me that there's one other officer that he used to work with in Seattle, who is now working with Marquet. His name is Dave Asher. They all already know as much as we do, well almost anyway. There was another man, agent Katz, but I don't know if he's still working with them."

"Could he have been the leak? Do you think maybe..."

"No," Magdeline said, firmly. "I don't believe that any of them had anything to do with your mother's kidnapping Rosie. Rosie?"

Rosie looked up from her coffee.

"You have to trust people. I know it's hard, but these are all men who helped you before. They are not part of the projects. I think someone may be afraid of what your mother knows, and maybe it just took them three years to track you."

"What about the violinist from last night? She must be our sister too, but she looks healthy, and she's obviously talented. What if someone was there watching her? Someone was always watching me, and if someone watching her saw us then..." Rosie had started talking rapidly. "What if they followed us and they..."

"Rosie, calm down," Magdeline said, reaching to take Rosie's shaking hands in hers. "We weren't followed, and no one is watching the house. Soren checked the street this morning, and all the cars are those we know. It will be okay, but we need to contact Marquet."

"Right," Rosie said, taking a deep breath to calm herself. She felt as though all the tension of the past few days was suddenly hitting her full force.

"Let's finish our breakfast first," Magdeline said giving Rosie a few minutes to calm before she continued. "We need to agree on what to tell him. Do we just tell him about your mother, or should we tell him about the Victoria, the violinist?"

"I want him to focus on my mother, but what do you think?"

"I think we need to tell him everything, but then there's a part of me that wants to find out more about her myself first. You're right too. I wouldn't want Victoria to distract from finding your mother, and neither one of us want any more people involved."

"Then let's just stick with my mother. We didn't know about Victoria before and if we weren't followed, we can pretend, just until my mother is safe, that we still don't know about her. I feel like mom should hear about her first."

"Okay," Magdeline said, "Let's call Marquet now."

Lyon, France

Larry was with Dave when Magdeline called. They had been going over some interesting research Dave uncovered at the Bibliotheque Nationale de France, (National Library of France), Bibliotheque Genealogique et d'Histoire Sociale de France and the Archives Municipales de Lyon (Archives of Lyon)

Dave was researching his theory about how everyone in the projects seemed to somehow be related. Jonathan's letter to Magdeline had emphasized the term family, but was it all genetic? The term family is often used to bond people in cult situations too. However, they had already discovered numerous literal familial ties that had been shown throughout the known participants in the projects. They were worldwide and even Jonathan had only been able to give a general list, saying that there were many that he did not know the actual locations of, and he was certain that once he disappeared, those he did know would be moved.

Richter was the only brother who was supposedly privy to all the project locations and objectives. For some reason, France seemed to be key. Jonathan said that as far as he understood, the Paris Project was the most advanced and most dangerous, but as they had already discovered, it did indeed vanish before they arrived there, after Sophie had been kidnapped three years before.

Sophie's adoptive parents had also gone underground with the Paris Project, it was believed, to keep her safe as well as possibly infiltrate, but like all the others, they had not been heard from in three years.

In fact, the past three years had been eerily quiet, given all that Jonathan's letter claimed was happening, until now.

Larry, put Magdeline and Rosie on speaker phone so that Dave could hear, and listened carefully to everything they said had happened. Afterwards, they all agreed to call Shane.

Seattle

The apartment was empty of life when Shane arrived home, and a couple of bags Patty had packed for their move were gone. He assumed she had taken them to the new house and called the school to see if Daniel had been picked up. He already knew Kenneth would be with Patty, as she insisted on working with him one on one using online teaching programs.

There was no way that Kenneth could ever go to a regular school. His differences would be too obvious and his aggression too dangerous. There was also no way that Daniel would be safe at home with Kenneth unless Shane was there. So, they had looked at alternatives and discovered none, except to enroll Daniel into school as a kindergartener that they already passed him off as. Daniel was all smiles about this, as he loved to play with other kids, and there would be friends in his class from the playground at the neighborhood park.

That was probably going to be the most difficult thing about this move. Daniel had made actual friends. His growth, unlike Kenneth's, had slowed to a normal rate, and he fit in well at the school.

Finding that Patty had not picked up Daniel, Shane took some boxes to his car and headed to the school to get his son and join Patty and Kenneth at the new house.

Upon arrival, he wondered where Patty's car was. She must have gone to get something for them to eat. They had not brought over any food, and Kenneth was always hungry.

Entering the house, Daniel ran to play in the yard. There was a funny quiver going on inside Shane's nose as he looked around. He could see no signs of Patty or Kenneth. Her bags were not there, and none of the books that she always kept out for Kenneth to study were anywhere in sight. He knew it, even before he finished checking the house. They were gone.

He sat, staring out into the yard where Daniel was playing on the slide Shane had put up just the day before, when his phone rang with Larry Marquet's number.

***

It had been two days, and Suzanna Morgan was at a loss. Though a part of her knew what he had done, another part still refused to believe and half expected him to walk through the door with a bouquet of flowers and an apology.

They had enjoyed a lovely afternoon, with Edgar even volleying with her on the tennis court. It was the most time he had taken out to spend with her, one on one, for far too long. They had grown distant over the past three years, and Suzanna longed to bridge the gaps, and if not as a family with Alice, at least get back the closeness they had shared as a couple.

After their picnic and play on the courts, Suzanna had gone upstairs to shower, while Edgar said he was going to check in on things at the office with Charice. After her shower, she had come down and knocked on the door of Edgar's office. When he didn't respond, she had knocked again and listened, with her ear against the door, in case he was on one of his private calls. She heard nothing.

"Edgar?" she called, but when there was no response, she went outside to look for him. It had been a lovely afternoon, and since the office door had been locked, she could only assume he must have gone out the French doors to the garden. She walked the circumference of the house and then through the open French doors to his office, where everything was neatly arranged. She felt a foreboding sense of déjà vu.

There was no smell as there had been three and a half years before and it was broad daylight, yet... Suzanna picked up an antique letter opener. She would keep her guard up. She checked the door to the house again and found it still locked. She checked the closet after pre dialing 911 on the Edgar's phone, her finger poised on the call button, the letter opener ready in her other hand. There was nothing and no one there. Going back to the French doors, she locked them securely and laid the phone at the ready on the desk as she searched for some clue. It was then that she noticed his desk calendar, which was always full, was blank from that day.

Then it hit her, he hadn't been trying to renew their relationship, he'd been saying goodbye.

Now, as she sat at his desk, her phone rang. Suzanna looked down to see Shane's name on the screen. She hit the answer button. "He's gone," she said. "Edgar is gone."

The reply shocked her.

"Patty and Kenneth are gone too."

An hour later, Shane was back at the Morgan's home, and detective Lidia Yarnok was on her way to join them.

The next day, Shane finished clearing out the Seattle apartment. He had debated about what to do with Daniel. He considered leaving the boy with his sister, but in the end, they were both on a flight to Paris, where they would meet up with Dave and Larry, re-cover what they knew of the Paris project and then head back to Lyon, where Margot, Larry's wife, was eager to meet Shane and Daniel

face to face. Shane would then stay in France while Larry
and Dave flew out to Austria.

***

Suzanna couldn't bear to stay in the house alone. So,
packing her bags, and with Lidia's help, she moved into
Alice's old condo in downtown Seattle. It had been left just
as it was before Alice disappeared.

The neighborhood had seen better days, and she was
thankful that Lidia was with her as she looked at the
homeless on the street corners, who seemed to have
multiplied a hundred-fold since her last trip into the city.
She needed to be here though. There were still things
Suzanna wanted to know. She was certain that she would
be able to discover things about Alice that the detectives
had missed. What she wasn't sure about was, if she should
enlist Lidia to help.

Lidia had been one of the initial detectives that had
already been through Alice's condo. She would know what
was where, but not necessarily, what it meant. She also was
privy to what had been removed and stored in evidence.

Suzanna had no doubt that Edgar left on his own accord,
but Alice? Even though it seemed clear that she did not
want to be found, perhaps, just perhaps, there was a way
that Suzanna could get Alice, who she still thought of as her
daughter, back.

Suzanna had lost so much. Alice, her sister Claire, and
now Edgar. She had no other family. Yes. She would talk to
Lidia. She had grown to like Lidia, and there was Charice.
Charice would help her.

Suzanna had never felt so alone as she did after Lidia left
her at Alice's. She almost asked her to stay, but instead she
had decided it was better to be there alone for a while first.

She set the alarm and walked through the rooms, trying
to remember Alice's manner, trying to picture herself as

Alice. Eventually she found a restaurant menu in the kitchen and ordered one each of the items circled by Alice. It was a lot of food, but aside from some bottled drinks, the refrigerator was empty.

Suzanna looked through the cupboards and discovered the bottles of wine Alice had tucked away, knowing full well that Suzanna would not approve. She had wanted Alice to be perfect, with never a lapse in her mental focus. She had been rigid as a mother. She saw that now. She hadn't really been much of a mother at all but had treated Alice more like a prized possession.

She thought back to her own mother and found that what she remembered most was how much she'd been away. Often, she would take Claire with her, leaving Suzanna with their father.

At first, she had liked it. She enjoyed helping at her father's firm and having her annoying little sister gone. It was only as a teenager that she began to consider that it was odd and began to harbor jealousy toward Claire. It wasn't Claire's fault though. She couldn't say the same for what she had later put her sister through. That had been her fault, or rather her selfishness.

The door buzzer interrupted her reverie, and she went to open the door to the delivery person.

She dished out the curry and popped open a bottle of wine. At first, she sat in the kitchen, then she moved to the living room and opened the drapes. It was too cold and wet to eat on the balcony, but she pulled a chair next to Alice's desk and sat there. Staring into the dark night, she ate and wondered how she could ever find light in her life again.

Chapter 5

Austria: May 15th

Larry landed at Salzburg, and Dave would arrive in Bern, Switzerland the next day after going over his research findings with Shane. Then Dave was planning to drop in on the Martinson's before meeting Larry.

The Martinson family story was the odd one out that they felt was important to connect.

Larry wished that Katz was available but knew that he was on paternity leave. Philip Katz and Dr. Monica Campuso had met on the Martinson case in Brazil three years before. They married one year later and two months ago, welcomed their first child, a daughter, Alexandria. Katz, like Larry, had left INTERPOL and now worked with Monica's uncle at the French embassy in Brasilia, Brazil.

He was one of the few who knew the case. He had even stayed at the Martinson's guest house with Sebastian when Ana was returned. And he knew the connections between the Martinson case and what was going on with Rosie and the Anglistan family.

It was the 'Why' with Ana's abduction that was still a big question mark. And her mother, Larry was certain, had been less than forthcoming. The lack of any real closure over the years and more and more questions, was overwhelming.

Larry decided to at least call Katz. The man was a genius, and even from a distance, Larry knew that he, Shane, and Dave, could use his insight.

Larry pulled over for a bite to eat before continuing. He looked at the time. He wanted to get a first-hand look at the house where Claire was abducted before heading on to the Anglistan home. By the time he would get there, it should be a decent hour in Brazil to call Katz.

When he neared the house, Larry parked on the roadside, approximating where Rosie said the van had parked. He then called Katz, who was just cleaning up from breakfast.

Philip was glad to hear from Larry. While he loved playing daddy, he also missed having something to work on mentally. The work he did at the embassy was hardly the challenge his mind craved.

He asked Larry to forward what they had, and he would think on it. Even though it had been three years, the situation was never far from his mind, especially now with his own daughter. Philip also had been keeping an eye out for any leads to Leona Himminger, the woman who had kept Ana for ten years. So far there had been nothing, but like Larry, Shane and Dave, Philip couldn't let it go. The implications of what they knew were too far reaching.

Larry was surprised to be greeted by two very hungry dogs when he entered the house. There was a well-chewed bone on the kitchen floor along with a mess from the refrigerator. He guessed that one of the dogs had managed to open the door.

Larry tiptoed around the mess and snapped photos throughout the house. It appeared that aside from the food mess in the kitchen, the house had been well cleaned. He took a blue light out to check for blood spatter, which is next to impossible to completely clean, and was relieved when he found none.

Although the lab in the Marianas had been scrubbed of all usable DNA traces, he doubted that whoever had taken Claire would have had sufficient resources to clean that well here, especially within the time frame given by Rosie.

Before Larry left, he sent the pictures to Shane, Dave, and Philip, and looked for the security cameras Rosie said they had installed. He wasn't surprised to find them missing. Then he put the dogs on leashes he found by the door and led them around the yard, just in case their noses may lead

to any clues, but the only place they took him was out back
to a small, enclosed area where they had been doing their
business via a dog door Larry had not seen inside.

Peering in, he saw why. The dog door was not set in a
regular door, as most, but cut into the wall with a couch in
front of it. A hidden escape route. They had been ready, just
not ready enough.

Loading the dogs into his rental car, Larry called
Magdeline to ask what he should do with them. Rosie was
ecstatic to learn that they had survived and relieved to
know that no blood traces were found.

Seeing as they had a large yard and knowing that not just
Rosie, but all the boys would be thrilled, Magdeline told
Larry to just bring the dogs with him. Soren would pick up
some food for them on his way home.

Later that evening, after Magdeline insisted he stay for
dinner, Larry checked into a bed and breakfast in town. He
was climbing the steps to his room when he saw her. It was
just a glimpse, as she set her dinner tray outside the door
of her room.

Was it? Could it be, Alice?

***

Victoria cancelled her next concert. She needed to stay
here, needed to find out who the woman she had seen in
the auditorium was. After the concert, she had reviewed
the seating chart and reservation list and found the name
Anglistan listed for two of the three seats that had later
been deserted. The other seat was under the name of
Jenkins. When she looked up the names, she discovered
only two Jenkins listed in Vienna and no Anglistan. Upon
googling Anglistan however, she found articles on both
Soren and his wife Magdeline, one of which included a
small group photo. It was enough. A few not so legal

inquiries via hacking into public records, gave her an address. In the morning she would post the letter, which she had carefully constructed, in hopes of setting up a meeting with Magdeline.

Sweden

The train ride had been difficult for Alice and the flight to Kiruna even more so. The biggest concern was being stopped in customs and having Alice quarantined, especially after the worldwide virus scare, which many still feared a new strain of.

Fortunately, Brother Archibald had been able to send ahead to a medical doctor friend of his in Athens, who was willing to write an official note on his behalf. The note stated that the passenger in question was suffering from a non-contagious condition known as hydrocephalus and may experience fever due to inflammation.

Even with this note, the concern remained, as it was written in Greek. Fortunately, Swedish customs was nowhere near the ordeal it is in some countries, and they passed through without issue at the Stockholm-Arlanda airport before transferring to their final flight into Kiruna.

When they arrived, they rented a car under Nick's name and Jonathan drove them to the lodge where they had reserved a room for a week. In the morning Jonathan would go to the lab. He hoped they hadn't moved it.

The complex in Sweden was even larger than the one in the Marianas, and with Meschner's death, it was technically Jonathan's project. He had not listed it in the locations he gave in the letter to Soren and Magdeline. All the less reputable doctors and scientists had been sent to other projects. It was one thing he had made certain of before his disappearance. The lab had to stay operational there, because of what Meschner had done years before.

He wondered if there had been any progress in restoring Oscar Noostrom to health. Jonathan remembered all too well, watching Oscar's wife, Berna, and knowing that Meschner had no real intention of helping the family, but the legitimate scientists, with Meschner gone and no longer sabotaging their efforts, perhaps they had had more success. He hoped so, for both Oscar and Alice's sake, because that was the kind of treatment that would be needed if she were to survive without becoming more machine than human.

Jonathan had no idea what to expect, but what he discovered, the next day, was far beyond anything he had imagined. After some brief confusion, Carl arrived.

At first Carl feared Jonathan's reaction. Afterall, he had taken over his brother's identity. Thinking for a minute, and feeling the gaze of security scrutinizing the situation, he decided the best response was to simply greet his brother with a smile.

"Richter! What a surprise! You should have let me know you were coming."

"It was spur of the moment," Jonathan responded. From the look on security's face, he decided it was best to play along with Carl.

"It's all right," Carl said, nodding to security and praying it really would be all right. "It was just a brotherly practical joke. We always have liked to try and impersonate one another to see how far we could go with it. I'm afraid the beard was a giveaway Richter. Won't you follow me?" Carl said, motioning to Jonathan.

They proceeded into the elevator, both leery of the other.

"So, how long have you been me?" Jonathan began.

"Three years."

"All right. And you think it safe to have me here as Richter?"

"Safer than you think. I can guarantee he won't be protesting."

"And Mathias?"

"I haven't seen him since I last saw you."

"But you have seen Richter, and he knows you are here as me?"

"You could say that."

"What's going on here Carl?"

"It's a long story," Carl said, as they continued down a corridor "And where have you been? Or more to the point, what brings you here now?"

"Another long story," Jonathan responded, as he watched Carl type something into a mobile.

They passed several people along their route and Jonathan was surprised at the atmosphere of friendliness, especially that displayed by Carl, as he introduced Jonathan as Richter. Social skills had never been Carl's strength before, but Jonathan could see that the past three years had been positive for his baby brother, and he was beyond curious, especially when Carl led him to the apartment of Berna Noostrom.

Berna was concerned by Carl's message, but she also knew that the real Richter, the most dangerous of the brothers, was no longer a threat. Opening the door, she took in Jonathan. The beard disguised his face well. It was his eyes she focused on though. You could tell a lot from a person's eyes.

"Jonathan," Carl said, turning to his brother. "I'd like to introduce you to my birth mother. I found the records just before I came here," Carl continued, "and it's changed my life."

"I can see that," Jonathan said, holding out his hand to Berna.

She took it and squeezed as tightly as she could, while giving him an intense stare, wondering if he would respond. Jonathan only nodded and turned back to Carl.

"There is something very important that I came here for and would like to talk to you about privately Carl."

"I don't keep secrets from my mother, Jonathan, or my brother," Carl said. He still wasn't certain he could trust Jonathan and wanted Berna and Ivan present when Jonathan revealed the purpose of his visit.

"Brother?" Jonathan asked.

"Yes, well, half-brother, Ivan. He was in the lab but should be joining us momentarily."

Jonathan took a deep breath. He didn't want to play games, and he didn't trust Carl any more than Carl was ready to trust him.

"Carl," Jonathan started. "How much do you know about P2P?"

"Adam Hisdak, Nadier's son, took it over and it's gone underground."

"That much I knew. What I need to know is what they did to Alice and why they would have kidnapped Sophie."

"They didn't, kidnap Sophie that is. That was me. As for Alice, I don't know how she got there or what they did to her."

"*You* kidnapped Sophie?" Jonathan asked. "I don't understand."

"That's in the past," Berna cut in. "It's the future, the work he's doing here now that matters. Please just let him be," she begged.

Jonathan turned to Berna, just as Ivan arrived. Seeing his mother's face, Ivan hurried to her side.

"Why are you here?" he demanded, staring Jonathan down. "Why can't you leave us alone? Haven't enough people been hurt by your experiments?"

Jonathan took in the accusations, the stares of recrimination, and then glanced back to Carl.

"Look, I don't know what's going on here, but I'm not here to hurt anyone."

"What are you here for Jonathan? Where have you been for three years?" Carl asked.

"Hiding," Jonathan stated simply. "I didn't want any part of this, our father, Meschner's schemes. Mathias was right. We should have listened to him. We…"

"I know," Carl said. "I couldn't agree more, but why are you here now?"

"Alice. She's dying, and aside from Paris, this is the only place I could think to bring her for help."

"Alice? Where is she? What's happened to her?"

"She's not far. We met quite by coincidence. Until a few weeks ago she was fine, but something Nadier did to her is causing her entire system to malfunction. She needs help."

"Is Sophie with you too?" Carl asked, trying not to think of what he'd done before. He had only meant to help her, but now Carl realized the truth. Sophie hadn't needed his help.

"No," Carl replied. "It's Sophie's husband who is with Alice now. Look, it's a long story. Please, we're the only ones that can help her. If you've really changed Carl, then…"

"He has," Berna broke in again. "He's bringing my Oscar back. Do you remember how many times Meschner lied, how he manipulated me? Do you? I remember you."

"He manipulated all of us, made it impossible for us to live freely. We, my brothers, we were all just part of his sick dreams to dominate the world. We can change that though, Carl," Jonathan said, turning back to his little brother. "We can use Meschner's work to help people, but we need to work together."

Carl looked from Jonathan to Ivan and Berna.

"If he's telling the truth, we have to try and help her," Berna said, fearing if she were to refuse mercy to someone, and there really was a God, then all her prayers for Oscar would be for naught.

"Bring her here," Carl said, "but not Nick, assuming it is Nick that Sophie married?"

"It is, and I agree, he doesn't need to be here, but I'll need help to bring her."

"I'll go with him," Ivan volunteered.

"Ivan," Berna started, "Someone else can..." then she stopped herself. She knew that there was no one else that could go. It would have to be one of her sons, either Carl or Ivan, and if something happened to Carl now, then all really would be lost. Yes, there were hundreds of others, scientists and technicians working there with them. Many were close friends, but none, aside from them and Ivan's wife, knew the truth. They didn't dare risk exposing Carl or what was going on in the lab with Richter and Oscar. Nor, from what she understood, could they risk anyone else seeing Alice.

"Okay," Carl said. "Take the truck in bay seven. It's fully equipped. I'll ready a place for her."

Seattle

Suzanna stood on the balcony, watching the ferry make its way across the Puget Sound. The dark night and the glittering lights hid a multitude and created an apparition of the city she once loved. The emerald city. That's what it had been called, emerald, like Alice's eyes. Suzanna wondered where those eyes had come from. It wasn't Suzanna's sister Claire or Edgar. She briefly wondered where he was. Was it possible that he now knew where Alice was, or did he really not care anymore?

Lidia brought over the I-pad that they confiscated from the car at the condo three years before. Alice wasn't wanted as a criminal, and it had contained no evidence against her or Edgar, so there was no need to hold it in evidence, and Lidia was just as curious to find out about Alice as Suzanna was.

The I-pad had been Alice's secret and contained mostly personal data, almost like a diary. Only, it didn't seem to be the diary of the Alice that Suzanna knew. It had hit her like a slap in the face. She really didn't know Alice, because she had only paid attention to the daughter that she and Edgar were trying to mold her into. She knew only the Alice she saw at the offices, meetings, and events. Somewhere, somehow, even as full as they had kept her schedule, Alice had managed to lead another completely different life.

She looked out towards the ferry again and made a decision. Just as she had ordered all the items circled by Alice on the takeout menu, she would visit the places Alice wrote about. She didn't know where all of them were, but she would find them. She would find the people who had known Alice and then, just maybe, she would find Alice.

The first thing she would do is go to the gym where Alice had a membership. Lidia had been there when Alice first went missing and had already met with some of the people who knew Alice. Yes, that was where Suzanna would start.

She took in a deep breath of the cool night air, went inside, and opened a curried chicken entrée and a bottle of wine from the pantry. She felt better now that she had a plan, some kind of action she could take. Even if it didn't lead her to Alice, at least it would help her to know her.

Sitting on the sofa with her dinner, Suzanna opened the I-pad again and scrolled through the movies in Alice's library. She chose one titled "Away Again Away". It was an adventure film about a young woman who had been trapped, first as a child, growing up in a mafia family. She escaped into the witness protection program only to marry a man who abused her and their daughter. With the help of some passing gypsy's, she escapes with her daughter. she winds up falling in love with the brother of the gypsy woman who cared for her daughter. They marry and ride off with the caravan into the sunset.

Suzanna was surprised by how enthralled she became in the film and wondered if Alice had met someone new. She hoped so. She always regretted helping Edgar to push the relationship with Albert, and she only knew of Jack as Sophie's cousin. Perhaps Alice has started a new life with a family of her own, Suzanna thought. Was it possible? Yes, it was, and Suzanna hoped, even if she never saw her again, she hoped that Alice was happy.

Sweden

Alice opened her eyes and the first thing she felt was terror. She knew the man in the room with her was not Jonathan. That meant that he had to be one of Jonathan's brothers. She wasn't strapped down on the bed, but she was sedated and had no strength. Her body felt like a drained battery. For three years she had run on high power, but now she could barely open her eyes, much less defend herself.

She tried to remember how she got here. It wasn't like before. She had the vague memory of Jonathan coming to where she was waiting with Nick. He had brought another man with him. They told Nick he had to stay behind, that he should go home to Sophie. They had helped her into a large vehicle and hooked her to IV's. There must have been something in the IV drip that knocked her out. The last thing she remembered was Jonathan saying it was going to be all right. She trusted Jonathan. What if he had been betrayed though? She had to see him.

"Jonathan?" she whispered.

"He'll be back soon," Carl said. "I'm Carl, the youngest brother. I promise you, you're safe, but I do understand if that doesn't mean much to you. I understand you went through a lot in Paris. I've examined the visual implants and stopped the tracking, but when you're up to it, it could help if you tell me about the experience. You may have guessed that one of the drips is a sedative. The more you can rest, the better. The other drip is a special immunology therapy. Right now, your body is attacking itself. Once we slow that... Well, I won't overwhelm you now. You should regain some strength in a couple of days. Ah," Carl said, as Jonathan returned. "She was asking for you."

Jonathan sat down next to Alice and took her hand.

"Is everything okay?" she asked, worried by the expression on his face.

"Yes, it will be. You just rest and get well," he told her. He didn't dare tell her about the source of the treatment they may need to use. He had just returned from what was now Carl's lab. Ivan had explained to him how Richter had come to be there and how he was being used to heal Ivan's father, Oscar.

They believed that using some of the genetic extractions from Richter may also be the way to treat Alice. He knew he would have to tell her eventually, but not now. He could barely take it in himself. It was the first time in his life that he could remember Richter looking vulnerable. He had to smile at how the tables had been turned. He also had to wonder where Mathias could be.

Richter could hardly believe his ears as he had listened to Ivan and Jonathan discussing Alice and how they might use him to help her too. Alice, his perfect mate, the one that Meschner had meant for him. Together they would have ruled. They were meant to be immortal together, but she had left him. He thought back to their time together in the cabin in Canada. She had saved his life, but then she had left him.

Now they were saying that he could save her life. For the first time Richter could remember, he felt conflicted. If Alice could be saved, would she still be sufficient? There was no one else, not yet anyway. He had to save his strength the only way he could, by using his mind. At the moment, his mind was the only thing he still had control of, but the mind is powerful. His will was powerful. In that, he was always the strongest of his brothers.

N. France

Laura lit the candles, and for the thousandth time, wondered what she was doing, as she made her way down the hallway and the spiral staircase to her wine cellar. She held the lighter in her left hand as she felt the curve of the iron railing with her right. She had a package of tea candles in her pocket that she placed on the shelves as she went. She wished she had a flashlight, but she had taken that out to the garage earlier to work on her bike.

The storm had come up rather unexpectedly, the winds knocking out power, and even though it was only two in the afternoon, the day had gone dark. There was a generator that was hooked up to the new section of the house, but this section had been built in the seventeen-hundreds, and it was where Laura had chosen to live, turning the new section into a café and wine bar.

Since she still worked at the family restaurant, she only opened here three evenings a week. It was enough. Her great-grandfather had left the house to her, which had been a surprise to all, since no one in the family even realized he owned it. Great-grandfather's will had been full of surprises as had his death, or rather the way it occurred.

Laura had lived in the house three months now. There had been nothing out of the ordinary aside from the fact that it seemed so well cared for. All she had needed to do to get started, aside from the usual licenses, was to pick out tables, chairs, tablecloths, and order supplies.

She looked around the wine cellar. Nothing appeared to have been disturbed, and she no longer heard the noises. She almost laughed aloud at herself. The cellar was just that, wasn't it? It was probably just rats, except, rats don't make mechanical sounding thumps and thuds. There was something else niggling at the back of her mind too, something an old friend of her great-grandfather, Ferdinand, had said as he spun tales of the community and its supposed secrets.

He had claimed that the Nazi's used underground tunnels to move between properties and that some of the tunnels ran for hundreds of kilometers. That wasn't anything odd. Almost everyone knew that they had used underground tunnels for smuggling and hiding stolen art and other treasures. Many of the tunnels had been dug by the French themselves during the first world war as bunkers. From what she had learned, all of the tunnels nearby had been blocked off decades ago or converted into tourist sites after they had been searched and thoroughly updated their safety standards. The closest one she knew of had been under a school and supposedly caved in back in the 1970's. Ferdinand swore that there were other tunnels that had never been discovered and that they were still in use.

He once told her great-grandfather he saw men moving equipment in the middle of the night. He also claimed to hear odd noises, much like she had heard earlier.

Ferdinand had passed three years earlier. He was a hundred and five years old, but still, her great-grandfather refused to believe his old friend had died of natural causes. Everyone, including Laura, had only smiled indulgently, but

now she wondered. Even though her great-grandfather had
been a hundred and two years old, his death, much like
Ferdinand, was sudden and very similar.

She remembered her great-grandfather repeating the
account to her several times about the men Ferdinand had
claimed to see carrying large machines that seemed to
vanish into the night. One of the most repeated stories was
about two women though. Two women that her great-
grandfather said had been long dead. He said they had
grown up together and the women had disappeared in the
war. The strangest part of the story was that Ferdinand
claimed he saw them just months before he died and that
they hadn't aged. It couldn't be right.

What had really caught Laura's attention when her great-
grandfather died, were the words the doctor used to
6describe his death. They were the same as those he had
repeated about his friend. It was too similar.

Neither man had any known health issues, aside from
occasional gout, and even before Ferdinand's death, her
great-grandfather had stubbornly avoided seeing the local
doctor. Instead, he would make the trip into Calais, often
with Laura, for annual checkups and to renew his glasses
prescription. Laura was probably the only one in her family
that really knew just how heathy he was. He had been
given a clean bill of health, just two weeks prior to his
death. That wasn't all though. He had also told her that he
had all of Ferdinand's notes locked in a safe. He had not,
however, told her where this safe was. He had, however,
left her what she believed was the combination in the
safety deposit box with the deed to the house. She had
searched his house and most of this one, without luck.
While she was down here, she would search the cellar
again.

Another "Kerthump!" came from behind the opposite
wall. Making her way over, she pressed her ear against

what should have been cold stone, only to find it oddly warm. She touched the other walls. All were cold. The cellar was completely underground. She went back to the warm wall and held her ear against it longer. She could just barely make out a faint, but steady humming sound.

She nearly jumped out of her skin when she heard the doorbell ring upstairs. Blowing out candles as she went, she hurried up the steps to the main entrance of the café. The rain was beating down in torrents as Mathias peered through the window. Laura hurried to let him in, debating about mentioning all that was going through her mind and what occurred in the cellar.

"Hi! What are you doing here? You're soaked! Come in the kitchen and I'll make some tea," Laura said.

"I wanted to come over and give my condolences. I just returned this morning and heard about your great-grandfather and this place from Tony. It looks great."

"Thank you. Where were you? I haven't seen you in months."

"I was in Paris for a while and then Switzerland," he started, saw more questions in her eyes and continued. "It was mostly business and some family matters."

"That happens in a family business. Is everything okay?"

"Not really, but as you know, my family is a bit complex."

"I take it you still haven't heard from Carl?" she asked.

Mathias sighed, "No, and at this point I don't expect to," he replied. It always pained Mathias when Laura mentioned Carl. He knew it shouldn't, because he knew that neither he nor Carl were good for her. Still, Mathias envied Carl. Even if for a short time, Carl had known something that Mathias never could, no matter how much he wanted to. And the truth was, he wanted Laura.

The kettle whistled and Laura rose. "Would you like tea or coffee?"

"Neither. Thanks. I should be going. I'm sure you have a

lot of work to do."

"Not really. I'll be at the restaurant tonight. Have you moved back to the chateau?"

"No, I'm staying at Tony's. The Chateau is a bit big for one person."

"Ah, well..."

"What is it, Laura?"

"I don't really know. It's probably nothing."

"No, it's not. Something's bothering you. Did you hear from Carl?" He wasn't sure why he asked that, but he had and realized his mistake almost immediately.

"If I had heard from Carl, I would have told you, not asked if you had heard from him. What sense does that make?" she said, stirring her tea and turning to stare him down. "I don't understand either one of you. You come and go, and I've never been able to pinpoint just what "the family" business is. I know your father was some kind of doctor and that he had a mean streak, but what exactly is it that you do, Mathias? Who are you really, and what do you do? And don't talk in circles. I've Googled your family, and do you know what? According to Google, you don't exist."

"Not under my real name, no."

She just continued to stare at him.

"I can't explain any more, except to say that my father was not a good person, and my work is to try and right some of the wrongs he committed and prevent some that may yet be committed by those who worked with him."

Chapter 6

Austria: May 18th

Larry would stay at the B&B another couple of days to investigate the woman he had seen, before moving to the cabin Dave had booked and where they were now meeting. They decided that a private short-term rental would be better than a hotel so that they could set up boards and not worry about leaving files about. It would also save on their budget. Going private was great, but the income was sorely lacking, and both men wished they had paid more attention to and invested more in the digital currencies that were becoming more and more mainstream.

The world was changing too fast for them to keep up. Half of what Edgar Morgan and Dr. Meschner had done was legal now, even considered normal in some countries. Why shouldn't you be able to customize your child, people reasoned, much as they tried to reason why you should be allowed to decide, even after birth, if your child was worthy of life at all. What scared them even more though, was how oblivious the majority seemed to what they considered obvious moral atrocities.

"Sometimes I wonder," Dave started, "I always wanted a family. You know, a wife, a couple of kids, but I'm torn. I look through the history records and see what humans have done to each other over the millennia. This didn't start with the Morgans or Meschner. I mean, our world is becoming more and more like the sci-fi horror flicks I used to watch growing up. I think about what Shane is going through, and I'm scared shitless of what the world would be like for my children. On the other hand, I look at Magdeline and Soren and their three boys, and I think, wow! I want that."

"I know what you mean, and I hope to God that those boys are able to have, what we would consider, a normal life. I have to say, I'm impressed with Magdeline and Soren's ability to handle all this as well as they have.

I definitely worry about my daughters too. Chelle and Mary were telling me about some of their classes. Chelle said they are asking students to be chipped starting next term. Thank God she graduates this year. Then, Vivian called me last night. She had a job offer, but it required all employees to be chipped. I told her that her mother and I would send her some funds to get by while she kept looking."

"Is her boyfriend the one who majored in blockchain technology?"

"That's him. Thad or Thatcher, or something like that. I met him once when I went to visit her. I didn't like him. I even found myself wondering if he was a GMO male. First food, now people. But we need to focus on the full-fledged human person of Rosie's mother, Claire. Judging from history, my guess is, they weren't out to kill her."

"But why take her? I mean, sure, she knew things they might want kept quiet, but aside from talking to Magdaline, she'd been quiet. She and Rosie both, neither of them even wanted what happened known. They just wanted to live in peace. It really doesn't make sense. One thing that occurred to me was to trace Claire's ancestry, looking for some special genetic trait they could be interested in, but the family genealogy, so far anyway, looks fairly boring. We'd always thought that she was only used as a surrogate for her sister, Suzanna, but there must be more."

"Or maybe," Larry said, "They didn't want Claire at all. From what Rosie told me of where the van was positioned, it was her they were waiting for. My thought is that Claire was only taken as bait for Rosie."

"I thought that too, and I agree, Rosie was likely the main target. My thinking though, is that they want both of them for some reason. Otherwise, why did they enter the house before Rosie's normal bus? Remember? Rosie said she had arrived early, but they were already in the house. These guys would be sure to know Rosie's regular schedule."

"You're right. It's almost like when they took Sarah Martinson, except with her, there had been the abortion. It's even possible, and I hadn't thought of this before, that the baby survived. I don't want to take us off on a tangent though."

"It is a possibility to think about," Dave said. "One of their goals is to be able to prolong and regenerate life indefinitely. What if, now that Claire is healthy again, just what if, they plan to impregnate her again?"

"She's nearly eighty!" Larry said.

"Sarah in the Bible was supposedly older than that and if they want to become as gods..."

"Which Jonathan said they do. So, I guess it is a possibility," Larry admitted. "And honestly, if I hadn't known, I would have placed her in only her late fifties or early sixties. So, let's take a look at where they could have taken her. Is there a legitimate facility that might be working on that type of project?"

"There could be," Larry said. "I remember back around 2007 or 2008, there was an experiment done with mice. They gave older mice something that enabled them to produce more eggs, and there were healthy pups born. By now, there must be somewhere trying it with humans."

***

Magdaline opened the letter. She thought it was odd that it had a local postmark. Nobody sent mail locally anymore. In fact, they rarely received mail at all except for a card from her parents and an occasional event invitation. But this was local, very local in fact. The stationery it was

written on was from the same B&B where Larry was
staying.

"What is it?" Soren asked as he came in from the yard
where Rosie and the boys were playing with the dogs.

She handed him the letter.

Magdaline looked out the window, into the yard. "She
doesn't seem to have noticed Rosie."

"You did well with her disguise," Soren said, watching
Magdaline worriedly, as she paced the kitchen. "What are
you thinking?"

"Probably exactly what you think I'm thinking," she
replied, looking at him with a half-smile. "I need you to
keep Rosie distracted, as well as Larry and Dave, if they
arrive before I get back."

"Oh no! I'm not letting you go alone. You should tell Larry
and Dave."

"I told you, we want to keep focused on her...our mother."

"Judging from this notepaper, she's staying at the same
B&B as Larry. What if ...?"

"He's moving into a cabin Dave rented. If he'd seen her, he
would have said something."

Soren raised an eyebrow. "I'm going with you. She won't
know I'm there unless you need me."

Magdaline raised her eyebrow back at Soren and looked
outside.

"They'll be fine. She's great with them, and they adore
her."

"I'm just trying to decide if I should tell her."

"How about this," Soren asked, "I'll tell her you need to
run out for something before Larry and Dave arrive, and if
she's okay, I'm going along to help. It's mostly true and
leaves you in the clear."

Magdaline cocked her eyebrow at him again and moved
to get her sweater and purse, while Soren talked to Rosie
and the boys.

***

After meeting with Dave, Larry headed back to the B&B. When he pulled up, he noticed a young woman, whom he didn't recognize, coming out the front. Something about her made him watch, and when she looked both ways to cross the street, he knew it was her. She was wearing a black wig, cut short in back and longer in front, to hide her profile. Larry parked and followed her at a safe distance, while he sent a text to Dave.

She walked a long way, and Larry was starting to feel out of shape, as she turned off the road and onto a footpath leading up to a scenic viewpoint. There were a few people at a nearby picnic table and the occasional walker passing by, but it was otherwise isolated and not somewhere that provided Larry with any real cover. There was a porta toilet past the picnic tables. So, as she sat on a bench looking out, Larry casually strolled toward the toilet. He didn't really fancy hiding inside, so he ducked around behind it and into Soren.

The two men stared at each other, both of their mouths forming to ask what the other was doing there.

"You first," Larry said.

"Magdeline had a letter asking her to meet here," Soren answered, and he glanced to the right as Magdeline made her way to the viewpoint. "And you?"

"I saw her at the B&B and followed her."

Neither man said anymore, as they focused on watching the meeting.

Victoria was nervous. She had no need to look up. She could feel Magdeline's approach.

"It's a beautiful view," Magdeline said, as she sat on the bench overlooking the vista.

"Yes, and one I hope to be able to continue enjoying freely," Victoria replied. "I've done nothing to jeopardize anyone. I just want to be left alone and for my family to be left alone, as agreed."

"Me too," Magdeline replied, and Victoria looked up at her. "I only found out about the projects three years ago."

Searching her gaze, Victoria's sense was that Magdeline was telling the truth, however, her medical background along with that of her husband, still made her suspicious of their involvement in the projects.

"You?" Magdeline asked. "How long have you known?"

"Since I was a teenager, but how can you be in the field you are in and not have known? I can't picture you or your husband, from your bios, not being a much bigger part of this."

"Fair enough. If you look closely, you'll find that I was one of my first patients. I used to be paralyzed from the waist down. I was a reject at birth. I understand how it would seem unlikely, but both my husband's and my career are coincidence."

"How did you find out then?"

"I was mistaken for someone else and kidnapped three years ago," Magdeline answered, not ready to involve Rosie or mention Alice and Sophie yet.

"How much do you know? Are you being watched?"

"Not as far as I know, but I have learned a lot over the past three years. It sounds as though you know a lot as well. Maybe we should pool our knowledge?"

Magdeline sensed an instant defensiveness.

"How am I supposed to trust you?"

Magdeline knew she needed to make a choice and hoped that Rosie would understand and that she wasn't going to be taking too much focus off finding Claire. If she could get Victoria talking though, perhaps she might even know something that could help. She obviously knew more than she was meant to.

"What if I tell you that there are two former police detectives from the states and a former INTERPOL liaison investigating the projects? Would you trust them?"

Victoria was surprised by the idea, but still suspicious.

"And how do I know they aren't another part of it? I'm not stupid. I just want to know that my family is safe."

"It sounds like we have the same priorities. Look, you can search Larry Marquet. He's a former INTERPOL liaison. Look at his profile, and if you want, I can call and ask him to meet us here."

Magdeline had already typed Larry's name into her mobile and handed it to Victoria.

"This says he lives in France."

"Yes, but he's here on other business. In fact, he may be at my house right now. We invited him for dinner."

"If he'll come here, I'd be curious to meet him. Just meet. I'm holding to my promise, as I always have. You can't report otherwise."

"I won't report anything," Magdeline said, taking her phone back and calling Larry.

Both women turned in surprise at the ringing that came from behind the toilet. It quit suddenly as did the ringing at the other end of Magdeline's phone, which fortunately Victoria could not hear, as Magdeline shrugged and kept the phone to her ear. She couldn't imagine that Soren would have contacted Larry, but she had a strong suspicion that it was Larry's phone they had heard. She could hear his breathing and then the closing of a door.

Larry grabbed his phone, quickly hitting the answer icon, and after the women turned back to the viewpoint, he ducked around the back side and into the porta toilet to answer it.

"Magdeline, is there something I should know about?" Larry asked.

"I was wondering if you would mind meeting me up at the city park viewpoint. It's a hike, but just up the trail after the park across from your B&B. There is a stairway that you can take as a short cut from Park Lane…, You know it. Good. About how long?"

"Five seconds soon enough?"

"I see. Fifteen minutes will be fine. I'll explain everything when you arrive," Magdeline finished and hung up.

"You had better," Larry sputtered and wondered if he dared to sneak back outside but thought better of it.

"He's not far. He hadn't quite left for my house yet," Magdeline explained, biting her tongue and looking at Victoria, rather than toward the toilets. "Where did you grow up?" Magdeline ventured.

"Didn't you see my bio?"

"I did, but I assumed it was fabricated."

"You really don't know?"

"No. Like I said, I didn't know anything until three years ago."

"You seem awfully calm about it. Who did they place you with growing up?"

"I didn't really get to know the couple I was given to. The people I used to believe to be my biological parents were killed in a car crash when I was only a month old, and I was adopted by another family. They were the only parents I've ever known about until three years ago as well."

"You said that you were paralyzed from birth?"

"Yes,"

"And you healed yourself with your work?"

"Yes."

"Who did your kidnapper think that you were?"

"I really think that we should wait for Larry. By the way, I meant to tell you, you played beautifully the other night."

"Hardly my best, but thank you."

They continued in awkward conversation until Larry, who thought he was going to be asphyxiated, looked at the time and stepped outside. He took in three cleansing breaths of fresh air, looked around the back, where Soren was still crouched, and gave him a look that said, they would definitely be talking later.

Soren tried not to laugh and then hoped that Magdeline didn't think he had called Larry behind her back. Then, realizing that they had already been gone longer than expected, he left his post to phone Rosie and see if Dave was there.

Victoria's eyes went wide as Larry approached, and she got up to leave. Her heart was beating a million miles an hour. That man was following her. He must be. She had seen him earlier at the B&B and then in the mirror of her sunglasses as she walked to the park.

"What's wrong?" Magdeline asked.

"Liar!" she spat, jerking away and hurrying to the path. A group of students had arrived and were blocking the trailhead. Looking around frantically, Victoria hurried toward the steps, praying she wouldn't be ambushed at the bottom. If they were waiting for her there would be no place to go from that route. She looked back toward the bench and saw that they were both looking at her, but neither made a move to follow. They must have someone to intercept me at the steps and probably at the trailheads as well, she thought. Not knowing what else to do, she hurried into the woods behind the toilets.

Soren was talking to Dave as she passed by. He looked back toward the viewpoint to see Larry and Magdeline talking. Unsure of what was going on, Soren followed. She wasn't an easy woman to follow, Soren thought. The way she zigged and zagged, was like trying to follow all three of his boys at once, and she was fast! He didn't think she even realized he was there. It looked almost as if she were running in a trance, eyes focused straight in front of her as she made her way this way and that through the trees until she came to the edge of the park. She stopped abruptly and turned.

Soren was certain she must have heard his footsteps. He had stopped in a kind of skid, ducking behind a large rock. He could hear where they were. The sound of the water was distinct. The falls ran down into a small garden area and then under the road and into a creek the other side.

Victoria listened. She was sure she had heard something behind her. She scanned the area, and two rabbits chased from one bush to another. She sighed. "I have to get a hold of myself," she said to herself, as she tried to decide her next move. The falls was probably a good thirty-foot drop, but there was a safety railing that led down to a relatively flat rock. And no one was on the road below, which appeared to be blocked off for repairs. Could she climb down? Did she have a choice?

Not knowing what else to do, when he saw Victoria climb over the railing above the falls, Soren dialed Magdeline to let her, and Larry know.

Nova Scotia

Jack was surprised, when he dropped by Nick and Sophie's, to find her home already.

"I thought you two had another week?" Jack asked. "Where's Nick? Out with Jeremy?"

"Hi, Jack. I was just thinking of you," she said truthfully. "She had been intending to just wait out the original timeframe of their trip at home, without anyone being the wiser. She would pick Jeremy up from Nick's parents the day after tomorrow. They had come up with a backup story for her to come back without Nick, but that was for his parents, if he had not returned by the time she picked their son up. Jack showing up was completely unexpected. "Weren't you in New York?"

"I was, but Robby came down with the flu from his daycare and passed it on to Beth. Quill is sleeping in the game room downstairs. I asked if he wanted me to stay and help, but he has extra staff already that he's training for summer. So, not wanting to be in the way or hang out in a hotel by myself, I came back early. Your turn Soph."

Jack already knew she was hiding something, and Sophie knew that he knew. She had to think of something fast. He was giving her the no excuses stare down.

"Okay, Jack, you caught me. It was meant to be a surprise, and if you'll just trust me and stop asking questions, it still can be."

"A surprise for what?"

"A surprise for you. You weren't supposed to be back yet, remember?"

"A surprise for me, why?"

"A surprise for your birthday, now will you stop?"

"My birthday isn't for over a month."

"These things take time. Nick is away right now trying to arrange his end of it, and I am here doing mine. Now, no more questions or you really will ruin it, and I'll have to explain to Nick. Don't you dare put me in that position!"

"I wouldn't dream of it," Jack said, "I will be awaiting my birthday most anxiously. Where's Jeremy?"

"He's with Nick's parents. Have you ever tried to plan and watch a two-year old at the same time?"

"Okay, I'll buy that. Maybe."

"And no letting on to anyone that you know there's a surprise, because they may or may not be involved. Promise?"

"Okay. So, how was Greece?"

"Beautiful, but we'll tell you all about it when Nick gets back."

"How long is he away for?"

"Not long," she replied, as Jack's eyes bored into her with suspicion. "He'll call me tonight to let me know how it's going. Now, you tell me, what are you doing here?"

"I told you..."

"No, I mean here, at our house."

"I was just going fishing. Nick said I could borrow some lures to try. I was headed for the garage when I saw you."

"Oh, okay, go ahead. Don't worry about returning them, Nick and I will come by to see you soon," Sophie said, praying that it was true.

Sweden

Nick had stayed in Sweden until Jonathan returned to update him on Alice and set up a line of communication. Not only did he want to stay updated on Alice, but Jonathan said that they could use his assistance in procuring certain supplies and information.

Jonathan debated telling Nick about Carl and Richter's role in the treatment. On the one hand, knowing that Richter was no longer a threat would put both Nick and Sophie at ease. On the other hand, it may not be wise for them to become too at ease. Jonathan knew there was an almost endless array of connections, any of which could decide to target Sophie again.

Jonathan was especially concerned about the current involvement of her parents and what may be going on with P2P. While he had learned through Carl that part of the P2P operations had been returned to the institute, he knew that the vast majority would have been kept underground and spread out through any number of locations. He had given many locations in his letter, but he knew that there were likely many he was not privy to.

In the long run, he decided against mentioning either Carl or Richter. He knew that Sophie didn't trust him. He could only imagine if she knew about Richter or Carl's involvement. No, it was better for them to stay alert, especially with a young son.

Neither Sophie or Nick had told him about Jeremy, but he had deduced his existence, first from Sophie's lack of protest in going home, and then from doing a standard search of birth records. No matter that Sophie wasn't considered project viable, it was his heritage. Jonathan knew that, just as they had abducted and used other children, unknowingly related to the family, Jeremy would be a prime target. This was something that he did warn Nick about.

"How did you know about our son?"

"It's a matter of public record, and it's important that you and Sophie stay aware."

"But Jeremy is a normal little boy. He has no connection to the sick experiments your family conducts."

"He's still family. An unfortunate point, but it's the spine, if you will, of all the projects. Sophie still carries the genetic strains and depending on how much of who she may have passed on..."

"Look, I appreciate that you're helping Alice, but leave Sophie and Jeremy out of this."

"It's not me who made them part of this. You know that. Her parents..."

"Adopted parents..."

"Are still part of the family code. You know that too."

"Just how far does this family code travel?"

"It's global. I can't escape it either and God knows I tried. I even succeeded for a while, but I knew it couldn't last. I can never be free, and neither can Alice, but your family, Sophie never underwent any of the therapies or implants. That gives you a freedom you can't understand, but because of the genetic code she carries, you need to be diligent in protecting that freedom."

"Tell me more about the projects. I need to know what I'm dealing with."

Jonathan shook his head, "There's a lot that even I don't know. Richter was the one groomed to take over, but only the pieces that our father was part of."

"I thought he was the head of all. I hoped when he died that the nightmare was over. I know that I was very wrong in that, but..."

"But the scope is broader than you can imagine. Family is everywhere. Different branches have started their own projects. It's like a tree. The seeds were planted long ago. My father's family was one of them. Now the seeds have sprouted into intertwined roots and branches. I heard him refer to it once as the tree of life.

"I think you know that he fancied himself as God incarnate. As I said, even I don't know the full extent, but I do know that even without my father or Richter, there are others who are vying for that same god status. They want to form the world to their view. The next world war won't be between separate nations, but among those vying for control of the entire world.

"I said that you still maintain freedom because Sophie was never given the treatments or implants, but just look at the world, Nick. People have already been getting chips implanted here in Sweden, voluntarily, for a few years now. Much of the work of the projects is becoming legal. It's all connected. The family is just an interwoven aspect, a part of the whole that is working to advance what the world is already beginning to accept."

"Dear God."

"I think you do understand. I said my father had referred to the family as the tree of life. If you know your Bible, which I think you do, you'll remember that there were two trees in the midst of the garden, the tree of the knowledge of good and evil and the tree of life. After man ate of the tree of the knowledge of good and evil, God blocked him from the tree of life, lest he never die. The family never dies, or at least that's the goal. I doubt very much that my father is really dead."

"Meaning?"

"Meaning that not just his DNA, but his actual body is probably somewhere right now, waiting to be regenerated." Jonathan took a deep breath. "I've said too much, but I truly do want you and Sophie to have what I never can. I tasted it for the past three years. Guard your freedom. Don't dig any deeper into the projects. Go home. Use this and only this phone. I'll send a code and a number when there's any news or if there is anything you may be able to help with. Sophie shouldn't know about this."

"I don't keep secrets from my wife. I'm the last person who wants to involve her more, but she won't stay away, not so long as her parents are missing. She's already been in contact with her aunt Josephine's daughters."

"She what?"

"They actually contacted her. She hasn't heard from them for some time, but she's always thinking of them and her parents."

"You should get back to your family. Forget about the phone."

"But…"

"I should never have asked for your help."

"And if you need information or supplies that you don't want to go through the project for?"

"I guess I'll have to put my alias back to work."

"And Alice?"

"Sherman will find a way to contact you."

"Sophie will…"

"Sophie isn't here. Go home Nick. Fly back through Greece in case someone besides Sophie is watching for your return, and then go home."

"And what do I tell Sophie?"

"The truth, that I'm doing all I can. There is one thing you can do that won't connect back to you. I'll give you a package to mail from Athens. It will help me maintain Sherman's existence while I'm here."

Switzerland

Sarah watched her husband set the table and wondered if Ana would come home for dinner or not. They had both tried to call her, but as usual, she ignored them. She had been distant before, but ever since Sebastian left, it seemed as if they had lost her all over again.

"Can I use the car tomorrow, Stephan?" Sarah asked.

"You haven't driven in years. I don't mind taking you wherever you need to go?"

"I drove just last week. Remember?"

"That was just up and down the hill from Ana's work."

"Yes, and now I'd like to drive myself around some more. It's high time I did, but if you object..."

"I didn't say that. I just..."

"Stop worrying, Stephan. I know it's hard for you. We were both gone a long time, but that doesn't stop us both from being independent adults. In fact, I should look for a car of my own."

"I didn't realize you felt so strongly. You should have mentioned it before. Of course, you can use the car, but I do worry, Sarah. I love you."

She turned, struck with guilt by the catch in his voice. Why did he still love her? Any normal man would have moved on long ago. Stephan was no normal man though. He also still hadn't realized her betrayal. She had wanted to confess, to tell him the truth about Ana, but she couldn't. She couldn't, because the fact was, she still loved him too. That, and she was still scared for both herself and Ana. Knowing would also put him in danger. No. She had to keep the secret. It was bad enough that Trudie knew.

She needed to see Trudie. She knew Stephan wouldn't object, but she didn't want him to know. The less he knew, the better.

Stephan wanted to ask where she wanted to go but knew that he was already walking on thin ice. Sarah was an independent woman, who had never liked being coddled or questioned too much. It was one of the things he had admired in her when they'd met, her strength and independent spirit. That was something that Ana had inherited from her mother. It had just been so long since he'd seen it. He told himself that he should be happy. Sarah was just becoming more herself again.

"Here," Stephan said, reaching into his pocket and handing Sarah a set of keys.

"Thank you. I promise to be careful, and I'll call if I'm going to be late," she said, as her phone buzzed with a text. "It's Ana. She's staying up at the lodge. She says she's helping Aida with dinner and has an early tennis lesson in the morning."

"At least she's made a friend. Aida may be older, but she seems nice, down to earth. Maybe she'll be a good big sister like influence," Stephan said. "Has she talked to you, Sarah?"

"You mean about Sebastian?"

"I mean about anything. I know you play tennis together, and I've seen you talking. I was just wondering if she ever shares anything important with you, and if she did, would you tell me?" he asked, his voice faltering on the last.

"She's talked a lot about Sebastian, and frankly," Sarah added, with more than a hint of venom, "I'm glad he's gone!"

Stephan stopped, surprised at the harshness of her tone. "It wasn't his fault," he ventured.

"Why do you defend him over Ana?"

"That wasn't the way I meant it. I know it was hard for her. Her insistence is the reason he came to live here. She wouldn't leave Brazil without him. You know that."

"I know that you admire his seeming piety. He hurt Ana though," Sarah said, as she went to the pantry.

"Not on purpose," Stephan said under his breath, so that Sarah couldn't hear. He hated arguing, and the fact was, she had a point. He did want to defend Sebastian. Partly because he was the reason that they had Ana back and partly, and this is the part he felt guilty about, because Sebastian had felt more like his son than Ana did his daughter.

Sarah's heart ached from her own guilt. While she loved Stephan, she resented his god and that Sebastian had left Ana for that same god. They were delusional. They must be, especially Sebastian, after growing up as Ana had described. And Stephan happily fed his delusions. Still, to try to improve the mood of the evening, Sarah chose a bottle of Chardonnay from the wine cooler, she knew was Stephan's favorite.

"We can still have a nice dinner together," she said, turning back toward the dining area, with a smile she hoped he wouldn't see through.

Stephan smiled back, but the pain in his eyes still showed, as he said, "I'll get the wine glasses."

Austria

Soren made his way through the woods and down a staircase to the road below, somehow beating Larry and Magdeline, and just in time to see Victoria slip.

The sun had already started going down and the stones were slick. She had turned at the sound of someone approaching and lost her footing, sliding several feet and hitting her head. Cold water trickled over her. She opened her eyes, trying to focus. There was more than one person below her now. She felt trapped, as she grabbed at the cold stone of the falls, unable to get a grip.

"Don't try to move," she heard an unfamiliar man's voice call up. She tried to feel for a foothold, but all she felt was slick rockface. She couldn't even use her heal to leverage herself up. She tried again to grab the stones so that she could at least lift herself out of the awkward angle she was lying at. Her fingers were going numb from the cold water. She hadn't felt this helpless in years. She had vowed to never be helpless again. She could hear more voices now. She recognized the one voice as Magdeline. Making a last-ditch effort to push herself up, she tumbled down.

Magdeline rushed to her, checking her vital signs.

"Pulse is steady, and I don't think anything is broken, but it's hard to tell. She'll have some nasty bruising, but I think most of the scratches are superficial. She must have hit her head pretty hard. She's out cold. Speaking of which, help me get her out of this cold water. Soren, get under her shoulders while I hold her head. Larry, grab her legs," Magdeline directed.

Together, they carried Victoria to a bench on the other side of the road, and Soren hurried to bring the car.

Larry had moved the road barricades, while Magdeline rubbed Victoria's arms and legs to warm her. A few minutes later they positioned her across the back seat with Magdeline, and Soren drove them to the house.

"So?" Larry asked.

"She's a concert violinist. We saw her by chance at the theater where we arranged to meet Rosie," Magdeline responded. "Rosie doesn't know I went to meet her."

"A concert violinist?" Larry asked.

"Here," Soren said, as he pulled a concert program from the glove box and handed it to Larry.

"We didn't tell you because we didn't want focus distracted from Claire. I'm sorry. It all happened so fast. We assumed she had left with the rest of the musicians. They're on tour. And then she sent a note wanting to meet."

"Okay," was all Larry could think to say, as he browsed the program and read her bio.

"She's clearly scared to death of something," Soren added.

"She told me that she's known about the projects since she was a teenager. She's worried about her family. If I understood correctly, she knows things that she's made a deal to keep secret in exchange for their protection. She was extremely suspicious of us because of our professions," Magdeline said.

"Well, I guess that's understandable," Soren replied.

"And she must have seen me at the B&B and thought I was following her," said Larry. "This is going to be an interesting evening," he added, as they pulled into the drive.

Inside the house, Dave asked Rosie to keep the boys busy while he went to talk with Soren.

Rosie wanted to follow and find out what was going on. She'd been suspicious that Magdeline was keeping something from her, and now she was certain, but currently being the only adult with three three-year old boys, she wasn't even able to sneak a peek out the window.

Back outside, they decided to take Victoria in through the French doors of the master suit and place her on Magdeline and Soren's bed. Magdeline was concerned that she hadn't stirred, but she was more concerned about hypothermia. So, she sent Larry to the garage for a heat light while she stripped off Victoria's wet clothes and tucked the comforter around her.

"You can plug it in there," she said when Larry returned. She was checking Victoria's eyes with a pin-light for signs of concussion and or bleeding. As soon as she shown the light in Victoria's second eye, a vice like hand gripped her wrist. Fortunately, Larry was there and able to hold her down on the bed as she struggled, and Magdeline injected her with a sedative.

"Now what?" Larry asked.

"Not a clue. I didn't give her a high dose. She should wake up soon and I'll give her a muscle relaxer. Hopefully we'll be able to talk to her. I need to talk to Rosie too."

"Okay. I'll guard her, but send Dave in."

Magdeline nodded and went to the living room. Soren was making dinner for the boys as she asked Dave to go back to the bedroom, and Rosie stared at her.

"Mommy!" chorused the boys, running to her.

"Mommy needs to talk with Aunt Rosie," she said, as she greeted them with hugs and kisses. "Go get your dinner and I'll be back soon."

"So?" Rosie queried, following Magdeline into the hall.

"I received a note from Victoria."

"You went to meet with her."

"Yes. I'm sorry I didn't tell you. I wanted to talk to her first. She doesn't know about you."

"She's here. Isn't she? And I'm guessing Larry knows. What happened?"

"She was staying at the same B&B as Larry. He just happened to follow her to where we were meeting. She saw him, darted, and fell. She knows about the projects, and she's terrified for her family and of me, Soren, and Larry."

"Why did she want to meet with you then?"

"I think she just needed to know, but then she saw Larry and..."

"You said she fell."

"I think she'll be all right."

"Is she alone with Larry?"

"Larry and Dave. She's extremely strong," Magdeline said, rubbing at her wrist. "She grabbed me when she woke up while I was examining her."

Rosie nodded and said, "You should be with her then when she wakes up again. If it were me, and I woke up alone in a strange place with two strange men, I'd be pretty scared. I know how scared I was in the hospital."

"Your right. I'm sorry Rosie. I…"

"I understand. I'd have done the same," Rosie said and hugged Magdeline.

"Thank you," Magdeline said and hurried back into the bedroom, where Victoria was starting to stir.

Larry and Dave looked up at her.

"It's probably better if it's me and not you she sees first," Magdeline said and traded places with Larry.

"Well, definitely not Alice," Dave said. "What do we know about her? Anything besides this bio?" he asked, setting the program aside.

"I know where she's been staying," Larry offered.

"You want me to go through her room?" asked Dave. "I could say I'm her boyfriend and she asked me to pick up some things for her?"

"Not a bad idea," Larry consented.

"Kidnapping is a felony," came a low moan.

"We're not kidnapping you. I know you don't believe it, but you're safe here. Let us help you," Magdeline said.

Victoria's muscles felt like limp rags. All she could do was stare at Magdeline with a look of combined fear and rage. "You drugged me."

"Just a safety precaution. I need to finish examining you too."

"Where are my clothes?"

"On the floor. They were pretty messed up from the fall you took," Magdeline answered, as she lifted Victoria's eyelid and shined the penlight.

Larry had gone to the soggy pile of clothes to search the pockets for her room key. "Here," he said to Dave, "and make sure to bring her a change of clothes."

"Who else is here?"

"Larry, and one of the former police detectives I told you about from the states, Dave Asher."

"Hi," Dave said, coming over where Victoria could see him.

"I told you the truth," Magdeline said. "Larry staying at the same B&B is just coincidence. He saw you and thought you were…"

"You know others?" Victoria asked, as her eyes looked to each of them and then back at Magdeline.

"Yes," Magdeline answered.

"Bring the brown leather bag. It's under the pillows," Victoria said.

"Okay," Dave said. "Anything else you need?"

"My laptop. You'd probably try to get into it anyway. I'd rather you do it in front of me," she said, glancing at Dave and then looking back at Magdeline. "So, what's my prognosis?"

"A slight concussion. We need to make sure you stay awake for the next couple of hours. I'm sure we can find plenty to talk about, and if you want, we'll even let you ask the questions. Won't we Larry?"

"For now," he said.

"Who did you think I was?"

"A woman called Alice Morgan. Do you know who she is?"

"I ask the questions."

Athens

Sophie was thrilled when Nick called her from the airport in Athens to say he was boarding a flight home. He had just made it, after the flight from Stockholm had departed nearly two hours late, and because he had to leave the airport to mail the package for Jonathan, he also had to go back through a full security check.

Taking a deep breath, Nick settled back in his seat and reached to open the water he had gotten from the machine in the boarding area. When he turned the lid, water began to spurt out. He hadn't realized it was carbonated. He clamped the lid back on, placed it in the seatback pocket, and covered the wet spot on the crotch of his pants with the in-flight magazine, as a woman, in a very form fitting dress, sat a pet carrier on the seat beside him.

He felt guilty, not offering to help her with the overstuffed carry on she struggled to put above, especially when an elderly gentleman in the opposite row gave him a look before getting out of his own seat to assist her.

The carrier beside him moved, causing him to look. A very fluffy black cat stared at him with yellow eyes and hissed. The woman finally sat and made cooing noises to the cat, and it licked something from her finger, presumably a sedative, before she placed it under the seat for take-off. As she did, her sunglasses fell at Nick's feet. He reached to get them, and the magazine slipped, revealing the wet spot as he handed them back to her. From the look on her face and the way she immediately wiped them down with a sanitizing cloth from her purse, he knew she'd seen. He considered trying to explain the water bottle mishap, but she already had headphones on and was flipping through her own magazine.

As the plane took off, Nick gazed down at the sea and out toward the acropolis where he and Sophie had enjoyed themselves before Alice had come back into their lives, not that she had ever left them. Nick wished he could stop thinking about what Jonathan had told him.

As the plane turned and leveled off, he realized how exhausted he was. He was still thirsty too. Taking the bottle from his seat, he very carefully unscrewed the top and drank, hoping he wouldn't need to climb over his seat partner later for the toilets. Then he lay his head against the window and fell, almost immediately, asleep.

Chapter 7

Puget Sound WA: May 19th

Suzanna looked out at the naval ship docked to the right, as the ferry pulled into Bremerton. The first thing on her list was a coffee shop Alice had mentioned in her blog.

She found it just up around the corner of the first main street. She wasn't sure what, or for that matter how to order after she heard the request in front of her. A lavender, quad venti, almond, no foam with a small swirl of non-dairy whip. What was that? She wondered. She was used to the espresso machine in the office and had even bought one for home. She had learned to make the occasional cappuccino Edgar liked, but she was generally straight up espresso or one of the many varieties of organic coffee pods kept on hand.

Stepping out of line, she scanned the menu board and decided to keep it simple and just order the number two breakfast special. It was a lavender latte and a blueberry muffin.

The cafe was crowded inside. So, getting it to go, she made her way outside to sit for a while at a table next to a heat lamp, where she could study the map and get her bearings. The lavender latte was unusual, yet surprisingly good, and she wondered if it was something Alice would have ordered.

The next stop was to try and find the camera shop. They hadn't found the camera, but according to the blog and photo entries, Alice had owned a high definition, Nikon ultra max zoom AX3. It was unique, as it was digital, but offered a film option. She was only guessing that Alice had bought it in Bremerton but knew that it may also have been purchased on Bainbridge, Seattle or anywhere else

Alice may have gone that she had not yet discerned. After all, she had had a car that they hadn't known about.

Suzanna made her way up the street to the first camera shop listing she had found. Fortunately, there weren't many, only three for the city and one walking distance. The others she would have to call for a car to.

She was both pleased and surprised when she hit pay dirt on the first one. The man behind the counter recognized Alice as soon as Suzanna pulled out her picture. What was odd, is that he knew her as Allie. She had never known or even considered Alice going by a nickname. Then again, the fact that she had never really known Alice was why she was here in the first place.

Brent, the owner, asked how Alice was doing. He hadn't seen her in over three years. Suzanna told him that Alice had moved to France, since that was her last known location, and he seemed stunned. Then he asked Suzanna to let her know she was missed, and he wondered why she disappeared so suddenly without saying goodbye. Suzanna wasn't sure, but she sensed that he was hurt. Had Alice had a relationship with this man? She couldn't possibly have had time, or could she? Suzanna still had a hard time grasping that Alice had found time for everything she had so far read about in the blogs.

After the camera shop, Suzanna took the ferry to Bainbridge and ate lunch at a café where Alice had taken one of the photos that showed one of the brothers watching her. A chill went up Suzanna's spine as she wondered which one he was.

The memory of her time on the island in the lab, three years before, made her shutter. Thinking of Richter's cold brutality and knowing that he had escaped, caused her to take a deep breath and carefully note the faces of those around. No one else was alone or looked even remotely out of place, and she let her breath out with a sigh, as the waitress came to take her order.

After lunch she walked around, trying her best to locate places Alice had photographed, then she headed back to Bremerton to go dancing.

She knew she would be out of place. Even if she didn't look her years, she would still be at least double, if not triple the age of most there. Still, she decided to follow through. She would go to as many places as possible that she knew Alice had gone to and going dancing today would cover the top three mentioned locations.

A few people did glance at her, but not quite as oddly as she'd thought they might, and when she made her way up to the bar, she recognized the owner of the photo shop.

"Well, hello again," he said, as she sat on the barstool beside him and ordered a glass of wine. "I've got that," he added.

"Oh, thank you. I haven't been here before. Alice told me about it," Suzanna replied, trying to relax as a techno beat reverberated through the club.

"Really? That's interesting. I'm sorry, but until today, I had the impression that Allie didn't have any family," Brent said, as the bartender brought her glass of wine and refilled his beer. "Anyway, to Allie!" he said, raising his glass to hers.

"To Allie," Suzanna repeated.

Another man came towards them and slapped his hand on Brent's shoulder. "Hey bro! You gonna introduce me to your date," he said, looking Suzanna up and down and then back over to Brent.

"Suzanna, this is my brother, Trent. Trent, this is Allie's mom. You remember Allie?"

"You know I do! Well, well, it's nice to meet you Allie's mom. What's Allie up to these days?"

"Apparently, she moved to France," Brent said.

"Well, what do you know? The world is full of surprises!" Trent said, and then he ordered a beer.

"So, now that you're at the dance club Allie told you about, you want to dance?" Brent asked, offering his hand.

"Sure. Why not?" Suzanna replied and was sure she saw Trent smirk.

"You familiar with Dolly Bali?" Brent asked, as a new song began.

"Who?"

Brent smiled, a big wide grin. "That's the artist who does this song. She was one of Allie's favorites."

"Oh," Suzanna said, watching how Brent danced as the floor crowded. Strobe lights beamed in different colors, and the volume was deafening, but she tried to move to the rhythm, standing in place, just moving her arms and hips as Brent did. There was really no room to move, and Suzanna focused on Brent. Eye contact. Maintain eye contact, she thought to herself, in order to stay steady. If she didn't, the close crowd and dizzying strobe lights would cause her to pass out. He just kept on smiling as she stared at him, wondering who he had been to Alice. It seemed both he and his brother were far more than just her camera source or mutual club goers. They knew Alice.

After another hour, Suzanna, mostly watching from the bar as the men danced with younger women, was ready to leave. She'd been ready to leave for some time, but her ferry was now just twenty minutes out. As she was headed to the door, she caught Brent's attention and waved. He broke away from his dancing and held the door for her.

"Thank you. You seem like a nice young man, Brent. I need to get to my ferry now," Suzanna said, turning to go.

"Wait, I wanted to tell you something. It had been so long it slipped my mind earlier. Allie had me develop some photos that she never picked up. Would you like them?"

"Yes, I would. Thank you."

"If you want to head to the ferry, I can grab them and meet you there in ten minutes."

"Okay..."

"See you in ten then," he said and hurried to his shop.

Suzanna made her way down to the dock and waited at the boarding ramp. She was worried he wasn't going to make it in time. Then she saw him jogging toward her.

"Here," he said, and he handed her a grocery sized paper bag.

"Thank you, Brent. It was really nice meeting you," Suzanna said, turning to go up the ramp.

Brent caught her arm. She fell into him, or he pulled her to him, it was hard to tell which.

"This is for Allie," he said and kissed her hard on the mouth. The force of his tongue searching her mouth shocked her. She stood stunned, staring as he walked calmly away. The horn blew on the ferry, marking its departure. Snapping out of her stupor, Suzanna picked up the bag she had dropped and hurried up the ramp, barely making it as they closed the gate and the ferry pulled away.

Nova Scotia

Sophie awoke with a start. She had been dreaming of Alice. In the dream, Alice was with Richter. Sophie shivered and pulled on her slippers and Nick's robe. His robe always felt warmer, and it smelled of him. She could hardly wait to get to the airport to pick him up.

She put the kettle on to boil and showered. She stood under the shower, trying to shake the fear she felt. Why would Alice be with Richter? It was just a dream. Get a grip, she told herself. Alice was with Jonathan. She had been with him the past three years. Sophie needed to believe that Jonathan would help Alice. She stood under the shower until it began to run cool. Then she dashed back into Nick's robe and her slippers, made herself a strong coffee and a bowl of oatmeal, before getting dressed.

The sun was just peeping over the horizon. His flight wouldn't land for more than two hours. She had plenty of time, but she wanted to get going. She needed to see him, to have him tell her that Alice was safe, and everything would be okay. Something inside knew that it could never really be okay, but still, she hoped. Just like she kept hoping that her parents would return.

After dressing, she pulled on a coat. She was layered, so she could always take it off later and be fine, but now, she was shivering. She got in the car and scanned the satellite radio. She needed something upbeat and tuned it to Caribbean Island beats. She made herself sing along. "Don't worry, be happy," she sang, as she turned onto the road.

Austria

They had all been up until past two in the morning. They went over each of their histories and gave evidence until Victoria finally began to relax and tell them about herself.

Originally placed with a family in Australia, she had what she would consider a normal life until just before her sixteenth birthday. Like Alice, she had been given vitamins all her life, only instead of oral, they had been injected. Unlike Alice, she had not been pushed further ahead in school. In fact, her parents seemed relieved when she had purposely dumbed down her class nerd participation at the suggestion of being moved to a more advanced school.

She explained that she had been active in both music lessons and track, with track being her favorite, and she didn't want to leave her team. The coach had even suggested her to Olympic scouts. She wasn't sure she wanted to go that far but running gave her an outlet for the pent-up frustrations she frequently experienced when having to bite her tongue to keep from correcting her teachers, and the extra charge of energy she seemed to carry. Her parents had also kept a close watch on her, though not as extreme as Alice's, and like Alice, she said that she had seen a man who seemed to be watching her.

Just before her sixteenth birthday, her parents woke her, and her then three-year old brother. They had all gone to the airport and flown to Shanghai. While there, she underwent numerous tests that reminded Larry of what Ana described happened to her.

One night, when they thought she was sedated, one of the doctors left his desk without logging out of the intranet. She had stolen a thumb drive earlier for just such an opportunity and managed to download several files and climb back into bed, with them none the wiser.

Once she realized what they had planned for her, she made her escape, or thought that she had, until she reached and boarded the train. There she saw the same man who was watching her back in Australia. He was sitting in the seat next to the one she reserved. He said that she needed to return. Her family's lives depended on it. Then she told him about the files she had read, and that she had made a copy, but she would not tell him where the thumb drive was. She said that if her parents or brother were harmed, she would reveal the projects and their true goals.

He laughed at her and held her arm, dragging her off at the next stop. He underestimated her though, and just as he was guiding her toward the front of the station, she broke free and ran. He ran after her, but it was dark, and she ran at more than twice his pace.

A few days later, she risked calling her parent's mobile. She knew it would be tapped, but she needed to know if they had been harmed. They were relieved to hear from her, but told her not to worry for them, but to run, and so she did.

She took the Siberian express from Beijing to Russia and hid out in the countryside, working for room and board. It was there that she acquired a new violin. She had started playing at the age of four, and when the people heard her, they helped her get to an audition in Saint Petersburg.

That was the beginning of her career. Of course, that also soon gave away where she was, but she had become well known, and her disappearance would not go unnoticed. And so, between that and the files she absconded with, they left her alone.

There were others they could use, and she kept their secrets, so long as they promised not to harm her family. What she had been too late to escape though, was having a trigger programed.

Until two weeks ago, she talked with her family at least once a week, and now she was afraid, not just for them, but that someone was trying to trigger her. She assumed that someone had discovered the contact she made. The person said they could help deactivate the trigger and release her family. Then she told them about the closing night at the theater in Elsbethen, the delivery, and the sense that she was being followed.

The only ones who had gone to bed, at even close to a decent hour, were the boys, which meant they were also the first ones up. Surprised to see their dad and Dave asleep on the couches, they hurried to wake their mother. But Magdeline, leaving Victoria to rest in the Master bedroom, was in the guestroom with Rosie.

Though she had been told about them, Victoria screamed as they piled onto the bed to shake the woman, they assumed was their mother, awake. Her scream was followed by a chorus from the boys as they took in the bruising to her face and arms.

Five seconds later, the bedroom was a chaotic scene of Soren, Magdeline and Rosie trying to calm both Victoria and the boys, who stared from their parents' arms, looking back and forth between their mother and the second newcomer, who looked so much like her.

"Why is there another you in your bed, Mommy?" Spencer asked, as he calmed, and Magdeline dried his tears.

"She's another aunt," was all Magdeline could get out, as Hamilton buried his head firmly in her shoulder sobbing, and Thadeus clung to Soren, eyes fixed on Victoria, who stared back at him.

Sensing Thadeus's fear, Rosie tried to bring Victoria's attention to her. "You're scaring him."

"Check his teeth," Victoria said. "I want to see their teeth."

Soren left the room with Thadeus, and Magdeline followed out with Spencer and Hamilton.

"I'm sorry Soren, but I need to..."

"I know," he said, as she put Spencer down and pried Hamilton off to transfer.

"Come here buddy," Dave, who had followed Soren, but stayed in the hall, said to Spencer.

"Did you and daddy have a slumber party like Mommy and Aunt Rosie? And what happened to that other woman? And why does she look so much like my mommy and why was she sleeping in mommy and daddy's bed?" Spencer questioned in rapid fire. "Mommy said she's another aunt."

Dave nodded, as Spencer went on.

"They look like me and my brothers, like they're triplets. Do you have triplets who look like you, Mr. Dave? You know the neighbor's cat had kittens, three! But only two looked the same. They were all born together, but one was spotted and two striped and my friend at school has an aunt that picks him up sometimes, but she doesn't look at all like his mommy!"

"Well..." Dave started, but was relieved when Spencer said, "I'll ask mommy. She's a genetic scientist. I know she can tell me why the kittens and Willy's aunt look different."

"Good idea!" Dave said. "You have a very smart mommy. I know she can answer better than me," Dave said, smiling as Spencer grabbed the remote for the television.

"Do you like Super Skunk?"

On hearing the television, both Thadeus and Hamilton let go of Soren's legs and hurried to join Dave and Spencer on the couch.

Soren looked at Dave and said, "I'll put some coffee on."

"Thank you!"

A few minutes later, Larry, who had gone back to the B&B to sleep, knocked on the door.

"I'll get it!" Spencer yelled.

"No. You watch Super Skunk," Soren said.

Larry bit back a laugh at the sight of Dave with the boys huddled on the couch. "So?" Larry asked, looking around and noting the absence of both Magdeline and Rosie, along with the somewhat, harried look Soren wore.

"So, the morning was a bit traumatic. We, meaning all adults, overslept and the boys went in to wake up Maggie to find a battered version of mommy in bed, who screamed when she saw them. Then they all screamed, and it was chaos for a while."

"They seem to be recovering," Larry noted.

"Yeah, nothing Super Skunk can't remedy. Maggie and Rosie are in with her now. She was literally shaking in terror at three-year-olds. Thadeus was staring at her, and I heard her ask Rosie to show her his teeth. I don't suppose you have any clue what that would be about?"

"She wanted to see his teeth?"

"That's what she said."

"I'll just go and…" Larry said, turning down the hall and throwing a wink at Dave, who looked like he had three new best friends.

Magdeline answered Larry's knock and ushered him in. He was surprised to see them looking at dental ex-rays.

"These are the boys dental scans on the right," Magdeline said to Larry, "and the others are from Victoria's files."

Victoria looked wearily at Larry and then explained, "This pile of the boy's scans are human. This pile is other mammals. The next is also a non-human mammal. You can tell from the rest of the skull structure, but they have human dental structure. Then the fourth is a human skull, but the dental structure isn't."

"Where are these from?" Larry asked.

"They were part of the file I told you was delivered to me. I had seen similar scans before, from the files in China. One of the projects is an experiment in not just altering and adding human genes in DNA, but in combining genes of various mammals, including human."

"You're not saying that you think they succeeded in that?"

"I know they have. My parents told me a few years ago, not in so many words of course, because our conversations are never private. They referred to a story book I used to have. You've all heard of werewolves, well this story was about animals, who could turn into humans. Anyway, I knew when my mother mentioned it, that she was telling me they had succeeded. Given the time frame, the first children would be about the age of the boys. I apologize for scaring them, but..."

"We should have set an alarm so that we would be up before they were," Magdeline said.

"Dear God," Larry said, "This reminds me of a story Shane relayed to me from Ralph, the man who helped us in Quebec, Canada."

"I thought no one else was involved," Victoria said.

"He isn't, not really anyway. He's a civilian, a freelance truck driver. He doesn't know about the projects, but he helped Shane and Alice out of some tough spots. And after she disappeared again, he keeps his eyes and ears open. Some of his deliveries are to a university lab where we know they perform, how should I say, various, questionable genetic experiments. Anyway, during a cargo transfer, one of the men suffered a bite from something. He went to a nearby emergency room and claimed it was a dog bite, but a nurse said it looked human to her. Then the guy just disappeared from the hospital, taking a suture kit and antibiotic. The company listed on the manifest was one connected with shipments to the project in the Marianas. That would have been three years ago too," Larry finished.

Soren knocked on the door and Rosie opened it. He came in with a tray of coffees.

"Why though?" Larry asked, taking a coffee and turning back to Victoria.

"Why not?" Victoria replied. "The doctors and scientists, where they held me in China, had only one goal. They are forming an army. Remember, they let lose the viruses just two years ago. Also remember that it was supposed to have originated in bats, then consider, did the virus really jump from bats to human or was it conceived in something that was both? Then that something could be used to spread it. It wouldn't have been this project specifically, but another under the control of the same power."

"What? You're not saying they created some kind of Dracula like entity that..."

"I don't know, but I wouldn't be so surprised. It's all tied together. Look at how much the whole world has changed in just the past few years. Think of the science of the projects and how much of it is now acceptable. How many other things that just a few decades ago were considered so immoral as to be illegal but are now so widely accepted that you would be criticized to speak against them. Science, society, the world economy, has all changed drastically."

"You said they're creating an army?" Larry asked.

"Yes, a hybrid army, part human, part animal, part computer. Soldiers that can both think independently yet be programmed. They have just enough skill and knowledge, yet they are not controlled by emotions, have brute animal strength and stealth. And they can be easily hidden both among people and animals."

"Dear God," Soren said.

Magdeline's mind was racing a million miles an hour, trying to absorb that something so extraordinarily horrible could be a reality.

Rosie stared at Victoria, as though frozen, and Soren squeezed Magdeline's hand.

"Do you think it's really possible? I mean, I believe you, Victoria, when you say it's been done, but to what degree?" asked Soren.

"I guess it would be possible, eventually, to achieve that goal. I know that there was a loosening of restrictions on chimerics about a year ago. That's the technical term for mixing DNA from more than one type of organism. It was connected to the Endless Frontier Act. Supposedly, the Chinese had already created human-primate embryos. This has been going on for far more than a year though. It's the goal itself that seems so incomprehensible," Magdeline replied.

"You mean, evil," Soren added.

"Exactly," said Victoria.

Rosie moved away to look out the window to where the dogs were playing in the yard. "What about my mother?" she asked. "That's why Larry and Dave came, why I'm here. What was she taken for? What are they doing to *her*?"

Magdeline moved to Rosie.

Larry was thinking about how to proceed. "It looks like this just keeps on expanding. We now have nine missing persons."

"Nine?" Rosie asked, as she and Magdeline turned back towards the others.

All eyes were on Larry, as he went on to explain. "Rosie's mom, Victoria's family, Sophie's parents, Shane's wife and son, and Alice's father. Mr. Morgan, along with Shane's wife and son have vanished now, we believe of their own accord, about the same time as Rosie's mother. We think Sophie's parents also left of their own accord, to protect her, but we can't be certain on any of them. In fact, I should up that number to fourteen, if we count Alice, Jonathan, and his brothers. We have substantial evidence to say that they left of their own accord as well. However, Rosie's mother, Claire, is the only clear kidnapping and still remains priority. I'll call Shane and ask him to check further on the Chinese angle."

Nova Scotia

Nick was sound asleep in the passenger seat when Sophie pulled up to the house. He yawned and pushed himself up and out to help Sophie with the bags. His luggage wasn't much, but she had wanted to stop for groceries on the way and had fully stocked up.

While Sophie could hardly wait to find out what happened in Sweden, she held back, steering Nick to bed, while she unpacked and put everything away.

A couple hours later, he wandered into the living room to find Sophie on the phone with Jack's mother, Anne. He poured two cups of coffee and took them to the table and sat down across from her.

"I'm sure he's fine. Nick just woke up and we were going to swing by his place anyway before we pick Jeremy up. You know how he is when he goes fishing. Everything without fins, including time, ceases to exist. If he's not home when we go by, we'll run up to the river and check a couple of his favorite spots. Okay? Yes, I promise we'll call to let you know."

"Jack went AWOL on the river again?" Nick asked.

"Sounds that way. He came by and borrowed your lure kit, and I called him last night to tell him we might be by today, but he didn't answer."

"What time?"

"Around nine."

"He was probably catching the last of the light. You know he turns his phone off so as not to scare the fish."

"How is Alice?"

"The last time I talked to Jonathan, she was stable."

He told her what he knew as they drove to Jack's.

Sophie knocked on the door.

"His truck isn't here, so I doubt he is," Nick said.

Sophie reached for her phone to call Anne.

"Hold up on that, Soph. Let me give Tom a call first."

"Okay, and I'll call Shannon. They've gone out a couple of times, but I think she's more into him than he is her."

Nick just nodded, as Tom picked up.

They hung up their phones at the same time.

"I'll call Anne. You drive. You know the hot fishing spots," Sophie said, a sense of unease settling in. This wasn't like Jack. Yes, he could get distracted fishing, but to not show up when he promised to come by his parents? And Shannon had been trying to reach him too. She only lived two blocks down and said she hadn't seen his truck for a couple of days.

They went to three of Jack's known spots before they found any sign of him.

"That's my lure case," Nick said, pointing to a log, a few meters from the riverbank.

"Are you sure?"

"Positive," Nick answered, as he walked over and picked up the kit, pointing to his initials on the corner. "I recognized the stain first," he said, pointing at a dark spot.

"It's even got my DNA. Blood droplet from catching my finger on a hook once."

"But where's his truck?"

"He may have parked at Tom's cabin and hiked in. From there, he's between a few good spots. It's not like Jack to be careless though," Nick said, as he scanned up and down the river.

"Look," Sophie said, "I see several footprints, but only ours that lead toward the road,"

"It is a popular spot. There's too much ground cover to see prints through the woods, but it's pressed down that way and over there. Come on. If we go right, we'll get to the cabin."

At the cabin, they noted two sets of tire tracks and what looked like a motorbike track.

"Now I'm really worried. Jack would never leave your kit behind. And where's his truck?"

"Hold on. I'll call Tom again and see if he knows where the tracks might be from. It's possible he had a renter, and if so, maybe they saw Jack."

"What if he fell in the river?"

"Not likely. There would have been more on the bank, and we probably would have found his truck."

"He could have been pushed."

"Hi, Tom. It's Nick again," Nick spoke to Tom, as Sophie inspected around the back of the cabin. Keeping an eye on her, Nick followed at a distance. "Yeah, okay. Thanks," he said, hanging up the call.

"So?" Sophie asked, as she inspected some broken twigs, trying to match them to nearby trees and bushes.

"He had a couple out here last week for a few days. Then he was up here to inspect it, make sure it was clean and nothing left behind. When did it last rain?"

"It's actually been dry since I've been back. What about the motorcycle track?"

"It could be from a delivery. Doesn't Shannon use a moped now? What are you looking at?"

"I was just thinking it's odd that there's no path here, but there are broken twigs from both of those bushes, like maybe someone had been hiding in them?"

"Possible, but they would most likely be from an animal going through."

Sophie sighed. "I just don't know what to tell Anne."

"Nothing yet. It may not be like Jack, but it is possible that he missed picking up my kit and moved on. Let's go check a couple more spots before we jump to conclusions."

Sophie called Nick's parents, who were happy to keep Jeremy another night, so that they could rest. Then a couple of hours later they drove up to Jack's parent's house. Both Ben and Anne came out to meet them.

"We still haven't found his truck, so he could have driven out of town. There's a lake down by Dartsmouth I know he likes, and we'll go check down at Sheet Harbor as well," Nick said.

"And maybe he wanted to try someplace new," Ben added. "It's possible Anne."

"Then why hasn't he called?" asked Anne.

"His battery could be dead," Nick offered.

"I'm calling the police," Anne said.

"I'm calling Shane," said Sophie. Anne hung up the phone and all eyes turned to Sophie. "It could be connected."

"Connected?" asked Ben.

"I think we should tell them what we learned about Jeremy."

"How much?" Nick asked.

"All of it!" Anne said. "Who told you what and when?" she demanded.

Nick looked to Sophie.

"We...I...," Sophie tried to start, her mind darting a million miles an hour on how to explain what she needed to without giving away what she knew about Alice and Jonathan. Anne had almost been killed once already for knowing too much. "I think it could be related to the same projects that I was part of," she began.

"But Jack was a normal birth. Trust me, I remember," Anne said.

"Yes, but I think it's possible that there's still a connection. I mean..." she stammered, searching for the best way to continue. "What I mean is, maybe someone thought that Jack knew too much."

"I think he's still investigating Alice's family," Nick added.

"You mentioned Jeremy," Ben said.

"Jack was concerned that Jeremy could be a target because of the genes he shares with Sophie. After all, she was kidnapped, and well, you know about her parent's and Josephine's involvement. Jack is genetically related to them. If you take that along with whatever he may have discovered, then..."

"Exactly," Sophie added, "and we never did find the man who took me."

After an awkward silence, where Sophie could feel Anne's eyes boring into her soul, as though she knew that Sophie hadn't admitted the whole truth, Sophie phoned Shane.

She was surprised when he sounded like she had woken him. It was still early in Seattle, but Paris was a different matter. And after Shane explained that his wife, Patricia and one son were missing, Sophie told him about Jack. He didn't even question her reasoning in calling him.

It fit in with Dave's theory of family and Claire's abduction. Jack was Sophie's cousin and even though Sophie had been adopted, her aunt Josephine, who was a prime player in all of this, was also Jack's aunt. They had already deduced that Josephine's lineage played a role and Jack's mother was her first cousin.

Chapter 8

Seattle: May 20th

Suzanna sat on the floor of Alice's condo with Detective Lidia Yarnok and Charice, going through the photos that Brent had given her.

"There's just so many!" Suzanna exclaimed, overwhelmed.

They were trying to categorize them by general locations, setting aside those where they spotted one of the brothers watching her.

"I don't think they're the same man," Lidia said, holding up two of the photos. "Look at his ears and the hair line. I know it's a small image, but when you use the magnifier, it looks like his hair is more than two days of growth lower to his ear. The sunglasses are different too. Can I take these? I'll bring them back, but these are the best photos we have of any of them, and even though the one only shows half of his face, I'd like to scan them and run them through our facial comparison program."

"Do whatever you want, Lidia. Send them to whoever. Charice?"

"Yes?"

"Can you go through all the company portfolios and photo archives? I want to see every photo attached to a file or taken at a party since Alice was born."

"It sounds like you're trying to do my job now," said Lidia.

"No, I'm just trying to do what I should have done a long time ago; be a mother. Edgar walked away and right now, I don't even want to know where, but Alice, I do want to know. I want to get to know her as well as I can, and if possible, I want to do all I can to protect her, wherever she is."

"I'll pull it all up, whatever I can find, but what are you hoping to find?" asked Charice.

"I'm not sure. I'd also like to go talk to Brent again, but not alone."

"I'll go with you," Lidia volunteered. "I haven't been that direction for a while, and he sounds like an interesting character. I'll run a background check on him too. To be honest, I'm thinking of following in Shane and Dave's footsteps and going private. I avoid the station as much as possible. The only one I'd miss would be Selma, in forensics, and she's trying to get a transfer."

"If you do, I'll be your first client," Suzanna said.

"And you can count on Max as a military source," added Charice. He's developed quite a penchant for investigation himself."

"And what about you?" Lidia asked Charice, "It seems you have a touch of the investigator too."

"I'm loyal to Mrs. Morgan and Alice. You know I'd do whatever I can to find out what happened to her and know she's okay."

"And Edgar?" Lidia asked.

Charice looked at Suzanna and shook her head. "I still can't believe he disappeared like he did, but like Suzanna, I don't doubt he left of his own accord. He left everything too well arranged for Morgan Acquisitions and Morgan Enterprises. All the funding is in place, everything was moved completely into Suzanna's name more than a month before."

"My husband was very efficient in his arrangements."

"Who is actually running Morgan Acquisitions and Enterprises now?"

"Technically, me," said Suzanna, "but that just means I have final approval. Edgar was more hands on in the decision making. I approved a turnover of that to the board. They all have equal say. Lately we've been working more with smaller merchants, trying to help some of the businesses that couldn't hold on during the virus. We developed a kind of co-op to help similar businesses band together. They each keep their own branding, but funds are pooled, and they are officially owned by Morgan Enterprises. We distribute the budget for each. The founding owners receive an annual percentage of profits, based on how much Morgan paid to buy them out."

"Interesting," Lidia replied.

"For all of his faults, Edgar always had good intentions," Suzanna said, wiping away a tear. "Excuse me."

"They really loved each other," Charice said to Lidia.

"I know. And now she's alone. I feel bad for her. I'm glad she has your loyalty, Charice. The more I get to know her and the more I learn about Alice, the more I really want to be able to focus on helping them."

"I can understand that. What about you?"

"What do you mean?" Lidia asked.

"You're young, single. Is there anyone special?"

"Not really."

Charice gave her a questioning look.

"Can you keep a secret Charice?"

"Of course."

"There's another reason I want to stay on this. I miss someone too sometimes, and he's working this case in Europe. We never dated, I was with someone else, but we were partners, and I miss working with Dave."

"You mean you miss Dave."

Lidia smiled and blushed, as Suzanna came back in.

"I'm sorry about that. Sometimes it just gets to me," Suzanna said.

"That's called being human," Charice said.

"And that's a good thing," Lidia added.

Switzerland

Trudie was worried. She picked up the phone twice to call Soren but didn't. She knew he didn't want to be part of this, whatever this was. And she wanted him and Magdeline to have a normal life with their boys. After all, that was why they moved to Austria. After the incident in the vault and the death of Professor Crabben, things had almost returned to normal until Sarah came around and told her the truth about Ana.

Yesterday, Sarah told her, what Trudie could only pray was, the rest of the story. Just knowing that Ana was the product of an affair had been enough of a shock. What Sarah had come to talk to her about last week had put Trudie on red alert.

It started out normally enough, though this was the first time Sarah had driven into Scangentech. She said that she wanted to see some of the people she used to work with and that it wasn't fair for Trudie to always come to her. Sarah had been warmly welcomed by the few who were still around that she had worked with. Then Trudie took off early. She wasn't comfortable talking about anything personal related to Sarah in her office, which she still worried was likely under surveillance.

Sarah began with telling her about the visit from Dave Asher, who worked with the man who had been an original agent in charge of her and Ana's disappearance. She said that he had come before and asked about family genealogies. Of course, Stephan was friendly with him, and they chatted easily. Dave inquired about Ana, who had been at work. He asked Sarah and Stephen more about their family history too, telling them that he was still trying to draw genealogical connections.

"I know he was trying to connect our family history to why they wanted Ana. I had to bite my tongue from

screaming that he was barking up the wrong family tree,"
Sarah said. And for a moment, Trudie thought that she was
going to reveal who Ana's true father was. Instead, Sarah
then asked about Dr. Crabben. She wanted to know whose
samples he was accused of taking and if they had
discovered anything more about who had been in the vault
with him or about his death.

"You know I'm not at liberty to tell you that," Trudie
replied. Then Sarah went on to say that she believed it was
all tied back to the Cryogenic DNA Conservation or CDC
program.

That was why Trudie wanted to talk to Soren. She knew
that he believed that the program may not have really been
ended. But what could that have to do with Ana or Sarah's
genealogy? When she asked Sarah that question, she again
mentioned the man she had seen at the conference in Paris,
just before her abduction. She said that she didn't know his
name, but he was tall with dark hair, and she felt he was
watching her. She had also seen him talking with another
man that she knew to be working with Professor Crabben.

Trudie's first thought was to encourage Sarah to go to the
authorities, but the police were only involved in what was
considered a car accident. The DNA theft investigation had
all been kept internal, and she believed that it had to be
someone internal who was working outside of
Scangentech's protocol that was responsible for what had
happened to Soren in France and the DNA theft, which
meant the likely murder of Crabben.

She picked up the phone again to call Soren. He didn't
answer, so she left a simple message for him to call her
back as soon as he could.

Austria May 21st

"Hey Trudie, what's up? I'm sorry I couldn't get back to

you yesterday. It's a little hectic here right now."

"Is everyone all right?"

"The boys and Maggie are fine. We have some unexpected company. Is everything okay there?"

She told him what Sarah had told her.

"I think you need to talk to Dave Asher on this. I happen to know that he was just there last week to check in on the Martinsons."

"How would I get in touch with him?"

"If you call back in about an hour, he'll be here. It's a long story. Both he and Larry Marquet, the former INTERPOL liaison, are here."

"I don't want to go to anyone official. That's why I called you. I'm sorry, I shouldn't be bothering you with this, but..."

"No apologies needed. I get it. It's all connected. Both Larry and Dave have gone private and started working together. There's more tied to this than you know. You did the right thing calling me. They need to know about this. Should I ask them to call you when they get here?"

"Please."

"Okay Trudie, will do."

"What was that about?" asked Magdeline, coming up behind and wrapping her arms around him. "Is Trudie okay?"

"She's fine, but she has some information from Mrs. Martinson. I'm going to have Dave and Larry give her a call when they get here. It has to do with Professor Crabben," Soren said, turning and brushing back her hair as he kissed her forehead.

"Breakfast was delicious. Thank you. Thank you for putting up with all of this. Rosie, Victoria..."

"You're welcome," he said, kissing her mouth. "You know I can put up with anything, so long as you promise to keep putting up with me."

The boys were all showing off to Rosie, hanging spoons from their noses, and Soren was just about to pull Magdeline around the corner for a longer kiss when Larry and Dave knocked at the door. Spencer ran to let them in. He knew it was them, because Dave had made up a secret knock with the boys the other day.

"When this is all over, do you think your parents could come stay with the boys for a week, Maggie?"

Magdeline smiled and went to help Rosie with the boys, while Soren went to talk to Dave and Larry about his call from Trudie.

"I'll call Trudie. We've spoken before," Larry said, "but I want Dave to sit in, since he had the last contact with the Martinson's. Is there someplace quiet where we can talk privately?"

"Why don't you two use my office," Magdeline offered.

They kept the call with Trudie as short as they could, while making sure they wrote down all the information and asked a few pertinent questions regarding Professor Crabben. Trudie scanned a copy of his personnel file and sent it to them. They now had his date of birth, place of birth and the person who had been his emergency contact. That, of course, had been his son Aaron, who still worked in the vault, maintaining data on all samples, from the history of the individual during their life, to the history of any movement or information requests of their DNA.

Larry wanted to look at Aaron more closely and send Dave to investigate deeper into Sarah's genealogy. It did seem that the genealogy of the women was more involved than that of the men. That meant finding out the background on both of her parents. This was basic information that Dave had, but because her biological father was out of her life at such an early age, Dave had focused on Sarah's mother and Stephan's family background. Now it seemed that the research on Stephan could be scrapped. They needed to know more about Sarah's biological father.

Just this was enough on its own, but add on the original case of Claire's disappearance, throw in Victoria, and yesterday, Shane called to tell them that Jack had gone missing. How were they going to handle it all?

"I feel like we were walking in some rain and suddenly got dumped on by an avalanche," Larry said. "We definitely need Katz help."

They spent the rest of the day going over the files Victoria had and maps of the area where Rosie and Claire had been living. They needed a plan for Victoria. She was healing well and had been formally introduced to the boys as their other aunt. She couldn't stay there forever though.

Even though she had cancelled her current concert engagement, she still had others. It was decided that she would keep the room at the B&B rented until she was due to meet for her next concert, which would be in Bern, Switzerland on the following Saturday.

Larry was also continuing to stay there just in case he saw anyone who may be watching Victoria. Soren and Magdeline insisted they pay for the lodging of both Larry and Dave as officially employed private investigators.

"It's only right," Soren said.

"I'm the one who called you about Claire and brought Victoria into this," Magdeline added.

Later that evening they met at the cabin and did a video meeting with Shane.

"What I don't understand is why Mrs. Martinson didn't tell me about the connection between the man she saw in Paris and Professor Crabben. Unless she was afraid that it would somehow give away her affair," Dave said. "I had a feeling that she was holding back. She seemed so detached when I was questioning Mr. Martinson about his genealogy. Do you know how much time I spent looking into him? And now we find out he's not even Ana's father."

"I know," Larry said. "I wish Trudie would have filled us in on that sooner too, but I doubt she realized the relevance and was just staying loyal to her friend."

"So why let the cat out of the bag now?" Shane asked.

"Because she's also a loyal friend to Soren and Magdeline," Larry explained. "She did ask, and we agreed, to try and not let on that we know. We don't want to alarm Mrs. Martinson or cause a rift between her and her husband. The affair itself is a private matter. But we need her to tell Trudie who it was with. For now, we'll focus on Sarah Martinson and why she would have been chosen."

"The hard thing is, I can't seem to get a lead on her birth father. We have his name, but after her parent's divorce, he just seems to vanish. No photos, nothing, and about seventy-five possibilities of men in the right age range in Europe. Her mother is a dead end too. It seems that after her daughter had been sent to Reflect de L'esprit for treatment, she moved back to Marseille, where she stayed."

"And since Mrs. Martinson has been home? Hasn't she even come to visit Ana?"

"No. From what Mrs. Martinson told me," said Dave, "They had been estranged since her mother married husband number three. Sarah had been close to her step-father, who she is in touch with, and he came to visit once, but he lives in Spain and has zero genetic connection."

"I talked to her mother, Paula, whose maiden name is Bernard, which, happens to be the second most common surname in France. The last name of Sarah's father is Mueller and covers about half of Germany.

"Paula also didn't seem to know or care much about any of her family. She did give me the name of her parents, which I already had from Mrs. Martinson. Then she said she needed to go. She was what you might call stonily polite. So, right now I'm looking for a needle in multiple haystacks."

"We're passing the genealogy research all over to Philip," Larry said.

"That makes sense," Shane said. "He's already looking more deeply into Jack's family. Fortunately, Sophie was able to collect family records from his parents. So, most names and dates are already there. You said he wanted to stay busy," Shane laughed.

"I think he was hoping for something a bit less monotonous," Larry replied, "But we need to get some lead on Claire. So far, we've got nothing. Rosie gave us a partial plate, but it gave us three possibles, two of which are owned by a large fleet. The third is a medical lift van, owned by a rental service that loans out to medical facilities. We're waiting on the rental records. Not being official makes getting them a little slow, and most of my contacts are in France. Fortunately, one of them has a brother-in-law who works for the Austrian Federal Police. Hopefully, we'll be able to get a look at those Monday. I'm also looking into getting camera footage from Nova Scotia border crossings to see if Jack's truck shows up."

Nova Scotia

Anne knew that they were doing all they could, but that wasn't going to stop her from doing what she could too. Jack was her only son, and he was missing. She couldn't sit back and do nothing. She knew that Ben was just as worried, but he was distracted by the necessary work on the farm. Besides, it was her side of the family that had somehow gotten messed up in all of this, her side.

The records, family Bible and photos were strewn over the table. She had given copies of it all to Sophie, but still,

Anne was the one who had been there when many of the photos were taken. She was the one who had grown up with her cousins, who were key in this and had listened to stories told at the dinner table. Maybe, just maybe, something here would bring back a memory of a conversation or event that would shed light on why someone would take Jack.

She had to believe that was what happened. It was far better than the thoughts of him being in an accident.

Her first fear was that he had slipped in the water and drowned, but when his car wasn't found, she worried that he might have crashed somewhere. Nick had searched for two days now, with no sign of Jack's truck. She knew he wouldn't have gone far. That made it all the more likely that he had been abducted, which meant that he was most likely alive.

Nova Scotia was only accessible by a few points, and they were looking for a way to gain access to traffic cameras.

She looked through her pictures, sorting aside those that included her cousins Josephine and Lily or their immediate family.

Sophie was also going through family photos and taking an especially close look at the photo Jack and Nick found of the parade with the millennium countdown clock. She saw the girl who was supposed to be her, but wasn't her, and then thought of Pollina. It couldn't have been her, but could Josephine have fostered another look alike? Then there was Amber, who looked a lot like Sophie's adopted mother, Lily. What did it mean?

She shook her head. She needed to think about Jack. Instead, her mind drifted to Alice. At one point, after they first met in New York, they had been so connected. Then again in Greece, Sophie could feel Alice. Even when she and Jack were in Seattle for Alice's memorial, Sophie sensed she was still alive. Right now, when she thought of Alice, all she felt was confusion.

Alice had asked about Jack. She knew Alice didn't want to drag him into all of this, but it seemed she didn't have to. He was already family by extension. *Family*, that word wouldn't leave her alone.

She went to the bedside table where she kept her mother's Bible, then she went online and did a genealogy search. Even though she had also given these records to Dave, she wanted to look at them again herself. She thought about sending copies of all the photos to Dave too, but he wouldn't know the places or people like her. So, she decided not to waste time. She needed to feel like she was doing something.

Nick had gone out again to look for signs of Jack's truck and then went to Jack's cottage to look through any personal correspondence.

Sophie had just typed her great grandmother's name into the ancestry app and came up with only the names of her great-grandfather and their children, which she already knew, when Nick called.

"Did you find something?" Sophie asked.

"It's more what I didn't find that has me worried. His laptop is gone. I know he doesn't use it for fishing, so that tells me that whoever..."

"Took Jack, took his laptop too. Which tells me that someone thought he had something important on it. What though? And is anything else missing?"

"It doesn't look like it. I know that Jack had scanned and downloaded everything he had on Alice, including the file that I burned. My hope is that he may have made a backup. I don't suppose you know his password to check the cloud files."

"No, but Jack wouldn't have stored that there. If anything, he would have put it on a thumb drive."

"I checked the desk and shelves and..."

"Check his underwear drawer or under his mattress."

"Okay, going there now."

"And?"

"Nothing in the underwear. Hang on a sec while I check the mattress."

"Anything," Sophie asked a few seconds later.

"Maybe, but not under the mattress. I found his computer bag under the bed. It's empty except for two thumb drives and a notebook. I'll bring it home. How's Jeremy?"

"Being an angel and making me some more family pictures. They're interesting. We look like we're in a punk rock group. You have green hair and mine is purple. He gave me lots of jewelry too. Oh, and there's a P-U-P-P-Y."

"Oh my. I'll be home soon. Should I pick anything up?"

"Actually, that would be great. Maybe some S-P-A-G-H-E-T-T-I from the pub and some M-U-F-F-I-N's from the café. Make sure you keep..."

"I know. I'll smuggle the muffins in in Jack's computer bag."

"Is that daddy?" Jeremy asked, his wavy dark rust colored hair bouncing against rosy cheeks, as he left his drawing and ran to Sophie.

"It was, but daddy's busy. He just called to let me know when he'll be home."

"And is he getting the M-U-F-F-I-N's?"

Sophie looked in shock for a moment at the two- year-old, who stood grinning in front of her, then asked, "Do you know what that is?"

"No. I hope it's food though. I'm hungry!"

Sophie smiled.

"Why don't you have one of the little bananas and some milk, and I'll clear off the table so we can eat when daddy gets home. You still have half a bottle from lunch in the door of the fridge."

"Okay. Can I have chocolate milk?"

"No. Finish what you already opened. We can talk about chocolate after dinner."

"Okay," Jeremy sighed, and Sophie started to move the pictures off the table, making sure to keep them all sorted.

She was just picking up the last pile when one caught her eye. It was from the pile that had been part of her memory book and included the parade photo. It was a polaroid of a birthday party and was marked, "Sophie- 8years old". At first glance, it was just a picture of children sitting on the floor while Sophie opened gifts. She remembered this day.

Some of the children were her cousins. No, *all* of the children were her cousins. That's why she remembered. She'd had two parties that year. One was with her friends and this one for her cousins and other family, but why?

She remembered being confused as to why her mother didn't want her to have her friends at the party. Her mother had said something about there not being enough room and it being more fun to have two parties. Then Sophie quickly looked through all the photos marked as her 8th birthday. This was the only one of her cousins. The piles were in chronological order, and she looked to see if there were any others. There weren't.

Tucking the polaroid into her Bible, she finished clearing and setting the table just as Nick got home.

Chapter 9

Switzerland, May 22nd

Sarah followed Stephan into the sanctuary. It was only a couple of hours a week. It was the least that she could manage for him. Today was also a rare occasion because Ana was with them. It seems that her friend Aida had the day off and wanted to come.

Usually, the lodge was too busy over the weekend for Aida to get away, but it had been a long time since she had been to a Sunday service, plus she hoped it might be a way to help Ana reconnect with her parents and eventually get over her resentment about Sebastian's leaving.

Aida understood Ana's pain, but Ana was too young to keep pining as she herself did. Also, Sebastian had been her stepbrother and left of his own desire, whereas Kristor believed he had no choice. That was why Aida couldn't let go. She believed that Kristor felt the same for her and that if he could come back to her, he would.

One part of her realized that she could hardly be the only woman he'd ever meet, and that in three years, it was very possible that he no longer gave her a second thought. She didn't believe that though. Her heart wouldn't let her let go. She'd gone out with a few other men that her brothers had deemed worthy to set her up with, and she'd even had fun with a couple of them, but there was no spark. Fortunately, the lack of spark seemed mutual, and they didn't pursue her. Her brother Fredrick, the only one she had confessed to about her trip to Verona, said it was because they could always sense the other man on her mind. Verona, such an ironic place for them to have parted. A tragic love story, just like Romeo and Juliet, only they weren't dead, which meant there was still hope.

Aida pulled her mind back to the present. She could sense Ana's tension and wondered if there was more to it.

Aida knew Ana had been kidnapped as a child, which was why she wasn't in the regular school system and had been able to come to work for them at the lodge. She also knew that Ana's mother, Sarah, had been hospitalized from the trauma, but Ana never talked about it further. What Aida didn't realize was that it was during that time that Sebastian had come into the picture. That was something that had confused her, but Ana had clearly said stepbrother, not half-brother, and so she let it go.

The music started and Aida glanced at Ana and her mother as they stood. Mr. Martinson was on the other side of them, and Aida couldn't help but notice the difference of their attitude. She had the strangest feeling that neither Ana nor her mother wanted to be there. Not that it was really her business, she thought as she sang along.

Sarah had learned to relax. She knew he wasn't there. It wasn't even the same church. Stephan said they had moved services into this new building five years ago. She had told Ana as much, but still, even though Sarah had been through a lot, it was nothing compared to what Ana had gone through.

After church, Ana went back up to the lodge with Aida and Sarah took the new car that Stephan had gotten her. Why did he have to be so good to her?

It was there when she had returned from meeting with Trudie the other day. He had even tied a bow and put a card on the wipers. It was a brand-new, red, Land Rover, with all the bells and whistles. She hadn't known what to say or do. When she'd gone in the house, she found him in the kitchen, making dinner, the table set with candles and her favorite wine. At first, she had just stared, and then, still focused on the vegetables he was chopping, he had asked if she liked it or if she preferred a different color. She wiped at her face to stop the tears that had gathered in her eyes from running down and told him that it was wonderful, that he was wonderful, which was true.

For the rest of the evening, she had just let him take the lead, while she tried to blot out all the fears racing through her mind. Ana was eighteen now, and Sarah wasn't sure if that made her more or less safe.

Trudie had called her the night before to ask if she would like to have lunch and go shopping at the new outlet stores that were almost midway between them. Sarah had jumped at the excuse to not join Stephan for lunch with the Trent's.

Trudie was trying to think of ways to coax the identity of Ana's father out of Sarah. Could it have been somebody from Scangentech? That would make the most sense, but then she remembered that Sarah had said it happened at home. If she didn't get it out of her, then tomorrow, Trudie would go back through the employee files to see who else lived near Sarah.

There was another comment Sarah made when she first confessed that Stephan wasn't Ana's father. At first, Trudie put it off as the effect of drugs and that Sarah simply hadn't been thinking clearly. When Trudie had asked outright about Ana's father, Sarah said something about it being *both of them.* Both of whom? She had also said that Ana wasn't normal.

Trudie had only seen Ana briefly since her return, but considering all she'd been through, she sounded like a normal enough withdrawn teenager, and before the abduction, Trudie remembered her as a sweet child, a little shy, but nothing unusual.

Grabbing her purse, she kissed her husband, Russell, and headed out to meet Sarah.

On the drive, Sarah ran into road construction and was forced to make a detour. Traffic was slow and when she reached the first intersection, instead of following the detour, she made her own detour. She had only set an approximate time to meet Trudie, and she wasn't planning to go too far off course. She just wanted to see it, see where professor Crabben had supposedly driven or been blown off the road.

Trudie said there was evidence of a bomb, and they hadn't even bothered to look for remains. Who would want to kill Crabben though? She knew it must have to do with the CDC program, but why now? Was it because she was no longer locked away and they feared what she might remember? Why not kill her then? Was it a warning to her or could she be wrong? It had been ten years. Perhaps the vault breach and his death were about some new project he'd gotten involved with.

She couldn't shake the feeling though, that it was all connected. The timing of his death was just too much of a coincidence to only be a coincidence. Dave Asher knew everything was connected too, he just didn't know how or through who. They had to have picked her to have Ana for a reason.

She didn't want to think about it, yet she did, because she had to. She needed to understand as much as possible to protect Ana. At eighteen and distraught over Sebastian, there was no telling what she might do or who she might inadvertently come into relationship with. Aida did seem nice, but one friend wouldn't hold Ana back if she decided to leave.

Sarah knew that she must have a decent sum of money saved up. Stephan had given her a crypto wallet not long after she started at the lodge. It hadn't had much in it to start with, but Ana was thrifty and worked a lot of overtime. She had also confessed that she had some funds, though she wouldn't disclose how much, from Brazil, that she had invested.

Investing seemed to be the only common ground Stephan and Ana had found. And they were both good at it. Ana had admitted that if they ever had to leave, her portfolio was increasing steadily. At least she had included Sarah in her thoughts of leaving.

The lake came into view just as she turned around the corner. It wasn't a large lake. In fact, it was almost just another part of the river that flowed down toward the French border.

She pulled over just the other side of the bridge that spanned the river. Getting out, she stared down. She wished that she could talk to Crabben again.

An hour later she was having soup and sandwiches with Trudie and wondering why Trudie seemed so curious. The questions weren't direct. Sarah had avoided answering the direct questions of who Ana's father was, but she knew Trudie was fishing and wasn't sure how long she could swim around the answer. So, she told her a partial answer, which she thought was true.

"I don't think he gave me his real name because he was married. And to answer your next question, no. He didn't work at Scangentech and was no one you would have known. I didn't want to confess that I don't really know who her father is. I'm ashamed enough," she told Trudie.

"Well," Trudie said, when she called Larry Marquet that evening, "She answered me about Ana's father, but I'm afraid it won't help much, except to eliminate any Scangentech employees."

"Did she say how she met him?"

"Only that it was at a dinner party, which was to do with work. So, odds are, he's part of the scientific community."

"Still, it would be like looking for the right needle in a stack of needles," Dave said.

"Thanks anyway, Trudie. I appreciate the effort," Larry said.

Lyon, France: May 23rd

Shane hung up the phone with Larry and went to pack. They had discussed it over the weekend and decided that it would be best, at least for now, if Shane was in Austria with Dave, while Larry accompanied Victoria to her next concert. Margot was also planning to join Larry in Bern for the weekend.

Knowing that Daniel loved trains and wanting to see as much as possible himself, Shane made a booking to leave after lunch. Soren would pick them up after work and they would all eat dinner together. Shane was anxious to meet Victoria, and Daniel was anxious to meet Thadeus, Spencer and Hamilton.

He couldn't imagine what it would be like to have four three-year-old boys in the house, but Magdeline had insisted, and Daniel had been excited to meet her too. He had met them all during Patricia's video calls, but to have three new playmates!

"Remember, you're bigger than them, so make sure you play nice," Shane reminded him.

"I will daddy. Will mommy be there too?" Daniel asked,

"No, remember I told you that mommy and Kenneth had to go someplace special for treatment."

"Yeah, because of the pains Kenneth has, because he grows even faster than me."

"That's right," Shane said, and wasn't sure if Daniel looked disappointed or relieved as he stared out the window. Shane imagined, that like him, it was a mix. He missed Patty, but then he had plenty of time to get used to that during the five years she was missing before, and at least this time he was sure she had left of her own free will, otherwise she wouldn't have taken Kenneth and left Daniel.

Eventually, he knew that Daniel would start asking why mommy didn't call. In fact, he had already asked if mommy stopped loving him because he made Kenneth mad.

Shane told him that mommy would never stop loving them both. He only hoped it was true. The going away for treatment story was the only thing he could come up with when Patricia disappeared, and he prayed that somehow this could all be resolved without hurting Daniels's heart as much as it hurt his own.

Nova Scotia

Jeremy was at the skate rink, with Nick, while Sophie took the photo over to Jack's mom.

Ben served the coffee and insisted on warming up some cinnamon raisin buns for them before going into town to pick up the groceries that Anne gave him a list for.

"He's just trying to be helpful and stay busy so that he doesn't think on Jack, but he's making me crazy! Now what was it you wanted to show me?" Anne asked.

"This photo. I remember that they're all my cousins, but Jack isn't there. He came to the other party with my friends. Do you recognize them?"

"Do you have any of their parents?" Anne asked.

"I'm afraid not. This polaroid is the only one of them. All the rest are of the other party."

"I wonder," Anne started. "I do seem to recall Josephine visiting that year, but I don't remember your party being delayed."

"So, maybe this party was before my birthday."

"Yes, that would make sense. What I started to say though, is that I wonder if these cousins are from Simon's side of the family. That would explain why I don't recognize them, except for that one. The one boy looks familiar. I know I've seen him before. Those two with the dark hair look like twins. I don't suppose you remember who was taking the photo?"

Sophie thought for a minute. "No, I'm afraid not. I only remember the party and that they're all cousins because Mom said that I was having two parties. Another thing that bugs me is, I remember visiting Josephine in France and meeting other cousins, but I'm certain that it wasn't any of the children in this photo."

"Some of them could be foster children who weren't there when you were. They might also be Simon's side of the family," Anne said. "Between you and me, I always thought Simon was a little odd."

"You have no idea," Sophie thought, remembering Pollina and Amber.

"The one boy could be Simon's son," Anne said. They look a bit alike, and I remember, Josephine did mention he had a son before, but no, that can't be it. Unless he's a lot older than he looks here, Simon and Josephine would have already been married when he was born. Let me just check their wedding date."

As Anne got up, her cat, Pudding, was displaced from her lap. The butterscotch-colored cat yawned, looked up, and a few seconds later had made herself at home on Sophie's lap.

Sophie smiled and stroked the contented feline, who began to purr, as Anne returned.

"Here we go," Anne said, "They were married in 1988? So, I suppose it is possible. He would only have been a baby and Simon couldn't have been divorced for long."

"That's the same year I was born," Sophie commented. "Are you sure he was married to the mother?" Sophie asked.

Anne sighed. "I'm not sure of anything about him. You're right, I shouldn't assume he was ever married before. I guess, I'm just old fashioned. That must be who he is though. I vaguely remember Josephine mentioning him, and I must have seen a photo of him or met him the last time I went to visit."

Sophie was debating on whether to tell Anne about Pollina and Amber, but wouldn't she already know? Jack had told her that Anne kept in touch and had been the one to call Josephine after Sophie's parents disappeared.

"When is the last time you saw Josephine?"

"It must be close to twenty-five years. Jack wasn't quite a teenager when we went to France last. When is the last time you saw her?" Anne asked.

"When I was sixteen. We all went to visit. I don't remember much about Simon. I think that he was gone a lot while we were there."

"Sophie…"

"What is it?"

"I know that Josephine has to be mixed up in all of this, I'm guessing, maybe even as much as Nigel. You forget, I'm the one who knew the truth about you before you knew. Josephine was a nurse. I highly suspect she didn't give up medicine for a vineyard. In fact, I have a feeling, and I think that you can confirm it, that she is still in the medical field. Am I right?"

"I believe you are."

"I used to call Josephine at least a few times a year. New Year, Christmas, Easter, Birthday, but since Lily and Nigel last went missing, I've only heard from her once. When we were teenagers in Ireland, we were all fairly close, though, I was always closer to Lily, your mom. Josephine was the more independent and often rebellious one."

"Anyway," Anne continued, "I got a postcard from a village in Switzerland. Josephine apologized for not giving me their new phone number and left a number at the bottom of the card. I rang it and it was answered by someone who identified themselves as a restaurant. I thought I must have dialed wrong, so I tried again. The same thing happened. I don't know. Maybe she wrote it down wrong. It struck me as odd though to have received the card at all."

"When was this?"

"About two or two and a half years ago. Hang on a second and I'll get it, then you can read the whole thing. it should be in this basket," she said, turning to the shelf behind them.

Sophie took the postcard and read, *"The skiing is great! I'm so sorry that I forgot to give you our new phone number.* 33-989-122-340." Sophie stared at the number for a minute. "Do you remember the name of the restaurant?"

"No, why?"

"I don't know. It just seems strange."

"This whole business is strange. You know I'm not one to anger easily, but I'm angry at Josephine. I used to admire both her and your mother for adopting and fostering children. I was never sure about the reasons they didn't have their own though."

"I thought my mother couldn't have children."

"That's what she told me," Anne said. "but I... I don't know. Actually, I do know one thing, but it happened a long time ago and Lily told me in confidence."

"What is it, Anne? Anything could be relevant."

"I don't see how it would matter, but Josephine had a baby. She was only seventeen and it wasn't as accepted then as it would be now, especially in Ireland. I don't know if it was a girl or a boy. Anyway, Lily said that Josephine never even saw it. The doctors took it away immediately, and supposedly, it was adopted. Soon after, Josephine started her nursing studies."

Sophie was silent.

"Are you okay Sophie?"

"Yes. I think I just realized something. I have a secret too. Only Nick knows about it, but it has to do with Josephine, and as I said, anything could be relevant."

"Okay then, spit it out."

"It may sound a little crazy."

"No crazier than anything else."

"You have to promise not to tell anyone else. If the wrong people found out, like Simon..."

"I wouldn't tell Simon a secret if my life depended on it."

"Three years ago, I got a letter from Scotland. It was written by two girls who said they were my cousins and that they were twins. The one looks just like me, the other like my mother at their age."

"And?" Anne asked.

"They wanted to meet me. They had overheard their parents, Josephine and Simon, talking about me. So, I flew over and met them in secret."

"In Scotland?"

"Yes."

"And Josephine and Simon were there?"

"Yes, well for part of the time. Simon left for France, but Josephine was there with the girls."

"You saw her?"

"From a distance."

"And what did you just realize?" Anne prodded.

"I'm sorry. I'm trying to articulate it. I think that Josephine may have actually given birth to both of them. I think the one though, must have been implanted? I mean, the one who looks like me can't be hers, but the other looks so much like an old picture of my mother that it would make sense if she were Josephine's. Still, both girls are being treated as part of the same program. So, I am really confused about that."

"You mean an experiment like you and Alice were part of?"

"Exactly. They both have increased IQ's and abilities like us as well. You know, I consider myself normal, but do you remember how easily I learned to skate?"

"I do," Anne replied. "I assumed it was just a God given talent."

"It was a gene given talent. Alice was able to skate the first time on the ice with Jack in New York."

"Jack," Anne sighed. "I just want to know where he is and that he's okay. I don't really know how this helps. Can I get you some more coffee?" she asked, already refilling both of their mugs.

"Thank you." Sophie said, turning the postcard over in her hands. Then she got her phone out and searched the locations both on the card and on the postmark.

"What are you looking for?" Anne asked.

"Did you know that there's another one of us in Switzerland?"

"What do you mean?"

"Another woman who looks like me and Alice, but she's like me. Dr. Marshall saved her, and she was adopted."

"I wonder how many there are."

"So do I. Here's the strange thing, like my cousin in Scotland, she's not the same age. She's two years older. Nick also showed me this picture," Sophie said, showing the picture from the parade. From the countdown clock, we know this is not me either. She's still an unknown. My cousin is too young and the woman in Switzerland was raised in Italy."

"I agree, it's a mystery, and I wish Thomas Marshall were here to give us some more answers. It sounds like they had major operations in Quebec, Paris and maybe around here," Anne said, picking up the postcard."

"I'm not so sure that Josephine mailed that card," Sophie said.

"I recognize the handwriting, but what makes you say that?"

"The girls. I don't believe that Simon would have let them leave Scotland. When I was there, they were being kept pretty much isolated and I can't believe that they would be left alone, though they are perfectly capable of taking care of themselves. They were closely watched, like Alice was. I also can't picture Josephine leaving them with Simon to go skiing. Can you?"

"No, I can't. But, who and why? And the handwriting."

"When I first contacted my cousins in Scotland, they had sent me the number to a friend's phone and a time to call. They weren't even allowed their own phones." Sophie paused. "They were afraid. They had overheard Simon and Josephine talking about injections they were supposed to start getting. They discovered that they could replace the drug with saline and that Josephine was none the wiser. Being a nurse though, I would be surprised if she hadn't figured it out, but the last time I talked to them was after this card. We lost touch after the virus lockdown, and I haven't heard from them since.

"My feeling," Sophie continued, "is that Josephine may be being manipulated by Simon. Maybe she's afraid of him, and like the girls, she may have used someone else to mail this. Maybe this was her way of trying to contact you about something more than a phone number. I'm going to call and find out the name of that restaurant," Sophie said, as Anne handed the postcard back.

France

Laura hurried to answer her business phone. "Café La Famille', Commet puis-je vous aider?" Laura asked.

Sophie switched into French and asked if Laura knew anyone by the name of Josephine Chedaux.

"Oui."

After asking who Sophie was, Laura explained the restaurant and her café's connection with the Chedaux vineyard. Laura said, "I don't understand why she would give you this number. We only see her if we have to go to the estate, which is rare, and the last few times I was there, she wasn't. In fact, this line is only used for our suppliers. Perhaps her new mobile is just so similar that she wrote this one by mistake."

She then gave Sophie the addresses for both the restaurant and the café before heading down to the wine cellar.

Since the storm passed, she had not heard any more of the odd 'kerthumps' from the cellar. The one wall was still warm though. It was odd.

Choosing two reds and two whites, she headed back up the stairs. Tonight, she was doing a test kitchen and Mathias had volunteered to be her guinea pig. She had been surprised that he was an excellent cook in his own right, and she valued his opinion.

As usual, he was right on time and had come baring two wine bottles of his own.

"One to try and one to add to your cellar if you like it. A gift from Tony."

"A new wine from the Chedaux estate?"

"It is. It's from a little experiment Tony conducted. You will be the first, beside him, to try it."

"Speaking of the Chedaux estate, I don't suppose you've seen Josephine Chedaux?"

"No, I haven't. I don't think she's been there for the past three years. She pretty much left Tony and his father in charge. Why do you ask?"

"I had a strange phone call. A woman who claimed she got this number from a postcard her aunt, Josephine Chedaux, sent. She asked if I knew her, and when I explained the relationship of the restaurant with the vineyard, she asked for the addresses of both."

"What was her name?"

"Sophie. She said she had lost contact and the postcard was all she had to go on."

"She asked for the addresses? As in she was in the area and might come by?"

"No. She said she was calling from Canada, Nova Scotia. Why? Do you know her?"

"I know who she is," Mathias responded. He felt suddenly on edge.

"Are you all right?" Laura asked.

"Fine. I'm just surprised. So, tell me what is on the menu?"

"First, tell me who Sophie really is."

"There's nothing to tell," he replied, consciously relaxing his voice. "She really is Josephine's niece."

"Is she also your ex-girlfriend?"

"What? No, no. I've never even met her. I just know who she is. Let's just say that her family has a connection with mine. You know that my father and Josephine knew each other."

"Yes. It still seems odd that *Sophie*," she said her name intentionally, to look for a reaction from Mathias, "that she would call here, on the supplier line, from Canada, to look for her aunt. And it seems even stranger that her aunt would send a postcard with that number, claiming it was hers. I thought that perhaps she had a new phone with a number that is close, but that sounds highly unlikely."

"I agree." Mathias said. "It's a mystery. Now, about that menu?"

Mathias needed to find out what was going on. A part of him still thought of Josephine like the mother he never had.

Sometimes he even thought that perhaps she was his real mother. She had been unusually close to his father and Meschner had never been known for being close to anyone. He wondered what else the postcard had said. He knew there must be a reason she'd sent it.

He had seen her husband, Simon, at the institute in Paris and even followed him a few nights. He had been hoping that Simon would lead him to Hisdak, but the only thing he learned from following Simon, is that Josephine did not appear to be living in Paris with him, and that Simon was far from faithful.

He knew that Josephine and the girls who lived with them hadn't been at the vineyard for three years now. Where were they and why was Simon staying in Paris?

Nova Scotia

Sophie typed in the addresses of the restaurant, café, and vineyard. They were all within a small triangle. She pulled up a satellite image of the restaurant and showed that to Anne.

"Do you recognize it?"

"I can't be certain, but it may be a restaurant we ate at on my last visit to France. It's been such a long time ago."

"I am going to go with the assumption that Josephine sent you this for a reason. And I am praying that somehow finding out where Josephine is can help us find Jack and maybe my parents."

"What about the girls in Scotland? I know you haven't heard from them, but you know where they were living. Perhaps they're still there."

"You're right, but I can hardly hop a flight to Scotland right now."

"True, but I could."

"What would Ben say?"

"He'd say no, if I told him why, and I already promised not to tell anyone about the girls."

"It wouldn't be safe for you to go alone."

"I've been to Scotland before. I have a few cousins there myself."

"But Ben would never let..."

Just then, Ben came in.

"Did you ladies realize it's past lunch time?"

"Oh," Anne said, "I'm sorry. I haven't started anything."

"No need to worry about that. A sandwich will hold me just fine, and I know where everything is. I'll make you each one, if you like."

"I'm good. Thank you. I've been nibbling and sipping coffee all day," Sophie said.

"Same here, Ben," Anne said.

"Okay."

All was silent while Ben made his sandwich. He grabbed a beer from the fridge and headed to the door. "Unless you two have found anything you want to tell me about, I'll leave you be and join the sheep for lunch."

"We'll find something. I know we will," Anne said.

"This really is hard on him, on you both," Sophie said. "And I can't help feeling it's somehow my fault."

"Never! You were a victim in all of this, and I feel more and more certain that it started when Josephine married Simon."

"This has been going on long before Simon."

"True, but what if he's the one who started the ball rolling in our family? Think about it. You were already four when Nigel and Lily adopted you."

"But there was Meschner and Dr. Marshall. I know my da' already had a connection to the university where Meschner did much of his research."

"True again, but I just can't help feeling like Simon is the key. And why haven't we heard from Thomas, Dr. Marshall? I ran into his son the other day at church and asked if he'd had any word. He hasn't, and I know he's worried, but he felt that if anything had happened someone working with his father would have found a way to notify him. He's working on the assumption that no news is good news. But what do I do about Scotland?"

"Let me call Shane again. He'll probably read me the riot act, but maybe I can put him onto Scotland without mentioning the girls. I don't know. They're nearly eighteen and it could be a wild goose chase."

"Then there's the postcard from Switzerland and the restaurant in France. This card was sent a long time ago though," Anne said.

"Yes, and it's been just as long since I've heard from my cousins. We know she's not in France, at least not at the vineyard. And it seems strange that the girls haven't made some form of contact, unless they moved again. That leaves Switzerland, maybe somewhere near where this card was mailed. If we go with the assumption that they moved again, then maybe Josephine did send this card herself." Sophie theorized.

"But then, why the number to the restaurant in France? Is there something about it or someone who works there that she was trying to tell us about? What if we're wrong? what if she doesn't know anything about where Jack is?"

"I don't know, but it looks like I'll need to get going," Sophie said, as Nick and Jeremy pulled up the drive. "Did Jack have anything personal that he kept here?"

"You mean like he did with the files he found on you?"

"Exactly."

"Not that I know of, but I'll take a look. There are a few places he liked to stash things when he was a boy."

"Speaking of boys."

"Mommy, mommy!" Jeremy called, as Nick opened the front door, and Jeremy ran to Sophie and Anne. Pudding, who had been sleeping on the back of the couch, dove underneath it as he plowed past. "Guess what mommy?"

"What?" asked Sophie.

"I got to pet a sheep!"

"Wow!"

"Did Uncle Ben tell you the sheep's name?" Anne asked.

"Her name is Daisy!"

"Well then, you are special if you got to pet her. She only lets really special people touch her," Anne said.

"Did you and daddy have fun at the ice rink?" Sophie asked, as Nick came over.

"Sometimes it was fun, but daddy had to work too much."

Nick smiled, "It was a busy morning, but we got to skate some in between my classes, and I'll tell you, our son is a natural!"

Sophie smiled, "Just don't go sending him off to Olympic training camp yet."

"No need. He has me to coach him. Right buddy?"

"Right! I'm going for the gold!" Jeremy said, shooting his arm up in the air.

"Have you two had lunch yet?" asked Anne.

"We dropped in over at the new deli, but thanks."

"Does that mean he's all set for a N-A-P?" Sophie asked.

"Should be," Nick answered.

"What's a N-A-P?" Jeremy asked.

"The fourteenth, first and sixteenth letters of the alphabet," Nick responded.

"Huh?" Jeremy shrugged, giving them all a weird look.

"It's daddy's unique sense of humor," Sophie said.

"Why would I be ready for that?" Jeremy asked, and everybody laughed.

"What's so funny?" Jeremy wanted to know.

"You and your daddy and how much alike you are," Sophie said, picking him up. "I'll call you later Anne," Sophie said, and they hugged goodbye.

By the time they were home, Jeremy was snoring in his car seat.

"I have another class at three," Nick said, after putting Jeremy to bed. "Did you two find anything?"

"No and Yes."

"I expected nothing less," Nick said. "But you know what? Why don't you tell me all about it tonight? Right now, we probably have a safe half an hour to ourselves."

"And I could use a distraction," Sophie said, smiling, as she followed Nick to the couch.

Austria

Daniel, Thadeus, Spencer and Hamilton raced around the yard, playing tag with both the dogs and each other.

"I don't think I've ever seen a three-legged dog run so fast!" Shane commented.

Rosie and Magdeline were sitting in back with them and Soren had fired up the grill for dinner. Both dogs ran to Rosie in search of reprieve.

Inside, Shane was formally introduced and updated on, Victoria, and the plans for her upcoming concert.

"How do you like your steaks?" Soren asked.

"Rare," Larry said.

"Same here," said Shane.

"Well done please," Dave answered.

"Victoria?" Soren asked.

"Medium, Thank you."

"Okay, I'll do my best, but the only guarantee is on Dave's."

After dinner, Dave & Shane went to the cabin, and Larry went back to the B&B to pack for the trip to Switzerland. Magdeline had insisted on letting Daniel stay overnight.

"I think it would be good for me to observe him, and you and Dave have a lot to talk about," Magdeline said. "How's he been about Patricia's absence?"

"He wants to know when she's coming back. He was worried that maybe she didn't love him because he made Kenneth so mad."

"No acting out?"

"No. I told him that mommy and Kenneth went away to get treatment for Kenneth. I didn't know what else to say. How do I keep explaining why she hasn't even called?"

"I don't know, but he seems like a good boy. We can talk more later."

"You're positive you don't mind him staying over?"

"We have two bunk beds in the boy's room, and to see them playing together, I think that separating them now would be a lot more stressful for all of us."

"Thank you," Shane said and went over to where the boys were playing to tell Daniel goodnight and that he'd see him in the morning.

Nova Scotia

"So, Switzerland? I don't see it," Nick said.

"We don't know if it connects to Jack. The day turned into more of a how to find Josephine in hopes that she could help us find Jack."

"I know she's your aunt, but she's been playing on the wrong side of this for a long time. You were there when she took the girls to that clinic. What makes you think she would help?"

"There must be a reason that postcard was sent to Anne. I think, and so does Anne, that Josephine is being manipulated by Simon. Didn't you say that he used her last name to disguise himself in online searches?"

"He did, but she was on that hospital board. I'm sorry, but she's in just as deep."

"Maybe she's changed sides. I think that she's afraid of Simon. I know Amber and Pollina were."

"If we pull back and look at this rationally, focusing on Jack, it makes more sense for them to take him somewhere that doesn't require a flight."

"They took me to France from Quebec."

"Okay, you have me on that. But his truck is missing too."

"That could have been hidden anywhere."

"So, do you have a plan?"

"I called Shane, and it turns out that he is in Austria now, and Larry will be in Switzerland soon. I didn't mention Amber or Pollina, but I took a picture of the postcard and sent it to Larry. Don't worry. I'm not planning to take off, at least not without you. You have proven yourself indispensable."

"I'm glad to hear that."

Chapter 10

Austria

Larry and Victoria had just left for the train. In the back yard, Daniel was playing with the boys and dogs, while Shane and Magdeline discussed him, his brother and Patricia in her office. Meanwhile, Dave went over everything about Claire's abduction again in the living room with Rosie.

Soren had been in the yard with the boys but came in and said he needed to leave for work, and Dave and Rosie took his place along with a hot pot of coffee.

The morning was cool, and Dave gave Rosie his jacket when he saw her shiver.

"Thank you. I meant to get a sweater, but I've been sharing clothes with Magdeline and didn't want to disturb her or go through her closet without her. Will you be warm enough?"

"I'll be fine. I'm from Seattle. This feels like summer," Dave said, smiling.

"I grew up north of you, but I was never really outside much. Anyway, I'm not sure what else I can tell you."

"Why don't you run me through a typical day and the places you went, people you may have met while you and your mother lived at the house. Did you have a weekly routine for groceries, church, etc.?"

"Mom was never a big churchgoer, we did go on holidays and talked with a few people at Easter, mostly Mrs. Bantan, who runs a shop on the edge of town. We didn't go out much. A few times we went to touristy sites, and I took riding lessons."

"Riding lessons? I used to ride. Did you meet many people at the stables? And what about your job?"

"The stables where I rode were related to my job. Employees at the animal rescue got free lessons. It was a small group of people. I took the bus, usually the same one, with mostly the same people. Sometimes we would go to the park or the library. I know a lot of people would call it mundane, but we enjoyed a calm life. It was nice."

"Did you ever have guests over?"

"No. I think the only person who ever came to the house was the local plumber a few times."

"Tell me again why you were on an earlier bus that day."

"It was a beautiful day. I had finished helping clean the cages early. Most of the animals were outside that day, which made it easier. We usually have animals that need extra attention because of injuries, but that day everyone had been tended to, and there were no wounds to change or other issues to deal with. I thought about going to the park, but then I saw the earlier bus coming and decided to just head home."

"What about your mother? She must have done something besides sit in the house all day."

"She volunteered a couple days a week at the food pantry, and she was growing a nice garden. We were going to get a booth for the farmers market this year. If you're asking if she had a social life though, then no. Neither of us really did. She would go to the pool sometimes, and I met her there occasionally. They had a nice heated indoor pool in town, with saunas and jacuzzi tubs. We had a membership. There really isn't anything else. We never went out with other people."

"Okay," Dave said, as Magdeline and Shane came out.

"I need to go into the lab for a while," Magdeline said.

"And I want to get Daniel settled in at the cabin," Shane said. "Will you two be okay here alone?"

"I can take the boys to daycare," Magdeline said. "I shouldn't be gone for more than two or three hours though."

"You can leave them. I don't mind," Rosie said.

"I don't mind," said Dave. "I've noticed that they keep each other occupied."

"True. Well, okay. If you're both sure. There are some sandwiches already made up in the fridge and soup for their lunches. You can both feel free to help yourselves to whatever you find in the kitchen. If you think of something you want, just text me and I'll pick it up at the market on the way home. They should all sleep for an hour after lunch, especially since they seem to be running off so much energy now."

"Daniel! Come on buddy, we need to head out," Shane called, and Daniel came to Shane, followed by all of his new friends.

"Do I have to go?" Daniel asked. "I was going to teach them the pirate game."

"We'll come back later, and you can teach them then."

"When?"

"Soon, I promise."

"Can I have a dog?"

"Maybe when we get back home,"

"When?"

"I don't know right now."

"Will mommy and Kenneth be there when we go home?"

"I don't know. What I do know is that you will love the cabin. You'll have your own loft."

"Can Hamilton, Thadeus and Spencer come too?"

"Not right now. Come on. I think you'll really like it."

"Okay," Daniel said, turning and waving to the boys, who had gone back to playing tag with the dogs."

"Magdeline took Shane and Daniel to the cabin, then went

into the lab. She wanted to run tests on samples that Shane had brought from both boys and run comparison tests of her own genetic code against Rosie and Victoria. She had run a comparison of herself and Rosie three years before but wanted fresh results to compare between them all. There were several new developments in the field of genetics that would allow her to see even more subtle details.

Somewhere

Jack paced the corridor. Even with the large landscape view windows he still had no idea where he was. The last thing he remembered before waking up here was snagging a really nice trout. He'd been making dinner plans for it, but instead of it landing in his frying pan, his frying pan had landed firmly against his skull. He had a vague, blurry memory of a man standing over him and being administered a shot of some sort.

The window looked out over a forest and a river. There was a mountain not far off that he didn't recognize. The only things he could tell, was that from the placement of the sun, he was facing south-west, and looking toward the mountain, he felt that he was at a higher elevation.

The corridor he stood in was long with five rooms off it that faced north-east. The window in his room gave him no further hints to his whereabouts either. That window overlooked an unfamiliar lake, and he could see what he thought was a church steeple on the other side of the lake and, he thought, a campground, but he'd need binoculars to be sure. Since there was a church, he figured there must be a small town hidden amongst the thick trees.

He had decided that he was no longer anywhere in Nova Scotia, but where? And why?

The doors at either end of the corridor were shut tight via electronic locks. The other four rooms contained a gym, a lounge with kitchenette, and two other bedroom suites like his own. His own room had a large bath and its own kitchenette as well. He had been left with plenty of food and drink, and the lounge area was filled with a pool table in the center, a dart board and various board games and reading materials.

The gym equipment was incredible! And there was a sauna, jacuzzi, toilet and shower, as well as a washer-dryer. It was like he was locked in his own mini resort. Nice, if you're there by choice.

He hadn't seen a single soul since he had woken up with a hell of a headache. Aspirin and a bottle of water had been left for him on the bedside table. They had also left some new clothes for him.

When he woke up, he was naked under the sheets and later discovered his fishing clothes in the dryer. Whoever had taken him had been thorough. The question was who? Who hits someone over the head, undresses them and leaves them in a place like this?

He knew that it had to be about the project that Alice and Sophie were part of, but why him? He hadn't even seen Alice in over three years, and everything had been normal, well, as normal as possible under the circumstances, at home. The only strange thing had been Sophie's early return from Greece without Nick. He knew her story of a birthday surprise was probably a lie. Had she been taken again too, he wondered?

Alice, it must have something to do with the snooping he had continued. Why did he still feel so much when he thought of her? They hadn't even known each other that long. It had been a whirlwind romance. In fact, aside from the few days journey between New York and Nova Scotia, it hadn't even been much of a romance. They had shared a few kisses, hardly any reason to be mourning more than three years later. He had tried to talk down his feelings, tried dating Sophie's friend Shannon, but it wasn't fair to her. Of course, if he had accepted her last offer to go out, he might not be here now.

He looked out at the view as he replayed that chance meeting in New York. A meeting that had turned both his life and Sophie's upside down. He prayed that Sophie was safe and again wondered where Nick had really been that last day that he spoke with her.

Then he thought about his mother. She was first cousins with Sophie's mother, and both of Sophie's parents and her aunt Josephine were part of this and missing. Had his mother been taken too? Was his abduction because he'd gotten too close to something, or was it aimed at family connections and if so, where was everyone else? He half expected to see Sophie's dad walk through the door at the end of the hall.

He paced the corridor again, trying to think of some way out. Even if he could break a window, without a parachute, there was no safe way down. He'd tried playing with the handle of the electronic lock, wondering if he could dismantle it. The only thing he accomplished was nearly electrocuting himself.

Going into the lounge, he made a pot of strong coffee, heated a frozen muffin, and slumped down in one of the cushy lounge chairs facing the windows. He randomly grabbed a newspaper. It was in French and a year old. He put it back and looked through the magazines. There were multiple languages, but he settled on a DIY magazine in English. Then he sat it down and got up to pace some more while the coffee finished brewing.

He perused the individual shelves of English, French, German, Italian and Chinese. What the hell was this place?

The coffee pot beeped that it was ready, and he sat back down again with a large mug, just staring out of the window, trying to focus his restless mind.

Austria

Dave looked at the rental records on the van he suspected may have been used by Claire's abductors, only to have it show the van in for repairs on that day. He needed to find out exactly what time period that day it had been out of service. If it had been in for repairs in the morning, he saw no reason why it couldn't still be the right one.

He was feeling desperate to get some kind of lead on Claire. He had spent the day with Rosie and the boys until Magdeline and Soren came home, and he could almost feel her pain. She'd been through so much. The first thirty years of her life, all but lost. She got three years of attempting to live a normal life and now this. The only person in her life who has ever mattered to her is taken.

He imagined her lying on the floor of the truck, hiding, wondering what they were doing to her mother, her dogs, and when they might find her.

"Are you okay?" Shane asked, coming down from the loft where Daniel now slept.

"No," Dave said, shaking his head. "Honestly, this insanity is beyond me. And do you know what I hate most of all? I hate how damned helpless I feel to do anything about it!"

"I get it, Dave. Trust me, I get it," Shane said, as he grabbed two beers from the fridge and sat down in a chair across the table from Dave.

"I'm sorry Shane. You're the one who really has to deal with it. I can't even fathom what you must be going through."

"You know, in a way, I've almost become numb. And the really crazy thing is that it's that little boy up there, who is one of the products of this insanity, that's keeping me sane. He's not even mine, but he is. He's mine by choice, and I wouldn't trade him for the world, no matter how he came to be."

"And Patricia?"

"She made her choice eyes wide open this time. Like I said, I'm numb. The worst part of her leaving now is how it's hurting Daniel. Anyway, how is Rosie holding up?"

"She has a tough outer shell, but inside … I don't know how she, how any of them are holding it together as well as they are. Magdeline and Soren manage to maintain as close to a normal happy life as any people I've ever met. Even after taking Rosie in and then Victoria.

"The things Victoria said, the files she showed us, how much longer can the world go on like this? And so much of it is becoming legal. I can hardly find a place that takes cash now, and there's no way in hell I'm letting anyone stick a chip in me. Yet, so many people seem oblivious. The kids that were born after the dot com era don't have a clue that for thousands of years humanity survived without phones, much less 5G. People used to grow their own food. There was no microwave, no instant artificial everything. I'm sorry. I'm ranting."

"Don't worry. I'm sure I'll have a few rants myself. I can put up with yours if you can put up with mine," Shane said.

"Deal. To top the day off, I got the report back on the one van that seemed most likely to be the one used to abduct Claire, but it's listed as being in for repairs that day. I don't have a clue how to find out where or what time it was being worked on."

"And now Jack is missing," Shane added. "Sophie called me again today."

"Is there something new?"

"Anne received a postcard, over two years ago, supposedly from Josephine. It's postmarked from a little tourist town in Switzerland."

"What does that have to do with Jack?"

"Maybe nothing, but Anne and Sophie put their heads together and came up with the idea that Josephine was trying to tell Anne something because she wrote the wrong phone number on the card. The phone number she did write is the number for a restaurant that buys wine from her vineyard. They went on to suppose that she's afraid of her husband, Simon. Remember what Jack found. Simon was on the board of the hospital in Quebec with her, but everything listed for him is using Josephine's maiden name. He took her name to hide himself. That itself says a lot. We know at one point, Josephine, her sister, Sophie's mother, Lily O'Hare, and Jack's mother, Anne, were very close."

"And Sophie's parents have already disappeared, we believe to protect Sophie, which means Nigel is probably working at one of the projects, possibly led by Simon? If we believe that, then the idea that Simon is responsible for Jack's disappearance isn't too far-fetched.
They did almost kill his mother because she knew too much. We've already seen all those files though. However, if Simon or someone else is concerned about Anne or Sophie, or if Sophie is right and Josephine is afraid of Simon, then Josephine could be turning against the projects and threatening to expose more. In that case, Jack would make the perfect pawn," Dave concluded.

"Exactly."

"Does Larry know about the postcard?"

"I sent him a copy of what Sophie sent me. He's hoping to check out the area where the card was postmarked. It's not far from Bern. As far as finding Jack, since we have nothing else to go on, maybe looking for Josephine will lead us to him. It's a hell of a long shot," Shane said.

"But better than a non-shot," Dave added and took a slug of his beer.

"We're still hoping to get some traffic cam footage that could help locate Jack's truck, but our resources are limited and even if we find the truck, the only thing we might gain would be the general direction they took him. It is also possible that Jack was taken one way and his truck the other as a mislead. Unless we get footage of Jack behind the wheel somewhere, it would probably be useless, especially since we know that they use private planes that could be listed under any multitude of names. When I went looking for Patricia, I wound up in Quebec, and she had been on the other side of the world."

"What about the Paris project that Hisdak was, and probably still is, running somewhere? Even though we couldn't come up with enough to hold him, we know from Mrs. Martinson that it's related to her and Ana's abduction. It's also probably a safe guess that wherever it went is where Sophie's parents are," Dave said, getting up and bringing over a map and a marker.

"What are you thinking?" asked Shane.

"I'm going back to the family. We believe Sophie's parents went to Paris and are likely somewhere in France still, and we know that Sophie and Alice were taken to Paris. Wouldn't it make sense that Jack is somewhere in France as well, and that Simon is probably working with Hisdak?"

"Go on."

"The Chedaux vineyard is in France, but north, outside of Calais, whereas the Chateau I was at and where Soren was, is south." Dave circled the areas on the map, then went to get another file. "These are the locations of known properties in France," he said, pulling out a list and circling those locations.

"It's all over the place," Shane said, standing and pacing the room, while Dave studied the map.

"Where is that restaurant located?"

"It's close to the vineyard."

"Okay, that's not on our list, but God only knows how many names they have property under, and it may be what Josephine was trying to tell Anne."

"You mean that you think this restaurant may be used as a location for part of the Paris project?"

"There must be something there," Dave said. "Back to my point about family though, if I had to guess, I'd say that Jack is somewhere in France."

"Well, that narrows it down from somewhere on the planet, which is where we were before," Shane said, as he looked at the postcard. "Can I see the Swiss property listings?"

Dave handed them to Shane.

"The town on the postmark is different from the photos."

"The photos are a collage of towns."

"True, but this one corresponds to this property of the Morgan's."

"You're right. Larry and I have already been in touch with Saville, the agent I was Guarding Richter with, in Halifax. He also worked on the original Martinson case. He met Jack once and offered whatever resources he has to us. He's also worked for the French and Swiss governments as well as INTERPOL. So, this would be a good area for him to help."

"Agreed."

Chapter 11

Switzerland, May 25th

Cora hummed a haunting tune as she carefully manipulated the two safety pins in the lock of the window.

Claire kept her ear to the door, to listen for anyone coming.

France

Adam waited until he heard the moped leave and then chose three bottles of wine, the three she had just put away. He wanted her out of there and he had a plan to make it happen.

Seattle

Suzanna, Lidia and Charice caught the 8:45 ferry to Bremerton and walked into the coffee shop at 10:00. After that, they would all head over to the camera store to meet with Brent Levar.

"So, I did it," Lidia said," I have officially handed in my badge."

"Are you going to call him?" asked Charice.

"Who?" Lidia asked.

"You know who," Charice teased.

"Europe is lovely this time of year," Suzanna added.

"Okay you two. Now I'm sorry I said anything. I was just feeling nostalgic. We're colleagues, but he's only come back once in three years, and it certainly wasn't to see me."

"Ah, now we come to the truth," Charice said.

Suzanna nodded. "Believe it or not, I was worried that Edgar was interested in someone else right up until he proposed."

Lidia was blushing and relieved when the waitress brought their orders out. She was just taking the first sip of her latte when her phone rang. She looked at it, didn't recognize the number and shoved it back in her purse. A minute later it began to buzz with a text message. Lidia stared at it.

"Anything wrong?" Charice and Suzanna asked almost at once.

"I don't believe it," Lidia replied. "It's a text from Dave. He's in Austria with Shane, and they want to talk to me. He says he'll call right back."

Suzanna was nervous.

"Are you Okay?" Charice asked her.

"I was just thinking about Edgar and wondering if..." She shook her head. "I really don't know where he is."

Just then, Lidia's phone rang again, and this time she answered, "Well, hello to you too...Okay, well why don't you ask her yourself? Here," she said, passing the phone to Suzanna. She turned to Charice. "Wasn't really me he wanted to talk to after all," she said, and focused back on her crepes.

"I can't say that I recognize any of those places," Suzanna said, looking at the photos Dave sent to Lidia's phone. "I can have Charice look back through the business files, but we gave you all we had on our property listings. I'll pass you back to Lidia. She has something to tell you."

"No, I...", Lidia started, as Suzanna passed her phone back.

"Hi, it's nothing really, just that since Shane left, I started to think I might follow in his footsteps and go private myself. Today is my first day as a free agent. Tell Shane I said hi," she finished and hung up.

"So, what did he say?" Charice asked.

"I believe the only syllable he came up with was, "Wow",

followed by silence, which is unusual for Dave. Anyway, you heard the rest. Now, let's enjoy this, before it all goes cold."

Brent was more than a little surprised to see Allie's mother again. She'd brought friends this time too.

"Hello ladies, how can I help you all today?" he asked, wondering just what Suzanna may have told them about their prior meeting.

"If you're not too busy," Lidia asked, looking around the store that, aside from them, was empty, "We'd like to ask you a few questions."

"About?"

"About your relationship with my daughter," Suzanna said.

"Okay, ask away, but I'll have you know, I don't kiss and tell," he said, looking directly at Suzanna.

"I have a confession," Suzanna said. "Alice is missing. The last I knew, she was in Paris, but it's been a long time since I've heard from her. So, I've hired a private detective," Suzanna turned and indicated Lidia. "You were so nice before, I hoped that maybe you could tell us a little more."

"How would I know anything about her disappearing in Paris?"

"We believe," Lidia said, taking over, "that someone was following her here, and he is in some of her photos. That same someone may be involved in her disappearance."

"Okay. Well, I'm glad to help, but I still don't see how or what my past relationship to her has to do with anything."

"Did she ever say anything to you about being followed?" Lidia asked.

"Sure. She said her boss was keeping tabs on her."

"It wasn't us," Suzanna said, but I want to find out when and where it happened. I brought a few photos that I believe he's in and was wondering if you recognized the locations, and if by chance you could get us a clearer view of his face."

"Let me have a look." He stared at the pictures she handed him, "I might be able to do something with this one," he said.

"I'd appreciate it," Suzanna said. "I'm also curious to know how long you've known my daughter."

"That's a better question for Trent. He knew her first."

"Okay, but judging from your message to her, I'm guessing you knew her best."

"Nobody *knew* Allie. That was part of what made her so interesting, but yeah, okay, we developed a bit of an on again off again relationship. It was mostly off. She was more interested in taking pictures. I think I was... I don't know what I was."

"Did you care about her?" Suzanna asked, needing to know.

"If I didn't, I wouldn't have given you that message for her."

"Fair enough."

"Where can we find your brother?" Lidia asked.

"Here, in about an hour."

"Did you know who she was?" Lidia asked.

"What do you mean? I just said nobody really knew her."

"Did she give you her last name?"

"Sure. I ask every customer for their last name, so that I can index what belongs to who."

"And?" Lidia prompted.

"And it's been a while. I put those photos I gave Suzanna aside a long time ago. So just let me check. Here it is, Allie Wallace."

"That's my sister's married name," Suzanna said to Lidia.

"Okay then, thank you for your time," Lidia said.

"Oh, is that a good camera for wildlife shots?" Charice asked. "My husband is an avid photographer."

"What you probably want is the one next to it, on the left."

"Okay, thank you. I'll think about it. Maybe when we come back."

"Here," Brent said, handing her a couple of pamphlets. "These are the specs on that and another. I guess I'll see you in an hour."

"That was a little surreal," Lidia said.

"What do you mean?" Charice asked.

"I felt like he was holding back but being very conscious of not looking like he was holding something back."

"I had the same feeling," Suzanna said. "It's like when we used to have a deal ready to propose and right before the meeting the company would drop a bomb, usually that they were in a lot more financial difficulty."

"I'm really curious about the brother," Lidia said. "You met him, didn't you, Suzanna?"

"Only to say hello. The nightclub was way too loud to hold a conversation. He gave off a different vibe from Brent though. Let's just say, I wouldn't want to be alone with him in a dark alley. He looks a lot like Brent, or rather Brent looks a lot like him. He told me that Trent is two years older."

They walked down to the waterfront and decided where to have lunch, then made their way back up to the camera store only to find it locked tight.

Austria

Dave hung up the phone and tried to focus again. They had talked to Saville, who said that he would do what he could. However, his hands were somewhat tied by the fact that he was still an official agent, and this was not an official case. He would make unofficial inquiries and check with the land registries.

Restless, Dave got up and walked to the coffee pot. That was the last thing he needed. He left his mug by the sink and headed outdoors to breath in the fresh air.

The cabin was a private owner rental, and the closest neighbor was probably a good three miles down the road. It wasn't completely rural, no livestock in sight anyway. It was on the outskirts of Hinterbruhl, about fifteen minutes from where the Anglistans lived and only half an hour outside the main city center of Vienna.

Europe had grown on Dave. It wasn't perfect. No place is, but he loved the history and the contrast between old and new was like night and day, yet, like night and day, they managed to blend harmoniously together.

The evening was warm, but the sun was heading down, and a light breeze was blowing. So, with the thought of clearing his mind, which currently felt like it was in a round-about with twelve exits, he grabbed his phone, took a water from the fridge, and walked toward town.

Dave knew Shane would be at the Anglistan's for dinner and sent him a text to say he was eating in town and asked if Shane could pick him up on his way back.

He couldn't believe how easily he had lost track of time as he looked over the same notes that he had read through a thousand times. Only this time, he was looking at them in relation with the new notes he had. It still didn't seem any clearer.

He walked past a museum and made a mental note to check it out when it was open. Then he noticed a small café and bar attached, which was still open, and he found a table overlooking the main street. He ordered and sent Shane a text of where he was.

The restaurant closed a half hour before Shane arrived, but his table was outside, and the waitress said that he was welcome to stay while he waited. She even gave him a free glass of wine, as it was the end of the bottle. Then she finished up inside and chatted with him while she wiped down and swept the outside area.

Thinking of Leti, the waitress who had helped them in France, he asked her about any legends of the surrounding area. He wasn't asking for work's sake since Austria itself had no known links to the projects. He liked that and just wanted to enjoy a couple hours of unrelated investigation of the area.

As it turned out, Gretchen, the waitress, was a fount of local historical legends, from five-hundred-year-old ghosts to modern financial scandals.

By the time Shane picked him up, he felt as if his brain had been given a much needed, deep tissue, stress relieving massage, until that is, Shane asked if he'd spoken to Lidia.

He wasn't sure why it unnerved him so much when she told him about leaving the force and going private. Maybe it was the possibility that Shane might ask exactly what he did when Dave relayed the conversation.

"That's fantastic. You know, we could really use her help. I don't suppose you asked how she feels about Europe?"

"It didn't come up," Dave said, "She was with Suzanna Morgan and Charice when we spoke. That's why I was able to get what I did, which is really nothing," Dave replied, feeling the tension creeping back. "We may be able to use her better from Seattle."

"Possibly, but with Edgar gone, I don't see that there's much there. I feel bad for Suzanna. I still have my doubts about how much she really knows, but I know what it's like to have your spouse vanish. She's lost her daughter and sister too. It's good Lidia's spending time with her, especially with Charice married now. The only other people that seem to be in her life are a few other wealthy women who come by to play tennis or ask her to help organize fundraisers to solicit donations for whatever their charity of the month may be.

"From what Lidia told me, last time we spoke, Suzanna really wants to find Alice now. She even moved into her condo because her house was just too big and empty, and she's still holding out hope of finding some random clue somewhere."

They parked at the cabin and Dave held the door, while Shane carried the sleeping Daniel up to bed.

Dave didn't want to think about Lidia. In fact, the one trip he'd made back to Seattle, he'd barely popped in at the station long enough to say hello and then joined Shane for lunch. Dave didn't want to move backwards in his life. Sure, Shane was here, but that was different. He had never had the slightest impulse to kiss Shane. He had barely restrained himself when he left three years before, but what would have been the point? She had been with Rick, who he considered a friend. And the only interest she had ever shown in Dave, was to harass him over every little thing. It had been even worse than usual after he returned from Canada. He had been thrilled to go to France and work with Larry. Now, he needed to be able to stay focused and help Rosie find her mother.

Shane came back down and took a beer from the fridge. "You want one?" he asked Dave.

"No, thanks. I had wine with dinner. So, what happened today?"

"For one thing, relief. All of Daniel's tests came back normal and Magdeline thinks he's doing great. As for Rosie, she remembered something, or at least thinks she did. She had a dream last night that she's sure is a memory of hearing the men who took her mother say something in French. It doesn't necessarily mean anything, even if they were speaking French. French is a common second language pretty much worldwide, but we go with what we have. I also had an interesting call from Larry, who had an interesting call from Katz."

"What does he have for us?"

"He took the work you had already done of tracing Lily and Josephine's family, and he found a link. On a whim, because of Ana being brought to Brazil, he ran a search through their databases and found a Lilianna Fontaine, Josephine's grandmother, who arrived in Brazil in 1945 and gave birth to twin boys. In the same month that Lilianna gave birth, there is another woman, registered under the name Marta Fontaine, who gave birth at the same hospital to a daughter. The daughter, however, is listed as Analina Heisenberg. There are also records showing that a woman under the name of Marta Heisenberg, later gave birth to two sons and another daughter. One of those sons, was named Simon. He moved from Brazil to France, where he attended medical school in Paris between 1971 and 1977. In 1988, when he married Josephine, records show that he legally changed his last name to hers, Chedaux. What is even more interesting, and this is the part Larry said you'd really love, is that he discovered Josephine's mother had a sister named Marta. In France, however, she was declared dead, along with Lilianna, in 1947. So?" Shane asked Dave, who was lost in thought, totally dumbfounded by the implications.

"Shane, you know Fontaine is the name on the chateau I was taken to by Hisdak. The story was that when it was taken over by the Nazis, all the men were killed, and when they left, both mother and daughter were pregnant. I was also told that Lilianna died there in 1989. So, at some point, she must have come back. If this is right though, then..."

"Josephine Chedaux married her cousin or uncle?"

"First cousin," Dave said, getting up and walking to the fridge. "You know, I think I'll join you in that beer after all." He grabbed a bottle, and Shane passed him the opener. "It's not likely that Josephine would have known, but if Simon knew, that could be why they never had children together."

"There's more."

"More?"

"Analina Heisenberg shows up later in Sao Paulo, Brazil, where she disappears after marrying a, Hans Meschner, in 1970. That's as far as he got there, but we can't forget the other brother and sister that Philip is still trying to trace. He did, however, trace the twins that Lilianna gave birth to. They immigrated to the United States in 1956 to live with their uncle in New Orleans.

"So, both Lilianna Fontaine and her daughter, Marta, ran away to Brazil with the Nazis who may have been responsible for the death of their husband, father, and brother," Dave contemplated. "Stockholm syndrome?"

"Maybe, but we'll probably never know."

"I really hope he can trace Hans. My guess is that the name Meschner isn't a coincidence. Also, even though Sarah grew up in France with her mother, her father is German. So, both of Ana's parents are of mixed German and French descent. This could link them into the family as well. What was Analina's father's first name?"

"Let me look," Shane answered, taking a small notepad from his rear pocket. "Old habit," he said, as he looked down at his notes from Larry's call. "Herbert Wilhelm."

"Herbert Wilhelm Heisenberg," Dave repeated, as he wrote the name in his own notes.

"And the twins Lilianna had, were Peter and Ulf."

"Wait! Ulf?"

"What is it?"

"Stephan Martinson's father's name was Ulf. There was nothing about him coming from America though."

Dave stared into his beer bottle. "Do we have first names for Analina's other brother and sister?"

"Natalie and Wilhelm."

"Well, we may still be missing a lot of pieces, but at least some of the picture is starting to connect."

***

Soren was lying in bed, considering everything he knew and had seen over the past years, from his concerns at Scangentech to the files from Jonathan and now Victoria, and the night he had followed a cooler to Paris.

"Maggie?" Soren asked, as she came in and sat on the bed beside him.

"Yes," she answered, putting her head on his shoulder.

"What do you think of taking the boys to your parents for a few days?"

"Are you worried because Rosie's here?"

"No. I was actually thinking that Dave, Shane and Larry are spread too thin, and that with three more people helping them out, the odds of finding Claire would be a lot better."

"Oh, so, you want to pawn our boys off on my parents so that you can play detective," she said, as she ran her fingers down his face, turning his head so that he was looking straight into her eyes. "Tell me, what else you were thinking about, because I know that you wouldn't even think of what you just suggested if there wasn't more to it."

"I was remembering when I followed the cooler to Paris."

"And?"

"And thinking about everything else, from Jonathan to Victoria, and that, like it or not, our boys are connected. You're connected. If they came for Rosie, then..."

"You think they'll come for us next?"

"Maybe. I want to help put an end to this, to keep you and our boys safe. I can't help thinking that the people I saw in Paris may be important in helping to connect the pieces."

"I don't suppose you would be able to remember the faces well enough to do sketches?"

"Not particularly good sketches. I should have tried right away, but I didn't know just how much a part of this we already were, and I dropped the ball. I only really saw them from behind or in profile when they got off the train. So, what are you saying Maggie?"

"I don't like it, but... I know that Rosie is constantly worried that she's putting us in danger. I feel the same way you do about protecting our boys, and you're right about Dave, Larry, and Shane. I also think that they won't like the idea, but at the same time, let's face it, they need us. We have the medical insights and living here, as well as having lived in Switzerland, gives us some added benefits too."

"True," Soren chuckled. "I was listening to Dave on the phone to some archive in France. He was attempting to speak in French. It hurt my ears."

Magdeline laughed. "I know. Larry's German did the same to mine, and I don't think either of them speak Italian. Shane's French isn't terrible, but Daniel's is better, and his German is non-existent aside from what he said he picked up watching old war movies. Daniel is already picking up German too."

"Poor guy, I can't imagine what he must be going through. And his wife didn't give you any sign that she was planning to do a disappearing act?"

"None that I saw, but I'm a geneticist, not a psychologist. I'm just relieved that Daniel seems to be doing well. I mean, he's still big for his age, and clearly advanced in other areas, like language. But he seems to adapt well, and if I didn't know better, I'd never suspect he wasn't Shane's."

"Me either," Soren agreed.

"Back to the original question though, I'll call my parents tomorrow and see what their schedule looks like. And you need to come up with a reason to give them."

"Already done."

"Really?"

"Uhuh. I want to take you on a second honeymoon."

"Do you?"

"I do. Unfortunately, I doubt we'll get much time alone any time soon."

"Which means you'll have to take me on a third honeymoon." Magdeline smiled.

"Completely agreed."

Sweden

Alice was sweating profusely, and Carl had hooked her up to another IV, while Jonathan continued to sponge her forehead with a cold cloth.

"What I don't understand," Jonathan said, "is why we don't have these problems. Granted, her implants are advanced, but did Hisdak never suggest you or himself getting them?"

"No, he didn't. Not that there was much time, but you're right. Meschner never tried to upgrade us, except for Richter. He was given injections, and you know he injected me in his own sick experiment," Carl replied, "My own fault really, for wanting to impress dear ole dad."

"I learned a lot, being free of him, and one of the things I learned is that he was never a dad to us. Think about it. We're all just his guinea pigs, his grand science experiment. You're lucky. You at least have a mother now," Jonathan said, smiling at Carl. "I wish…"

"What?"

"I'm not sure. It doesn't matter."

"I have the files."

"What files?"

"I stopped at Meschner's old office at the college in Malmo on my way here, and I found the files that list our full genetic profiles. After I met my mother, I locked it away. It's in the safe in my apartment. It's up to you if you want to see it." Carl said.

"I'm assuming you read all of it."

"I saw enough. A lot was encoded. There are thirty-three thumb drives, labeled for the different projects that Meschner oversaw. I did look through yours, as well as Richter and Mathias. It's something you need to decide to read for yourself though. We've both learned a lot in the past three years, and I learned that we are who we decide to be. At one point, I wanted to be like him," Carl said, pointing to Richter, "But I thank God I didn't succeed. Genes influence us, but they don't make us."

"Wise words, little brother," Jonathan said, as he gently used a freshly cooled cloth on Alice's forehead. "I found out who my birth mother was five years ago, along with my full genetic profile. After Mathias turned, I did some of my own digging," he explained. "I didn't find as much as you though, and what I did, I wish I hadn't" he added, looking up at Carl.

"I was lucky," Carl replied.

"Still," Jonathan continued, "We should look more closely at those files. There may be other information that could help us."

"If the triggers are listed, they're encoded in the files I haven't been able to decipher."

"I was thinking about Alice. Meschner must have kept more information on her, especially if he meant for her and Richter to be together. It doesn't make sense that any of their parentage would be the same. Yet, we were led to believe that Mr. Morgan's DNA is a part of all of us."

"There are a lot of things that didn't make sense in those files. What did, is that Mr. Morgan was a much lower percentage donor for Mathias. It wasn't until he decided to turn against the projects that Richter took over." Carl said.

"Which means she was originally intended for Mathias. We need to find her file. Still, if Meschner's plan was to give Alice to Richter... What if the reason he...? No."

"What?"

"Well, maybe he was working on a way to reverse engineer genetics? Think about it. We know that one of the aims that has been successful is to reverse aging, but what if you could also simply, not only slow the genes, but completely remove them? What if some of the procedures performed on Alice and Richter were meant to remove the genes of Mr. Morgan that would have made them too closely related to safely mate? Think about it. With our multiple parentage, we're really genetically more like cousins than full brothers."

"You're right," Carl agreed. "I know that our mitochondrial DNA was manipulated for us to look alike, but from what I read, a part of the looking alike was to differentiate who is part of which project. In that case, what you're saying would make sense. He would really only need to water down the genetic code, so to speak, leaving enough to maintain the aspects of why those genes were chosen in the first place."

"Exactly!" Jonathan said, looking at Alice. "We need to understand the full genetic profile of Alice and the others."

"You mean Sophie."

"And Rosie and Magdeline and whoever else."

"Who is Magdeline?"

"Presumably one of Claire's babies that she thought had died. She was in the news three years ago, when Albert, the man who worked for Edgar Morgan, kidnapped her, thinking she was Alice."

"You think there may be more?" Carl asked.

"I don't know how many times they tried before Alice was born or how many babies Dr. Marshall may have rescued. It would have been before we were brought to the island. You do realize that this all started long before us."

"Of course. Just look at Oscar."

"Yes. What do you think his prognosis is?"

"I can't really say. I have to stay hopeful for my mother's sake. There's been some good progress, but he's been like that for so long. Even when we're able to give him the new organs, there's no telling how his mental and emotional health will be affected. I mean, can you imagine waking up and discovering that so many years have passed? The world has changed so much just in the past decade. To be honest, I feel confident about bringing his body back, but I'm scared that it may not bring him back. Does that make sense?"

"It does, but you can't do more than what you are," Jonathan said. "There has to be a way to get that thing out of her," he continued, looking at Alice. "I think the fever is going down again, but..."

"Are you in love with her?" Carl asked.

"No. Not the way you're thinking anyway. I did have someone, briefly, like you had Laura."

"What happened?"

"I couldn't put her in that situation. Carl, we have to be very careful. If we don't know our triggers, and even if we do, we may not be able to control ourselves, and the last thing that I could deal with would have been hurting her. Even if it meant leaving and hurting both of us. I know she'll find someone else. I pray she already has. What I'm trying to say is that..."

"That even if Laura forgives me, I can't be with her?"

"Not unless there's a way to disarm ourselves, and even then, our genes have been programmed to stop aging or at least slow to a hundredth of normal age. We wouldn't be able to grow old with them. It would be selfish. Alice has become like a real sister to me and that's how I care about her. She has someone that she fell in love with too, and if we can get that, so called upgrade out of her, maybe she can find happiness. From what I understand, her genes are meant to have stopped aging as well, but she was also reliant on a special herbal vitamin to fight rejection..."

"What are you thinking?"

"I'm wondering, if her aging has started again and if hers can, then..."

"I think the idea was to stop everyone from aging. Maybe we could make that happen with Laura and..."

"You're right and you're wrong Carl. Right in that the idea is to stop everyone from aging, but wrong to assume that everyone will want that."

Later that evening, Carl was considering what Jonathan said. It had never occurred to him that someone would wish to grow old. He understood that it could make sense if they couldn't stop the aging of loved ones, but could there be such a thing as living too long?

Methuselah supposedly lived nine hundred and sixty-nine years. Had that been long enough for him? Had he looked old? Carl did the math of what he and his siblings would look like at that age, and they would look about the equivalent of a fifty-year-old. Not bad, but what if you simply tired of living? He knew it was possible, especially after everything that happened two years before. The world had been engulfed in chaos until what had been called by many, "The Great Intervention." Things hadn't gone the way that the instigators had hoped. It was hard to believe that it was less than a year since it all came to a head on September 14th, 2021. During the year and a half before, many had chosen to take their own lives.

Could he ever feel like that? Yes, still, Carl had never entertained thoughts of suicide. It made no sense to end your life based on temporary circumstances. But what if those circumstances were to go on, for say, decades or even hundreds of years? He wondered.

Switzerland

Cora had taught Claire all she needed now, and with two of them, it might just be possible. It would all depend on what condition they returned Claire in today. She would need to be able to walk, run if possible.

The door beeped open, and Cora watched through one drooping eyelid as she wiped spittle from her mouth. She knew they thought she was completely out of it, and it had deemed to be an even greater advantage today than she had hoped.

The nurses had Claire in the usual straitjacket but had not yet injected her to numb her legs. So, as the one finished prepping the needle, Cora dove forward at him as Claire kicked out at the other.

Quickly, Cora used the injection on one nurse. The other nurse went to restrain Cora only to be kicked back again by Claire as Cora grabbed a section of bed railing, she had disconnected, and gave him a good solid whack on the head. She had just enough time to prepare another syringe before he came back around.

Claire managed to position her legs in a semi choke hold around the man's neck. She couldn't hold on long, but she managed just long enough for Cora to drive the injection into the base of his spine.

The door was wide open and neither nurse would be following them. If they could leave via a rear facing window, their odds were much improved.

Cora used a piece of metal that she had managed, over the decades, to file into a kind of knife, more than sharp enough to help cut Claire free.

Tucking the makeshift knife up her sleeve and grabbing a couple more syringes, Cora filled them, and Claire took the pass cards off the nurses and stripped the bed sheets. Then they simply walked out the door, locking the nurses within.

They knew there was no one else on this floor. So, picking the closest rear facing room, they used the pass card to enter and began knotting sheets together. Between them, they were able to lift the bed into a position that allowed them to bash the metal legs against the window until it broke. They swept away the glass from the bottom of the sill and tied the makeshift rope to the bed frame. It was secure but still left about a ten-foot drop.

They held their breaths as they heard footsteps in the hall. Cora went first out the window and dropped onto her side. She was sure her arm was broken, but she could live with that.

Claire stared down, as Cora got to her feet. She heard the beeps and knew there was no time to think.

Claire started out the window and had barely swung her legs out when the door opened. She grabbed a jagged piece of window glass, cutting her own hand in the process, but she felt nothing as she held it in defense of the man storming toward her. She wasn't sure where she cut him, only that it had been enough to get away. She hurried down and dropped as Cora had, making sure to angle her body to land on her left side.

There was no time to think about the pain that reverberated through the entire side of her body where she hit the ground. She pushed herself up with her right hand, which was bleeding profusely. She saw no sign of Cora but knew that she had only seconds before they would catch her. There was a wooded canyon in front of her, with a steep slope that was surrounded with an electric fence and topped with barbed wire. To the side were garbage dumpsters. She lifted the lid to one and climbed inside, lowering the lid.

It was dark and smelled worse than a sewer. It was all Claire could do not to vomit. It was also very warm inside the metal container, and she stripped off her top to remove the light undershirt she wore, tied that around her face and replaced her top. It smelled like her own sweat but was still better than the trash surrounding her. She didn't want to think about it. Fortunately, it felt as though it was all tied up in plastic bags. So, she wasn't coming into direct contact with it.

She could hear people searching outside now with dogs.

Cautiously, Claire rolled the trash bags on top of her to help hide her scent even better as well as to hide herself, should the lid be lifted.

She must have passed out, because the next thing she remembered was waking up, shivering with cold, and what little light had made its way into the dumpster before, was gone. The night was deadly silent, aside from an occasional hoot of a nearby owl.

It was hard to move as pain coursed down her left side, but she slowly made her way to where she could peek out from the lid. She inhaled deeply of the fresh night air. The area appeared deserted. Still, she waited, listening for any voices or footsteps. Nothing.

She almost passed out again from pain, as she tried to hoist herself out of the dumpster. Squeezing her eyes tight, she inhaled deeply again and fell to the ground. Her right hand ached where she had cut it, and she worried it was becoming infected.

Hobbling silently around the building, she saw a parking area and drive. A guard was stationed in a booth at the entrance. Claire watched him as she crept between the cars until she was no more than ten yards from him. She watched as he poured himself coffee from a large thermos. She was trying to decide how fast she could get through the entrance and into the woods. There was no way unless something distracted him longer than refilling his mug.

Then she saw him exit the guard booth, radio in hand, and she feared he would check the parking area. Instead, he ducked into the woods. That's when she realized, she had her chance and took it.

The guard zipped his pants and hurried back at what he thought had been footsteps. Getting back to the guard booth, he took a high beam flashlight and made an arc with it around the parking area, woods, and drive.

Claire lay flat as the beam passed over her. She waited, heart pounding painfully in her chest until she heard music.

The guard had not seen her. There was no more light, only the calming sounds of classical music drifting from the guard booth.

Looking up, she watched as he turned to pour fresh coffee, and she made her way deeper into the surrounding woods.

Seattle

After returning home that night, Suzanna made a decision. She knew Alice was likely in Europe. So, she should be too. The dilemma was where to go. France or Switzerland?

Suzanna was confused about both Brent and Trent and wondered why the shop had been closed when Brent knew of their intention to return. They had all agreed that they were probably the reason, but why?

She would try one more time before leaving to get in touch with Trent. Not that she believed he could help at all in leading her to Alice, but she felt certain that there was something in their relationship that he was hiding. Both Lidia and Charice agreed.

Suzanna looked over the pictures Brent had given her again. There were so many, but at least they were now somewhat sorted.

She went to the group labeled as still unknown. Most of these were simple outdoor scenes, some with people in the background, like at a park or lake. Several looked to be on a hiking trail, but there were no signs or other people in them. Then there was the cabin. That was the location Suzanna felt drawn to find out more about.

Lidia was having a friend do a property search for both Brent and Trent to see if it matched up to them. What was strange, was that there were several photos that she believed to be the same cabin, both outside and in.

After returning on the ferry in the afternoon, Suzanna went to the YMCA and spoke with Alice's friend, Melinda.

She asked Melinda about the cabin, but she knew nothing. Then Suzanna had stayed for a yoga class and a sauna as she tried to focus her mind.

That was when she had really decided on the trip to Europe.

Suzanna poured herself a glass of wine and looked at the time. Why wait? It wasn't that late, she thought, and she called Lidia.

Chapter 12

Austria: May 26ᵗʰ

Rosie awoke and stared at the bedside clock. It was only 4:00, and all was shrouded in darkness, just as in her dream. Rosie shivered as she remembered how the tree branch snagged her in the dream, ripping at her. There was a wind and leaves swirled around her ankles like mini tornados. Her feet felt stuck. She'd had to drag them along step by step. She had felt lost. Every direction looked the same. The dark silhouettes of trees danced in the wind, taunting her, their branches reaching out to capture her.

Rosie rubbed her eyes and moved to look out the window. The night was clear and still. Closing the curtain, Rosie turned on the bedside light and pulled the blankets to her chin.

Her mother was out there. Rosie knew it, knew that the dream had been some kind of connector. She had always had strong dreams that connected her to her mother. She had known about the cancer even before Claire did. She knew this dream was telling her something too.

Shane was restless. It was only 5:00 and Dave was still snoring away. He tiptoed into the kitchen, started a strong pot of coffee and sat down. He was staring at the board that Dave had put together, but he was thinking about Patty. He'd had another dream about her. He had them frequently, but he only remembered shadows. What was odd about this one was that Kenneth had been crying, not his usual crying either, but an earnest crying, for his mother. Shane's nose had also been itching like crazy until he had given up and gotten up.

Could she be in danger? He wondered. He knew she left of her own free will. The fact was, she had the first time too.

Could she have been tricked again? There had been so much tension between them, and just knowing that she had left willingly, he had never thought beyond that.

He felt an overwhelming sense of Deja'vu, and he got a tissue to blow his nose just as the coffee pot chimed.

He had just finished his first cup and was headed for another, when Daniel climbed down from the loft.

"Hey buddy. You're up early."

"I had a bad dream about mommy," Daniel said, coming over for a hug. Shane stroked his head, trying to comfort him. He almost told him it was just a dream, but was it?

A few minutes later, Dave woke up to the smell of breakfast and after eating, they all headed over to the Anglistan's, where they would drop Daniel for the day, before following up on the van that may have been used to kidnap Claire.

***

Cora had spent the night on a bench she found. She had managed to grab a set of nurse's scrubs from a laundry truck she saw as she made her way around the building. Pulling them on over her clothes, she used the distraction on the other side of the of the building, to simply walk out through the main gate. They would have looked straight at her and not recognized her in an upright position, head held high and eyes wide open. She could have helped in the search for herself without them being any the wiser. She laughed at the thought as she looked out at the open countryside in front of her.

It had been so long since she tasted freedom. She had never really known it. She had been too rebellious as a girl. She had learned too late that sometimes you had to pretend to play along if you ever wanted to get away.

What now? There were so many things that she had always dreamed of, but she'd be a fool if she thought she was truly free. She needed clothes, money, food, all things she had none of. She literally didn't have a penny to her name. She had no family. All she knew of the current world was what she overheard and what she had learned from Claire, and it was a vastly different world from the one she had grown up in.

Claire, that was her answer. Claire did have family. She had people that she was certain would be looking for her.

Cora tried to remember the names Claire had mentioned. Her daughter, Rosie, but she would be in hiding. And then there was the doctor, another child that had been taken from her. Claire said she had healed her. She was a genetic scientist, Madeline? No, Magdeline, in Vienna. That's who she had to find. The question was, how?

First, Cora needed to find out where she was. She looked up at the mountains, trying to recall the different peaks of the Alps. The bench she was on was along the side of a trail. It must lead somewhere that would tell her where she was.

Her broken arm ached, but while weak from the years of incarceration and sore from her long hike through the woods, her legs worked fine. And so, she started out walking the direction that, the sun told her, was opposite of her escape.

***

Claire had no clue where she was. She had been running on shear adrenaline until she came to a stream. She took a, much needed drink and collapsed under a nearby tree. It was the chirping of birds that woke her. She knew she must look a mess. She was stiff and sore, but it was nothing compared to how she had felt with the cancer. She had made her escape, and now she would follow the stream until she found out where she was and could contact Magdeline.

She stripped off the stinky clothes she wore and washed the best that she could. It was a nice day. She guessed around seventy degrees. Wringing out the clothes, she hung them across some branches.

Naked in an unfamiliar wood was not something she ever imagined being, especially in her late seventies. She was pretty certain there was no one around but the birds and squirrels to see. So, she did what she could to tend to her hand. The palm was only slightly swollen, and she made sure there was no dirt in the wound. When her clothes dried, she could use strips from her undershirt to bandage it. In the meantime, she looked around at the different plants.

After about an hour of foraging, she had a decent array of berries and nuts. She wished she had coffee or hot tea, as she shivered in the light breeze. For now, she would have to settle for cold stream water.

The clothes were thin and dried in another hour enough for her to dress and set off. If only she knew where she was heading, or even how far. Thinking about that would do her no good though. The most important thing was to not be caught. Even if she didn't make it, at least she would die free. She thought of Rosie and everything they had been through and felt a surge of adrenaline and determination.

Sweden

Carl looked at the 3D scans that showed Alice's implants from different angles. Could they disconnect it? Carl thought through all the staff. He had already memorized their credentials, but none were experienced with this. Even if the surgery didn't kill her, it could leave her paralyzed. That was something they would risk. Alice had already been told the risks and agreed.

Jonathan also told her about Magdeline, so she knew that it was likely she could recover. She would need to be stronger first.

Carl had temporarily diverted more of the cellular energy directed at Oscar from Richter to Alice. She didn't want his genes, but his were the most compatible and he didn't know of another way to help her.

She didn't understand why Jonathan couldn't be a donor. He had told her that they didn't have the equipment needed to use both Richter for Oscar and Jonathan for her, but the truth was that Jonathan's genes would be much less acceptable if she were ever to discover the truth.

While Carl also knew his own genetic pool, he wasn't as familiar with who they came from as he was with Jonathan's. He had considered looking them up but had avoided it. He knew it wasn't good, and like he told Jonathan, who you are is more than your genes. It's who you want to be. Carl was just getting comfortable with who he was becoming, and Jonathan was a good man. The only things that could change that were his own decisions or his trigger.

In fact, after considering what he knew of his brothers, it was even clearer that Richter, not his genes, had chosen his path. Genes could only provide certain elements of persuasion, boost propensities and talents. They couldn't make you evil. If they could, well then, there really was no hope.

Carl's thoughts turned briefly to Laura. The painting was now on its way. He would likely never know her reaction. Perhaps it would wind up back in the Jacuzzi. What mattered was that he had tried.

Switzerland

Cora had walked most of the day, only passing on the outskirts of two small villages. At one, she snagged some clothes off a line and some apples from a basket next to a barn. A brown cow had given her an accusatory look and a warning moo just before a woman came around the corner.

She managed to duck behind a bale of hay, and as the woman was frustratedly looking for the missing clothes, she sneaked out, back into the woods, and onto the trail.

She now knew that she was in Switzerland, but that wouldn't help much. According to a map at a fork in the trail, she had two choices. She could either hike for a few days and get lost in the Alps, or she could continue on to the next village, which she hoped would be bigger.

Now, the sun was starting to sink, and a cool breeze was blowing. She needed to find somewhere safe to spend the night. A drop of rain told her that it needed to be someplace under cover.

She heard the bells chiming in the distance. A church was the last place anyone would think to look for her, and so she turned off the path in the direction of the chime.

An hour later, she saw the steeple and the chimes sounded again. The rain had turned into a shower and her broken arm ached as she hurried toward the church. There was no one in sight, and she made her way past the gate and up the front steps.

She tried the large wooden doors, tugging as hard as she could with her left arm, but they were locked tight. She thought about looking for another entrance, but the rain had started to pound down and at least she was under cover.

Curling up in a corner, she felt the stones, cold and damp, underneath her. Her mind fled back to another time when she had fled. They had caught her that time, but only because she'd been taken to a hospital.

Cora stared up at the night. The glow of the moon was just visible through the clouds, and as she stared at it, she vowed that no matter what, they would never take her again. Somehow, she would be free.

She looked up as the door of the church opened and a young man came out.

Sebastian didn't see her and was startled by her approach behind him. She spoke in French, telling him that she was homeless and asked if he knew of a place where she could stay the night out of the rain.

He wasn't sure what to do. He knew he couldn't leave her, but as he took in her features, he found himself wanting to run. Instead, he called the director at the seminary and asked if he knew of a place for her.

There was an empty block of dorms that were sometimes used to house guests as well as those down on their luck. Usually they only took in men, but given the time and weather, the director asked Sebastian to bring her there.

He led her to the car, filled with trepidation. He knew his feelings were irrational, but she reminded him so much of his mother. She was shorter and nowhere near as fit or youthful, but her face. It was what he imagined his mother would look like if she was a normal person and down on her luck, as this poor soul was.

On the way, he tried to make small talk and find out more about her. She told him that she had left her husband. That he beat her.

It was a believable story that would readily explain the bruises and broken arm from her fall.

Sebastian asked if she had reported him, but she said she had tried that before, and it only made things worse. This time she was determined to simply disappear and start a

life far away from him. She told him that she had used all
her money to take a bus from France. She claimed she was
from a village outside Lyon.

As he showed her to the dorm room, he asked if she
needed a doctor, but she refused, claiming that the arm
was only sprained. She told him that her husband had
connections in the medical field, and she didn't feel safe
risking it, as he might be calling around, expecting her to
have gone to a doctor.

He sensed she was genuinely terrified of being found, and
he chased away his fear. Everybody had a doppelganger. It
just so happened that this woman was his mother's.

He brought her blankets, toiletries, and a plate from the
kitchen.

"Can I get a name, just a first, for the registry?" he asked
her.

"Cora," she said, as she sipped the coffee.

She must have felt his shock. She stared at him.

The look in her eyes paralyzed him. His mind told him his
feelings were ridiculous, but his spirit was filled with
warning.

"Do you need something else? Is there some requirement
for you to call the police?" she asked, "Or are you just
having a fit?"

"No, no, I'm sorry. I... You remind me of someone," he
said, understanding that she must sense his desire to run.
It was something he knew to be cautious of when working
with the homeless. They could sense the repulsion of them,
that was the sentiment of many. Sebastian had never been
repulsed. This was a personal issue. Perhaps it was God
sending him a test.

"Who do I remind you of? A demon?" she asked, "By the
look on your face, I ..."

"No," he said, cutting her off, "Not at all. I apologize. It's
just that..."

"Well, spit it out! I know I look awful, and I don't smell good either. So…"

"You look like my mother," he blurted out. "I'm so sorry. I know that probably doesn't make sense," he hurried on. "You might say that she was like your husband, abusive, and I had hoped never to see her again. I understand what it's like to need to escape he said," coming closer. "May I," he asked, motioning to the chair.

Cora nodded. There was something about this young man, something she'd been trying to place since he began speaking in the car. His voice. She studied him as he sat.

"I never talk about her, accept with my sister."

"Was she abused too?" Cora asked, feeling a softening towards him.

"Yes, we escaped together."

"I'm sorry then that I remind you of her. If I can be honest, you remind me of someone too."

"Not your husband, I hope," he said, and Cora laughed. The laugh made Sebastian's spirit quicken again, and he tried to push down his trepidation.

"You remind me of my sister."

"You have a sister," Sebastian said, his mind racing.

"Not anymore. She died when we were teenagers," Cora said. She had no idea if her sister was dead or alive, but she was dead to her. She had left her and gone with them long ago. Cora could barely remember the good times they had as young girls. Well, not really good times, but they had had each other's back.

"I'm sorry," Sebastian said, feeling a guilty sense of relief. "I should leave you to get settled now. Breakfast is at seven in the hall we passed next door. You'll hear the bell. You are welcome to join us until eight. If you would rather not, I understand, and can bring you a plate afterwards."

"That would probably be best. Thank you," she said. "I really do appreciate this, Sebastian,"

"You're welcome, and if you need anything, you can use the in-house phone in the hall. If you push two, it will link you to the director's office. Good night," he said, going to the door.

"Good night," Cora replied, as he left.

That night she dreamed of her childhood. They had been eleven. They had just been caught and received a shot. The examination was next. It was like this every week. There was always an examination. Cora hated the poking and prodding and the private questions that the doctors asked. The next day would be a different doctor, the psychologist. He only poked and prodded at their thoughts and feelings. Cora wasn't sure which she hated more.

They were going to separate them soon. She had overheard the doctors discussing it. They were meant for different purposes. Her sister would be sent away to a military school, and she would be sent to the hospital.

They were fifteen now, and the yard was filled with military vehicles. Her sister was home, but just for the weekend. They passed notes through a hole in the wall they had made beneath the baseboards. They were never left alone to talk privately. Cora had an examination that morning. They were getting ready to implant her. She was scared. She didn't want to be pregnant. She was planning to run away.

They had caught her at the place where she was hiding to wait for the train. That's when she knew it was her sister who ratted her out. Her sister was one of them.

***

Claire was freezing. She had no idea how far she had walked, following the stream. She could see lights in the distance, but they were too far away. The rain had soaked her to the bone, and the only cover was the bridge she sat under now, watching the lightning crack the sky after each roar of thunder.

She couldn't have come this far just to die of hypothermia under a bridge in the middle of a wood. Realistically, she knew it wasn't really as cold as she felt. It was just that she had no protection from the elements. If only she had found the bridge before getting so wet.

The bridge wasn't for cars or people, but a railway, and she wondered what train may pass. She thought of Rosie. Had she made it to Magdeline? Was she safe? Where had Cora gone? Who was Cora? Claire kept herself distracted from her discomfort with these thoughts until sleep finally overtook her.

Washington State

The plan was tentatively made. Suzanna knew that Lidia was secretly thrilled. Charice had told her as much. Still, she had at first made excuses, but under encouragement from Charice, she soon agreed. They would leave for Switzerland the next week.

They were all going to take a little drive today up the Hood Cannel. One of the real estate agencies Lidia had mailed the pictures of the cabin to believed it may be one of their listings. They couldn't give a name or even be certain it was the same, but the agent had said that the trim was very familiar. If nothing else, the architect was probably the same. That would be their next step if they found nothing today.

They pulled up to the cabin and used the key that the real estate agent had left with a neighbor to let themselves in. They had been warned that no one had been in to clean yet, and they all wiped cobwebs from their faces.

Suzanna knew as soon as they pulled up the drive. They may have been a mess, but the roses outside were the same as in the pictures, and inside there was a mug by the kitchen sink that matched the mugs that were on a table in another photo.

It made sense. No one had been here in three years. The cabin had been repossessed by the bank. Lidia was doing more digging to get the owner's name, but Suzanna knew. She knew as soon as she opened the cupboards and saw the same wine and the same canned goods that Alice kept at her condo.

The questions were how and why? When? was another question that Suzanna couldn't grasp. How many times had they thought Alice was somewhere else when she must have been here? When she wasn't at the office, or event with them, they had been in frequent phone contact, but never thought Alice was lying to them. She must have been.

They went through all the rooms, and Lidia took hair from a brush along with the mug for Selma to do a DNA analysis.

Charice was shocked by the idea that Alice could have managed to keep a place here. The drive alone, including time on the ferry, had taken over two hours. Coming here would have meant at least five hours round trip.

Suzanna opened the closet in the bedroom and discovered a violin. She remembered that Alice had wanted to learn the violin.

"Music teachers," she said.

"What?" Charice and Lidia asked in unison.

"She did have a natural talent, but I'm wondering if maybe she hired a music teacher."

"There can't be that many around out here," Charice said.

Lidia googled for music teachers in the area. "There's more than I thought," she said. I have five listed within twenty miles. Shall we pay them a visit?"

They took more photographs both inside and out, and Suzanna took the violin. Then they went to ask the first instructor if he had ever met Alice.

They were at the third instructor, when someone recognized the picture of Alice.

"She didn't look like that. Her hair was black and straight, and she sometimes wore glasses, but that's her. That's Allie," a woman said. She had just come out of her lesson and introduced herself as Gale. "My parents named me after the winds that were blowing the night of my birth," she said.

"How can you tell for sure it's Alice?"

"I saw her adjusting the black wig in the lady's room once. It was definitely her, but I haven't seen her in forever."

"Thank you," Lidia said. "That explains why the instructor didn't recognize her."

"No," Gale said, turning back to them. "She didn't take lessons from Mrs. Barns. She was a friend of her son. The few times I saw her, they came together. He used to help his mother teach. That's why I remember her at all. She always came and left with the son, mostly on weekends. I assumed they were a couple and had broken up."

Mrs. Barns came out a few minutes later and they asked her about what Gale had told them.

"They weren't a couple. I didn't really know her at all," she said. "I know he liked her, but Rob said she was seeing someone else. They were friends from college. He met her when he was working in the school's library. She told him about her interest in music, and he offered to help her. She came over here when she could on weekends. Sometimes it was pretty late, but she said her parents had a cabin nearby, so it wasn't a problem. The last I heard, he said she had to go on some business trip, but she never came back. That's all I know."

"Do you think we could talk to your son?" Suzanna asked.

"What is this about?"

"She's missing," Lidia said. "I was on the original case three years ago when she disappeared from the business trip you mentioned. We would have come to talk to you sooner, but we weren't aware of the friendship. I've since gone to working as a private investigator and am trying to help her mother." Lidia motioned to Suzanna.

"I'm truly sorry, Mrs.?"

"Morgan," Suzanna said.

"I don't see how Rob can help, but I'll give him a call if you like. He lives in Port Townsend now, married, and just gave me my first grandson," she said, smiling "Here's his card."

"That would be great. Thank you," Lidia said, handing Mrs. Barns her own card.

They got back in the car and Charice drove, while Lidia dialed the son's office. He was a dentist and was able to make a few minutes for them between appointments.

"I wondered what happened to her, but then I saw the article about her parents," he said, looking at Suzanna, "and I figured that she was worried about you. I never heard anything more. I did try to text her, but she never responded. I didn't really follow up. I'm sorry I can't be more help."

"Do you know the name of her boyfriend?" Lidia asked.

"No, I don't think it was really serious. She said something about finally having someone that she could let her hair down with. Dancing, she liked to go dancing when she didn't have any work events. I usually didn't see her until Sunday, but she did come up a few Saturdays. I think she came up with the guy she was seeing. I'm not sure. I just remember when I picked her up that there was a different car in the drive once. Usually, we'd meet for coffee at the "All Night" diner before the lesson and sometimes after.

"A couple of times she said some guy was following her. She thought you knew where she was, because she was sure that he was reporting to you.

"Feel free to call if you have more questions. I have to see my next patient now," Rob said, as a tech signaled him from the reception.

"Just one more question," Suzanna said.

"Yes?"

"Do you remember what kinds of books she used to check out?"

"Sure, it was a lot of stuff on law and investigative stuff. She even special ordered international books sometimes."

"Could she do that?" Lidia asked. "She wasn't a student anymore."

"Alumni members have borrowing privileges. I'm sorry, I've got to go."

"Thank you for your time," Lidia said.

"I think we should go to the library," Charice said.

"I agree," said Suzanna.

Lidia googled the hours. "They close at eight. I don't see how it will help though. She can't have checked out anything since she's been gone, and I doubt they'd keep records."

"Unless she had some unreturned from before," Charice said.

"That's a good point. As her mother, I should go and make sure that any past due or lost book fees are paid," Suzanna said.

"Okay," Lidia said. "I have errands to run tomorrow. And I should probably tell my sister and parents I'm going to Europe. Not that they'd notice, but I'm hoping to leave my cats with them."

"If it's a problem," Charice said, "I'd be happy to take them."

"Really? That would be fantastic. Both my dad and sister are allergic. Half the time they start sneezing when they see me, just from the stray hair."

"It's settled then," Charice said. "I'll go through the files to see if I can figure out how Alice bought that property. I wish we knew how long she'd had it."

"My guess is Trent might know. I do want to try again to talk with him. I have Brent's cell number, but it always goes to voice mail, and he doesn't return my calls." Lidia said.

"I could go back over and ask about that camera again. I really was interested in buying it for Max."

"Not alone," Lidia said. "I don't know what, but he and his brother are hiding something. Neither one of them has a record though."

"I wish I knew what Trent's relationship was with Alice. It bothered me, what Rob said about him being up at the cabin with her," Suzanna said. "I also know that it probably won't give us anything to help find her, and I would really just like to get away as soon as possible. I feel like everything we do only leads to more questions, and the only one who can really answer those questions, is Alice."

Chapter13

Switzerland: May 27th

Claire was woken by the rumbling on the tracks above. Her whole body ached, and she was stiff both from the cold and her fall. The rain had stopped, and the sun was peeking up over the tree line.

She washed up the best she could, wetting her hair and tying it in a lose top knot. Her right hand was redder than she would have liked and sore. Gently she squeezed and a small trickle of puss oozed out of the cut. This wasn't good. She had to get to Magdeline. She let the cold water of the stream run over it, not sure if she was helping or risking worse infection by whatever bacteria may be in the water. She also risked taking a drink. She really had no choice.

Yesterday had been fine, she'd been higher up, away from towns, trains, and other pollutants. She found and pressed some rain cleaned leaves against the infected cut and held them there with her fingers as she continued downstream.

The lights she had seen last night couldn't be more than another hour or two walk. She hoped there would be a public phone where she could make a collect call or maybe a kind person would let her use their mobile.

She knew she needed a doctor to look at her hand, but she didn't dare trust that any aside from Magdeline, wouldn't contact wherever it was she had managed to escape from.

Cora had warned her that the family, as she called them, had tight connections throughout the world and a network of doctors who may or may not know the truth about what was going on.

Austria

Soren discussed taking some time off with his job and was told that he had three weeks of paid time, that he could take free and clear. He was ahead of everyone else on the research team. He was also currently in a position where, as long as he read his emails and responded in a timely manner, he didn't need to come in until the next project, which was slated for whenever the funding came in.

Magdeline was a bit busier at her own lab, but they were all her personal projects. She really only needed to be there to run private tests or if there was some kind of emergency. The students she worked with would be off for the summer starting next week, but she knew a couple would be happy to acquire more work-study hours. None of them were paid except when she offered an additional job. She was considering that now.

She had come up with a theory that went beyond mere gene editing to actual gene separation, and she had talked to Shane about using the DNA from Kenneth and Daniel for it. Her hope was that, if it proved out, and if they found Kenneth, it may be used to slow his growth and modify his propensity for aggressive behavior.

This was something that the students could work on that would also give them some good original material for their graduate thesis.

Today, she would go into her lab to discuss and make up the schedule for the coming weeks. Her parents had agreed to come stay with the boys, and Rosie was on board too. She hated leaving the dogs but knew that they'd be well cared for.

Magdeline's biggest concern was what the boys might say to her parents about Rosie and Victoria. Simply saying they were friends or Soren's side of the family wouldn't explain anything if the boys told the story about finding someone, they thought was mommy, in mommy's bed. If she told them not to tell, that was tempting fate that they would. They didn't talk about it, but having their grandparents with them, they would want to tell them everything that had happened since they last saw them.

The alternative was to come up with a story to tell her parents to explain any strange stories the boys may tell. She was still working on that one.

The tentative plan was that Rosie would help care for Daniel when Shane couldn't be with him. Leaving Shane and Dave to focus on finding her mother. Rosie would also be able to actively help by acting as a translator.

Soren and Magdeline would go to Switzerland. Magdeline wanted to meet Sarah Martinson and Trudie was the link to introduce her and Soren. Then she could also get together with Heather, who was not only one of her best friends, but had been the lead doctor in charge of Claire and Rosie's treatment.

Switzerland

Cora woke late after a restless night of dreams. She had just returned from combing her hair for herself for the first time in years. She hadn't been allowed her own toiletries since the time she tried to escape by eating soap. She had been quarantined in the medical ward as they pumped her stomach and strapped her into a straitjacket. That's when she knew, her best chance to be free was to cooperate. She wondered, had cooperation made her sister free?

She started at the knock on the door, caught her breath, and when they didn't enter, she called, "Who is it?"

"It's Sebastian. I have a breakfast plate for you. I can just leave it out..."

She opened the door to Sebastian, just as he was bending to put the plate down.

"Thank you. Would you like to come in?" she asked.

"Oh, thank you, but I have a class I need to get to. If you like, I can come by at lunch."

"Yes, please do," she said, taking the plate from him.

She couldn't get over his voice. Every time she heard it, she heard the echo of her sister calling, "Ready or not, here I come." They had played hide and seek a lot, hoping to find the perfect spot where no one would find them.

Cora put the tray on the small desk. He had been considerate and brought her two coffees. It didn't make sense. She knew the research on voice patterns and how children learned to recognize that of a parent verses a stranger. Voices were nearly as unique as fingerprints, and his was uncannily similar to the voice she recalled as her sister's. Add to that what he said about her looking like his mother, his abusive mother, and it was too much to just let go. She needed to find out more about him.

She hadn't seen her sister since they took her from Brazil. She had been taken to the institute in Paris, after another attempt to run away.

Cora tried to tell herself that she should just move on. She needed to find Magdeline. She wondered briefly if Claire had made it. She doubted it. She had heard the nurse at the window yelling. Surely, they had caught her.

A part of her felt guilty for leaving her behind, but once she found Magdeline and Rosie, surely, they would rescue her. If she had allowed herself to be caught, neither of them would have stood a chance.

When he came back for lunch, she would ask Sebastian about making an outside call and if there was any internet that she could use to look up Magdeline.

Nova Scotia

Sophie hung up the phone. She and Nick had been talking to Larry, and a decision was made. They were all heading to Switzerland. The biggest decision had been what to do with Jeremy. In the end, they decided to bring him.

They had already been away from him long enough, and there was no way to explain to Nick's parents why they would leave again without him.

Margot, Larry's wife, had said that she would be more than happy to watch him when needed. She had no intention of going back to France without Larry, which meant that she would be there as long as the rest of them. She would need something to keep her busy, and when it came to everything going on, watching Jeremy was the only job that Larry would agree to let her do.

They would fly out on Monday and meet in Bern. Then they would head out to one of the towns in the postcard.

Bern, Switzerland

"Have I told you how glad I am you're here?" Larry said to Margot. "I almost wish that Nick and Sophie were coming tomorrow so I could have some extra eyes at the concert."

"Speaking of, I didn't see Victoria at breakfast today."

"She went to coffee with some friends. They have a rehearsal before the lunch reception this afternoon. That means we have about three hours to ourselves. What would you like to see?"

"How about here?" Margot said, pointing to one of the villages on the image of the postcard, Larry had on the table.

"I was thinking someplace not work related."

"It's not work to me. It looks like a lovely village, and I would like to get out of the city for a bit."

"I guess it can't hurt anything."

"Of course not. We'll just be tourists."

"Why that town? If I may ask."

"Like I said, it looks like a lovely village."

"Okay, well, we better get going then if you want to have any time to look around."

Seattle

Suzanna was surprised when she saw the email. It was sent to Charice and included information on the camera she'd looked at along with an attachment for Suzanna. Charice sent her a text to let her know she was forwarding something important.

The attachment was enlargements of the photos and a note apologizing for closing the store when they had come before. Apparently one of the men watching Alice had threatened Trent once. Thinking that the man worked for Alice's parents, Trent wanted nothing to do with Suzanna. Brent only learned this when he told Trent they were coming to talk to him, and Trent had insisted that they close the store.

With that mystery solved, Suzanna headed off to the University of Washington campus. There was more than one library building, and while she knew which one Rob had worked at, she wanted to cover all the bases.

Chapter 14

Switzerland: May 28th

Cora was in the library. She had found information on Magdeline Anglistan, but was she ready to contact her yet? She should at least send a message about Claire. What should she say though? Should she explain who she was? She had learned that Sebastian was from Brazil, which cinched what she suspected. Should she tell him the truth?

The director had told her that since the entire block of dorms was currently empty, she could stay. He only asked that she attend chapel and that, if she were still here when her arm healed, she help in the kitchen and gardens.

If she decided to stay on working there, they would move her into the workers quarters. She was basically being offered a job with room and board. These were the things that she needed. Perhaps this was a better way to start over. She was basically protected here, and Sebastian, whom she was now certain was her nephew, was here.

Logging off the computer, she made her way outside to the garden. It was the first time in her life she really felt free. She was tired, so tired of hiding and pretending, always looking for an escape route. But here, there was no one after her. There was no reason to look for her here.

She wondered again if she should tell Sebastian the truth about who she was.

After some time of contemplation, she went to the director to ask if there was some way that she could mail a message to a relative in Austria. He had given her some paper, a pen, and an envelope, and told her to simply have it to their mailroom by 13:00. No need to worry about postage. It would simply be processed with the other mail.

Cora could hardly believe the kindness she was being shown. A part of her wondered if there was an ulterior motive. Were they that desperate to find workers? Or perhaps, if there was a God, He was finally making up to her.

She hurried to write something that would help Claire. After all, without her, Cora would still be there herself. She didn't know how to give directions, but she could give names and a description of the building and location. She was going with the assumption that Claire had been caught. She gave nothing away about herself and needed to be sure they wouldn't know where she was. That meant that when she took the letter to the mailroom, she would need to explain that she couldn't risk being found, and make sure that the school's address would not be on the envelope. She was assured it would not be and so, leaving the letter, she headed off to the chapel.

She had been inside a church only a few times growing up, mostly for Easter celebrations. She knew the basics, but she had never known any real believers before Sebastian. At least he seemed to be one, though how that had occurred was something she knew could only have happened after he escaped.

***

When Claire arrived at the edge of the town, she was suddenly afraid. She didn't know where she was or who might be looking for her. If any normal person saw her, they might call a hospital. Her German was passable, but still not that great. What if they didn't understand her? Should she just use English? How could she explain her condition in any language? She knew she was a filthy, smelly mess after sleeping on the ground and walking for two days, not to mention the way she was walking, stiff and bruised. Then there was her hand. She didn't want a hospital or the police called, or worse yet, some social service organization. She just needed to get in touch with Magdeline. Did she even remember the number correctly? And if she was in Switzerland, what was the country code to call Austria?

She had to find some clean clothes, but how could she without being seen? What story could she come up with? She was still down beside the stream, but she could see a road running alongside, just up a bank.

She followed the stream a little further until she saw what looked like the back side of a supermarket. She took a chance and looked around the side of the building to see if there was a phone. She didn't see one, but pay phones were so rare anymore, she wouldn't be surprised if there were none in the town.

She made her way back into the woods and splashed water on her face from the stream. There were some fragrant flowers growing nearby and she plucked a few blooms to rub on herself, in a desperate effort to at least smell decent.

Then she sat on a rock beside the stream and did something she hadn't done for a long time. She prayed.

A few minutes later she heard footsteps coming down the bank behind her. She froze. Then, turning slowly, she saw a man. He wore a hat with the supermarket logo and carried a lunch cooler as he headed toward her.

"Are you all right?" he asked in English.

She couldn't move or make her mouth work to respond.

"Were you in an accident?" he questioned, coming closer. "Can I call someone for you?" he asked, caution seeping into his tone as he pulled out a mobile.

"I'd like to call my daughter," Claire managed, and the man came closer, holding out the phone to her.

"Here," he said, "What happened to you?"

"Long story," she replied, taking the phone as a tear rolled down her cheek.

"Did you have an accident?"

She only looked up and asked, "How do I call Austria?"

"Where in Austria?"

"Outside Vienna."

"That's a long way away."

"I need to let her know I'm all right. Please," she said, hearing the desperation in her own voice and wondering what he must be thinking.

"Plus, forty-three."

She dialed the number, but then remembered it was to text Magdeline's tablet. She looked for his texting app.

He looked at the cut on her hand and the cringe on her face as she tried to type a message.

"That looks pretty bad. I can take you to a clinic in town."

"No," she said simply, trying to decide what to say. "Where are we?" she asked.

"Schwyz, Ibach, more specifically."

She looked at his hat and typed in the location he gave her along with the store name and hit send. Claire audibly sighed in relief when it sent.

"Look, I don't want to leave you here. It would be after dark before your daughter could get here."

"She'll come, and I'll be fine."

"Look, I don't know what happened and if you don't want to tell me then..."

"I don't. Here," she said handing the phone back to him. "Thank you."

"Hang on to it, in case she replies," he said, unzipping his lunch bag. He took out an apple. "Do you mind if I join you? My wife packed plenty to share. Juice or water?" he offered, sitting on a nearby rock and pulling out two bottles.

"Water. Thank you," she said, taking it. She cringed as she tried to open the cap.

"Here, let me get that. Do you like shrimp salad on Rye?" he asked, pulling out a gigantic sandwich that made Claire's mouth water.

She smiled, as the phone vibrated with a reply from Magdeline.

Austria

Magdeline and Soren had just gotten the boys in the SUV and started out to pick her parents up from the train station when she saw the message.

"Pull over Soren."

"What is it?" he asked, moving to the side of the road.

"It's from Claire. She said she escaped and she's behind a supermarket in Ibach, Switzerland. I think that's near the border."

"It is," Soren replied. "Check the train schedule. It might be best to tell your parents I have some last-minute business, and I take the train to go find her. I'm fairly familiar with the area. Larry, Shane and Dave aren't."

"Good point. Driving will be faster though. Go on to the station and I'll let Claire know you're on the way."

"Call the station too and get me a rental car," Soren said, as he pulled back into traffic.

Magdeline sent a message that Rosie was safe, and Soren was on his way to Switzerland, but it would be at least nine hours, probably ten, before he could get there.

"Have I told you lately that you're wonderful?" She said to Soren.

"Not today," he smiled "Are you boys ready to see Grandpa and Grandma?" he called to the back seat.

"Yay!" came the cheer of all three.

Magdeline called the rental car desk, then called Larry to tell him about the message from Claire and Soren's plan to go get her. Then, Magdeline called Shane just as they turned the corner toward the station. She asked him not to say anything to Rosie until they had Claire to safety.

Switzerland

Claire handed the phone back to the man who introduced himself as Roger.

"You can't wait out here that long," he said, looking at the message reply.

"I'll be fine. It's not like I'm dressed to go anywhere else."

He wasn't sure what to say to that. She wasn't dressed in much at all, except what looked like a hospital scrub top and grubby sweatpants.

"I was abducted," she said. It was the truth after all.

"You don't want to call the police?"

"No. My abductor may have someone in the police."

"I see. You know, at first, when you didn't speak, I wondered if you were an escaped mental patient, but I can tell from the way you talk that you're not. Where are you from?" he asked. "I grew up in the USA myself, Oregon. I took a study abroad class in Germany, business administration," he said with a laugh. "I forgot to take the high-tech block-chain classes though, and I wound up working as a manager here. I met my wife in Germany too. She's from here. Anyway, you sound American?"

"Yes, but I live in Austria now with my daughter."

"And you were abducted."

"It's a long story. It was my daughter they wanted. They took me to find her."

"Then she's in danger?"

"When I was taken, she knew where to go."

"Wow. Well, I have to get back to work in a few minutes, but I think I can come up with a clean tee-shirt and some sweatpants for you. I'll bring it out on my break, along with something for your hand. You hang onto the phone."

"Are you sure?"

"I'm not supposed to take personal calls at work anyway. If someone needs me, they can call the office phone."

"I don't know how to thank you."

"Just prove me right and still be here when I come back."

***

Larry thought he was going crazy. Margot was obsessed with something she overheard in the lady's room of a coffee shop they stopped at in the town from the postcard. It was about some exclusive resort or spa of some sort, and she was determined to go there. Soon, Sophie and Nick would be there to help look for Jack, because of the same postcard and now Magdeline and Soren were coming to meet Sarah Martinson.

The bright spot was the message from Claire.

Victoria had also been asking him to double and triple check security, which he had no say in here. He offered to act as her personal bodyguard, but she didn't want him to do that. No one else could know anything. She insisted that everything appear normal, but that he still secure her safety while she went off with friends, playing the 'normal' game. She was also worried about her family, whom she had still been unable to get in contact with.

Feeling overwhelmed, Larry called Dave to fly into Bern and join them at the concert. It seemed that he wouldn't be needed to help look for Claire now and Shane would be basically playing guard to Rosie and Claire. The cabin seemed as safe a place as any for them.

Dave should arrive just in time to go to the hotel, change and get familiar with the concert venue. He and Larry, with Margot, would take up posts on either side of the lobby as the guests arrived.

Finding a ticket for Dave was problematic. So, the plan was that after Larry and Margot entered, Margot would stay seated, and Larry would give Dave her ticket to hold. He wouldn't go inside the auditorium though, he would stay in the lobby, supposedly waiting for someone, ticket in hand. He only hoped that they didn't do a head count and notice the auditorium was already full.

"Take a deep breath, Darling," Margot said, "At least Claire got away. That's one less missing person to worry about."

"That depends on what Soren finds when he arrives at the location. We don't know her condition or what she's been through. She said she was okay to wait, but she may send another location later. Rosie still doesn't know, and I'm not sure what this may be letting Shane in for. I wish Soren and Magdeline were staying there and not coming here. They still don't know that Nick and Sophie are coming with Jeremy. I know they're all trying to help, but..."

"You need their help," Margot said, "and you know it. Just like you know you need mine."

"You'll have enough to do watching a two-year old."

"I raised three daughters. You don't think I can multi-task?"

"I don't want you to multi-task. I can't have to worry about your safety too. You already know too much. You should have stayed in Lyon."

"I wouldn't know any less there. Here, I'm just a tourist, interested in checking out a resort. I bet Sophie, Magdeline and maybe Victoria would come with me too."

Larry rolled his eyes. "Just what we need, all three of them, with you snooping around. You do realize that the idea is to investigate inconspicuously?"

"What is more inconspicuous than a girl's day out at a nice spa? They can even wear disguises. You said Victoria has one with her."

"Yes, but I still recognized her. I'm just glad that Rosie is still in Austria, or I'd be seeing double doubles."

Margot laughed. "And what if Alice decides to turn up too?" she asked.

Larry closed his eyes and took a deep breath.

"Come on, let's go and find some lunch."

"I'm not really hungry, but that being said, Victoria is meeting her friends in the lobby in half an hour to go to lunch. If she wants me to keep her safe, she'll need to get used to my being her shadow."

"You mean us? It's far more inconspicuous if you don't follow alone. And I am getting hungry."

"Okay. I want to head down in fifteen. I figure it's better if I'm there ahead of her rather than following her."

"If you're ready, I'm ready now, and I'd like to tuck into the gift shop."

"You know I can't include your shopping in the expenses."

"I know. You seem to forget that I have my own resources."

"No, I can't forget. Your father reminded me too many times before he let me marry you," Larry replied, as he reached around her to open the door.

Money had never been an issue for Margot, and he knew she thought of it as their money, but still, he was old fashioned and felt the need to be able to support them. Not that it had ever been easy with three daughters, especially when they lived in Paris during their high-school years. He could hardly wait for Dave to arrive. He needed a male confidant, and Dave was still single without a wife of his own to worry about. His presence would help balance things out.

France

Laura double and triple checked the wine list for the

night. She hadn't heard any more of the strange noises in the cellar, but the wall was still, if not as warm as before, warmer than the other walls. That wasn't what was bothering her tonight though.

She had decided a few days ago on this evening's wine list, but when she went down to the cellar to retrieve the bottles, they weren't there. They weren't missing exactly, meaning, there were bottles in the spots, just not the bottles her list showed should be there. Aside from the two she had discovered on the opposite wall of what her diagram showed, the other bottles she wanted were nowhere to be found.

***

Mathias was having dinner at Laura's family's restaurant with Tony, before going over to help Laura. He had volunteered to make some hors d'oeuvres and play waiter, so that she could socialize, observe, and get to know her customers.

They had just ordered when a young woman showed up carrying a large rectangular package. She said it was for Laura and was told that Laura wasn't there. Tonight, they told her, Laura was at her new wine bar. It wasn't far, if she wanted to go, or they could deliver it to her.

Mathias excused himself from the table and went to the reception area where the woman was speaking to Laura's brother.

Chantel looked up when he spoke and was at once struck by the voice similarity. She looked closely at Mathias, noting the similar facial structure.

"I'll be going to the wine bar right after dinner and would be happy to take it to her," Mathias said.

"Oh, well, maybe I'll see you there?" she said, her curiosity high. She knew about Richter, but surely, this man was a brother as well. She knew that there were four of them. "What did you say your name was?"

"I didn't, but it's Mathias."

"Well, it's nice to meet you Mathias. If you give me directions, I can just head over there."

"They aren't open yet. I'll be going over after dinner to help. Laura is a friend of mine. What did you say your name was? And if I may ask, who is that from?"

"Chantel. I'm visiting with family nearby and told... my boss, that I would bring this to Laura. They're old friends."

"Well then, Chantel, would you like to join me and my friend Tony for dinner? There will only be hors d'oeuvres tonight at Laura's."

"Won't your friend mind?"

Mathias motioned to Tony, who came to join them.

"Tony, this is Chantel. She has a gift from a friend of Laura's, and I invited her to join us for dinner, and then she can follow us over after. Is that all right?"

"Of course. Come, we've only just ordered. May I recommend the chicken La' Fleur? It's the chef's special tonight."

"All right, but I need to make a quick phone call first."

"No problem. I'll put your order in. What kind of dressing for your salad?"

"Italian, thank you. I'll be right back," she said and headed for the parking lot.

Mathias took the package to the table and sat it on a chair.

"I have a funny feeling I just found out how to find Carl."

"You think it's from him?"

"I think it's a painting. He would think that to be a safe way of contacting her without anyone else being able to track it. What's interesting is that she said it was from her boss, and I don't think she was lying. I think she was trying to explain without mentioning his name."

"That would mean he's here."

"No. That I doubt. He's not in France. I would have found him. She said that she's here visiting family. Can you find out from where?"

"Me?"

"I don't need her to get suspicious, although, I think she already is. She may even be calling Carl now. I gave her my name, and if she's working with him, odds are she knows about me."

***

Chantel pulled out the burner phone Carl had told her to use in an emergency. Was this an emergency? She knew he wouldn't want Mathias to know where he was, but she hadn't told him and there was nothing on the painting to give it away. That was why she was delivering it. The painting was with Mathias. All she had to do was leave. What if she ran into them while she was out with her friends somewhere? She didn't want to be looking over her shoulder for the next two weeks. She didn't have to tell them the truth. Yes, she would tell them what her friends and cousins believed, that she was working in Switzerland. That would even help lead Mathias away from Carl.

She tucked the phone back into her bag and went inside to join Mathias and Tony for dinner. She could make a call tomorrow, when she knew more about what his brother was doing here.

Somewhere

Jack was mad at himself. Someone had come and he'd slept through it. How? He had to have been drugged, but how had someone even come in without him being on alert? The last thing he remembered was tying his shoes to start his workout. He had been wide awake. Then, two hours later he woke up in bed again. He looked up at the vent that was blowing cool air as he ran on the treadmill. Had they put something in the vent system?

He got off the treadmill and went back to his room. The vent covers were welded on, not that anything larger than a rat could fit inside of one. Where did the vents go? He hated being trapped like this. He couldn't see where an entrance was at the bottom or where any other part of the building may be. Surely there must be more to this complex than just these rooms off this corridor.

Jack ran his hand through his hair and slinked his way, like the caged animal he was, back to the gym.

He did another five miles, then showered, grabbed a water, and sunk into the jacuzzi. He had to think of something.

His guess was that they must have cameras to watch him, but as of yet, he had found none.

How long would they keep him? What could they have planned for him? Was all this just to get him out of the way?

He played with a remote that controlled available music selections, mostly classical and jazz. There was nothing with lyrics. Perhaps this was a psychological test to see how long he could last without so much as another human voice. He was already talking to himself, but that wasn't anything particularly new. He figured it was something most people, especially single people, did.

As he switched the music off, another switch flicked on in his head. A radio. Maybe he could build a radio, to somehow reach the outside world. He had rebuilt radios in the garage as a boy. It wasn't that far-fetched, or at least no more so than the situation he was currently in. "Far-fetched situation, far-fetched solution," he said to himself, as he climbed out of the jacuzzi.

Switzerland

The concert was about to start, and Dave did another round of the lobby, whilst pretending to talk on the phone. All seemed normal, until after, when they arrived back at the hotel. There was a letter waiting for Victoria at reception.

Dave asked the man at the desk if he could describe the person who left it, but he had not yet come on shift when it arrived. Then Dave asked whether he recognized all the people in the lobby and surrounding shops and restaurant as hotel guests.

"I am sorry, Mr. Asher, but again, I only arrived less than two hours ago, and I did not work the past two days. I am sorry. Perhaps I can ask Gwen. She is the head of housekeeping for the evening shift," said the man behind the desk, whose name tag read, 'Henrik'.

"Yes, please do. Thank you, Henrik," Dave said.

Victoria had not opened the letter. After the last note from the delivery driver, she was worried. Though she knew a part of her verbal trigger, she worried that after the last failed attempt, something else could be contained on the letter. Poison, some other phrase that may also work as a trigger. She couldn't be certain how many methods could be used to trigger her. She was certain that there was more than one and it could be anything sensory. She wasn't even certain what the trigger would do, only that it would be destructive to others and or herself.

***

On Roger's afternoon break, he took Claire a set of lounge wear that they carried at the store. It was nicer than sweatpants and a tee-shirt, cooler too. The day had gotten quite hot. He also grabbed some stretchy slip-on shoes, sunscreen and a first aid kit.

She did a quick change behind some bushes, then they cleaned and bandaged her hand.

Roger had called his wife, telling her that a woman was traveling and had car trouble and was waiting for family to pick her up, but they wouldn't arrive until after dark. She had agreed with him that it would not be safe for her to wait outside alone, and Roger told Claire that they insisted she come to their home for dinner. It didn't matter how late. He wasn't going to leave her out alone in the night. She could wait on their couch until her ride arrived.

Claire was relieved. The last two days had taken their toll. She only wished she could wash her hair. The clean clothes felt wonderful, but wet wipes could only do so much to clean her up. She was flooded with thankfulness though, mostly at knowing that Rosie was safe.

She typed in a message with the new location to pick her up.

Soren replied that his estimated time of arrival was between ten and ten-thirty that night. He would call from his own phone when he reached the town and gave her the number so she would know it was safe to answer.

***

Gwen wasn't able to tell Dave much more than Henrik. She did recognize everyone currently in the Lobby and surrounding areas. She also described to him the occupants of the rooms surrounding Victoria, but these were all other people who were part of the concert. Victoria had already checked, and there was no one new to her working this show.

"So, what do we do?" Dave asked Larry when he returned from taking Margot out after the concert and they were all in Larry and Margot's suite.

"Could you transcribe it, but use different words or word orders so that I can read the message?" Victoria asked.

Larry went to a bag that Margot had brought and removed a pair of gloves. He then used a dropper to apply a liquid agent that would react upon most dangerous substances that may be invisible to the naked eye. There was no reaction.

Larry took the envelope out onto the balcony and opened it. He then placed the pages in two plastic sleeves, that had also been in the bag, and he came back into the suite.

Victoria and Dave watched, as Larry sat and read the letter, and Margot brewed some tea.

"It's Poetry," Larry said. "The whole thing. It's all one long poem." Larry handed it to Dave.

"I think I'll say goodnight now," Victoria said, and rose to leave.

"Victoria?" Margot said, "Are you sure you should be alone? The tea is almost done."

"I...What type of poetry is it?"

"I'm afraid that literature has never been my strong suit," Dave said.

"Nor mine," Larry added.

"Let me see," Margot said, as she brought the tea. Dave handed her the letter. She scanned it. "It's a ballad. That means it tells a story. This kind of poetry is often put to song. Look Larry, here at the bottom. It's a set of notes. Perhaps it was meant for Victoria to play it?"

"They can't be dumb enough to think that I would."

"It's a love ballad. Is it possible that it has nothing to do with the project? Are there any ex-boyfriends, perhaps?" Margot asked.

"No," Victoria answered, shaking her head. "I haven't even allowed myself to think about that since I left Australia."

"There is something familiar about this particular ballad too," Margot said, as she continued to read it to herself. I think you should run it against know ballads. I don't think it's an original, at least not in full. I think it's based on a well-known ballad and that they altered it."

"I'll take it to my room and see if I can find anything," Dave said, as he sipped his tea. "This is really good, Margot. You know I'm usually more of a coffee man."

"I know, but nothing beats a nice Darjeerling to help relax the mind and body before bed."

***

Roger's wife, Helena, insisted Claire help herself to their shower.

Much refreshed, she towel-dried her hair, put the lounge wear back on, and headed down the stairs. It smelled terrific. She was surprised by a girl coming in the front door as she entered the living room.

"Claire, this is our daughter, Livy. She occasionally blesses us with her presence when she has nowhere else to go. Livy, this is Claire. She had some car trouble and is joining us for dinner while she waits for her ride."

"Hi," Livy said, smiling at Claire and going over to give her dad a peck on the cheek. "Don't listen to him too much," she said, turning back to Claire. "I'm a student at a culinary school in Lichtenstein. More often than not, they come to my apartment for my cooking. I have finals this week to cook for. So, tonight I am on vacation. My mother is a great cook too, so don't worry."

Claire smiled at the girl, who must have been about twenty. "I'm just thankful for the hospitality, but it does smell delicious!"

"It will be. Where are you from?" Livy asked. "Your accent sounds a lot like my dad."

"That is because I am also originally from America. I live with my daughter in Austria now."

"Where in America?" Livy asked.

"I've lived in a few places. Mostly the Northwest, like your dad."

"So, what are you doing in Switzerland?"

"Let's not subject guests to twenty questions." Roger cut in, sensing Claire's discomfort.

"It was only three, but okay," Livy said, giving her dad an odd look and turning back to Claire. "I'm sorry. I only meant to make conversation."

"Don't apologize," Claire said. "It's just been a really long day," she said with a yawn that she didn't need to fake. "Your dad knows I'm tired."

"Why don't you go give your mom a hand in the kitchen," Roger said.

"Because I'm taking twenty-four hours of kitchen free time," Livy replied, as Helena came in to tell them all that dinner was ready.

"Livy, honey, I didn't know you were coming tonight."

"I didn't know either mom, until Janie got a call and suddenly had a date. I didn't feel like going out alone. And as I was just telling Dad and Claire, I am taking a kitchen break until I cook for finals. Plus, I know you always have plenty."

"Well, it's good to have you. I'll just set one more place," Helena said, as they went to the table.

Livy left after dinner, saying she was on a diet and didn't dare stay for dessert. Helena had made chocolate truffles in plum sauce and that was what they were enjoying now, along with espresso.

"That was too good for words," Claire said, hoping to keep the conversation limited to the food. Soren should arrive in less than two hours now, and Claire was trying to cling to consciousness over her desire for sleep.

"Thank you. I'm glad you enjoyed it. You know, you are welcome to rest in the spare room if you like," Helena offered, as Claire tried to stifle another yawn.

"Oh, thank you, but no. It won't be that much longer. Is there any chance of getting the recipe for these?" Claire asked, as she took another truffle.

"Of course. I'll go get it, but you must promise not to tell Livy. It was her great-grandmother's. Most of her recipes are. She does change things up to make them her own though. I, on the other hand, tend to stick to the original," Helena said and disappeared into the kitchen.

"I can't thank you all enough, Roger," Claire started.

"I'm just glad to be able to help."

"If there's ever any way that I can repay..."

"Just give us a call to let us know how you and your daughter are doing. I had a sister, Tina," Roger started. "Her husband used to beat on her. She left him and took her daughter, but he found them. He's in jail now, but my sister is in a hospital, permanently. A brick to the head can cause terrible damage. Livy is really my niece. She was only two, and I have no idea why I just told you that story other than I want you to understand why I would do anything to keep that from happening to someone else."

"I'm so sorry. Is she still in the states?"

"Fortunately, we were able to bring her here. There's a top-notch facility in Lichtenstein."

"Does that mean there's hope?"

"Only that she'll live out her days in relative comfort. She recognizes Livy when we visit. I'm not sure about me. She can't talk, but you can see it in her eyes that she knows her daughter, and I like to think that knowing her daughter is safe helps her."

"It does. That I promise you. It does," Claire said, as Helena returned.

"Here you are," Helena said, handing a recipe card to Claire.

"Thank you!" Claire smiled.

"What time again is your ride supposed to arrive?"

"About an hour and a half now, but don't feel like you need to stay up and entertain me."

"Nonsense," Helena said. "Do you play Rummy?"

"I used to,"

"Then, why don't I pour us some more coffee and we can have a round."

"I'll grab the cards," Roger said, "and a dash of rum for the Rummy. Ladies?"

Both women passed on the rum, and they played cards until Soren called to say that he was only ten minutes out.

Roger gave Claire a list of their contact information and made her promise to let him know how she and her daughter were doing.

"I think I may just believe in God again," Claire said to Soren, as she collapsed against the seat. "How is Rosie?"

"She's fine now, but she'll be even better when she sees you. I hope you don't mind, but I booked a hotel just over the Austrian border," he said, yawning.

"I understand. You look almost as tired as me,"

"So, can I ask what restored your belief?"

"I was sitting by a stream, lost, dirty, hungry, and with no way to contact anyone. I had just prayed in desperation, and along came Roger. He let me use his phone, no questions asked and then... They were so kind," she said and wiped at a tear as she thought of Roger's sister.

Chapter 15

Austria: May 29th

Rosie woke up well rested. For the first time in days, she hadn't had a nightmare.

She went into the kitchen and started the coffee. She didn't look up, but she could feel Daniel watching her. It was only 6:00 in the morning, and she could hear his father, Shane, snoring away in the other bedroom.

She couldn't remember the last time she had felt so relaxed, but why? What had changed?

Light was starting to trickle in the windows through the trees outside. Pouring herself some coffee, she opened the front door. Aside from Magdeline's back yard, she hadn't gone outside since the day her mother was abducted.

She stepped out onto the small porch but stayed by the door. Looking out at the forest, she inhaled deeply and took a sip of coffee. Two rocking chairs sat to the right. Scanning the area, she took a seat in the chair closest to the door. Across the drive, she spotted a racoon. He spotted her too and they had a stare down until something moved in the bushes behind it, and the racoon dove into the bushes. Rosie laughed, then startled as she heard a noise to her left.

Gripping the arms of the chair, she turned to see Daniel, still in his pajamas.

"Hi," he said, "Can I sit with you?"

"Sure," Rosie said, relaxing and smiling at the little boy.

Daniel giggled as two squirrels chased each other up a tree.

A minute later, Shane came out, carrying his coffee, to join them. "Nice morning. Can I share your seat, Daniel?"

Daniel moved to let Shane sit and then climbed onto his lap.

"Good coffee, thank you," Shane said.

"My mom always said, a teaspoon of cinnamon makes all the difference."

Shane smiled. "I didn't even know we had cinnamon."

"It was behind the filters."

"We found your mother," Shane said.

It took a moment for Rosie to respond. She turned and stared at Shane. "What did you say?"

Shane smiled. "Soren is bringing her here as we speak. He just messaged. They should be here by two."

"But how? When?"

"We wanted to make sure it was really her and she was safe before we told you. She contacted Magdeline yesterday, and Soren went to get her. She was in Switzerland, which is why it took so long."

"She's okay?" Rosie asked, smiling at the same time her eyes filled with tears.

"She's fine, a few bruises from jumping out of a window, but fine, and she can't wait to see you."

Rosie's tears of relief flowed freely now, and she wiped at her face.

"Thank you!" she said, looking at Shane.

"Are you okay?" Daniel asked, not understanding why she was crying at the news.

"I'm fine," she said, as Daniel climbed off Shane's lap and went over to her.

He climbed onto her lap, put his arms around her and whispered in her ear, "I hope they find my mommy soon too."

Rosie hugged him tight. She could feel his pain. It didn't matter that his mother had left by choice. He was just a little boy who wanted his mommy.

"How about I make us all some pancakes," Shane said, getting up.

"Can I help?" Daniel asked.

"Sure, you can help mix the batter," Shane said and turned to Rosie. "Can I get you a refill?"

"I can...," she started.

"You deserve to relax," Shane said.

Rosie handed him her mug. "Thank you."

A minute later, Daniel came back out with a tray of coffee and a glass of milk. He sat it down on the small table between the chairs.

"Dad said he could mix the batter if I wanted to sit outside with you."

Rosie smiled and took the coffee, while Daniel took the milk and climbed back up into the other chair.

They sat in silence, watching and listening to the birds sing, until Shane had breakfast ready.

After breakfast, they drove into town to get groceries and some clothes for Claire.

Switzerland

Dave had found the poem. It was an old Scottish ballad about a battle, only the words had been altered to modernize it. He sent it to Shane to see if he could make something of it.

Then he had a call from Sebastian.

"This is a surprise! How is seminary?"

"Good, but I've discovered something, or rather someone, that could be important."

Sebastian decided to be direct with Cora. He told her that his mother had a sister named Cora, who she said had died. Then he showed her a photo he had found and hidden long ago of his mother and her sister smiling on the veranda of a large house. It was the only memory of his mother he had taken, because he wanted something positive to remember her by.

Cora hadn't denied that it was her in the photo. She couldn't. The tears came too quickly.

They were up the better part of the night talking, and for Claire's sake, she had told the truth about where she had escaped from and asked him to call Dave to see if he could help.

Cora's hardest decision was whether to let Dave in on her relationship to Sebastian. She wanted peace, but she realized, if all she had gone through was only to protect herself, her life really had been lost. If she wanted those years locked away and all she had learned to matter, she needed to let it be known. Sebastian assured her that Dave and Larry could be trusted to protect her secrets.

Dave didn't tell Sebastian that Claire had already been found, because he hoped to find out more about Cora first. Could she even somehow lead them to her sister?

Larry, Margot, and Victoria had gone to the pool and Dave decided he could use a nice sauna to relax and went down to join them. Then he and Larry left the women by the pool, while they found a private sauna, and Dave filled Larry in on Sebastian's call.

Somewhere

Jack looked at the conglomeration of components that he had removed from various kitchen appliances and work out equipment. He had kept the treadmill intact for his sanity, but the rowing machine & bike were out of commission, and he would have to heat food on the stove, as the microwave had proved the most useful.

He flipped through the DIY magazine, hoping that he was reading the French correctly. He was using this along with a Popular Mechanics magazine in German to put together what he hoped was a functioning transmitter.

He had made kitchen utensils into makeshift tools and wore rubber gloves that he found under the sink. He thought he had all that he needed now, and it was just a matter of connecting it all correctly and praying a signal could get out.

France

Chantel had not stayed long at the wine bar. She had let Mathias buy her one drink, while she sat with Tony and checked out Laura. As soon as she was sure Laura had the painting, she made her excuses to leave. It had been too busy for Laura to talk, and Chantel had no desire to get to know the woman.

Tony discretely followed her out and waited for her to leave before getting in his car to follow.

She stopped at a chain hotel, about an hour away, outside of Calais. It was nearly midnight when he called Mathias with the location.

After closing, Laura stared at the package, thinking the same thing Mathias was, that it was a painting from Carl.

Now, she still stared at it, only it was no longer covered in the brown wrapping paper but hung on the wall of the wine bar.

"He has so much talent," she said, as Mathias and Tony helped her install new wine racks so she wouldn't need to make so many trips to the cellar. "I hate to think that he's hiding out somewhere because he doesn't want you to find him," she said, looking at Mathias. Couldn't you send a message back through Chantel and invite him to come here? The two of you could make amends. Maybe he could even help you in undoing whatever it is your father did."

"If he hasn't taken over working on some of the same atrocities," Mathias replied.

"If you really believe he would do that, you don't know him," Laura defended, giving Mathias a look that pained his heart.

"I don't like thinking it either, but aside from the past three years, I lived with him his whole life. I think I know him pretty well. I know he was different with you, but that was only a few weeks. Even you saw how he can overreact," he said, casting a look to the painting.

"I'm going down to get more bottles," Laura said.

"I'll help you,"

"No, you won't. Stay up here and help Tony."

Adam had just finished switching bottles and closing the hidden door behind him. He would be glad when she was gone, so that he could stop making the long journey back and forth from Southern to Northern France. He didn't dare leave the pods, that contained some of the most important people of the projects, in the hands of another while she was there.

Once he got rid of her, he could let someone else take over the maintenance. There wasn't much required. They could monitor the pods remotely, only needing to come if there was need of an on-site check, like making sure the generator functioned properly during the storm. Then he would be free to go back and focus on his family.

He didn't like leaving Mel in charge. She had begun taking far too much authority after the twins were born. In some cases, she had even challenged him, and that could not be allowed.

Laura noticed the change immediately and sat on the steps. How? Mathias and Tony had been with her from the last time she came down. She pulled out her phone. She didn't need reception to take a picture and show the difference from the one she had taken just half an hour earlier.

She grabbed a bottle, not for the new rack, but one of her favorites for herself. Even though she was irritated at Mathias, a part of her knew he had a point, and she was glad that both he and Tony were there to keep her from drinking the whole bottle. Normally she stopped at two, but now she understood why some people drank too much.

Between receiving the painting, being crazy busy with the bar and restaurant and whatever was going on in the cellar, she wanted nothing more than to disappear to some far away island, lay in a hammock, and drink.

"Grab a corkscrew. We're taking a break," she said, as she entered the kitchen. "I need to show you both something and prove to myself that I'm not going crazy."

Tony washed his hands and came over, while Mathias brought glasses and a corkscrew.

Laura poured and showed them the photos.

"How is that possible? We're the only ones here," Tony said. "Yet, I know those bottles were here." He pointed at the screen. "I put them there myself when we went down before, and we were all together since."

"Thank you!" Laura said, "I was starting to doubt my sanity, and this isn't the first time."

"When did it start?" Mathias asked."

"A couple weeks ago. The moved bottles aren't the only strange thing."

"What else has happened?" Mathias asked.

"Nothing happened. I heard a rumbling, something mechanical, but just twice and one of the walls felt warm when I put my hand against it and listened."

"Sounds like some sort of secret chamber to me," Tony said. "Let's all go take a look."

"I have a better idea," Mathias said. "Let's put cameras up."

"Cameras?"

"Just in the cellar. I'll bring and set them up tomorrow," Mathias said. "For now, let's go get the bottles to fill up the new rack. Then you won't need to go down there alone anymore."

"Okay. I confess, I'm not sure if I preferred the idea that I was losing my mind or that someone was sneaking into the cellar."

"You shouldn't be staying alone here either."

"I'll lock my bedroom door. Besides, it only seems to be the cellar that is bothered."

"Mathias is right," Tony said. "You shouldn't be here alone."

"You can stay at the Chateau. It's close and it will give the housekeeper more to do than dust."

She thought of arguments against it, but she really wasn't comfortable staying until this mystery was solved. So, she conceded to Tony and Mathias and packed a bag.

After they all ate, they went over to the chateau and enjoyed the jacuzzi before saying their goodnights.

Laura wandered the rooms at the chateau, then she settled into the bedroom she knew Carl had used.

"This is crazy!" she said to herself. Nothing in her life had been the same since they'd met. Before she even realized he was gone, Mathias had shown up looking for him. Mathias, who was clearly interested in her too, yet came and went for weeks or months at a time. Now, Carl had sent her that painting.

She lay back on the pillows, his pillows, closed her eyes, and willed sleep to come, but when it finally did, it was far from peaceful.

Chapter 16

Nova Scotia: May 30th

Sophie finished packing and Nick loaded the car while she finished getting Jeremy ready.

"Where are we going again mama?"

"Switzerland."

"Why we go to Swislan?" Jeremy asked.

"For an adventure!" Sophie said, hoping her smile looked genuine. "You know how mommy and daddy went to Greece?"

He nodded.

"This time we wanted to take you on an adventure! We're going to find Cousin Jack."

"That's easy mama. He'll be fishing."

Sophie couldn't help but laugh.

"You may be right Jeremy, but if he is, it's someplace new that nobody knows how to find."

"In Swislan?"

"Maybe. That's where we are going to start looking."

"Why isn't his mama going to look for him?"

"Because she and Uncle Ben have to stay at the farm to take care of the animals. We're going to meet some other family too. You remember the picture of Aunt Alice?"

"The one that looks like you."

"That's right. Well, you have other aunts that look a lot like mommy too."

"Are they looking for Jack too?"

"They might help."

"I bet I can find him before any of you do. I'm good at hide and seek!"

Sophie smiled. She wanted Jeremy to keep that innocence, that positive attitude that still believed he could do anything. She grabbed her purse and his backpack for the plane, and they were off.

Sophie wondered about Josephine, Amber and Pollina. Then she wondered about her parents. They had finally found Alice, was it possible that she could find them too and Jack? Could they be together? She hoped against hope.

Austria

It was a joyful reunion when Soren pulled up to the cabin with Claire. Shane and Daniel had gone for a walk, giving Rosie and Claire their space, while Soren went home to help Magdeline get ready for their trip back to Switzerland.

Later, they had done a conference call with Larry and Dave, who told them about the call from Sebastian. And Claire told them all about the experience with Cora.

Now, Rosie and Claire were playing with Daniel while Shane took another call from Ralph.

"There was another incident this morning I thought you would find interesting Shane."

"Okay Ralph, I'm listening."

"The same airport, different company, but I recognized the guy. The same guy who was bitten by something three years ago. He was doing the inventory. I don't know if he saw me, but I made sure he didn't know I saw him. I spotted him in my rearview before I got out to go inside, and I made it a point to say hi to another guy I passed, but I didn't even turn toward the guy from before.

What I have for you my friend, I have on record. As soon as I saw the guy, I turned on my phone's recorder and hid it in case one of them saw it. I left the windows down and I don't know what it means, but I'm sending you the recording now."

"Thanks Ralph! How's the family?"

"As crazy busy as ever, but wonderful! My boy is growing like a weed and the girls love being big sisters! And how are you doing?"

"Hanging in there."

"There was one more thing. When I dropped the load off, a doctor came out with the loading crew."

"Can you describe him?"

"Shane, I've become more of a pro than that. His photo is on its way."

"I think you have just earned official private eye status Ralph. You're like James Bond in a semi."

"I'll take that! If I find out anything more, I'll let you know. Oh, I almost forgot, the name of the company. I'll text you that too. I have to sign off and go to my daughter's dance recitals."

"Which one?"

"Both of them. One tap and one ballet."

"Have fun, and thanks again," Shane said as they hung up."

"First he looked at the photo and the name of the company. Neither were familiar. Then he listened to the recording. He heard clear animal like sounds, but there was something about them. He loaded the audio file to his computer and slowed the speed. He didn't speak Chinese, but what he was hearing now, definitely sounded more human.

"What was that?"

Shane turned, startled to find Rosie staring at him.

"I'm not sure. It's an audio file I received, but I couldn't make anything out."

"I think I can."

Shane looked at Rosie.

"I may have been deformed, but I still have acute senses, and I learn quickly. That was Chinese," she said.

"You speak Chinese?"

"No, but I understand a fair amount. There were a lot of Chinese doctors who visited the home where I grew up."

"Do you know what they were doing there?"

"I have a few guesses. When they left, the most beautiful children were always soon adopted. I used to overhear them discuss shipments from various ports all the way from San Diego to Kodiak."

"Are you coming back? It's your turn," Daniel called, coming into the kitchen. "I can help you carry snacks."

"Thank you, Daniel, but I'll be right there. I can just bring it all on a tray. You can skip my turn, and I'll take two when I come back. Okay?"

"Okay," Daniel said, giving both Rosie and his dad suspicious looks, before turning back to the game he, Rosie and Claire were playing.

"Can I listen to it later?"

Shane just nodded. The difference in Rosie from three years before was incredible. And just over the past three days, her confidence was visibly stronger. He had to pull his gaze away, as she fixed a tray of snacks and drinks to take back to their games.

***

Magdeline & Soren had been on the road for two hours when they received the call from Larry asking about picking up Sophie, Nick, and Jeremy from the airport. They had originally been planning to fly into Bern, but they had needed to land in Paris due to mechanical issues and were being rerouted to Innsbruck.

Magdeline and Soren would be passing at almost the same time the plane was due to land, so agreed to pick them all up for the rest of the drive into Bern.

"This will be good," Magdeline said. "We can get to know each other a bit before being thrown together with Victoria."

"Do I sound paranoid when I say, I don't completely trust her?"

"No. I've had the same thoughts. What bothers me, is how scared she seemed at first of us, yet she's spent years traveling and performing. At first, I thought it was because of the package she received in Salzburg, and her concern for her family as well as about her trigger."

"And now?" Soren asked.

"Larry says that she has been going out constantly. Granted, she wants everything to look normal, especially after cancelling her previous appearance, but I think she's keeping something from us."

"What though? Dave brought over all of her files and her computer himself."

"I think it's something that isn't in any file, except the one in her mind."

"Well, whatever it is, I'm glad we're agreed that something about her is off."

"Maybe Sophie can give us some better insights. According to Shane, her intuition is usually pretty spot on. She knew that Alice was still alive before there was any evidence of it. Shane said that she was even the one who insisted on additional DNA tests from the helicopter crash. Let's not share our feelings about Victoria until after they meet. I want to hear her unbiased views."

Sweden

Carl looked through another pile of resumes. The talk he went to in Uppsala before Jonathan's arrival had been on his mind, and he was looking over the speaker's colleagues. While she was only part of the research team for a project in China, he knew she must work with others who practiced the actual surgeries, and he hoped one of them had the expertise needed to help Alice.

They had finally gotten the infection under control, but for how long? And how long could he take away from Oscar without putting his treatment in jeopardy?

Nova Scotia

Anne and Ben both needed a change of scenery and had taken a drive along the coast where they enjoyed a picnic at a park with a view of Battery Point lighthouse and Anne tried to figure out how to broach the idea of going to Scotland.

She had already checked flights and put a story together about how with all her family gone, she felt the need to visit cousins in Scotland. She knew Ben would not leave the farm, especially without Jack there to help.

Jack. She needed to do something to help find him. Sophie and Nick were in Switzerland following up on the postcard, but Sophie was right, Josephine was not likely to travel with the girls, much less leave them on their own to go to Switzerland. That meant the odds were best that she was still in Scotland or had gone back to France. She felt that Scotland was the more likely answer. She had the name of the inn where Sophie had stayed and had already reserved a room. She could cancel up to forty-eight hours in advance, but she was determined not to.

She had rehearsed it a thousand times, but now that they were here, where she planned to talk to Ben, she was uneasy. She knew he would pretend to understand, but he would be hurt. How could she leave him behind, knowing he was just as worried as she was about Jack?

She didn't dare tell him the truth. Did she? She hated to lie, but it was for his own protection as well as the girls and Josephine. If they found her, Anne wasn't sure how she would react to her cousin, much less Ben.

"You know we should get away more," Ben said, laying down his ham sandwich.

"How about a trip to Scotland?" Anne spouted, before she could stop herself.

"Scotland?" Ben asked. "Where did that come from?"

"You know I still have family there. And when you mentioned getting away, it just popped into my mind. This is the time of year to go too! It would be lovely, if only we didn't need to do so much at home to maintain the farm."

"Well, that's something I have actually been meaning to talk to you about."

"What do you mean?"

"I had an offer on the farm. Not our house, that lot we could keep and maybe the one behind. The field and the livestock are all we'd be selling. Lane Maxwell is looking to expand his flocks, and he made a surprisingly good offer," Ben concluded and looked at Anne. "What do you think? I mean, it's not like..." he sighed. "It's not like Jack is going to want to take it over."

Anne's mind was racing. "I think. I don't know what to think. When did this happen?"

"The day Sophie came over. I know I should have told you sooner, but you've seemed so distracted. Look, Anne, I think it would be a great idea to go to Scotland together. When did you want to go?"

"Would Friday be too soon?"

"This Friday?"

The look on her face gave Ben a sudden feeling of suspicion.

"What aren't you telling me?"

"It's just that I feel so helpless to help Jack. He's our only child and..."

"I know. I feel the same way," Ben said, putting his arms around her. "You know you can tell me anything Anne. I'm here for you, and as long as it's in my power, I always will be. So, tell me the whole reason you want to rush off to Scotland."

Switzerland

That evening, Larry was feeling more than a little overwhelmed. At least Sophie and Magdeline had agreed to wear wigs. Victoria couldn't while she was around so many people she knew. He just had to remember which one was which. Magdeline was wearing the straight brown wig and Sophie had chosen to put her hair up and wear a shorter honey blond wig, in what Margot called a shag style.

Until the rest of the orchestra left, they would avoid all being seen together, but then they would carry out Margot's plan of a girl's spa day, going together as sisters and Margot as their aunt. She really was still far too young to play their mother.

While Larry still wasn't crazy about the idea, he had to admit that he was looking forward to a day with more men. Even if they would have two-year old Jeremy. He smiled and took a deep breath before heading into the suite.

Sophie and Nick had booked a larger suite, on an upper floor, with a separate bedroom, where Jeremy now slept.

Victoria and Margot had gone out and brought food back for everyone and now they were all gathered. Three virtually identical women. And then there was Rosie, and somewhere there was Alice, all from different parts of the world. Three of them had not been meant to live, one of them was missing, and then there was Victoria.

Shane had called earlier too and relayed the story from Ralph. He also sent the files. Larry was tempted to play the audio for Victoria, but Sophie and Nick didn't need to know what Victoria had told them concerning the Chinese project. Margot didn't know either and he didn't think Victoria would say anything to them.

It was odd, he thought, as he watched them. Sophie and Magdeline seemed at ease with each other, and Larry felt at ease with them, but he still felt tension between them and Victoria. It wasn't just them and Victoria, he thought. Everyone except Margot seemed... Cautious?

There was just something about Victoria, a standoffishness, that made him uncomfortable. Could it be the fact that she had been more involved with the projects? Margot seemed to think that was the reason, but Larry wasn't so sure. He wasn't so sure that he trusted her any more than she trusted him, which still wasn't much.

Chapter 17

Tuesday, May 31ˢᵗ

They had all, except for Victoria, stayed up until two in the morning. Then Dave and Larry had gone over the plan for him to meet with Cora and Sebastian. They were still the only two who knew about Sebastian's call.

Sebastian told them that he could be free on Wednesday, but Cora's one request was that she not have to leave the grounds of the seminary. It was the only place she felt safe, Sebastian told them.

They had a lot to go over before Wednesday, which Larry, still half asleep, realized was just the next day. It was also the day that the women had chosen for their spa day.

Later today he had scheduled time with Victoria and Magdeline to listen to the audio from Ralph. Then he and Sophie were going to attempt to do a call with Anne. He said attempt, because the weather reports for Nova Scotia were calling for storms, which meant that Ben was likely to be inside, leaving Anne unable to talk freely.

"Are you sure you don't want me to just bring something up for you Larry?" asked Margot as she came out of the bedroom to head downstairs for breakfast.

"No. I want to observe her, and I know she is planning to meet with some of the orchestra members before they leave," Larry said, and followed Margot to the elevators.

There were only a few people that Victoria seemed truly friendly with, and Larry wanted to observe them almost as much as her. He needed to understand her. The thought crossed his mind, that in that way, at least from what he knew, she was remarkably similar to Alice. Perhaps Margot was right. Maybe the fact that they had been so much a part of the projects was what made them different. Though, Alice had been unaware of the fact until three and a half years earlier, she had still undergone some of the same experiences growing up under tight control. Ana was the same. So, he guessed his wife must be right again. She usually was, but like Soren had confided, that still didn't mean that they could trust her.

Nick and Sophie were already in the restaurant with Jeremy.

Jeremy perked up from his plate of crepes as Larry and Margot approached. It wasn't them he was looking at though, but Victoria, who had just come off the other elevator with her friends.

"Remember what mommy told you Jeremy," Sophie said, as Nick made room for them to join the table.

"Are you looking for Jack too?" Jeremy asked Margot, as she sat beside him.

"I'm going to try."

"Look at all the lakes and rivers first and then ice rinks. Jack is always skating or fishing," Jeremy told her, very assuredly.

"Well, there is a lake near where your mommy and I are going tomorrow."

"I should come with you to help. I can see in places you can't because I'm still small."

"That's very true Jeremy," Margot said, "but the place we're going doesn't allow children. I'm sure you'll have a fun day with your dad though."

"Can we go fishing tomorrow dad?"

"Well, I think that Larry and Soren may have other plans," Nick said.

"Why do we have to do what they do?"

"Jeremy," Nick reprimanded.

"Sorry," Jeremy said and turned to Larry. "Do you like to fish Mr. Larry?"

Margot had to nudge Larry to get his attention.

"I'm sorry, what?" Larry asked.

"You're not supposed to be staring at her," Jeremy said. "Mommy told me not to."

"Your mommy's right," Larry said, taking a sip of coffee.

"Do you like to fish Mr. Larry?" Jeremy tried again.

"I used to, but I haven't been for a long time."

"You should come fishing with me and daddy tomorrow,"

"Jeremy, we are not going fishing tomorrow," Nick said.

"Why not? Don't you want to go Mr. Larry?"

"Well, I didn't bring a fishing pole," Larry said.

"And I don't have any for us either," Nick said. "Now eat your breakfast."

Thankfully, that seemed to end the fishing debate, until later that is, when Larry was the one to bring it up again.

Seattle

Charice picked up Suzanna and drove to Lidia's.

All the luggage just fit, and Lidia rode with her cats, Miss. Marple, a tabby calico mix and Mr. Frost, a gray and white of unknown breeding, on her lap until they arrived at the airport.

Lidia and Suzanna sat in the Air Swiss lounge, where Suzanna insisted, they drink a toast.

"What are we drinking to?" Lidia asked.

"New beginnings."

"New beginnings?"

"This is the first time in a long time I have gone anywhere without Edgar. I just feel like I'm starting a new life. I have a feeling this trip will be a wonderful experience for you too!"

"Well then, to new beginnings," Lidia said.

Somewhere

Jack connected the red wire and double checked what was in front of him with the picture in the magazine. It was a little rough, but it could work. It had to work. He had fashioned an antenna out of one of the refrigerator racks and just needed to finish wiring the plug.

Switzerland, June 1st

The women left first, and the men followed a half hour behind. They hadn't told Jeremy where they were going until they arrived at the lake.

"Yes! I know we'll find Jack now! He'd love it here!" Jeremy shouted with joy.

The night before, all the men had agreed. None of them were comfortable with their wives going it on their own, especially with Victoria.

Dave was disappointed that he couldn't go. Like Larry, he hadn't gone fishing in years. Unlike Larry, Soren, and Nick though, he didn't have a wife playing detective with a lookalike who had been part of some twisted Chinese human and animal genetic experiments.

The day before, Victoria had vanished, missing the time she had agreed to meet Larry to listen to the recording. She said that she had been trying again to get in touch with her family, but Larry wondered. He had gone to her room. She hadn't been there, and why did she need to do it at the same time she agreed to meet with him?

The pier was directly across the lake from the spa, and they had bought extra binoculars for all, even a small pair for Jeremy. The plan was just to be close enough. They were already supposed to meet the women at the village for dinner after their treatment and would spend two nights in town.

The next day, they would check out another nearby village from the postcard, while Dave went to visit the Martinsons. Magdeline and Soren would meet Dave later and spend the weekend visiting with Trudie, during which time they would also be introduced to the Martinsons. The following week, Victoria had another concert engagement in Geneva.

Larry baited his line and cast out. They were taking turns driving, fishing, and watching Jeremy. Soren started out at the tiller, while Nick helped Jeremy bait his line.

Larry set his pole and took out his binoculars. He scanned the coastline until he spotted the spa in the distance.

"Head port and straight," Larry called to Soren above the motor.

Geneva, Switzerland

Suzanna signed for the rental car, then she and Lidia went up to their suite. The car was promised to be waiting for them in the hotel garage by noon.

For the next three hours though, all Lidia wanted to do was sleep. Suzanna was busy looking at messages that Charice had sent, which included all property and client records for Switzerland, Austria, France, Italy, Spain, and Germany.

They had private bed and bathrooms within the suite, and Lidia closed the door to hers and flopped onto the bed. Then she forced herself up. She would be able to sleep longer if she prepared now. Taking a dress from her bag, she hung it in the bath to de-wrinkle while she took a nice steamy shower. Five minutes later, she had wrapped her head in a towel, set an alarm and buried herself under the covers. She couldn't remember the last time a bed had felt so good.

Suzanna looked up from the computer in the living area and smiled as she heard the low snoring coming from Lidia's room. Suzanna had slept the entire flight from New York and was excited to start checking out all the listings. She knew that Shane and Larry would have already done so, but it wasn't the same.

It had been a very long time, before they had taken Alice from Claire, since Suzanna had been here. And even then, she had only seen where Edgar guided her.

The first thing she was going to do was take Lidia shopping.

Friday, they would head up to the chalet that sat in the shadow of the Alps. A cleaning lady was supposed to come in and air everything, as well as stock the list of supplies Suzanna had sent to Charice from New York. She hadn't been certain at first where she wanted to start, but the chalet was one of the few places outside of Geneva that Edgar had ever taken her to. The A-frame also reminded her of the cottage that Alice had.

The last time she had been there was to go skiing after negotiations with clients in Geneva. Then they had gone to Alaska. It was the last time she actually saw her sister.

***

Dave met Sebastian at the gate of the seminary. Then he signed in at the office and followed Sebastian to the rose gardens, furthest away from the classrooms.

Cora looked up as they entered. She was nervous, but not afraid.

"Hello Cora," Dave said, reaching his hand out to her.

She took his hand. He had a gentle, but firm grip. She scanned his face. He had nice eyes. There was no hardness in him, like most men she'd met. She smiled and had a fleeting wish that she had cooperated with the program.

Then she would at least look the thirty years younger that she suddenly wished she were.

"Hello," she said and motioned for him to sit.

The benches where they met were in a circle, so they could all look at each other as well as see if anyone should be coming from any direction.

Dave took out his pen and notebook. "I understand you have had quite an ordeal over the years. What can you tell me about it?" he began.

"I wouldn't know where to start," Cora replied, "but just ask me what you want to know, and I'll do my best to answer."

Dave had a list of over a hundred questions that he and Larry had come up with and twenty-seven highlighted.

"What can you tell me about where you were?" he started, "How might I find it?"

"First promise that you won't try to go there alone. You won't be able to get Claire out on your own, they would just keep you."

"What do you think happened to Claire?" he asked, feeling guilty, but he was afraid if she didn't believe they still needed to rescue Claire, she might not risk telling him anything.

"They would have her drugged to the hilt as well as contained in a straitjacket. She may be in the same room, definitely the same, otherwise unused, section. They'll make sure she comes out of the drug induced stupors long enough for her to realize what is happening and try to force her to tell them where her daughter is. They will probably conduct experiments, possibly even send her to another project."

"I would go with Larry, the other man I work with, and others would be made aware of where we were going, if for some reason we didn't return."

"Here," Cora said, handing Dave a folded piece of paper.

Unfolding it, he found a very well-drawn and a very detailed sketch of a building. On the side of the building were diagrams of hallways. He studied it and looked back up at Cora.

"These are excellent!" he told her.

"I have an excellent memory. I've also drawn sketches of the doctors and nurses," she said, pulling out more pages from the bag beside her. "There are more, but these are all I've found time to draw. They are the most recent doctors that have been there and two of the primary nurses who were in charge of us."

Dave sucked in his breath as he opened one of the portraits and saw the face of Adam Hisdak staring back at him.

"What is it?" Cora asked.

"We've met before," he said, showing her the drawing.

"He's a nasty man. Where would you have met him?"

"We had an encounter, I'd rather not recall, during an investigation in France. How often did he come to you?"

"He came to check in every few months. He was always a nasty man, even as a child, I knew he would be worse than his father."

"You knew him as a child?"

"Since before he was born. He was born evil and developed into what I believe is considered a sociopath."

"Who are his parents?"

"His father is famous, or he was for a while, in the Brazilian and then French medical field. He went by Nadier."

Dave took notes as she continued.

"His mother was from Brazil. That's where I met her, but like me, she wasn't Brazilian. French and German, I believe. Natalie. Her name was Natalie, and Adam killed her."

"What do you mean? He killed his own mother?"

"Adam had a baby sister. When he was five, he threw her in a river. She wasn't quite two, but she was disabled, and she annoyed him, so he got rid of her. Natalie drowned in the same river, trying to save her. Adam never shed a single tear over his own mother. After it happened, his father took him to France. I saw him for the first time again, just five years ago. He's older than he looks, and I recognized him right away as he pretended to honor his father, while all along planning how he would take control. I wouldn't be surprised if his father is dead now too. Would you know?"

"No, I'm afraid I can't answer that," Dave said, trying to absorb what she told him. "You wouldn't happen to know the names of his grandparents?" Dave asked, thinking back to what Katz had discovered about Josephine's family.

"I'm afraid not, but I feel I've gotten us off the subject. I want to help you find Claire. So, I'll tell you, to the best of my knowledge, the route that brought me here.

For the next hour, Cora told Dave the route she took in her escape, and then she explained how she had come to be there more than fifty years before.

"1969, it was the last time I had even a taste of freedom. I was seventeen, and rebellious. The projects don't tolerate rebellion. I was sent to a special clinic first. And when they still couldn't control me, well..."

They took a break for tea, and then she talked about her sister, Leona.

"There are, or at least there were, two sides to the projects, the scientific and the military. I believe that they have reached the stage of being merged now. Leona was given to the military training. She wasn't always a bad person, not like Adam. When we were children, we were best friends. It was the training that changed her. She chose to cooperate, while I didn't. That is the main difference between us."

Dave left them for the evening, but Cora had asked him to return in the morning. There were things she wanted to tell him about that Sebastian didn't need to know, things that she had overheard about current projects. There were storms coming in, so they arranged to meet in one of the private study rooms of the library, after breakfast, when all of the remaining students would be in classes. Many had already taken their finals for the year and left for vacation and the few who stayed on, like Sebastian, were not likely to be at the library.

***

Sophie and Magdeline were enjoying the mud baths, while Victoria and Margot had massages. They would meet up for lunch and then head to a steam room they reserved and then mani-pedis before meeting the men for dinner.

It was Sophie who had snuck away into town for an hour earlier that morning. When they first arrived, there was only one Masseuse available. She told the others that she was going to the jacuzzi to wait, but instead, she went to the post office. She wanted to know if anyone could tell her where the postcard was sold. It unfortunately turned out to be a quite common card, but then she decided to show the woman at the postal desk a photo of Josephine and Simon that she brought.

"I know him," the woman had said, pointing to Simon. He keeps a post box with us. He hasn't been by for several weeks, but the box is all paid up. I expect he'll come by soon. It's getting a bit full. If you talk to your uncle, please let him know."

"I will," Sophie had promised and hurried back to the spa, where Magdeline found her sipping tea beside the pool and they headed to the mud baths, where they discussed Victoria.

Somewhere

Jack adjusted the antenna until he heard a faint static. It wasn't communication, but at least the makeshift radio appeared to work. He would need to increase the reach. At least he hoped that was the problem and not some kind of signal blocker.

Going to the refrigerator, he took out another shelf and worked to fashion it into an additional antenna.

Later in the afternoon he picked up what he thought was a weather forecast in German. It was a positive sign. If nothing else, perhaps he would at least discover where he was. The forecast itself was unnecessary, as the dark clouds rolling in spoke for themselves. He saw a flash of lightning in the distance as he paced the hallway, hoping for a better signal.

The center window that looked out toward, what he thought was a town, seemed to be the best so far.

He could see a couple of boats below and wondered what the odds were of them looking up and seeing him. Maybe he could write HELP on a sign and put it in the window. The two boats themselves were no more than specks in the distance, headed away from him to reach land before the rain hit. Someone would have to have some serious binoculars to even notice him, much less a sign.

Switzerland

They met at the restaurant just as the thunder clapped, followed by bolts of lightning striking out across the sky. They had barely been seated when the downpour began.

"Good timing," Margot exclaimed. "How was the fishing?"

"What?" Larry asked, as all the men gazed at her like deer in the headlights.

"Did you catch anything?" Margot continued.

Magdeline and Sophie tried to hold back their laughter, while Victoria stared at the menu.

"You really thought we wouldn't know?" asked Margot.

"But how could you?"

"Have you smelled yourselves?" Sophie asked.

All the men sniffed at their sleeves.

"We used wipes and anti-bacterial soap," Soren said.

"Even on Jeremy," Nick added.

"Maybe, but you forgot to wipe down your jackets," Magdeline said.

They had all been carrying lightweight windbreakers in case the storm hit before they got back to shore. And they were all hanging on the coat rack next to the table.

"I caught a trout mommy!" Jeremy stated with pride.

"Good job, Jeremy. Where is Mr. Trout now?" Sophie asked.

"We gave the fish to the nice man who let us use the boat and fishing poles."

"And how was your spa day, ladies?" Larry asked. "You," he said, looking at Margot, "smell quite nice."

"It's jasmine and lavender body oil," she said, "And you men can all relax, we already know you weren't really out for the fish today."

"I talked them into helping find Jack," Jeremy said.

"He's very convincing," Nick concurred, while Larry and Soren nodded in agreement. The women just rolled their eyes.

The waiter came to take their orders. Margot, Sophie and Magdeline ordered seafood, while the men opted for steak and Victoria and Jeremy went with chicken breast and chicken fingers.

When they got back to their rooms, and Jeremy was asleep, Sophie told Nick what she had discovered.

"I didn't tell the others. I was thinking maybe we can catch Larry alone in the morning to tell him. I don't see any reason for anyone else to know."

"I'm just glad you filled me in," Nick said. "Are you upset about the fishing trip?"

"No, because I figure it was collaborative, and it made Jeremy really happy."

"I got him a pair of binoculars to help look for Jack," Nick laughed, "but it sounds like you're the one who hit pay dirt."

"Only if he shows up while we're here."

"We don't have to all stay together. There's no reason why you and I can't stay here. Magdeline and Soren are going on to see people they used to know and help Larry and Dave. I don't see that they need us, and Margot seems to be the only one who really gets on with Victoria. How was she today?"

"Well, until the afternoon, I spent most of the day with Magdeline while Margot was with Victoria. We discussed her in the mud baths and agree, but Margot also made an interesting point and when I think back to Alice, I think she may be right."

"And she thinks?"

"That Victoria is more distant from us because she was a part of the project and grew up under more controlled circumstances, whereas Magdeline and I grew up like relatively average children. We can connect better. Remember how Alice ran away?"

"That was to protect Jack and you."

"And because she was never close to anyone while she was growing up. I don't think I could do that. Even though I pulled away from you, I could never just disappear like she did."

"Your parents did."

"Yes, but they did it together. Alice and Victoria are more of the lone wolf type. Victoria is fine with the people she works with, but with Magdeline and me, I don't know if she can connect. Alice was the same. It isn't that they don't want to connect. Alice and I did, and so did she and Jack, but they're more comfortable disconnecting. Does that make sense?"

"I suppose. Larry doesn't trust her. He was the one Jeremy actually convinced."

"I figured that. We also figured that you and Soren didn't put up any argument."

"Why would we?"

"Exactly," she said smiling, as Nick took her face in his hands and kissed her.

***

After dinner, Margot talked Victoria into going with her to the game lounge.

"Think of this as vacation dear. There is nothing else you can do right now to help your parents or brother. As a mother, I can guarantee that what they want the most is for you to take care of yourself. Clearly that ballad was intended to scare you, but..."

"But someone is watching me. They must realize by now who Larry is, and that means they could think I betrayed them, and they went ahead and killed my family. That's what I think has happened. It's my fault. I shouldn't have stayed and gotten in contact with Magdeline after I saw her in Vienna. I don't know what I was thinking."

"You had another note before you met her though," Margot reminded.

"That was my fault as well. I should have left well enough alone. I've always been too curious."

"Come on, let's have some distraction. Do you play twenty-one?"

"I played in Monte Carlo once," Victoria said. "We did a private concert for the royal family and some of us stayed and played. Roulette was my favorite though. It's more of a challenge. It's too easy to count cards."

"Really!" Margot exclaimed, "Would you mind playing a round on my behalf? Just one for two hundred Francs. And then we can move to roulette."

Victoria smiled and nodded. Larry's wife was an interesting woman, and she was unconnected to the projects, which made her feel safe. She knew that Magdeline, Sophie and Rosie weren't intentional threats, but they were still a part of it, but not a part with any information to help her. Magdeline shared the letter from Jonathan, but it didn't tell her what she needed to know.

The projects they were part of seemed distant from what she had experienced in China. Yet, they had been bred as part of the same project. All she had to do was look in a mirror to know that. They had been rejects though, but what about Alice, the fifth one? Could there be more? Had they been conceived as sisters? It was all just too uncomfortable.

She made the bet on Margot's behalf and took an easy win. They had just arrived at the roulette table when she saw Magdeline and Soren come off the elevator. Soren headed toward the bar and to Victoria's disappointment, Margot waved Magdeline toward them.

She reminded herself that it had been her idea to contact and meet Magdeline, as she placed her bet on red eight.

At least Larry hadn't bothered her about the recording he sent her. She hadn't listened to it yet. She needed to steel her nerves before she could face the implications of what she believed was on the recording after Larry's description.

***

Soren sat across from Larry at a table in the bar. "Magdeline will join us in a few minutes," he said.

"Okay. I just received an update from Dave, and I keep looking at what Shane sent. He just told me what Rosie thinks she understood from the recording. This guy," Larry began, turning his phone to Soren, "is supposedly a doctor who accompanied the shipment to Quebec."

"I know him," Soren said.

"Who is he?" Larry asked.

"That's Professor Crabben, the one whose car was pulled out of a lake in pieces three years ago."

"Are you certain?"

"Magdeline, Trudie, and I were all at his memorial. He led a program that was supposed to have been discontinued. It's the same one that Sarah Martinson was part of."

"That's why I thought he looked familiar!" Larry said. "I've seen his photo in her file. What was his name again?"

"Crabben."

"Drinks are on me," Magdeline said. "I just had a winning streak at the roulette table."

"How's my wife doing?" Larry asked.

"Breaking even. So, what have I missed?"

"This," Soren said, showing her the phone. "Professor Crabben, alive and well."

***

Lidia yawned, as she looked out the window at the storm and asked herself what she was doing there. She was, in a hotel suite almost as big as her house in Washington, and she was working for a woman she used to keep tabs on, because of the strangest missing persons case she had ever worked on.

She wondered if she should call Shane. She could really use a familiar voice right now, but he had enough on his plate. She wasn't even sure what it was she felt so uneasy about. She had spent days with Suzanna already. Still, she hadn't been alone in a strange country and totally dependent on her. Lidia hadn't even known how to exchange the new digital currency when they arrived. Suzanna had said she would take care of everything. Lidia did have a Mastercard, but if something happened, it wouldn't get her very far.

She knew she was probably being silly. Almost everyone here spoke English, and in a real emergency, she could always contact Shane or even Larry. She took in a deep breath.

Suzanna also insisted they were going shopping tomorrow, and that she was buying Lidia a new wardrobe.

"Great," Lidia said to herself, as she pulled back the covers to the king sized, bed. "New career, new country, new clothes, old case. I need sleep." She got up and looked in the mini bar, then poured herself a miniature beer and decided to call Shane in the morning.

France

Mathias felt weird being in Laura's home without her, but he needed to know. So far, the cameras had picked up nothing.

He went into the cellar and took two of the bottles that had been moved. Then he took the fingerprint scanner from his pocket and ran it over them. He had already loaded his, Tony and Laura's prints to its memory for elimination.

Nothing. Whoever it was had been careful.

He went to the wall that she said was warm. He had touched it himself and noted the difference when they came to set up the cameras. There had to be a door here somewhere. It took him nearly an hour to figure it out.

He thought about calling Tony, but he would need to go upstairs for a phone signal. So, taking the flashlight, he entered.

He saw the pods immediately and realized what he had found. He stared, stunned, at the face of his father under the glass. He half expected his eyes to fly open. He heard a noise coming from the left and swung the beam of the flashlight.

"Adam." It was the last thing Mathias said before the shock projectile hit him.

"Well, well, who do I have here?" Adam said, staring down at Mathias, "And what shall I do with you?"

Chapter 18

France: June 2ⁿᵈ

Tony was worried when Mathias didn't return by the morning and called Laura to meet at her place.

"He was going to come and check the cameras, maybe put up a few more," Tony said as they entered the front of the wine bar.

"Nothing looks disturbed, but that is his coat on the chair," Laura said, walking to it.

"His car isn't here though," Tony said, as they walked down the hall. "Let's check the cellar."

"It's locked," Laura said. It only locks from the outside. "Do you have the key?"

"Of course, here." She said, taking the key and turning it in the lock. "The flashlight I hung inside the door is missing," she said, as she flicked the light switch.

"Oh, dear God!" was the first thing Laura said, as they took in the broken glass that covered the cellar. Wine dripped like blood down the walls and shelves and pooled on the floor.

"It looks like a war zone." Tony said, moving forward, past Laura. "We can't walk down here. Too much glass."

"I'm calling the police. Before I would have just sounded like an idiot who couldn't remember where she put what, but this is... Yes, I'd like to report a break in," she said into her phone.

Switzerland

Dave went to meet Cora at the seminary's library. On the way he stopped to pick up some good coffee and pastries which caused a brief altercation with the librarian, who pointed to a sign that apparently read "No food or drink".

"I apologize," he said, "I don't read German, or Italian, or French, at least not well. We'll be in the meeting room the whole time and I promise, we'll be extra careful," he said, showing her the wad of napkins stored in his jacket pocket.

He couldn't tell if she understood him, but she pointed to the right, and he found the room Cora had reserved.

"I think I'm on the naughty list," he said, sitting down the food, coffee, and napkins.

Cora smiled and took a sip of the coffee.

"Sebastian mentioned you appreciate good coffee."

"And this is excellent! Thank you."

It was funny, Dave thought as they talked. He could definitely see the relationship between Cora and Sebastian. Both were congenial and easy to talk with, despite the years of suffering they had gone through.

The things that Cora told him that morning, were sufficient to fill a couple of novels.

"How did you find the will to survive?" he asked, as they walked out into the garden to where they would meet Sebastian for lunch.

"I don't know if it was as much will to live as it was refusal to die. When I lost the babies, I wanted to die, but then I remembered. One had been born alive. I have no idea what may have happened to her, but just the possibility that one of my babies was out there somewhere, was a huge motivation. I didn't know how I would find her, but I thought to myself, if I ever hear that they found her, I *will* find a way to rescue her."

"You never heard anything though?"

"No, which means that maybe they didn't find her."

"I hope that's the case, and maybe one day you can find her."

"All things are possible. At least that's what Sebastian keeps telling me."

Sebastian met them, and they all walked to the cafeteria, while Dave told him about his plans to go down and visit with the Martinsons.

"I don't suppose you remember a professor Crabben ever being mentioned?" he asked Sebastian.

"Not that I recall," Sebastian replied.

"Crabben?" Cora asked. "I think he was one who visited the hospital where they kept me. He may be in one of the drawings I gave you."

Dave unrolled the new set of drawing Cora had given him that morning and held them up to the picture of Crabben, Larry sent.

"Bingo!" Dave said. "This one. What can you tell me about him?"

"He wasn't so bad. Compared to the others, he was an almost welcome site. He used to talk to me while he examined me and took samples. He'd actually tell me about the current world. He never tried to keep me stuck in a time warp. He also talked about his son a lot and how excited he was about a project he was working on."

"Did you ever try asking for his help?"

Cora laughed. "I couldn't. It would have been too dangerous. He could have alerted them to my sanity. He definitely would have quit talking to me. Also, many of the samples were oral, and my mouth was often numbed."

They talked until Dave had to leave, and Cora promised to be in touch if she thought of anything else. During the morning, he confessed that they had found Claire. She was surprisingly understanding about him withholding the fact.

"She even said that I was probably right to do so," he told Larry over the phone. "I'll tell you, what that woman knows has both Victoria and Jonathan beat. I had to use shorthand to keep up... Okay, I'll see you tomorrow then."

***

"I think we may finally be catching some breaks. At least Dave is," Larry said to Margot. "Not that it will help us find anyone we're looking for, but it may give us a better understanding of what and who we are looking at and their plans."

"Just based on what you have told me, which I'm pretty sure is just the basics, I don't think I'd want to know."

"You wouldn't."

"On the other hand, I would need to know."

"Meaning?"

"Meaning, you're private now. You can talk to me."

"It's not my place to share a lot of it, Margot. And you really don't want to know."

"Maybe, but maybe if I knew more, I could help. I know, you don't want me to get involved, but one, I already am. I've met them. I've watched Daniel. Victoria is terrified of a ballad, because she thinks it hides a trigger of some sort that will cause her to what…? Spontaneously combust?

"I won't put myself in danger. I just want to know so that you can use me as a sounding board. Maybe I can see from a new perspective that could help."

"And maybe you could go missing too. I couldn't handle that," Larry said.

"What if they confide in me? What if I already know more than you think?"

"I'm sure you probably do."

"Wouldn't it be easier, and safer, if you just told me? Then you would know what I know, and I would know what to watch out for."

Larry took a sip of scotch from the mini bar and sat on the bed, defeated.

"If you really want to know, you may want some of this too."

"Share?" she asked, taking a glass from the table. "I have a feeling this will also require sobriety."

He poured the rest of the mini bottle into her glass.

"Where to start. This will take more than one conversation."

"Start at the beginning. I want to know everything."

"Oddly enough, that makes sense, because as weird as it was then, it only gets stranger. First, tell me what you already know, because I know, you listen in."

June 3rd

Margot and Larry were up until nearly four in the morning. It was now 8:07 and someone was knocking on their door.

Larry made his way to the door and opened it to find a frantic looking Nick.

"I can't find Sophie! I've looked everywhere. She left her phone in the room…I…"

"Calm down, Nick, and come in from the hall. When was the last time you saw her?"

"About a half an hour ago. She said she wanted to talk to Victoria and went down to breakfast ahead of me."

"Have you checked with Victoria?"

"Of course, I checked. When I went down to breakfast, she and Magdeline were both there. They hadn't seen her."

"What about Jeremy?"

"Soren is getting him breakfast."

"Okay, hang on, let's think about this."

"I am. What if Simon is here now? What if he saw her?"

"Do you think he would risk taking her with all of us here?"

"If he thinks she's a threat. Maybe he found out about the girls. I don't know. None of this has ever made sense!"

"What girls?" Larry asked.

"Oh boy," Nick sighed, "She still hasn't told you about them. I thought she told you about Scotland."

"She mentioned that she suspected Josephine was there because of family connections. I also know Simon and Josephine fostered girls in France, but what has Sophie had to do with them?"

"Can this wait? We need to find her!"

"There was another knock at the door and Margot, who had just finished dressing, answered it." It was Soren.

"You can call off the alarm. She's at breakfast."

"What? Did she say where she was?" Nick asked.

"She said she went to Victoria's room and when she wasn't there, she went back to your room, then she came down."

"But she was gone for half an hour? Victoria's room is three minutes, at most."

"And Victoria is always at breakfast early. It's speculation, but I think she was in Victoria's room. I know she and Magdeline were curious about some things, and it would be easy for her to pass herself off as Victoria and get housekeeping to let her in."

"Thanks for letting me know. Did you tell her I ...?"

"We just said you went back up to look for her. You must have passed in the elevators."

"She's going to kill me."

"What for?" asked Soren and Margot.

Nick looked at Larry.

"I'll see if I can ask some questions and get her to tell me herself. It's not like you actually told me anything yet anyway."

"Thank you. I guess I'd better get back down there."

Nick left and Soren began to follow, but Larry stopped him.

"Wait up Soren. What exactly were Sophie and Magdeline suspicious of?"

"They wanted to check her phone."

"Okay, not legal, but I'd be interested in that myself. Wouldn't she have brought it down with her though?"

"Probably. I mean she had her purse. I don't know. You'll have to ask them."

"I'll have to ask them a lot of things. Right now, I should probably get dressed."

"Do you mind if I head on down?" Margot asked.

"Not at all. I'll be there soon," He suspected Margot planned a little covert questioning of her own. He hated bringing her into this. If anything happened to her, he would never forgive himself. At the same time, he knew he couldn't keep her from investigating on her own any more than Nick could stop Sophie. Better to be open about it.

Geneva

Suzanna called ahead to make sure that the chalet would be ready by the time they arrived.

Lidia was still trying to decide what to wear. Suzanna had helped her find ten new outfits and three pairs of shoes to supplement her wardrobe for different occasions. Today they were stopping somewhere special for lunch on the way up.

Suzanna was curious to find out if she would recognize anyone or if anyone would recognize her. She smiled and reapplied her lipstick, then knocked on Lidia's door.

"How is this?" Lidia asked, as she opened the door.

"That will be fine. Just add some jewelry, do your makeup, and maybe put your hair up until we have time to get to a beautician. I'll be doing the same myself. I've neglected my routine since Edgar left. I have several nice hair clips if you would like to borrow one. We do need to head out in the next hour if we want to make the lunch reservation."

"I have a clip, thank you. I'll be out in a few minutes."

"I'll call the porter."

Lidia found some cubic stud earrings and a matching necklace, then pulled her hair up and put on a touch of mascara and lip gloss. "The hardest part of working with Suzanna", she said to herself, "is getting ready in the mornings."

She looked herself over in the full-length mirror and found she was actually pleased. Still, she didn't want to make this a habit. It was too much work. She had always been more of a get up and grab the closest clean item she found type of girl. Makeup and jewelry were reserved for dates, which she didn't have that many of since her breakup with Rick, two years before.

She still hadn't gotten around to calling Shane. They'd gotten back too late last night and now they were headed out again.

She grabbed her purse, phone, and roller bag, just as the porter was loading the luggage trolly. He smiled at her, as he took her bag, and they followed him down.

Not bad for a bell boy, she thought to herself. Who knew, maybe she would find a new beginning here.

***

Dave headed out of Bern. A part of him wanted to head back to Austria to find where Cora and Claire had been held, but he knew it wouldn't be safe to go alone, and the Martinson's were the opposite direction.

As he followed the signs toward Monthey, he took in the beauty of the Valais Alps in the distance. The views here had always been his favorite part of visiting the Martinson's. Their beauty could almost make him forget the ugliness in the world.

This was going to be an interesting trip. He knew Soren and Magdeline were probably on the same route, on their way to see Trudie, and he planned to be at the, hoped for, meeting of Martinson's and Anglistan's tomorrow.

Larry had called to give him the address of the chalet Soren and Magdeline arranged for them all to stay at. He and Margot would meet him there in the evening. First Larry was going to check out the post office where Sophie discovered Simon kept a box, and Sophie and Nick were staking it out from a café across the street. In deciding to do so, they sent Jeremy ahead with Magdeline and Soren.

Larry also told Dave that he didn't need to tip toe around Margot. As long as Larry heard any new information first, Margot was all in. For today though, her snooping would only go as far as Victoria, who she was returning to the spa with for a few more treatments.

Dave laughed when he hung up the phone. Sometimes he thought Margot was already ahead of them. This was going to be an interesting stay. He had also gotten in touch with Henri Saville, who had come across something interesting, which may or may not be related to Jack.

Dave yawned and picked up his coffee cup, which he noted was empty. He saw a sign for a Café Haus and pulled over. He knew they would look at him funny if he ordered a refill for his mug, so he went with a more culturally correct order of a 'kaffee-crème'. It was small, but more potent than the drip coffee from his hotel room.

He checked the time and decided he could relax for a bit on the patio. While his German and Italian didn't go beyond "dunkashane" and "grazie", his French, though not perfect, was dramatically improving, and he enjoyed being able to actually understand a few of the conversations going on around him.

He looked toward the parking lot as an Alfa Romeo pulled in. He had always liked those cars. He was just thinking to take a closer look and ask the owner about it when the man got out of the car and Dave sat back down. It was Simon.

Dave didn't think Simon would know who he was, unless Adam had sent him a photo, so he took a chance and followed him inside. Dave stood in line directly behind him and ordered another 'kaffee-crème'. Then he stood next to Simon while they both waited for the barista to make their drinks.

If Simon recognized him, he showed no signs, and Dave decided to make contact.

"Is that your Alfa Romeo outside," Dave asked in English.

"Why yes, it is," Simon replied, smiling.

"I've always wanted one, but they're not easy to come by in the states."

"No, I imagine not. Where are you from?"

"Los Angeles," Dave lied.

The barista finished their coffees and put them on the counter.

"Would you like to take a closer look at her?" Simon asked, gesturing toward the parking lot.

"Would I ever!" Dave said and followed him out. Dave took a mental note of the license plate, as Simon pointed out the different features.

"Here," Simon said, handing Dave a business card. "If you decide you're really interested, this company imports everywhere, and they can find you pretty much anything you want."

"Wow, thank you Monsieur?"

"Hallon. Are you staying nearby?"

"With some friends in Geneva, but I wanted to get up into some fresh mountain air."

"Well, I hope you enjoy your stay."

"I'm sure I will," Dave said. He felt dumbfounded for a minute as he watched Simon pull away. Then he sent Larry a text with a description of the car, plate number, surname Simon was going by and a photo of the business card.

He considered following, but he didn't want to risk being found out or missing his meeting with the Martinsons.

***

Larry could hardly believe it when he saw the message. He had just been on his way into the post office. Now, he turned back across the street to join Sophie and Nick. With any luck, they'd see Simon themselves in the next hour or so.

***

"I'm sorry," Stephan said to Dave. "Sarah and Ana went shopping this morning and haven't returned yet. I tried to call, but it keeps going to voice mail."

"That's okay. A lot has happened over the past couple of days. I want to tell you some things, straight out, and it will be easier without them here."

"What? Did you discover something about who took them?"

"Yesterday, I saw Sebastian and his aunt."

"His aunt?"

"Look, I'm not sure if I should even be telling you this, but my gut says that I can trust you."

"You can."

"This isn't something that I think either Sarah or Ana should know about yet. There's too much that I still need to look into."

Stephan nodded and sighed. "I don't want to keep secrets Dave, but..." Stephan paced the room and Dave waited in silence. "Sarah has been keeping secrets from me. She's been visiting Trudie, and I know that there is something, something important about Ana, she's not telling me. I think she almost told me when she was in the hospital, but she caught herself. Dave, I'm not sure that Ana is my daughter."

"I see."

"I'm not sure you do. Even if she isn't my biological daughter, I will always love her as if she were, but I've never felt truly connected to her. Sarah made me think of it the other day. She accused me of defending Sebastian over Ana, and she was right. I simply connect with and understand him better. What she doesn't understand is that no matter what, I love Ana because she is a part of Sarah, and I love Sarah more than my own life. I would do anything to help and protect them. So, if there is anything I can do to help, please tell me. Even if it means keeping it from Sarah. As long as it's for their protection, I will."

"Sebastian phoned me a few days ago to tell me about a woman he found wandering in the night. He took her to the dorms of the Seminary, where they sometimes take in people down on their luck. During their conversations, he discovered that she is his mother's sister. She escaped some kind of facility where she had been kept for decades because of her refusal to cooperate. I know it sounds far-fetched, but..."

"So have a lot of things. Just the fact that Ana was taken to Brazil. Is this woman from Brazil then?"

"Yes. She was sent to France as a teenager, but unlike her sister, she refused to cooperate. As you know Ana was subjected to several medical experiments, as was Sarah. Well, let's just say Sebastian's aunt gave us some valuable insights as to the intentions of those experiments.

"This is why I was asking so many questions about your and Sarah's genealogy. All of the experiments are related to what is called, the family. I've spent the past three years trying to link everyone together and Sebastian's aunt confirmed what I already suspected. Everyone involved is somehow related.

"You mentioned that Sarah has been talking to Trudie. Well, you have to promise you won't tell Sarah what I'm about to tell you."

"I promise. I want to get to the bottom of this, and I trust you. Trust me."

Dave smiled. "I do. Sebastian does too. You're aware of the Anglistan's who also worked at Scangentech."

"Yes."

"Trudie worked closely with Soren Anglistan, and they have kept in touch. They'll be here to visit with her this weekend, and Trudie has agreed to introduce them to Sarah. She'll be calling to invite you both for lunch tomorrow. I need you to make sure the meeting happens, and I'd like to be there too."

"Okay."

"What do you think the odds are of getting Ana to join?"

"Not so great. You know she's been working at the resort up the hill. She's gotten to be good friends with the woman she works with and works a lot of over time, helping in the restaurant as well as teaching tennis. We don't see much of her. I think the friendship is a good thing. Aida is like a big sister to Ana. She even talked her into coming to church with us."

"Maybe I should talk to Aida?"

"Maybe, but like you asked me not to tell Sarah and Ana about Trudie or Sebastian's aunt, I have to ask you to make sure that Ana doesn't know if you talk to Aida. Aida seems to be the only real grounding that Ana has, her only real friend. If you talk to her, please do it in a way that she doesn't know who you are. I wouldn't want to ask her to keep anything from Ana and risk that friendship. Ever since Sebastian left and Ana turned eighteen, I've been afraid that she would leave. Right now, her job and friendship with Aida is giving her something to stay here for. I don't want to risk that."

"I understand. I'll hold off on talking to Aida. It isn't so important for Ana to be there tomorrow."

"Thank you," Stephan said, as Sarah and Ana pulled up in the drive.

Over lunch they kept the conversation casual, with Dave hoping to get on Ana's good side by giving her the birthday present that Sebastian had sent with him.

She was as hard to read as ever, accepting it with just a nod, but being obviously protective of the box.

Dave knew what it was. It was a book of poetry. Sebastian had been concerned that she may take it the wrong way, but the poetry was all faith based rather than romantic, and he hoped it might reach her on a spiritual level.

Sebastian had even made Dave consider going back to church. It wasn't that Dave had ever disbelieved. He just wasn't certain how much he did believe. When the virus of 2020 had shut most churches down, he had started to question, but his research kept him distracted. Now, the questions were suddenly pouring through his head as he drove to the chalet.

No one else had arrived yet, and he chose a room and settled in. Then he went for a walk. He was coming back from exploring a local craft shop when he saw her. He blinked a few times in disbelief. What on earth was Suzanna Morgan doing here?

Dave didn't want her to see him, so he stayed back as he followed her until she came to another chalet. He watched her go inside and wondered if there was anyone there with her. Had she made secret arrangements to meet with Edgar here? He took note of the chalet number and turned to trace his path back to the one he was staying at, and then he saw his rental car. He had come in a full circle. She was staying right next door to him.

Hurrying inside, he called Shane. He was watching out the window and just about to tell Shane about Mrs. Morgan when he saw her.

"You won't believe this. I don't believe this."

"What don't you believe Dave?"

"I called to tell you that I saw Suzanna Morgan. I thought maybe she had arranged to meet Edgar, but she's here with Lidia."

"What? Lidia and Suzanna Morgan are in Switzerland?"

"About twenty yards outside my window. What should I do?"

"Well, if they're both there, I suggest you let them know that you are too. Talk to Lidia and find out why they're there. Maybe they have a lead on Alice or Edgar. With Lidia going private, I can see Suzanna hiring her. So, why don't you keep me on the phone and let's go say hello."

Dave was suddenly a bundle of nerves as he walked to the door. He checked himself in the mirror and took a deep breath. He was trying to remember if he had ever seen Lidia in a dress before. She looked fantastic, he thought, as he made his way around to where they sat on the back deck.

Dave cleared his throat as he approached, and they turned.

"Dave?" Lidia said, feeling her cheeks flush.

"What brings you two ladies all this way?"

"Long story," Lidia said, as Suzanna observed them.

"Well," Dave said, remembering the phone in his hand. "Shane would like to say hello too." He handed the phone to Lidia as he came up the steps to the deck. Wow! he thought, she even smells good. This is not fair. He realized he was staring and turned toward Suzanna, as Lidia walked away to talk with Shane.

"Mrs. Morgan. Welcome to Switzerland, but I'm sure you've been here before."

"Not for many years, but yes, Edgar and I used to stay at this chalet when we were in the area. I thought that you were in Austria," she said, motioning to another chair for him.

"I was, and I thought that you were in Seattle."

"We were. If you want to know why we're here, just ask," Suzanna said.

"Why are you here?"

"Ostensibly, to look for my daughter, but I have to admit I'm glad to see you."

"You are?"

"And so is Lidia."

"What?"

"Look, I do *want* to find Alice, but honestly, I think my odds of winning the lottery are better. In reality, I'm playing matchmaker. I was just about to call an old friend to see if her son was available to escort Lidia to dinner tomorrow, but with you here, I hope I won't need to."

Dave stared at her, unsure how to respond.

"Look, even with everything that happened, I was lucky. I had a wonderful marriage. I was a terrible mother though, and I don't know if I'll ever get another chance with Alice." She looked at Lidia, who was walking along a path behind the chalet as she talked with Shane. "I thought this would be good for her. You know, a fresh start as a P.I. Her first case in Switzerland. I can take her around, introduce her as a colleague. Maybe we discover something. Maybe she gets to meet someone and be as happy as I was, as happy as I would want Alice to be."

"So, you're taking Lidia under your wing as a sort of surrogate daughter?"

"You could say that," she admitted as Lidia returned.

"Shane sends his regards," Lidia said, and handed the phone back to Dave. She was far better composed now. "It looks like it really is a small world."

"Well," Suzanna said, "I invited Dave to join us for dinner tomorrow night. And he…"

"He has to go," he said, as he heard another vehicle pull up the drive and headed to intercept Soren and Magdeline before Suzanna saw her. This was going to be awkward enough without Suzanna spontaneously meeting Alice's double, or rather, doubles, he thought. Victoria, and possibly Sophie, would be here in a few hours as well.

France

Both Laura and Tony were worried about Mathias, but neither mentioned him when the police came to investigate the break-in of the wine cellar. The cameras Mathias installed were missing, but fortunately, the wine was insured, and Tony could give Laura enough replacements to get through the weekend.

"Mathias can fend for himself, and there was no sign of blood. I'm sure he's fine," Tony said, trying to convince himself as well as Laura.

"What about that woman, Chantel?"

"You know what, let's go and see. I know where she's staying. I don't know if she's still there, but we need to get out for a while. There's plenty of time before opening and…"

"I'm supposed to be delivering for the restaurant tonight."

"Call in sick. Or just tell them about the cellar, they'll understand."

"No. The cellar still stays a secret to them. Someone would be over here day and night to protect me. The last thing I need is my brother or cousins skulking about, intimidating the customers. I'll just tell them I didn't sleep last night, which I didn't, and ask if they could call my cousin Valerie in."

"It's almost to Calais. You can take a nap in the car."

They hadn't made it all the way to the hotel yet when they spotted Chantel. She was riding a bike with two other women and a man. They weren't certain if she saw them or not, but they continued on at a normal pace past the hotel and pulled up in front of a market. A few minutes later the other bikes passed, but Chantel was no longer with them.

"She must have stopped back at the hotel," Tony said.

"I don't think she saw us," Laura said, as Tony pulled out and circled back to park in a spot where they could observe the hotel. "Now what do we do?"

"Hope she goes out for dinner, maybe meets Carl."

"Do you really think he's here or that he had something to do with what happened in the cellar and Mathias disappearing?"

"I don't know what to think. I hadn't seen Mathias in forever until he showed up at the Chateau. It's been even longer since I've seen Carl, and he was just a little boy, but he was a holy terror. I'm sorry, but he was, and I don't think there was ever much love lost between them. Think about it. If Chantel told Carl about Mathias being here, then, what if he were jealous? It wouldn't surprise me at all if he would show up to get Mathias out of the way."

"The big hole in that theory is that something was going on in the cellar before Chantel ever arrived."

"We can't be sure when she really arrived," Tony countered.

"You said that she came to the restaurant looking for me. Don't you think if she had been here awhile that she would have known where to go?"

"Maybe, but who would want to destroy your wine cellar? A competitor would steal your wine, not destroy it."

"True," Laura sighed. "I don't know. Maybe Mathias disappearing isn't even connected to the events in the cellar."

"You don't believe that any more than I do."

"Maybe he caught someone in the cellar, and they caught him back."

"Look. There she is," Tony said, "She looks pretty dressed up and she's not taking the bike. Let's see who she meets."

A few minutes later, a Saab pulled up, and Chantel got in. They followed the car to a restaurant and watched as the same man they had seen her riding bikes with got out and they went inside together.

"Looks like a dead end," Laura said.

"I want to see if they meet with anyone else. I'll be right back," Tony said, and headed toward the restaurant. He came back ten minutes later. "You were right. Dead end. Let's get you back so that you can be ready for tonight."

"I was counting on Mathias to help make the canapes."

"I know a few of his recipes. I'll stop and pick up what's needed on our way back. Trust me. I can cover your wine and the food. You just relax and play hostess."

"Thank you, but I hardly think I will be able to relax until we know who's behind all of this."

Switzerland

It turned into a three-hour wait and a lot of coffee before Sophie spotted him.

"Are you sure?" Larry asked.

"Positive," Sophie said, as she zoomed in on the photo she'd snapped with her phone.

"Okay, you two go to the car. I'm going to buy some stamps."

Larry walked into the post office and pretended to look at some mailing options, while Simon collected a package and other mail from his post box. Then he followed Simon out and up the street, while Nick pulled out and followed with the car, parking it around the block until Simon turned the corner again. They did this a couple of times before they saw Simon get into the Alfa Romeo.

Larry joined them in the car, and they followed.

"Make sure you stay way back. I don't think he noticed he was being followed, but who knows, and we definitely don't want him to see Sophie."

"I think we should have just confronted him in town. It would have been three to one. God only knows where he'll lead us out here," Sophie said, as the road turned into woodland.

"Hopefully, he'll lead us to Jack. If we had confronted him in town, we would have lost that chance," Larry said.

"You're right."

"What did you just say Soph?"

Sophie glared at Nicks comment.

"I'm sorry Soph. I think it may be the first time Larry's heard that. She has admitted it on other occasions," he said to Larry.

Larry laughed and received a similar glare, but it was followed by a smile.

"Can you check where this road leads, Soph?" Nick asked.

"Please?" Larry added, and Sophie looked at the car's navigation screen.

"It looks like it hooks up with a highway in a few miles that will either go back towards Bern or to the French border. My bet is on France."

"Mine too," Larry said. "I'd better call Margot."

Larry had no sooner hung up his phone, than Simon's car vanished over a hill. They crested the same hill, but Simon was nowhere in sight.

"Maybe we'll see him around the bend up there," Sophie said.

Nick sped up before slowing for the curve. Nothing.

"I didn't see any turnoffs. Did you Sophie?" Larry asked.

"There was one, but I didn't see a sign. I think it was just a driveway."

"Keep going up to the border. If he just got further ahead of us, we should be able to see him there."

"I didn't think they stopped cars between Switzerland and France," Nick said.

"They usually don't, but it can happen, and they should slow down. Regardless, unless he sped way up, we should be catching up."

They got up to the border, but unfortunately the line was non-existent. They were only car number four that would simply slow down to be waved through by a bored looking guard.

"Ask if he saw the car," Sophie said, and Nick rolled the window down.

Nick received a negative response on the car, and they continued a few miles in until they reached a gas station, where they filled up and turned back.

"He could have turned off anywhere before the border," Nick said.

"But I'd bet it was where we lost him," Sophie added. "We should have been able to see him when we came over that hill."

"She's right," Larry said, and winked at Sophie.

"Stop sucking up to my wife Larry, or I'll have to tell Margot."

Half an hour later they were almost back to where they lost sight of Simon.

"Slow down. It should be on the right," Sophie said. "There!"

Nick slowed to the side of the road where another gravel road turned into the woods.

"What do you think?" Nick asked, looking at Larry.

"Let's take note of the location from the navigation system and go back to town. We can do a satellite search. I want a better idea of what's there before we go any farther. That, and Margot has been alone with Victoria all day. For now, I'll call Dave and let him know we won't be joining them tonight."

"Sophie?" Nick asked, as he pulled back onto the road, "Are you okay? You're awfully quiet."

"I was just wondering about Jeremy. Did we do the right thing, sending him ahead with Magdeline and Soren? I mean, I trust them and Dave, but Alice's mother is there."

"He'll be fine."

"I know you're right. And don't you dare say a word! I just miss him. We've been away so much."

"I miss him too," Nick said. "But we're not that far away, and we can call. He's probably having a blast. He and Soren really hit it off when we went fishing," Nick said.

Dave was relieved to know that Victoria and Sophie weren't going to be joining him yet. Soren was easy to talk to and Jeremy was a good distraction for him. They had just finished dinner, and Magdeline was helping Jeremy get ready for bed, when there was a knock at the door.

Dave answered it to find Lidia.

"Hi," she said.

"Hi back."

"Can I come in?"

"Where's Mrs. Morgan?"

"She's on the phone with Charice. Don't worry," she said, and Dave stepped out of the way to let her inside.

"Hi," Soren said, from the kitchen. "Can I offer you a glass of wine?"

"Hello," Lidia said, "I'm Lidia."

"I'm sorry," Dave said. "Lidia, this is Soren, Magdeline's husband."

"Oh, it's nice to finally meet you. I've heard a lot about you and Magdeline from Shane."

"Nice to meet you as well. Uhm?" he asked, holding up the wine.

"Sure, why not. I'll go with the red. Thank you," she said, as Soren handed her a glass and poured another, which he handed to Dave.

"I'm just going to go check on Maggie and Jeremy," Soren said, and left them.

"Well, have a seat."

"I thought they had three boys."

"They do."

"Oh. It's just that he only mentioned one. I..."

"Oh, Jeremy is Sophie and Nick's son. The triplets are with their grandparents."

"Oh. Where are Sophie and Nick?"

"They are with Larry, Margot and Victoria."

"Who is Victoria?"

"Ah, you have been out of the loop. Victoria is... I don't know if I should even be telling you."

"Never mind, I'm guessing that she must be the violinist Shane told me about. *He* thought it could be important for me to know there was another one."

"What else did Shane tell you?"

"That he had already considered calling me to come help and that I should ask you to fill me in."

"What did he think about Mrs. Morgan being here?"

"Well, since Edgar left, he thinks she could only help. He believes she knows more but was keeping quiet for Edgar's sake. But now, her focus is on looking for Alice. I've already met some of their old colleagues today. She insisted on taking me to a golf club for lunch. She hadn't been here since they took Alice home from Claire, but she still seemed to be well known. It was very interesting. I don't suppose you would be interested in the list of names I got of doctors who were there?"

"It couldn't hurt to look into. Does she know you're here?"

"It was her idea."

"Oh, and why are you staying *here*. I've never imagined Mrs. Morgan as the woodsy type."

"She said this was the last place she stayed in Switzerland with Edgar, and it had good memories. It is pretty classy for a cabin, sorry, a chalet in the woods."

Dave smiled. "I have to give you that. This place is four bedrooms and five baths. I've stayed in smaller hotels."

Lidia laughed, and they both took a sip of wine.

Chapter 19

Scotland: June 4th

Ben and Anne looked out the window of the plane as they descended into Edinburgh.

Neither knew what to expect. Anne had only contacted one family member that she knew was not in touch with the others. Sheila was her mother's niece, and not a blood relation. They had met as teenagers at a summer camp, and Sheila currently lived just twenty miles from the town where they were staying.

"So, why are we not contacting anyone else?" Ben asked.

"Because, if Josephine is here, and she had anything to do with Jack's disappearance, we don't want to risk tipping her off. Besides, Sheila's more fun and she'll be a great tour guide. She and her husband, Marco, ran a tour service in Italy for twenty years. They only decided to retire because the shutdowns were going to leave them at a loss. So, they took what they had and moved to her old family home she inherited from her father's side. Her stepmother, my aunt, died in a car accident in 1997. I remember because it was close to the time of Princess Diana's death. Sheila is the one who sent us that painting of Venice."

"At least I know she has good taste," Ben said, as they taxied to the gate and the fasten seatbelt sign blinked off.

It was only 8:00 am. And their car rental pickup was scheduled for 9:00. They would drive to Sheila's first, have lunch and a quick tour of the area before checking into their B&B.

Sweden

Carl had made an appointment to interview a surgeon that he met in Uppsala. Alice was holding steady, but he was concerned. He had needed to redivert some stem cell distribution from Richter back to Oscar. He was also concerned about how much more Richter could support.

No matter how evil their brother was, neither Jonathan nor Carl wanted to kill him. In fact, this had become the new topic of conversation. What would they do with Richter? Keep him in an indefinite cryogenic state?

First things first, Carl told himself, as he went through his folder of notes for the trip to Uppsala. He would be gone for over a week, going to seminars and learning as much as he could to stay up to date on the most current genetic therapies, as well as going to an AI convention in Stockholm the next weekend.

Ivan made him some excellent removable false teeth veneers to wear and custom fit, removable nose implants. They had taken time to get used to wearing, but they altered his sinus passages just enough, that with the teeth he would not be identified through a facial scan. He would also carry multiple pairs of brown contact lenses and a hair piece. He had been attempting to grow a beard, like Jonathan, but he couldn't quite get used to the feel of the whiskers and shaved.

He had decided to fly this time as well. It was only a domestic flight, still, he would borrow the passport Jonathan had in Sherman's name. The passport itself was real. Only the documents used to acquire it were forged.

Still, he would need to be extra cautious at the AI conference, as there were certain to be former colleagues of Meschner there.

He closed the folder and went to his apartment to pack. Jonathan and Ivan would take good care of everything, he reminded himself. He could trust these brothers. They even seemed to be getting along with each other. Jonathan had always been the charmer of them though.

Chantel was also due back at the weeks end. He should call and ask her to meet him at the conference in Stockholm. He would be less conspicuous with her on his arm. Then he thought about Laura and Mathias. A part of him wanted to contact Mathias, who he knew must be working to infiltrate P2P, but he didn't dare. Not yet.

He didn't like it when Chantel had confessed that Mathias and Laura seemed close. He also knew Mathias too well to dwell on it. Even if he wanted to, Mathias had too many scruples to get into a relationship. Carl wouldn't be that strong. He laughed at himself. He was no saint and probably never would be, but at least he had become someone, he hoped, was relatively likeable and he had gained his mother's…love? He doubted her feelings for him were that strong. He could never expect her to feel the same for him as she did for Ivan.

He shook his head, packed his toothbrush and shaving kit, and went to see his nephew and niece before he left. If he was sure of no one else, at least he knew Ivan's children loved him. They had been too young to know better when they'd met. The now, four-year-old Charlotta and six-year-old Elson, had taught Carl a lot. Three years before, he never would have imagined himself playing in a sand box, much less with dolls. They were just the distraction he needed.

Somewhere

Jack was frustrated. Aside from the weather report, he still hadn't been able to pick up more than static, and he hadn't seen another boat, aside from some canoes on the lake, since the night of the storm.

His guess was that the canoes were from what he figured to be a summer camp. He was too isolated. There probably wasn't a radio signal close enough or strong enough to pick up, even if he had a real radio. He was tempted to throw the conglomeration of electrical parts and wires that he had worked so hard on against the wall. It was a mess, and he had made a mess, taking items apart to make it. He glared at it, with its refrigerator rack antenna leaning against the window and went to work out on the one machine he hadn't dismantled.

Switzerland

Over breakfast, they decided that Margot, Victoria, and Sophie, would go ahead to the Chalet. Victoria was understandably nervous when they explained that Mrs. Morgan was staying next door. Sophie was nervous about that too.

Sophie also didn't like the idea of leaving Nick to possibly confront Simon. When they'd gone back up to their room, she wanted to beg him to come with them, but she knew it wouldn't be fair. It was her idea to come here and look for Jack in the first place. She had even pictured herself confronting Simon. But in that imagined confrontation, no one else was there. No one else was in danger.

She could handle putting herself in danger, but the idea of Nick or Jeremy being in danger terrified her. She knew that Margot was equally concerned about Larry, but he was trained. She wished that Dave or Shane were there to go with Larry when they went back to the turn off, but it was Nick. It was Nick, because she insisted they come. Simon was her uncle. This whole mess was, at least in part, because of her. If she had never asked Jack to look into her adoption, none of this would have happened.

Then again, if what was happening hadn't been brought to light, who knew where the projects would have gone by now. She hadn't felt this conflicted since before they were married.

"Soph? Are you alright?" Nick asked, coming up behind and wrapping his arms around her.

She turned and laid her head against his chest, listening to his heartbeat. "Just promise me you won't take any unnecessary chances. If he's with others, make Larry call Dave and Lidia. If you're not sure he has Jack, just leave."

"We'll be careful. I promise. And if he has Jack, we'll bring him back safe. He's not going to kill us. You know that. It's not their M.O. It'll be okay," he said, as she looked up at him. He cupped her face in his hands and bent to kiss her, long and slow. "To be continued when I return."

"I love you, Nick."

"I love you too, Soph, and soon we'll all be back together. Kiss Jeremy for me."

She nodded and took her suitcase.

Larry, Margot, and Victoria met them in the lobby. Then they got into separate cars and went in separate directions.

***

Lidia explained to Suzanna that Magdeline, Sophie and Victoria would all be next door.

"I didn't want you to accidently see them and have a heart attack."

"Thank you for the warning. I had expected to meet Magdeline, but three of them? Do you know where Claire and Rosie are?"

"I do, but I can't tell you without their consent."

"Would you ask Shane? I need to talk to Claire. I don't know if it's possible to make things right, but she is still my sister. I was terrible to her. The way we used her was terrible. I just didn't know how terrible."

"Okay, I'll ask."

"Thank you. So, other than shop talk, how was your evening with Dave?"

"Good. He agreed to come to the dinner tonight."

"Wonderful! Speaking of which, we have an appointment to get our hair, nails and makeup done."

"Someone else is doing our makeup?"

"It'll be fun. Trust me. If we get there by eleven, we can get a massage as well, followed by a light lunch."

"Okay," Lidia replied, as she looked through the window to see Dave outside with Jeremy.

Suzanna watched over Lidia's shoulder, as Dave played with Jeremy. "He looks like good father material. Don't let him get away. More coffee?" she asked.

"No, thank you. I should get dressed so we can head out. I know you want to make a couple of stops along the way."

"Nothing important. You could go join them for a while."

"Are you all right, Suzanna?"

"I was just thinking about Edgar. I don't think I could ever picture him playing like that. Go on, get dressed and join them. I'll let you know when we need to go."

***

Larry and Nick turned down the drive. They were about two miles in before they saw anything but woods. Then they came to a fork, and the trees cleared out. If they continued left, on the same road, they would come to a large cabin that was in the clearing ahead.

They turned to the right and kept going until they came to a lake with a boathouse and dock. They got out and were surprised to hear the sounds of children nearby.

Looking through the trees they saw, what appeared to be, a summer camp with cabins. The children's voices were coming from the other side of a group of cabins and there was a low wire fence marking the boundary.

Larry pulled out a map. "The camp must be at the end of this road here. It comes off the main road we were on about five miles further and traces back through the woods to this lake. I saw the camp on the satellite, but assumed they were vacation cabins. The turnoff we took isn't on here at all, probably because it's a private drive."

"What are you doing here?" came a voice from behind them.

Larry turned and saw a man of about thirty years of age, six foot tall, well built, and carrying a taser. "We must have taken a wrong turn," Larry said. "We were meeting some friends to go fishing."

"Which lake were you looking for?" the man asked, as he looked them over.

"This one, but obviously we turned at the wrong place, because they aren't here and judging from that taser, we shouldn't be either."

"This is private property. We caught your car on camera. If you're looking for fishing, you need to go about seven kilometers northwest on the main road and follow the signs to the national recreation area. You'll wind up on the other side of the camp. The GPS is terrible out here. Where you want to go is well marked though," he concluded.

"Thank you," Nick said.

"Yes, much appreciated," Larry added, as they got back into the SUV and started the engine.

They watched as the man turned up a path beside the boathouse. Then they turned back up the road.

"We should have guessed there would be cameras," Nick said. "At least the goons ask questions before tasing. I wasn't sure if he would buy the story though."

"I was surprised he did, which means, at least *he* didn't recognize us. I'm thinking it might be wise to invest in disguises. I'm also thinking that the best access to that house is going to be via the lake. Let's go find that recreation area and then do some shopping. I'll google costume shops."

"Search men's hair pieces," Nick suggested.

"Good call," Larry said, as Nick turned back onto the main road. "There were three hits in a twenty-mile radius, and one of them also sells costumes. It says they specialize in historical dress clothes and uniforms. I wonder if the uniforms are historical too or if they have something we can use."

Later that afternoon, after purchasing their disguises, they checked into a local hotel and rented a boat. They scoped out the shoreline towards where they had been earlier and noted a break in the trees past the boathouse and a log house set in, camouflaged, just behind the tree line.

"That must be private beach access from the house, and the trail our goon took was just a short stroll through those trees. We should try to pull up a satellite view again before we go tomorrow," Larry said.

"We'd better head back now," Nick said, looking up, as thunder rumbled in the distance.

***

Dave drove next door to pick up Lidia and Suzanna, but Suzanna insisted on taking the car she had rented.

"I did take mine through a car wash," Dave whispered to Lidia.

"Tonight's dinner is in honor of a man named, Seymer Lochande," Suzanna explained, "He owned one of the first companies that Edgar and I took over for redistribution. We worked closely until Seymer was able to buy back certain sectors of the original company, and he began to regrow it into one of the leading high-tech bionics companies of the world.

"His father had lost both legs in WWII, and his goal was that whoever had lost limbs to war or accidents, should be able to have them replaced with an even better bionic limb. He was one of the first to dream of connecting the bionics into the nervous system, so that the recipient would not only have feeling in it, but it would react to the brain impulses, just like the original limb. That dream is a reality now and they are working to replace not only arms and legs, but eyes, ears, noses, etc."

"Reminds me a little of an old TV show I watched as a kid," Dave replied.

"It's the same basis," Suzanna said, "Only now, ordinary people can receive them. That's what they are raising funds for in Seymer's honor. They want to provide enough funding to cover free bionics for one thousand people, who will be chosen by committee, based on applications."

"That sounds quite noble," Dave replied, while wondering in the back of his mind if it really were, or if the man being honored tonight could also be a part of the projects. After what Cora had told him, he wasn't sure if he could ever look at any doctor or scientist without suspicion again. The Anglistans being an exception.

He would be keeping his ears open tonight, at least to any conversation in English or French. Language seemed to be an advantage that most Europeans shared, being taught both their native language and English from a young age and encouraged to learn another as well. Dave hadn't even been offered another language until his sophomore year in high school, and he had only learned enough at the time to flirt with the girl sitting in front of him.

Half of the drive to the event seemed to be the driveway.

The dinner was at a house that reminded Dave more of a museum. Art covered the walls and statues were scattered throughout the garden, which was itself, a work of art. They were served champagne and appetizers in the garden, while musicians played on the veranda.

Inside, they were taken through a gallery and served dinner at three long tables that sat eighteen people each.

After dinner, the grounds were opened to more people, and more drinks and appetizers served, while they all browsed the items for the silent auction.

Once the sun sank, they came back inside to the room where they had eaten dinner. The tables had been cleared from the room and the musicians who had earlier been outside, were now playing from a small stage. A few chairs and cocktail tables had been set against the walls.

"I wasn't aware this was a dance as well," Dave said.

"Seymer loved to dance," Suzanna said, smiling at Dave and Lidia, as she picked up a glass of champagne and excused herself to chat with a couple they had sat across from at dinner.

The music started and a few couples began dancing. Then, Dave and Lidia suddenly realized that they were standing in the middle of the floor.

"Dance?" Dave asked.

"I..."

"I can't promise not to step on your feet, but I have improved since that time at the Policeman's Ball."

"Well, I guess. It looks like we're surrounded," she said, looking as more and more people filled the floor around them.

Dave worried his palms were sweating, but there was no way out now, he thought, as he took Lidia's hand in his and put the other around her back. He wished he had thought to use another breath mint after that last coffee.

Lidia could hardly believe what was happening. Had Suzanna known Dave would be there? It felt so surreal. Just over a week ago, she was sitting in Alice's Seattle condo, confessing that she missed Dave. She didn't know if she would ever see him again, much less be dancing with him in Switzerland.

"You have improved," she said, feeling herself blush and hoping he would just think it was from the exertion of the dance.

"Margot, Larry's wife, gave me a few pointers. I've learned quite a lot since I moved across the pond."

"I see."

"Shall we?" he asked, as the music picked up again.

Lidia gave him her hand.

They danced two more waltzes. Then the first winners of the silent auction were announced, and they went to find something cold to drink.

As they walked back through the gallery, Lidia paused to look at some of the paintings.

"That one, I believe, is a Claude Lorrain," Dave said.

Lidia turned and arched a brow in disbelief at him.

"He was a seventeenth century French artist. I've seen his work in the Louvre. It's nice, like stepping back in time."

"Who are you, and what have you done with Dave?"

"Still me, Yarnok. You're just getting a glimpse at my other side." He winked and walked to the next painting.

"I wonder where Suzanna is." Lidia said.

"I think she can fend for herself."

"You know she's setting us up."

"Yes, the detective in me guessed that last night. Have I told you, you look stunning?"

"No, Asher, you haven't."

"Well, you do."

"Thank you."

Neither said anything else as they went back into the dancing, where they waltzed until the next auction items were to be announced. The first was a marble fountain, the next, a print of one of Lorrain's paintings that lined the gallery walls.

Lidia still hadn't seen Suzanna anywhere and was legitimately feeling concerned.

"What is it?"

"You know how Shane's nose always tells him when something is suspicious. I'm have a similar feeling about Suzanna's absence."

"Let's go look for her then."

They wandered back through the gallery and out onto the veranda, where a few people were relaxing, enjoying the cool night air. It was cloudy, and even the moon was completely hidden. The only light came from the lamps on the veranda and the fairy lights that lined the paths through the garden.

They walked down the paths, between the statues, who now seemed to loom over them, like ghosts in the faint light. They walked all the way to the circle drive, where the valets waited, but there was no sign of Suzanna.

"This is strange. She's probably inside though." Dave said, and they headed back.

"Ah! There you are!" said a man of medium build with black hair and a goatee, that Lidia vaguely remembered from earlier in the evening. "Mrs. Morgan asked me to give you a message."

"And you are?" Dave asked, his detective's tone coming through.

"Maxim Duelet. It was I who invited Suzanna tonight. My father worked with Seymer and the Morgans. Anyway, she asked that I tell you she has left with a friend. She was unable to find you or contact you on the phone."

Lidia pulled out her phone and noted that the battery had died. "I forgot to charge it. Did she say where this friend lived or who they are? How long she would be gone?"

"I am sorry. I assume that when you are able to retrieve your messages, she will have sent you that information. She left the car for you. So, I would guess that she will not return tonight."

"Thank you. Thank you, for letting us know," Lidia said, the uneasy feeling increasing.

"Please enjoy the rest of your evening," he said and started to walk away. Then he turned back. "There is one more thing. Here, her tickets for the auction," he said, handing several ticket stubs to Lidia, before going toward a woman, who waved at him from across the veranda.

"We should go," Lidia said.

"I think we should wait until after the final auction announcement. How many bids did she put in?"

Lidia counted the stubs. "Twenty."

They continued back into the main hall with the dancing. The music was dying down and they were getting ready to call the final items for the night. Dave took out his own two tickets. "Did you get any?"

"No, I'm afraid I wasn't a very generous tonight. What did you bid on? I don't recall anything under a two-hundred Franc starter bid."

"There were a couple of items. Literally, two," he said, holding up his tickets. "I've never seen one done quite like this. Not that I frequent auctions, but like I said, I've been learning about a lot and my other side is developing."

Lidia looked at the tickets, as the numbers were called. "Oh no!" she whispered.

"What is it?"

"She won that last item. Why on earth would she bid so much on a book? What if I have to pay for it?"

"You won't. They'll message her for payment information. With everything digitized here, she can simply transfer cryptocurrency funds from her wallet to their wallet. I imagine it will be paid for before we have to pick it up."

Dave looked at his own tickets and double checked the numbers, a slow smile lighting his eyes.

"You won? Which one?"

"You'll see when we pick it up."

After the last item was called, it was announced that they would be ready for pick up after the final waltz. The announcer left the stage, and the music began.

"Shall we Yarnok?"

"Okay Asher. I guess I could use the practice," she said.

It was midnight when they left, and Dave showed her the Lorrain print he had won at the auction. "It's a smaller print, but I need to be able to get it in my suitcase."

Lidia plugged her phone into the car and retrieved her messages. She read for a minute, then handed it to Dave.

The people we were across from at dinner introduced me to a woman, who claims she saw Edgar in Davos. She didn't talk to him but was surprised to see me here tonight without him.

I told her we had an argument, and I came to our chalet in hopes of making amends but didn't realize he was in Davos.

If asked, please stick to the story that you are a Morgan employee, who came with me to visit your fiancé.

She is going to Davos tomorrow to prepare for a convention and invited me along. I hope you understand. If he is there, I need to find him.

"So, she's already telling people we're engaged," Dave quipped.

"Suzanna doesn't like to waste time. I just wish she had given the name of the woman she left with," Lidia said, as they turned onto the main road.

"Are you going to be okay alone at the chalet tonight?"

"I'll be fine. I just have a really bad feeling about this."

Part II

Chapter 20

Southern France: June 5th

Nigel watched, as the children ran through the caves, playing tag. What the hell was Adam planning?

They seemed so normal, but he knew they weren't. Still, he thanked God that from the beginning, he and Svend had gone against Adam, substituting the genes he had sent them. They were able to falsify the data using results combined with the other children in the nursery. He didn't know how long they could keep it up though, and he was positive that eventually Adam would confess to using Sophie's eggs. What better to hold over Nigel and Lily than their grandchildren?

Recalling the samples they were given to inject made Nigel's head swim. Adam was evil, pure and simple. And if possible, Mel was worse. They were building an army. That is what Adam called it. Sophie's children were intended to be leaders in it, while Adam and Mel's would be the heads.

If they were to succeed, which Svend and Nigel were determined to prevent, it would be an army more diabolical than any that had ever existed. The sheer knowledge base under the command of Adam Jr. and Eva Hisdak would supersede some computers. They would understand and fluently speak any language needed, giving them one on one negotiating ability with any nation. There would be no need for an interpreter who could leak the truth of secret conversations. The only teaching the children received was that which Adam and Mel deemed beneficial for their own end goals, and all the material was written from the perspective of them and others, such as

Meschner. At the age of three, they were already reading Mein Kampf and Mao's little red book.

He looked up as Celia, Gerard and Filipe ran toward Lily, who had brought their lunch. They were all smiles. He would not be able to hide their good nature from Adam or Mel much longer.

As soon as the training started, not to mention the hormone injections, they would be expected to behave as the genes they supposedly had would dictate. Next year was when the pullback was meant to start. The pullback being the diminishing of nurture. By the age of five, they would be expected to fend for themselves. It would go in levels, advancing through different scenarios like a video game, in which the children were the real-life characters. Each level would become more difficult and require real life use of the skills taught. These skills spanned everything from hand-to-hand combat to intellectual chess matches and negotiation skills. It was just part of basic training for an army born of scientific madness and moral depravity.

He wondered how Sophie and Nick were. Had they had a child yet?

Nigel hated this isolation. The nursery and his portion of the project had all been moved to underground caves in the south of France, that had been used and expanded during World War two. Whereas many such places would be a tourist attraction, these were closed to the public due to false propaganda, spread by companies supported by P2P. They were supposed to be contaminated by chemical weapons stored during the war. There were also rumors of mines, set as booby traps, if the allied forces should have come to investigate the caves.

The fact was, that the air here, even though underground, was some of the purest, and rather than chemical weapons, it was a primary hiding place for top officials. There were pools of healing thermal waters, and food was easily grown

in the mineral rich soil of an area between the caves that
opened up into the light of day. And if you needed to get
out quickly, there were also underground tunnels that led
under the border to Spain and Italy, as well as multiple
routes within France. He knew this, because the route that
Lily was brought in with the children began under a
vineyard, and the route that he and other scientists had
come through was via a tunnel in a forested area.

Granted, they had been blindfolded, but he could tell from
the roughness of the terrain and the scent of the trees,
moss, and other foliage as they were guided up a steep
path and into a damp cave, at which point the blindfolds
were removed so that they could make their way down
what appeared to be a mine shaft and through at least a
mile of narrow, winding tunnel, before coming up and into
one of the areas of thermal pools.

Stalagmites surrounded the pools like an obstacle course
and stalactites hung overhead, glinting in the shafts of light
that came through carved windows in the rock that looked
out on the garden area and were sealed with, what Adam
bragged was two layers of bulletproof glass, and at the
mouth of this section of cave was a sliding glass door, made
of the same glass.

Everything was powered by either thermal or solar
power collected from well-hidden panels.

What he, Svend, and Lily were working on was which
route they could safely get Sophie's children out and to
who? It was one thing if the children supposedly ran away,
but if Nigel or Lily were to disappear, Sophie would be in
danger. If Svend left, his sister was at risk. It was a complex
scheme, whose only hope of success was Lily's sister,
Josephine.

The problem was, her husband, Simon, was the only link.
He came from Paris on occasion with new gene samples
ordered through P2P, but Josephine had never come. While

they felt relatively assured of trusting Josephine, they knew that there was no way they dared to trust Simon. Lily believed, that much like them, Josephine's cooperation with the projects was based on fear of what Simon would do to the girls they raised, especially the two still living somewhere with Josephine.

Scotland

Pollina and Amber were excited about their eighteenth birthdays.

Simon had stayed away, only visiting on occasion, and life with their mother was far less restricted. In fact, Tabetha and Callie were even allowed to come to their house.

Josephine knew what the girls had been doing. She'd known from the lack of reaction after the first shot that they were replacing the hormone shots with saline, but she said nothing. In fact, she was impressed. She had almost spoken with them directly, but she decided against it. They were safer to not know and maintain their guard. It was an easy enough thing for her to fake the reports and test results that she sent to Paris.

Now that they were of age though, it would become much more difficult. Simon wanted to take them to Paris for the next stage, and if that happened, the deception would be exposed. That would put not just her and the girls, but the rest of the family's branch of the project at risk.

She needed to find a way to talk with her sister, Lily, and Nigel. She had also needed to find a way to keep Pollina and Amber from going to Paris. The solution to the last, presented itself in the form of Tabetha and Callie. Their friends had invited them to spend the summer with them, visiting family in Sweden, before Tabetha started college.

Somehow, Josephine needed to keep Simon from the girls until they left. Then she would have to convince him that they had snuck away without her knowledge. He would be angry, but she had learned to live with his temper long ago.

"Hello," Pollina said, coming around the corner of the kitchen.

"I thought you were over at Tabetha and Callie's."

"We were, but I left my new camera lenses, and we want to see if we can photograph with their new telescope tonight. Tabetha and Callie want to camp out on the ridge. Do you think..."

"It's fine. In fact, I may go out myself tonight."

"A meeting?" Pollina asked, concerned. Their mother going to a meeting was never good, and they were worried that something might happen before they would be able to go to Sweden. Their mother had been far too easily convinced.

"Did you tell Simon about Sweden?" she risked asking. Neither she nor Amber, referred to him as their father any longer. They had been told they were adopted, but Sophie believed that Josephine likely was their mother.

"No, but we need to talk. He's planning to be here for your birthday, and he'll want to take you to Paris."

"But we're going to Sweden. It's all been arranged."

"Not everything."

"Tabetha and Callie's parents have all the tickets. We'll be eighteen. You can't stop us from going!"

"*I* don't want to stop you. Listen to me. I am not your enemy. I want you to go camping tonight, but first, I want you to pack your suitcases and take them with you. Then, I want you to stay away. Your birthdays are Tuesday. If Simon comes back, you both need to be gone. Do you understand?"

"You're on our side?"

"There are things you can't understand. Things that are better for you not to know. That's why I didn't tell you this before, but he will come to take you, and you can't be here when he does."

"What about you?" Pollina asked, stunned, and scared by the expression on Josephine's face.

"I'll tell him that you ran away, and that's what you are going to do. Don't tell your friends where. It won't be safe for them to know. Tell them nothing, except that instead of picking you up, you'll meet them at the airport. Make up a story. I know you'll think of something. Make sure you take everything away from here tonight. He's in Switzerland now, but he could leave at any time. Will you tell Amber? Will you do that?"

Pollina nodded.

"Promise me. I won't be here. I need to have an alibi for not knowing you've gone. Please promise me, Pollina, you will come and get everything today and not come back."

"I promise," Pollina said, then turned and ran to get her sister.

Josephine went to a safe and pulled out two portable crypto keys and their passports, which she left on their beds. Then she took her purse and left before they could return. She had done what she had to do to keep them safe. "Maybe I should go too," she said to herself. Maybe, but what would Simon do to Lily, or Sophie, or even Anne if she did that? She had to convince him that the girls had outsmarted her and that she knew nothing.

***

Anne and Ben had slept late and were now getting ready to head out to meet Sheila, who offered them a tour along the coast and up to Dundee.

"I miss giving tours to people," Sheila said.

"Isn't Marco joining us?" Anne asked.

"He wanted to, but a neighbor threw his back out. Marco is helping him do some repairs and mowing. He's very handy!"

"I'd forgotten how beautiful it is here and all the history," Anne said.

"Well, you'll be getting a full reminder course. Here," Sheila said, handing them some brochures. "Just let me know which ones you're interested in."

"Let's start with the closest," Ben suggested.

Sheila turned down a wooded lane toward a lake.

"This home is still in use, but it is one of the loveliest in the area. Did I mention that I'm thinking of getting my real estate license? I would love to tour and show some of these homes. A lot of them need tender loving care. I would actually love to renovate some of them. Living in Italy gave me so many great design ideas! The house we're in now, well, as you saw, the low ceilings and beams are charming, but they don't allow much room for change unless you want to burn it down and start from scratch. And I wouldn't want to do that.

"I would love something like this to play with," she said, as they pulled over on a bluff, overlooking the lake with a grand house by its shore. "The location is ideal, and when I first saw it, I thought it was empty, but it wasn't listed. I've since discovered that people are here, but I can't say that they live in it. I only see vehicles in the drive randomly and usually several. I think perhaps it is used for entertaining or some kind of clubhouse. I don't know. I've only seen the cars, never the people. Of course, I don't stake it out, but there's a public lake access just down the road and Marco and I enjoy fishing. We've camped there a few times, and you can see the lake facing side from there. Only once out of, maybe eight or nine trips, did we ever see lights on. It's a mystery, and as hard as I've looked, I can't find any record of who owns it."

"Interesting. It is an idyllic location," Ben said.

"Yes, but let's go to something we can take a closer look at, as I see this is one of those times cars are in the drive."

Switzerland

Dave was heading out with Magdeline and Soren to meet
Trudie, and Lidia called Shane to let him know about the
development with Suzanna. She had tried several times to
call Suzanna, but it went directly to voice mail. She also
sent a text asking Suzanna to call her, but it had, so far,
gone unanswered.

A part of Shane felt torn. He wanted to be useful, but
aside from making phone calls, all he was doing was
playing guard to Rosie and Claire. Lidia had also told him
what Suzanna had said about wanting to see Claire.

"My nose is telling me that I should be there but let me
discuss it with Claire and Rosie." Shane said, "I'll call you
back. I need to touch base with Sophie and Margot too and
see if they've heard from Nick and Larry. I tried calling
them this morning, but like Suzanna's phone, it just went
straight to voice mail for both of them," he said.

Lidia hung up with Shane and was tempted to go next
door, but then she realized that she had never actually met
any of the people now there. She should wait for Dave to
get back. In the meantime, she decided to be nosy where
she was. It struck her as odd that Suzanna would just take
off without taking so much as her toothbrush. Granted, she
had plenty of money to buy whatever she may need, but it
just felt wrong.

She tried to remember the last names of the couple
seated across from them last night and bit her lip as she
looked at Suzanna's laptop. She was certain that the
contact information for the event would be in her emails,
but that would mean breaking not only into the computer,
but also her email.

No, she should wait for Dave to return. She paced the
floor, then decided to carefully look through Suzanna's

things. Maybe she had written the information down somewhere.

***

It was still raining, but Nick and Larry decided to make an early start of it and had been out on the lake from 8:00 that morning. The plan was to scope out the shoreline and go aground at a point further down, where satellite images showed another small dock protruding into the lake and a cabin. At about 10:00, they noted a family at the cabin, who looked like they were packing to leave. That would make it the ideal location to tie up at.

In their backpacks, they had night vision goggles with photography capabilities, stun guns and pepper spray. They were wearing ranger uniforms and hairpieces, which they were having serious debates about, because they were hot. It may have been raining, but the temperature was still a good eighty plus, Fahrenheit. Larry had also added a fake mustache, while Nick had opted for the more rugged look of a beard.

Larry was already concerned they may have been identified. Adam's arrest, three years before, hadn't exactly been low profile, and surely, Nick, as Sophie's husband, was in their files.

After the family left the cabin, they made their way to shore to scout out the woods between them and the house. They had just come to the tree line when they heard it. A few minutes later, a chopper was overhead. They watched as it departed.

"How much would you like to bet that Simon is onboard?" Nick asked.

"Probably pretty good odds, but let's not lose track of who we're really looking for. Simon wouldn't be threatened by us. We have no legal pull. However, if Jack is being kept here against his will, and we were to rescue him, then we could turn Simon in on kidnapping charges. The unfortunate truth, however, is we don't know if Simon is responsible for Jack's disappearance. We're still grasping at straws, and tonight, with or without Simon's presence, we need to either prove or eliminate this straw."

They made their way back to the cabin and Larry picked the lock. Leaving their boots outside, they went inside to dry out.

"Do you do that often?" Nick asked.

"No, but it's not like we're going to steal anything. We just need a dry place to lay low. They obviously aren't planning to come back any time soon," Larry said, noting the unplugged refrigerator. "Neither of us had much sleep last night. I think we should eat our lunch and try to catch a nap. I don't think we should play Goldilocks. So, let's take turns on the couch."

"I should call Sophie," Nick said, pulling out his phone.

"I guess, I should call Margot as well, or maybe I had better call Shane back first. He left three messages."

Ten minutes later, they both hung up their phones and looked at each other.

"You first," Larry said.

"Jack's mother called Sophie from Scotland. Apparently, they sold a part of their farm and decided to go check things out."

"You mean look for Josephine."

Nick nodded. "And Shane?"

"Mrs. Morgan has now run off, supposedly to look for her husband, whom she was told had been seen in Davos. Lidia can't get a hold of her though, and Shane talked to Claire. He told her that Suzanna wanted to meet with her, but now she's gone. He wants to come down and help Lidia, and Clair agreed. Rosie isn't happy about it, and I just realized that you haven't even met them yet, have you?"

"No, but I have been pretty well kept up to date. Sophie also told me that Dave was out with Lidia and Mrs. Morgan last night. She thinks there's a romance brewing."

"I think I'd better call Margot now and see what she might have to add to the story."

"I'll fix our lunches," Nick said, getting the food packs from each of their bags.

"Thanks."

An hour later, Larry was snoring on the couch, while Nick tried to pull things into perspective. There were so many different players in this, and like Dave said, they all seemed to be related. Unfortunately, they were too closely related to Sophie. He thought again of how Jonathan warned him about Jeremy. He was glad Sophie had gone on ahead and was staying together with so many other people. Victoria still made him uneasy, as did Mrs. Morgan being next door. A part of him was relieved she had gone. He just wanted to find Jack and go home.

He thought back to when he and Sophie had gone to Scotland and her cousins there. What was Josephine up to?

Was it Josephine or Simon, or someone else behind Jack's disappearance? Then he worried about Anne and Ben. He knew they would do anything to get their son back safe, but how?

Anne had already nearly been killed just because she found out about Sophie. Would Josephine hurt her own cousin? Sophie didn't seem to think so. Josephine had been in deep though. She'd served on the hospital board where Meschner worked. Hell, from what he learned from Jonathan, she may have even been intimate with him before she married Simon. Granted, that was a long time ago. Still, according to Dave she was related to Simon before they married. Could Sophie's mother really be so blind to her sister's life? And where were Sophie's parents? All these questions nagged at Nick.

The rain started pounding on the roof, and Larry rolled off the couch. "It's not the most comfortable, but you really should try to get some sleep. It could be a long night,"

"Yeah, thanks," Nick said, and headed to the couch. He doubted he could sleep.

Larry was concerned. Nick looked like he had been through the ringer. Between his concern for Jack, Sophie and Jeremy, Larry couldn't blame him. He just hoped Nick would be able to hold it together if there were any confrontations tonight.

The weather looked like it was going to be miserable too. However, Larry considered that to be an advantage. Had it really been Simon that left on the chopper? And what were the odds they would find Jack? Larry wasn't holding his breath. It was only a slight chance, especially since they weren't certain Simon was behind Jack's disappearance. What if it were Hisdak, or someone yet unknown?

They had never found any leads on Leona or Nadier. Then there was the supposedly dead professor Crabben, who had turned up very much alive in Canada. There were also the truly terrifying aspects of the Chinese project. He never had asked Victoria to listen to the recording again. Rosie gave them enough. Was it really possible that they had cross bred human genes with animal? Magdeline believed it was, or maybe, like some parrots, they had learned to form a few words. "Help, get out, no, go away, die, kill," the words translated by Rosie, hardly showed a high level of vocabulary. There were the bite marks too, but there was no way to confirm their origin.

Larry looked at his phone and saw a message from Dave.

Scotland

It had been a beautiful day. Tomorrow, they would explore some of the hiking trails near where they were staying. Mainly, Anne wanted to take the one Sophie had described to her, where she had met Pollina and Amber.

***

Pollina didn't bother hiding the truth from Tabetha and Callie. They already knew far more than Josephine suspected, because Josephine had no clue just how much Pollina and Amber knew.

Tabetha had already turned nineteen, so she had no problem booking a hotel room for them, which was perfect. Now Simon couldn't track them because nothing was in their name. Nothing that is, except their passports and plane tickets, and they would be safely on the way to their flight before those would register anywhere. They didn't know how far Simon's reach went, but they wouldn't be surprised if he had someone watching the train, bus, ferry, and airports, once he discovered them missing. Fortunately, the higher security and multiple airlines would make it almost impossible for them to be in danger after they arrived, plus they would be with Tabetha and Callie.

Switzerland

Larry and Nick made their way through the woods. The rain was beating down, forming treacherous slicks of mud. When they could see the back deck, they stopped to watch and listen. It was just past 21:00. The sky was pitch black and there didn't seem to be any lights on inside.

They made their way around to where they could see the parking area. No cars were in the drive, but they did spot the cameras. There was one mounted on the garage and another by the front door.

"Should we check the garage?" Nick asked.

"Let's go from behind."

As they made their way back towards the rear of the property, Nick slipped. "Damn it!" he exclaimed, under his breath, as he started to push himself up out of the mud. That's when he saw it. "Larry, stop!" Nick said, as he noted a glow of straight lines through his night vision goggles. "There's something here. I think it's some kind of wire. It's hard to tell in these things."

Larry bent down next to where Nick knelt and fiddled with some settings. "Shit! I came prepared for everything except this. It's electric wire. It looks like eight bands, spaced about a foot apart. My bet is that it encircles the whole property."

"I read somewhere that a monkey learned how to short out an electric fence with wet foliage," Nick said. "Shall we try it?"

"A monkey?"

"I'm just telling you what I read."

"Well, we certainly have enough wet foliage. Unfortunately, I didn't think to pack a saw."

"Maybe we can just break a branch off. It's worth a try."

"Okay. I'd hate to be outdone by a monkey. How about that one?" Larry said, pointing up to a fir tree.

Nick, being taller, grabbed the end of the branch to pull it down and between them, they eventually broke it off.

"What now?" Larry asked.

"We place it across the wires and pray they short out."

Ten minutes later, they were safely on the other side of the fence and peering through the garage windows.

"It's only the car Simon drove here." Nick said.

"Which means, either he is still here, or maybe we caught a lucky break."

"If Jack were here though, would they risk leaving him unguarded?"

"Only way to find out is to get inside."

"Won't there be an alarm?"

"Definitely, but that, I know how to cover," Larry said, and pulled out a small box from his pocket. "The alarm can go off all it wants. This will jam the connection to the police."

"I hope those aren't available on the open market," Nick said.

"You'd be surprised. Most security isn't half as secure as people think it is. I mean, we got through the fence with a technique learned from a monkey," Larry said, as they stepped onto the front porch, careful to stay behind the cameras. "If there is someone here, it's the cameras they'll be watching. So, as long as we don't get caught on those, we should be okay. Get your Taser ready though, just in case we do encounter someone."

The front lock was an electronic number combination pad. Larry took out another small electronic item.

"What's that?" Nick asked.

"Same thing safe crackers use to scan for codes."

The entry hall was huge, with a vaulted ceiling and a double-sided fireplace. A living room area was on the other side and story high, glass windows, faced out toward the lake. There were stairs to both the left and right, going up to a second level over the living room and a hallway, running behind the river rock chimney that extended down each side of the house.

"Let's finish checking out the lower level first," Larry said.

To their right, they discovered a large dining area and open kitchen that looked through the trees. On the other side they weren't sure what they were looking at. The walls were covered in charts and bookshelves. Larry took off the night goggles and pulled out a flashlight.

Nick did the same and took out his phone to take pictures.

They froze when they heard footsteps from above. Turning off the flashlights, they pressed themselves against a wall. The footsteps moved down the stairs. They recognized the voice of the man they had met by the lake, as he spoke on the phone.

"The short is probably from a deer again. I'll check it in the morning. I'm not dealing with a fried corpse in this weather," the man said. "I'm going to the hotel now. Room one twelve at the Ibis. Yeah, I'm good with that. I'm bringing two doses each. Should I take them to the same place? Oh, he's been very active. Very inventive. Yep, I'm leaving now," he said, and headed out.

Larry and Nick waited, listening as the garage door opened and closed, then the gate. Next the engine revved and sped into the night.

"Well, I guess they know who we are," Nick said.

"It's a good thing there's nothing in the room except some clothes and toiletries. He can't get to our SUV in the camp parking. It'll be closed for the night."

"What are the odds that he's the only one here?"

"I'm guessing pretty good, considering there were no other vehicles, but let's try to be quick. I don't think Jack is here. I do think if we keep tabs on our goon, he might lead us to him."

"Jack is inventive, if that's who he was talking about, but..." Nick stopped, as his light hit on a painting. "Dear God!"

Larry turned, and sucked in a deep breath, as he stared at a painting that looked like a renaissance version of Sophie, or several others, he thought.

Nick stared at it, as Larry snapped photos. Nick went closer to look for an artist signature, but it was just an indecipherable scrawl.

"Back up and let me get a shot. Let's work our way down the walls, photograph and video everything. Every book title, everything. Then let's get the hell out."

***

It was late when Shane finally pulled up to the chalet. Rosie opted to stay with the others, while Claire, Shane and Daniel would stay with Lidia.

"She doesn't want to be here if Suzanna comes back, and I don't blame her," Claire said, after Rosie was introduced to Lidia and said good night.

Dave walked Rosie next door.

Daniel was already asleep on the couch where he landed on arrival, and Shane lifted him to follow Lidia into the bedroom she had made up for them.

Then Lidia took Claire to her bedroom. "There's only three bedrooms and I didn't think we should disturb Suzanna's," she said.

Claire surprised her by laughing. "Perceptive," she said. "Even as children, I didn't dare to disturb Suzanna's bedroom. I hope you won't think I'm anti-social if I call it a night. It was nice to meet you."

"Not at all. It is nice to meet you too. Is there anything I can get you? Tea maybe?"

"No, thank you. I think I'm going to take a nice soak in that tub though and sleep like baby," she said, feeling the bedding.

"It is comfortable," Lidia said, "and I put clean towels in the bath."

"Where will you sleep though?"

"I'll be up late with Shane and Dave, then just crash on the couch. It's pretty comfortable too."

When she went back to the living room, both Dave and Soren had come over. Shane was still in the bedroom with Daniel.

"Shall I put some coffee on?" she asked.

"Please," came the reply, in triplicate, as Shane joined them."

"Has anyone heard from Larry or Nick?" asked Shane.

"No," Soren answered, "and Sophie's really concerned. Margot is holding it together for both of them."

"She's dealt with this type of thing from Larry's work for a long time," Shane said.

Just then, there was a knock on the door, and Dave went to answer it.

"We were just talking about you," Dave said, as Margot entered. "All good."

"I should hope so," Margot smiled. "Sophie is getting Jeremy down. Victoria is in her room. Rosie can share with me tonight, but then we'll have to sort something out when Larry comes back."

Just as she said that the phone rang. Larry and Nick had just made it back to the cabin and Larry called in to update.

"Perfect timing," Margot said. "We're all gathered, Shane, Lidia, Dave and Soren."

"*Good. Nick is giving Sophie a call and then he'll join in too.*"

***

Between the findings at the lake house, the lunch Dave, Soren and Magdeline had with Trudie and the Martinson's, along with Lidia's input about her time with Suzanna before they arrived, it was a full night.

Soren thought he recognized one of Cora's sketches as the man who left with the woman and girls in Paris. Yet, his instincts still felt something didn't quite match.

Margot mostly listened, but she had made a few observations herself, mainly regarding Victoria.

Nick had to remind himself that Alice's whereabouts was the one thing that he and Sophie had sworn to keep secret. A part of him wished they hadn't, but there was more than enough to deal with already, without throwing that into the mix. He trusted Jonathan more than he would trust Mrs. Morgan, whom he had never actually met, but felt he knew more than enough about. No, as far as he was concerned, and he knew Alice would agree, it was better to keep her out of it. Safer for everyone. He also felt bad that a part of him thought the same about Victoria.

Chapter 21

Switzerland: June 6th

Suzanna felt a sense of Deja vu as she stood at the window and looked down onto the lake below. She knew where she was. She came here after receiving a message that Edgar wanted to see her. It was a trap though, at least it seemed so. There was no sign of Edgar, and the car that brought her was gone. Her phone had also been taken, supposedly, at Edgar's request. She felt like a fool, and she knew she was a good ten plus miles from anywhere.

The lodge had been one of her favorites in the Valais Alps. The lake below, flowed down over the Italian border. There was a small village across the lake, that was a bustling tourist town in the winter, but now, the only inhabitants would be the modest population who called it home. The same went for the lodge and its spa. That was what made it extra special. In fact, the road up from the village was closed, from April 1st until November.

Its isolation was one of the reasons she believed Edgar might be here. She wished she had told Lidia more. She did still hold out hope that Edgar could come. The kitchen was well stocked, so there must be someone else here.

She paced the dining hall and went out onto the balcony that was fitted perfectly into the hillside, virtually hidden.

She remembered Edgar explaining the wonders of its architecture, how it had been carved out of the mountain, with tunnels that ran from one section to another. There were even private wings for dignitaries, who had their own entrances.

She sighed. It was a beautiful morning. Birds were singing. She may as well enjoy it. Edgar must be nearby. Why else would she have been brought here? Maybe he was delayed in Davos. After all, that was where she thought she was going until she woke up and found the message.

The note said that Edgar knew she was there, and he would send a car to bring her to him. It was the driver who asked her to leave her phone, otherwise he had been instructed not to bring her. It had made sense at the time.

She wondered if the resort was being utilized during its closing months for one of the projects. Morgan acquisitions had never owned the lodge, but like the shipping line that supplied the lab in the Marianas, it could be run by a company that owned a section of a redistributed acquisition. After all, she hadn't been here in thirty years. There was no telling how it may have changed hands or been divided up by the original owners. She didn't know who owned it originally. It may have stared at her from the books without her recognizing it.

That thought gave rise to another thought. She always considered herself and Edgar equal partners, but might he have been hiding more than she thought, even after all they went through three years before? After all, he had seduced her with a picnic and then vanished without a word. She hated the waring thoughts and emotions swimming through her mind, but she needed to look at the facts.

Somewhere

Jack looked at the weight he held as he flexed his arm for the twenty-fifth repeat. Would it shatter the windows if he threw it? He wanted to throw it, to throw something, and he needed it to be more than a dart.

He had become quite proficient at the dart board. If... No, when he finally got out of here, Nick would have to eat all those victories he had won over the years at the pub. The thought was a minute condolence.

Obviously, they didn't mean to kill him. He laughed, remembering that the projects were all about preserving life. "Ha!" he said aloud and was surprised by the sound of his own voice. Not having any human contact was really getting to him, and he wondered how so many people had survived solitary confinement. Granted, he wasn't in an eight by ten cell, but that was just logistics. He was still a prisoner. What were the plans for him? How long would they leave him here? He still hadn't located the cameras, but he knew they were there. He could almost feel the eyes watching him. Maybe watching him perform in this cage was what they wanted from him.

"If you can hear me," he yelled, "I'm not a circus monkey!"

"Hold it together Jack. You have to hold it together. Don't give them the satisfaction of watching you lose it," he coached himself. Then he took a deep breath, hit the shower, and then sank into the jacuzzi with a bottled water and a random novel from the bookshelf. "Women Of the Old World & How They Bred With the Immortal" He took a long drink and opened to the introduction.

Switzerland

The next morning, everyone seemed to be dragging, except Jeremy and Daniel. Daniel woke Shane up at 6:30, and guessing that Jeremy was likely up too, Shane went next door in hopes that maybe Sophie would be up as well.

Rosie opened the door and smiled at Daniel, who smiled back. She and Sophie were up, enjoying coffee, while Jeremy was eating a banana and playing cars with Dave on the floor, who had a large coffee by his side.

"I'm surprised you're awake," Shane said, looking at Dave.

"I don't think *awake* is the right word."

"Daniel, this is Jeremy. Remember, I told you about him?"

"He's her son," Daniel said, pointing to Sophie.

"That's right, Mrs. Rafferty."

"Why would I call her Mrs. Rafferty, instead of her name, like I call Rosie?"

"You don't," Sophie said. "Your dad is just trying to teach you good manners, but I prefer to keep it informal and be friends. So, let's compromise, and you can call me Miss Sophie."

"Can I still call you mom?" Jeremy asked.

"Yes, please."

"I thought you were married," Daniel said.

"I am, but the Mrs. sounds so formal. My music students still call me Miss Sophie."

"You teach music?" Daniel asked.

"Sometimes. I used to teach more."

"What do you teach?"

"Piano."

"Can you teach me?"

"I suppose I could, but there's a problem. I don't have a piano here, but maybe another time, if you come visit me at home."

"Where do you live?"

"Nova Scotia. It's in Canada."

"I know where that is. It's not as far away as our home, because it's on the Atlantic side and Seattle is on the Pacific side of the continent. Right dad?"

"Gold star in Geography. When did you learn that?"

"When I was looking at the map on the airplane," Daniel said, and sat down to join Jeremy and Dave.

"You look like you could use this," Sophie said, handing Shane a coffee. "Cream or sugar?"

"I think I'll go black for now. Thanks. Would you happen to mind if..."

"It's fine," Rosie and Sophie said, in unison.

"Dave?"

"I'm right behind you. You two have fun," he said to the boys.

"Should we get him something for breakfast?" Sophie asked.

"That would be fantastic," Shane said, "I'll owe you."

Once next door, Shane said, "I don't think we have any tight time schedules today. So, I was thinking we could catch a few more zees. If you don't mind sharing."

"I don't, but you might. I snore."

"I know, so do I. As long as you're not an overenergized little boy, I'm good."

"Ditto."

It was nearly ten, when they were all up and Soren came over. "You deserted me," he said to Dave.

"Sorry, I'm going to desert you even more. As per sleeping arrangements, I'll be bunking here, so that Rosie has a place to sleep."

"You would really leave me alone with all four of them?"

"We have great faith in your abilities. Besides, you have Margot and Jeremy. Larry and Nick may be back as soon as tonight, hopefully with Jack."

"Then where do we put him?"

"Well, if Mrs. Morgan chooses to stay gone, we may just have to utilize her room. She may not like it, but she's been out of contact long enough that we can call her a missing person. I'd like to get an inventory of her room today. Claire, I think you should be the one to go through her things," Shane said.

Claire couldn't help it. She smiled. "I know I should be worried about her, but I actually feel like a naughty child at the thought of going through her things."

"Lidia, do you mind helping?"

"You mean doing an unofficial, official inventory? I'm on it."

"Thanks."

The men went outside to talk about the situation with the Martinsons and the discovery of Professor Crabben, alive and well.

On the deck next door, the boys played, while Margot kept one eye on them and the other, plus both ears, on the interactions of the other four women, as they sat all together.

Victoria seemed to be making an effort. She was most social with Rosie, asking questions about the children's home she had grown up in, while Magdeline and Sophie exchanged parenting stories. Margot was most interested in the conversation between Rosie and Victoria.

"I'm wondering if Sarah Martinson knew anything about Crabben's involvement with the research combining human and animal genes," Soren said.

"Do you think he could have been behind the abduction?" Shane asked.

"I don't know. He told me that he had planned to ask her to lead the CDC program. If that was true, it wouldn't make sense for him to have her abducted. No, what we still don't know is, who was in the vault with him. And there is no way he faked his death and vanished without help. If he's working with the Chinese now, that could mean that the CDC program has been moved there. It was odd, when he told me about it, he caught himself. And the way he looked at me when he said it didn't exist anymore has always led me to believe that it does, just not at Scangentech anymore. What I find even stranger is the timing of his supposed car accident. It was right after Ana came back and Mrs. Martinson would have started coming around."

"Maybe we need to back off of trying to find Ana's biological father and focus on what Sarah can tell us about the time she worked with Crabben," Dave said. "I mean, we've sent Katz everything we have on the genealogy, and he has great resources. Also, with what Cora gave us, we have a better understanding of what's happening behind the scenes, particularly with the Paris project," Dave continued, "We also can't forget the footage that Saville gave us. He emailed it to me last night. We really should have Sophie look at it."

"That's a good point," Shane said. "If anyone could tell if it was him, it's Sophie. I hate to have to explain to her that the passport of one of the other men with him, matched her fathers, especially since none of the passports of the women matched her mother."

"It could, as Saville said, be a group using stolen passports. It's not like they really check. They were only looked at because there had been a murder nearby, and they were taking note of all the passports," Dave said.

"I understand there's been a rash of stolen passports in Italy. Maggie's parents were telling me about it. They're looking at instigating a mandatory chip ID. It's one thing to chip ID a cat or dog, but there's more than just the projects going on in this world, that is beyond disconcerting. Sorry, I think about these things a lot with the boys," Soren said, as he looked over at Jeremy and Daniel.

"I get it," Shane said, "But back to Jack. What do we think the odds are that the footage is relevant? I mean it was five days after he went missing and it seems like Larry and Nick have a pretty good lead, if Jack is who they overheard the man talking about. I just hate to put Sophie through more, especially with Nick not here," Shane continued, glancing over at Sophie. "Let's wait until we talk to Nick again, but my nose says it's not Jack or Nigel O'Hare."

"Always trust your nose," Dave said.

"If we go by instinct," Soren said, "mine says we need someone inside Scangentech to work with Trudie. She's been saying the place is bugged since before I left, and we know there must be an inside man, but the internal investigation was inconclusive. They only laid off a few people, and Trudie said they all left with good severance pay and references. In my opinion, someone inside the investigation is helping a cover up."

"I think you have good instincts Soren," Shane said. "Maybe you missed your calling. I don't suppose you would consider being the one to…"

"No. It wouldn't work for me to go back in. Whoever it is, would only be suspicious of me and more cautious."

"I suppose you're right," Shane agreed. "You're too obviously connected. Any ideas?"

"Not yet, but I'll discuss it with Trudie."

"That's something Saville might have an idea on," Dave said.

The women looked like they were dispersing, and Jeremy went inside with Sophie. Margot kept Daniel distracted for about another minute before he came running over.

"Okay, I'll touch base with Katz once it's a decent hour in Brazil and research that painting Nick found," Shane said.

"I'll set up another meeting with Mrs. Martinson," Dave added.

"I can't talk freely with Trudie until she's off work. So, unless you have something to assign me," Soren said, looking over at Magdeline, who was chatting with Margot, "I'm going to see if I can get some time with my wife."

"Can you play now?" Daniel asked. He had been patiently waiting, as they concluded.

"I think I can spare an hour or two," Shane said, checking the time.

"Can we go for a hike?"

"A hike? I guess so. Let's go get some drinks to take with us," Shane said, as Daniel smiled.

Scotland

Anne stared across the lake at the house. It had been in her dreams all night. Something about it haunted her and she couldn't get past the feeling that she had seen it before. She and Ben had enjoyed the hike up the trail, but they had only encountered the occasional backpacker or dog walker. It was a beautiful day, so she had convinced Ben to pick up something for lunch from a pub and take it to go.

"What are you thinking?" Ben asked.

"That I've seen that house before, before yesterday, but I can't place when or where."

"Where?"

"I may have seen it in a photo, but I feel certain that I have either seen it or been to it before."

"Could it have been a similar house?"

"I don't think so. I dreamed about it last night, and in the dream there was a secret entrance around the rear."

"Secret?"

"Yes, and I need to find out if I'm right."

"You want to sneak down behind a house you think you've seen before, maybe in a picture, to see if it has a hidden entrance that you saw in a dream? Did I get that right?"

"That pretty much sums it up."

"What are we waiting for?"

"There were still cars there when we passed."

"So, we go up where we can see the drive and wait for them not to be there," Ben said.

"Really? You'd do a stake out with me?"

"Might as well, unless there's someplace else you have a feeling about."

Anne smiled and kissed him. "Let's go!"

Two hours later, they watched as one car left, but two others remained.

"I wish we had thought to bring binoculars," Anne said.

"I'm guessing the sporting goods place down from the pub would have some," Ben said, "Instead of sitting here, why don't we go get them and come back? You can't make out the people at this distance without them. So, we wouldn't miss anything if we do, and..."

"We're sure to miss out if we don't," Anne finished, and Ben pulled back onto the road.

They were back in under an hour and Anne was anxious to see what she could see. She had just raised the binoculars to her eyes and was adjusting the focus when her breath caught in her chest.

"What? What is it, Anne?"

"Simon."

"Simon? Are you sure?"

"Positive. We can't let him see us and we can't lose him."

"You really think he would have taken Jack?"

"Let's just say, he's on my prime suspect list. And why is he here? What if he came for the girls?"

"What girls?" Ben asked.

"The ones that he and Josephine were raising. The girls that Sophie told me were here with Josephine and scared to death of him."

"I knew there was more going on than you'd admitted."

"Sophie swore me to secrecy on the girls, and I wasn't sure how you'd react if I told you everything. I didn't want you to go ballistic if you knew Josephine had been here."

"We can discuss that later," Ben said, as he pulled back onto the road to follow Simon.

"Where could he be going?" Anne questioned aloud, as they wandered down narrow winding roads that seemed to lead to nowhere. Then suddenly, they came around a bend and he was gone. They went on another mile or so before they found room to turn around.

"He had to have gone down that private drive," Ben said. "There is no place else."

"It must be the house where they were living," Anne said.

Ben looked at her. "So, now what?" he asked.

"Back to the lake. Then we call Sophie."

When they arrived back at the lake, the other cars that had still been there were gone, and they drove down the drive. Anne took pictures all around, while Ben, nervously stood guard as she made her way to the back. She was only gone five minutes, but Ben could feel his pulse racing. He was just about to go to the back himself, when she returned, a triumphant smile on her face.

"I was right! Look at this," she said, showing him the picture of the hidden entrance. "I almost missed it myself, and I was right in front of it!"

"Jack could be inside. We…"

"No," Anne said. "He's not here. You heard what Sheila said. There are only cars here on occasion. They were here this time for at least two days and now they're all gone. It doesn't make sense. Besides, if he were here, I would feel him. I know I would. We should get out of here, just in case, and call Sophie."

Switzerland

Sophie took the call and walked outside, glad that Jeremy was down for a nap. As soon as she heard what happened, she went to find Shane.

"He went on a walk with Daniel, but he should be back soon," Dave told her.

"I don't like this," she said, "and it's all my fault."

"How's that?" Dave asked, as Lidia and Claire came into the room. Claire caught her breath.

It took Dave a minute to realize that this was the first time, mother and daughter had met. Each knew the other was there but had been too occupied for it to fully register. Lidia stood beside Claire, concerned. The room was dead silent until Claire spoke,

"I'm very pleased to finally meet you, Sophie. I'm sorry, sorry about your cousin and..."

"It wasn't your fault," Sophie said, stepping closer. "I know that you didn't know about me."

"Still, I wish I...I want to help however I can," Claire said, stepping forward until they were only a foot apart. Claire bit her lip and shrugged helplessly, and Sophie hugged her.

They stood, embracing, for some time as Dave and Lidia stood watching in uncomfortable silence until the door opened, and Daniel hurried in ahead of Shane. Sophie and Claire broke apart. Shane realized what had just occurred, then followed Daniel to the table and opened the computer.

"Tell them what you told me, Daniel," Shane said.

"I remembered something mommy said once, when she was talking on the computer, about going to a lake with my brother. She said the name of the lake, but I forgot about it until we were on our walk and dad told me we're going to Geneva," he finished, as Shane worked to pull up internet.

Everyone stared at Daniel, waiting for him to continue. He stared back at them and then at the computer screen.

"Tell them the name," Shane prompted.

"Lake Genevieve."

"Lake Genevieve?" Sophie repeated. "Why does that sound familiar?"

Shane looked up at Sophie. "The only references I'm getting say that it's in Missouri or California, which doesn't help, unless we're way off base."

"I think I know the problem," Soren cut in. "There's some fancy spa that Maggie's parents like. I think it goes by that name, but the official name of the lake it's on I don't recall. I just know that the spa is here in the Valais Alps, the lake itself is on the border and flows from Switzerland into

Italy. I've never been there, but the pictures were beautiful."

"Saint Genevieve was the Patron Saint of Paris," Sophie said.

No one said anything for a minute.

Shane typed a search for the spa. "Odd," Shane said. "It says it's closed until November. It is possible Patty could have been referring to Missouri or California."

"I know I've heard of that lake before, not just the saint," Sophie said. "I'll call Anne. Oh! I almost forgot. Anne and Ben saw Simon. He's in Scotland."

***

Nick and Larry had changed rental cars and now followed the man from the house. At least in Simon's car, he was easy to spot and hear, as Alfa Romeo's defy Swiss noise pollution restrictions.

They stayed at a safe distance. Their only fear was that either he or they would need to stop for fuel soon, as they followed up and down endless winding roads. When they finally saw the man pull over at a diner, they realized that they had simply come around to the far side of the lake.

They waited in the parking lot, then watched as the man met another man and they walked to a boat launch a few meters down the road. The man they had followed gave the other a backpack and the other man took off in a motorboat. Soon, the first man climbed back in the Alfa Romeo and sped off. They followed and passed him, as he turned off to fuel up. Nick looked at their own gage, which was wavering on the red line.

"What do we do?" Nick asked.

"I'm looking for another station nearby. There's not much we can do without fuel. Okay, two miles up ahead, there should be a station. If we're lucky, he'll stay on this road and we'll see him pass and hopefully be able to catch up," Larry said.

"You do know I'm not a stunt car driver," Nick said, his knuckles already white with the tension of keeping up this far.

"Don't worry. I'll take over, but this may be one thing you can't tell Margot about."

They saw the car go by when their own tank was just half filled.

"It's okay. Fill her up," Larry said.

Two minutes later they were back on the road and Nick had to hang on, as Larry took the corners like a race car driver. Nick didn't even ask. He just prayed. If they lived, and Sophie found out, she'd kill them both.

Larry hadn't driven like this in years, and he wasn't sure if he was more exhilarated or scared, as he came around the bend. They spotted the Alfa Romeo turning up a side road, and Larry slowed to a normal speed, and soon, so did Nick's heart rate.

"Where did you learn to drive like that?"

"It was part of my training when I was in the French Foreign Legion. I admit, I was a little scared myself. It's been a good twenty years since I've driven like that. I guess it's like riding a bike. It comes back to you as soon as you hit the accelerator."

"Uh huh," was all Nick could muster, as they continued up a steep hill.

The man in front of them stopped at a drive with a chain across the entrance and they passed at a normal rate.

"See if you can pull up a satellite image," Larry said, as he pulled over at a viewpoint.

A minute later they were looking at an image. They could see the turnoff, but aside from that, they could only see trees.

"It's a lot denser up here than it was by the lake," Larry said. "I'll send the coordinates to a friend of mine and see if he can come up with any property listings."

***

Suzanna fixed herself another coffee and decided to take a look around. She didn't know if Edgar would come, or even if that was why she had really been brought here. She decided that the best thing to do was to become as familiar as possible with her situation. She thought she remembered her way to the spa and went to find the elevator that led to the underground tunnel to it. None of the elevators seemed to be operational, so she looked for the stairwell. She found it, but the door that should lead down to the tunnel was locked. She could only go up. All the doors to the upper floors appeared to be locked as well, until she came to the top.

The top floor was a glassed-in sunroom with a narrow pool that was only five feet deep. She was surprised to find it filled. She was definitely not alone here. Walking through the sunroom, she exited the other side and discovered the elevator there to be working. She pushed the spa level, then changed her mind and pushed the button for the room where they had stayed before. She thought it was four but pushed five as well. The elevator stopped, but the doors did not open and so she went down to four. The response was the same. On three, the doors finally opened, and she stepped into a hall with five rooms, all facing the lake, while the other looked down on the ski lift. As she looked down the hallway, she noted that one of the doors was open a few inches.

Suddenly nervous, she rummaged through her purse, looking for something that she could use as a weapon. It was between a pen and a pair of tweezers. Not helpful. She stood, staring at the open door, then reached up and pulled the curved clip from her hair. It was only about the length of her pen, but it had a point that she had stabbed her scalp with more than once. It was also diamond studded and would leave some serious scratches no matter how she used it. Ironically, it had been a gift from Edgar on their fortieth wedding anniversary. It was beautiful, she thought, as she looked at the diamonds, interspersed with pink rubies. She had worn it to the party, but now she gripped it in her hand as she walked to the door.

Carefully, she peered inside the room and slowly opened the door until she could enter. "Is anyone here?" she called, tentatively. There was no answer. Then she saw a familiar bag beside the bed. She walked over to it and found it to be her own overnight bag that she had left at the chalet. It had been repacked with a few changes of clothes and her jewelry box.

She went into the bath and discovered new toiletries, all her favorites. "Edgar?" she called? "Edgar?" He must have sent someone to the chalet when he heard she was here. That was the only explanation. No one else would have known about which toiletries she liked. He must be coming, she thought, sitting on the bed. Why was she not given a note or told about the room though? She very well could have sat up all night in the main lodge, waiting.

She noticed a room key sitting on a towel, folded beside the pillows on the bed. The towel, the spa, she thought. Looking through her bag, she found her swim suite, then she picked up the towel and key and made her way back to the elevator. She pushed the button for the spa and walked through the tunnel. It had plexiglass walls that allowed you to see the natural rock of the mountain behind. Overhead had been left rough, and the floor was overlaid with a non-slip, textured, waterproof carpeting, patterned to blend in with the surrounding stone and spotlights highlighted landscapes, hung along the walls.

When she came to the entrance of the spa, she paused, then punched in the key code from the back of her room key. The door slid open. It appeared to be empty. Not much had changed in over thirty years.

She checked to see if any saunas were occupied. Someone had to have been here recently, probably the same person who collected her clothes and bought the toiletries. She walked to the water cooler and poured a glass of rose water, then took it to sit by the full-length windows looking out onto the Italian side of the lake. The lake itself was thought to have magical rejuvenating powers and was known by several names, depending on how far back you went in history or which side of the border you were on. She sat staring, hoping Edgar would come.

It was nearly an hour later before she heard the door open. She sat still, feeling suddenly very vulnerable, as she listened to the approaching footsteps. It wasn't Edgar.

"You really should have stayed at home, Suzanna.".

Suzanna turned and stared at the woman standing before her.

"Who are you?"

"That is need to know, and you don't. The real question is, what should I do with you?"

"Where is Edgar?"

"He's somewhere safe and sound. If you had arrived a few days sooner, you may even have met."

"Where is he and who are you?"

"My husband attended Edgar's final treatment. Perhaps we'll have you join him, but I hate to waste the space."

"Why won't you answer me? Who are you? Who is your husband? Where is Edgar?"

"My, my, aren't you the curious one. I'm the one who gets to decide your life. Will it continue or will it not? In the meantime, I need to get some samples from you to help me decide."

"Don't touch me!" Suzanna said, getting up and edging her way toward the exit.

The woman smiled. "It won't open for you. I'm the one in control here. You do have a choice though. You can do this the easy way and give me the samples yourself, then relax and enjoy the services. Our AI assistants are quite good. I'll give you the sample list and kit to take them, or if you choose to not cooperate, I can take them myself. This stun gun has a fifteen-meter range, and its affects are most uncomfortable."

"Why did you bring me here?"

"You ask too many questions," the woman replied and pulled the trigger. Suzanna stumbled back into a chair, unable to move, while the woman came closer and injected a hypodermic into her armpit.

"Fortunately for you, your husband still holds some sway with certain people. Unfortunately for you, he's not currently in a state to argue if you don't prove to have any usefulness. In fact, if I had my say, neither of you would still be in the picture. I can be patient though. Soon enough I will be the one who has all the say," she said, smiling, as she opened Suzanna's mouth and withdrew the first sample of cells.

France

Carl had asked Chantel to meet him in Stockholm for the AI conference, and she was thrilled. If only he didn't still carry feelings for this Laura. She wondered if there was any way to help along Laura's relationship with Mathias. No, she didn't want to risk spending any unneeded time around either one of them. She had done what she came to do, deliver the painting, and spend time with her cousins, who all believed that she now worked in Switzerland.

It was only her mother and younger brother who moved with her to Sweden. Keeping the location of the move secret had been part of the contract. When he turned eighteen next month, her brother, Markus, who had been training alongside the lab techs, was promised a position.

She had to confess, it was a strange situation, but they were happy there. When they lived in Paris, they were poor. Her mother had never learned another language, and that kept her career choices to a minimum. She had been a happy housewife and mother, until Chantel's father died. Then, both her mother and brother depended on Chantel. Now they had a nice home in the nearest town, and Chantel had a private apartment at the labs. Soon, her brother would move there as well, and her mother had been given the option of living alone in town or having an apartment of her own on the campus. She still couldn't get over the size of the complex. It was like their own private city. She had never felt luckier than she did every day since they had met, and he saved her from the wrath of Dr. Hisdak.

No, she would drop by again, just as he had asked, and say that she needed to get back to Switzerland.

***

Tony couldn't stop pacing. The police had not discovered anything at Laura's and simply wrote it off to vandals. There was still no sign of Mathias either. Yes, he frequently left for long periods of time on mysterious trips, but he never just vanished without letting Tony know.

Whoever was in the wine cellar had to be responsible for his disappearance. If only they could tell the police, but for reasons related to his family, he knew that no matter what, Mathias would not want the police involved. Not that Tony had much faith in them anyway.

Tonight, Tony's wife had asked him to come stay with her and the kids at her parents, and Laura was going to stay at

Tony's, in Mathias room. Hopefully, things would stay smooth with his wife's family long enough for all of this to be sorted. Tony didn't feel it was any safer for Laura to be alone in the chateau than at her own home, and she still stubbornly refused to tell her family about the incidents.

He heard her pull up, just as he zipped his duffle bag and went to open the door.

"Welcome."

"I really don't know how to thank you."

"Just be safe. My father is just up the lane. He knows you're here and may come around to do a security check. So, if you see the beam of a flashlight in the window, don't freak out. If it's not him, the dogs will let you know."

"Tony?"

"I don't know. I don't think there's anything we can do. I have a feeling his family is involved. I don't think they'd hurt him. Make his life hell, yes, but I have to believe he's okay."

"Why would they be in my cellar?"

"Maybe they tracked him to you and realized he would be there and decided it was a perfect place for an ambush to keep him out of their way."

"What do you know that he won't tell me?"

"Nothing. He doesn't tell me anything either, but I know Mathias, and I remember his father and brothers. He doesn't tell us for our own safety. We have to trust that."

"What if they have hurt him?"

"Look, Laura, I know how you feel. I feel the same. I'll be back by tomorrow to finish helping you get the cellar back in order," Tony said, as he hefted his bag over his shoulder and headed out. "Help yourself to whatever you find. The kitchen is decently stocked, and I changed out the sheets and towels," he added.

Laura rolled her suitcase to the bedroom and then went to the living room and sat to watch television. Her mind wouldn't rest though.

She had noticed disturbances in the cellar before Mathias came back. There had to be something behind the wall that made it warmer, something that was making the noise. There had to be a secret door somewhere. Did Mathias find it? And what could his family have to do with it?

She started thinking again of the stories her great-grandfather had repeated from his friend. She felt more than ever now that they were more than just stories.

Scotland

Simon was furious and Josephine was scared. She had come up with a plan, but in order to execute it, she would be putting herself in mortal danger. It wasn't that Simon would kill her. No, he would do far worse. She shuddered as she thought about the woman she had met at the mental institute.

When he first arrived, she told him that the girls were out taking photos. He had gone to look for them but didn't find them. When he returned, he yelled at her for not keeping better tabs on them and questioned her about when they had received their last injections. She managed to calm him down, but he seemed more agitated than usual. When they didn't return by evening, she would need to be gone too.

She went to the grocer and bought both Simon and the girls favorites, making sure to talk about the special birthday dinner she was having for her daughters and to welcome her husband back from a long business trip. The cameras in the drive would pick her up coming home but not leaving. She fixed two glasses of his favorite, Glinlivet scotch, one with a special additive and took them into the study where Simon was waiting for her.

All the plans for the girls had been gone over at the meeting. Simon planned to take them back with him Thursday. He said he had already decided on the donor for the first impregnation. She asked him who, but he only smiled and suggested that they take advantage of the time alone before the girls return. His mood had changed, as it frequently did, between anger and lust. She could take advantage of this. She only prayed that the sedative would kick in before things could go too far.

Fortunately, Simon drank quickly. He'd just gotten his shoes off when he passed out. Josephine finished undressing him and used the handcuffs, he liked to use on her, to lock him to the bed frame. Next, she put on a wig, colored contacts, and glasses. Then she repacked Simon's suitcase, including both the passport he had come with and those that he kept in the safe. She took hers as well. She also took the crypto links, mobile phones, car keys and laptop.

She carefully avoided the cameras, as she hauled the baggage to the trail, and then she hurried into town where she caught a bus to the train station.

She would take the train to the airport, buy a ticket to Switzerland, then take the train to Portsmouth and a ferry to Calais. Then she would get another bus and ferry to Sweden. It wouldn't be what Simon expected. She hoped she might get an opportunity to meet up with the girls, but that would be risky. The most important thing was for Simon not to find them.

As her train pulled away from the station, she breathed a sigh of relief and smiled, as she thought of the humiliating position she had left Simon in.

Chapter 22

Switzerland: June 7th

Margot woke suddenly and noticed Rosie, who was still sharing her room, sitting by the window, getting dressed in the dark. The bedside clock read 4:44.

"Don't turn the light on," Rosie whispered. "I don't want her to know anyone else is awake."

"Who? Victoria?" Margot asked.

"She's outside, on her phone. I'll be back," Rosie said.

Margot pulled on her clothes and went to the window to see if Victoria was in sight. She caught a glimpse of movement in the trees. Silently, she pushed up the window, hoping to hear something, but all she heard were a few early birds chirping away in the tall surrounding firs.

She wondered if she should go outside herself, but opted to wait, watch, and listen. If they came back the same way the shadow disappeared, she was in perfect position.

It was nearly half an hour before she saw another shadow come from the trees. This one seemed to be hurrying. She didn't see another, but she heard the front door open and went into the living room. Rosie hurried towards her. Magdeline, Soren and Sophie had heard her come in too and came to see what was going on.

"They're here," Rosie said.

"Who?" they all asked.

"The Chinese doctors. They're in a cabin further down the hill. Victoria is meeting with them."

"We need to let Shane and Dave know," Soren said, heading towards the door.

"No, wait!" Rosie said. "We don't want her to know we know. She'll be back soon."

"Rosie is right. We should all get back to bed," Magdeline said. "Then you go over, as normal, and tell them," she said to Soren.

A minute later, they were back in their rooms, with all lights out.

Ten minutes later, Victoria crept back in and started a pot of coffee. She didn't want to do what they asked her to do, but what choice did she have? They had showed her live footage of her family. She wasn't going to kill anyone.

She looked at the herbs they had given her to add to the coffee. She thought about how her parents always told her not to worry about them, but to grab her freedom. She added two doses worth of the herbs. Ten minutes later she poured herself a large mug, sat on the couch, and drank. She could feel the toxin spreading through her limbs, until her entire body felt numb. Everything seemed to spin, as she lay back on the couch and closed her eyes. She could hear the pulse of her heartrate slowing. Her breathing slowed as well, and she felt nothing but the slight tingling of nerves in her toes and fingertips.

***

Lidia woke up with a start and looked at the time. It was 5:50. She may as well get up and put the coffee on. She pulled on shorts and a tank top and clipped her hair back.

Dave was still snoring away on the couch. She smiled. Something was nagging at the back of her mind. They had gone through all of Suzanna's things yesterday and she knew that one of her bags and some jewels she had seen her wear were missing. She couldn't be sure about clothes, as Suzanna had so many.

Could she have planned to disappear in advance? Maybe she had hidden the bag in her car, and that was the real reason she insisted on taking it rather than Dave's rental. Her toiletries all seemed to have been left, but she may

have packed another set. Lidia wished she knew. Had
Suzanna known where Edgar was and plotted an elaborate
scheme to meet him here, or had she been tricked herself
and kidnapped? Her phone had been off and the message
box full for two days now. A phone was easily replaceable
and the first thing you would get rid of if you didn't want to
be tracked. Lidia's gut told her that wasn't the case. She
had felt from the first that Suzanna could be in danger.

Dave stretched and rose from the couch, sniffing the air
like a bear coming out of hibernation.

"Morning," Lidia said.

"Morning Yarnok," he said with a wink. "It smells good. To
what do I owe the honor of this wake-up call?"

She knew he was teasing her, and a couple of witty
replies stuck on her tongue. She needed to be serious. She
pulled out some mugs for everyone, then set out the
creamers and sugar.

He moved to sit at the counter, watching her.

"I really think she's in danger."

"Okay."

"We need to talk to our host and get a list of the guests, find
out who she left with."

"I agree, but we also have to try and get up to the spa,
where just maybe, Shane's wife and son are. I also have
another meeting with Sarah Martinson. Jack is still missing,
and no one has heard from Nick or Larry since they
decided to check out an address up the road where they
lost track of Simon's thug. Sophie's aunt, Jacks parents, are
alone in Scotland where they spotted Simon, who is likely
behind the disappearance of both Jack and Sophie's
parents. Oh, and let us not forget the mysterious, Victoria,
and the half animal, half human atrocities that the dead,
but not dead, Prof. Crabben seems to be a part of. The same
Prof. Crabben that we are going to question Mrs. Martinson
about. And so, I have come full circle," Dave concluded,

shocked that Lidia hadn't interrupted. "Sorry," he added, "I know you two became close, but Suzanna Morgan doesn't rank as high on my priority list."

"It's all connected. They are all connected."

"I know. Remember, I'm the one who said that first. They're not only connected, but they're all related."

"I need to be doing something more than making coffee. I'm going for a walk," Lidia said, taking her coffee outside.

Dave thought about following her, but was stopped, as Daniel hurried over to greet him, and Shane followed sleepily behind.

"Thanks for making the coffee."

"I didn't. That was Lidia. She's really worried about Mrs. Morgan."

"So am I," Claire said, as she stepped out of the bedroom. "Maybe there's still a sisterly connection between us. I don't know, but I had nightmares about her last night. There are things missing from her room. They seem like items that someone else would have put together for her. Suzanna wouldn't leave this, especially if she was planning to meet Edgar."

"A keychain?" Dave asked.

"Not just a keychain. Look at it closely."

"It has a poem engraved on..." Dave started at a frantic knocking on the door.

Shane was pouring milk for Daniel as Lidia opened the door and Soren rushed in. "It's Victoria! We think she's dead."

"Daniel, wait here," Shane said.

"I'll stay with Daniel," Claire said.

"Actually, everyone should come. We should stay together. Daniel, can you keep Jeremy occupied?" Soren asked.

Daniel nodded. Shane took his hand, and they all went over.

"She's not dead," Magdeline said, as soon as they entered.

Everyone looked at Victoria, who lay on the couch, unmoving and very pale. Daniel broke free of Shane and went to Jeremy, who was attached to Sophie's leg.

"Why don't you two go play in our room? You heard Magdeline. She'll be okay," Sophie said to Jeremy, stroking his cheek.

"I'll teach you a new game," Daniel said, and the boys went into the bedroom.

"This," Magdeline said, lifting up the herb packet, "is a potent neurotoxin. She put it in the coffee."

Rosie picked up the narrative. "I heard her earlier this morning. She was on her phone, and I followed her down the hill to another cabin where she met with some Chinese doctors. I recognized one of them. He used to come to the children's home. I couldn't hear anything they were talking about, but I did hear what she said on the phone. She was speaking in Chinese. She was insisting on seeing her family. I saw through the window that she was looking at a computer screen. I don't know what was on it, but it may have been video of her family. Then they moved out of view, and I came back up here."

"It sounds like they gave her the herbs to give to us. So, why take them herself? Wouldn't that put her family at risk?"

"Maybe," Margot started, "She didn't want anyone hurt and taking herself out of the picture seemed like the only choice."

"You think she meant to kill herself?" Shane asked.

"I don't know. I know that none of you trusted her, but I don't think she would ever hurt anyone. I don't think she would have wanted to live with herself if she did. She was scared. She may have been as scared of herself as anyone. Think about it. She was sure that the ballad contained some kind of trigger."

"Jonathan's letter warned us about triggers," Magdeline said.

"I think she gave us an opportunity," Dave said.

"For what?" Lidia asked.

"What are you thinking, Dave?" asked Shane.

"I'm thinking that we should call for an ambulance. Not for Victoria, but for whichever of us wants to volunteer. They'll expect to see that. They may even be planning to come up here and find us themselves. It's still early though, so we can get ahead of the game. We should call and say there are several people ill and two unconscious. Sophie and Shane should take Victoria, with Margot and the boys, Claire and Rosie too."

"One of us should go with her too. She'll still need a doctor," Magdeline said.

"Okay," Dave said, "and the rest of us play victims."

"If they're watching, they won't buy it, unless we all play unconscious. It would be too hard to fake. If it's what I think it is, it numbs all your nerves. It's an immobilizer. We wouldn't be able to move our limbs," Magdeline said.

"We'd be paralyzed?" Claire asked.

"Not exactly. If it paralyzed, she would be dead. Think of it as when you go to the dentist, and they numb your mouth. You aren't paralyzed. If you try to eat and drink though, there's a good chance you'll wind up dripping the drink from your mouth and or, biting your tongue, because you lack feeling."

"I guess, I can volunteer to be unconscious," Lidia said.

"I would probably be a good candidate too. Then I can listen to what is happening at the hospital," Soren said.

"I can play the part as well," Dave said.

"Soren, you should come with us," Magdeline said, worried.

"I'm the translator Maggie, unless Lidia's German is better than Dave's," Soren said.

"Then I should go too," Rosie said.

"No. You've put yourself in enough danger," Claire said.

"Claire is right, and if I'm right, we need to get going," Dave said. "Soren, you be the one to not have coffee this morning. Let Lidia and I play the victims. You call for the medics and come with us to the hospital. That way you're less vulnerable and more useful to us both as a translator and a doctor."

"Okay, let's go," Shane said. "I'll get her to the car, while you get the boys," he said to Claire, Rosie, Magdeline and Sophie.

"You won't be able to fake unconsciousness when the medics come unless you take something. I have some of the sedative I gave Victoria before," Magdeline said, hurrying to get it. "I'll inject it under your arms, so the mark won't be obvious."

Fifteen minutes later, Shane had taken the boys and women in his SUV from next door, and the medics arrived. Soren explained that he was also a doctor and thought it might be some kind of food poisoning. He said that they had just been having morning coffee when they felt dizzy and passed out.

He had dumped the coffee made by Victoria, the herbs in it wouldn't match the symptoms. There was no way for Dave and Lidia to fake slowing their heartrates.

"Did you have any?" the medics asked Soren.

"No, I was going to make a pot and fix breakfast. They were staying next door and brought theirs over from there."

"Okay, their vitals are good," the medic said, but we need to get them to the hospital and do CT scans."

Another five minutes later, the ambulances left, and Soren followed behind. He thought that he saw movement in the trees. The neighbors on the other side were watching from their drive. It was when they passed the check-in that he noted two other cars pulling out and following behind him.

***

As they pulled onto the main road, both Sophie and Margot's phones buzzed with messages from Larry.

Nick was driving, following the same man from before. They would call later but wanted to explain why they hadn't been in contact.

Yesterday they hiked up to stake out a property they believed the man they followed was at. They confirmed it when they saw the Alfa Romeo, but after a while, both were ninety percent sure that Jack wasn't there. When they hiked back down to the road, their car had been towed and their phone batteries dead. They got a room for the night, but the phone chargers were in the car, and all the phone numbers were stored on their dead phones. They had just gotten the car released and were topping off the fuel, when they saw the man in a different car.

"I'm just glad they're both okay," Shane said, "and I know you must both be relieved," he said to Sophie and Margot.

"Do you want us to send them an update?" Margot asked.

"I don't want Nick to know and be distracted," Sophie said.

"There isn't really anything they can do. Let's just pray that we both find who we're looking for."

"You mean Mommy," Daniel said.

"And Uncle Jack," Jeremy added.

"Yes," Sophie said to Jeremy, then looked at Daniel and tried to give him a reassuring smile. She knew what it was like to have a parent vanish and could only imagine how he must feel.

Half an hour later, Shane turned up the road to the village that lay below the spa of Lake Genevieve. Rosie, Sophie, and Claire took the boys into town for breakfast, while he took Magdeline and Victoria to find a motel. It was far too early to check in, but by paying for the previous day, they were able to get into a room and reserve a few more for the others.

Magdeline said Victoria's vitals were stable, but she thought it could be several hours before she regained consciousness.

Then, after stopping back at the restaurant, Shane and Margot continued up toward the spa.

***

Suzanna stared out over the lake. She had woken up in her room, expecting to be locked in. She was surprised when the door opened easily, but not surprised when she found all the routes to the main level and exits blocked.

Now, she was on the balcony beside the spa and a small kitchen, where she had been able to order an omelet, prepared by an AI, named Andi.

Her coffee had just arrived when she thought she heard a car. Dashing out, ignoring Andi's calls, she hurried to the elevator and back to the third floor, where she could see out front.

She could hardly believe it! There was someone here, and she had never been so happy to see Shane McDougle! Now, if she could just get him to see her. She knew the upper halls were lined with privacy glass. All they would see was dark unless she could find something to break it with. She took a metal chair from her room and rammed it at the window. It didn't break, she saw Shane and the woman he was with look up. She was certain the building was soundproof, but maybe they had heard the reverberation. She kept banging into the window and calling Shane's name, as she watched him try the entry.

Her arms were getting tired and there wasn't even a crack in the window. That's when she hurried out to the balcony. She wasn't sure if her voice could carry enough, but she had to try. Somehow, she had to let them know she was there.

"It stopped," Margot said, but I'm sure I heard something."

"Me too," Shane said. "If it's sound proofed, then…"

"There's something there, on the chair inside," Margot said. "It looks like a scarf."

Shane looked to where she pointed. "Someone is definitely here. Patricia likes scarves," Shane added.

"I'll go look for another entrance, or a balcony," Margot said.

"Wait up! We need to stick together. Larry will kill me if I don't stick to you like glue. This place is huge! I'm calling Magdeline. Maybe she can find out more from her parents."

After calling Magdeline, Shane dialed Henri Saville, who said he was near enough and would call the town maintenance to request emergency entry assistance for himself.

"He's about an hour out, but he thinks he can have someone let us in, once he arrives, on the basis of an ongoing border investigation. He usually works the French border, but the investigation apparently encompasses all of the Swiss border."

Saville called back ten minutes later to tell them that an Italian officer with the Carabinieri, was on his way up. He would join them himself as well, but the Italian officer could be there in half the time and Henri had worked with him before. He sent his photo and name to Shane's phone.

"I know that you must be really anxious to find out if Patricia is here," Margot said.

"Anxious would be a good word for it," Shane replied, as they looked at a map posted by one of the buildings. "This place is even bigger than it looks. Apparently, there are tunnels that go through the mountainside. The spa itself is underground, but open onto the lake. They basically carved a resort into the mountain and added a few buildings."

"It is impressive. What is this?" she asked, pointing to a point on the far end of the diagram. "I don't see it."

"I don't think you're supposed to. It's probably a high-end wing for the rich to hide away," Shane said, trying to take it all in. "We know someone has been in there, and it connects to this structure and that one. Actually, it looks like a full circle, if I'm reading this right. You can take a tunnel from the spa level, under the parking, to the gift shop and ski rental. Let's check over there and see if there is any sign of life," Shane said, pointing to a glass fronted section.

Suzanna couldn't yell anymore. She was too center of the complex for her voice to go anywhere except out across the lake. No one but the birds would hear her.

She took a drink of water and went to look out the window again. To her surprise, the SUV was still parked below. She couldn't see where Shane had gone, but at least he was still here. That meant he must have some reason to believe she was here, but how could he have even thought to look here? She wondered, but it didn't matter. All that mattered is that she got out before that woman returned.

Southern France

Mel looked at the test results with distain. There was so much elimination that should have taken place long ago. The men who had run things were too soft and filled with altruistic dreams of nobody ever having to die again. Ridiculous!

Adam entered the lab. "So, my queen, what have you been up to today?" he asked, putting his arms around Mel. He considered how easy it would be to snap her fine boned neck, and he wondered what thoughts she had to get rid of him.

Yes, they were very much alike, perfectly suited.

Adam was excited about his acquisition of Mathias. He hadn't let Mel in on that yet. He enjoyed his little secrets.

"I think we need to eliminate the Morgans," Mel whispered in his ear. "We have the funding, and Mrs. Morgan is the only obstacle to the rest. They're not a strong part of the lineage."

"That may be, but there are still others who disagree. For now, they all stay alive."

"It's your father, isn't it?"

"I haven't heard from him or Leona in more than three years. You know that. No, it's Meschner's missing boys I want out of the way. They have too much tendency to grow consciences. Their genes, however, will be very useful and more resilient than those harvested at Scangentech or the CDC. Though the Chinese do seem to have fewer qualms about who they harvest from and just how, shall I say, fresh, their samples are."

"I don't trust the O'Hare's," Mel said, turning in his arms, to look him in the eyes.

"What can they do? Think about all we have to hold them."

"True, but what about Josephine?"

"Simon has his own ways to keep her in check. Let him. She doesn't even know about this location. Soon, Simon will bring the girls. Their lineage is the strongest on the European side. Just imagine, Mel. Soon, very soon, our dreams will come true."

"What about the O'Hare's daughter, not to mention Alice and the others. Why are they allowed to run around loose?"

"Simon made that bargain. You know that Mel. What has gotten into you today?" he asked, annoyed.

"I'm tired of waiting on you to take control," she answered, pulling away from him.

"Patience. The next generation has started. It won't be much longer before we can eliminate the old. We need to let the children develop. When we get to the next phase, we can start to phase out those of the previous generation who stand in our way. To do it now would put the children at risk, our children would be at risk. You don't want that. Do you Mel?" Adam said, stroking his hand down her cheek and continuing down her neck. Such fine bones, he thought.

"Adam is back," Nigel told Lily, "Svend thinks we need to move the children this week."

"Where? Who will care for them? How do we get them out?"

"We have a plan. However, it is dangerous, very dangerous."

"Yes?"

"You remember the earthquake, November 2019?"

"Yes."

"Several new active fault lines have been discovered since, and Svend believes we can utilize the thermal energy in the caves to trigger an earthquake. Earthquakes can be stimulated by a sudden release of stored energy. Right now, the project is harnessing and storing the released energy, but if we block it, it will build up. Just doing that though, will take too long. However, if we cut off the power, giving us dark cover, and at the same time redirect the power stored at the epicenter, which would be the thermal pools, we should be able to cause a sizable enough quake to collapse the passage and area around the pools. The trick is getting out, but making it appear as if you didn't. We'll do it at night, and you'll need to take the children out just before we cut the power and trigger the quake."

"What about you?"

"I can't leave Svend to do this alone. The hope is that enough damage will occur that missing people will simply be assumed dead. My biggest qualm is that many people likely will die. My biggest fear is, that the Hisdaks escape. I don't understand enough, but Svend thinks it's a reasonable option and that he and I can get out as well."

"Wouldn't it be easier to just kill Adam and Mel? I know it sounds terrible," Lily said, "but why should everyone else's life be at risk?"

"If we did that, then not only are we murderers, but fugitives. Simon and others would know we were behind it, and Sophie would be in even more danger. At least with the earthquake, everyone has a chance, and we can disappear with the children. Even Simon won't look for us if he thinks we're buried under tons of rock. He'd probably be relieved to have us gone."

"How do you get out? Where do we go, and how do we find each other?"

"We're still working on that. I just wanted you to know what we are planning. Look, Lily, we have two choices. We can either let them win, or we can fight. There are no guarantees. Life doesn't come with guarantees, but if we don't take a chance, then what would life be worth? Can you imagine what the world would become? What would become of the children?"

"You're right. I know. It just scares me to think of losing you."

"You won't lose me. No matter what happens, I'll always be with you, here," he said, touching his heart.

"I love you, Nigel."

Switzerland

Soren hung up his phone call to Rosie. She had given him more details about what she saw at the cabin, as well as the cabin number, which he passed on to Dave, who was now fine and awaiting doctor's release.

"You and Lidia are the trained police. Why don't you let me talk to Mrs. Martinson, while you check out the Chinese?" Soren suggested.

"That might not be a bad idea, but we won't say you're meeting her instead of me. I'll call and say I'm in the hospital for food poisoning and ask her a few questions over the phone. You take the car and just happen to be in the area and see if she's free. She should be, as I will have just cancelled. Maybe suggest having lunch up at the lodge where Ana works. In fact, go all in. Show her the picture of Professor Crabben. I'd like to know how she reacts to him being alive. Before you go, would you please go check on Lidia for me?"

"Of course."

"Thanks."

Soren walked down the hall to the room they had taken Lidia to. He was almost there when he saw the same man who had been following them from the chalet, dressed as a doctor, leaving her room. Soren hurried down the hall and into the room, where he found Lidia unconscious. Soren pushed the call button and checked her pulse, as a nurse entered.

"Get a doctor in here and call security. She's been drugged by a Chinese man, dressed as a doctor."

"What? Who are you?"

"Oh hell, try to revive her!" Soren shouted at the nurse, as he rushed out and back to Dave's room.

"I don't think so!" Soren shouted at the two men trying to hold Dave down. Soren picked up a chair and hit one of the men over the head, knocking him to the ground, while the other, who held the needle, rushed at Soren, jabbing him in the shoulder. Dave grabbed the man from behind, but the one Soren had knocked down was back up and shoved

Soren into Dave. Dave caught Soren just in time and
managed to maneuver him onto the bed and follow the
men into the hall. They disappeared into the stairwell, and
he hurried after them, grabbing a nurse, on the way, to
send to Soren.

They were only on the second floor, and the men were
fast. Dave burst out of the emergency exit just in time to
see them leave in a blue sports car. Noting the license plate,
he hurried back in to call Shane.

When he got back to the hospital room to get his phone, a
crash cart was being wheeled in.

Oh, dear God, no! He thought and turned to hurry down
the hall to find Lidia. He was met with the same scene as
the room where he had left Soren. He couldn't even breath.

Then he hurried to the nurse's station and tried to explain
that he needed to call the police. Finally, a doctor, who
spoke English arrived, and Dave was able to explain what
happened, and the police were called.

An hour later, Dave had given his statement, minus the
information that he knew about the men who attacked
them. He gave a good description, but claimed he had no
idea why someone would want to kill them, unless it was to
do with a previous investigation he and Lidia worked on.
Perhaps someone from Seattle with a grudge had followed
them, but he couldn't think who. He denied that he was
currently involved in any investigation and stated that he
and Lidia were on vacation, visiting friends.

Fortunately, both Soren and Lidia were now listed in
stable condition, while the doctors tried to figure out what
they were injected with.

"Just to get this all straight," the officer said to Dave, "both
you and your friend, Ms. Yarnok, are here on vacation
visiting the other man. You were brought to the hospital
after passing out from food poisoning. According to a
nurse, the man…?"

"Soren," Dave filled in.

"He found your friend, Ms. Yarnok, unconscious and told the nurse to call security for a Chinese man dressed as a doctor. Then he went to your room, where that same man and another were trying to inject you with whatever they had injected your friend with. Soren attacked the man holding you down and was injected by the other. They both fled and you followed, but they got away. Accurate?"

"As far as I know. Only Soren would know if it were the same man he saw in Lidia's room or a third."

"And you have no idea who they are or why they apparently tried to kill you?"

"No."

"All right, we'll check hospital camera footage and be in touch. One more thing."

"Yes?"

"What did you have this morning that could have caused the supposed food poisoning? Could there be a connection?"

"I doubt it. All we had was some instant coffee packets left over from a previous hotel stay."

"Which hotel?"

"I'm afraid I can't be sure. I always save those little packets with the cream and sugar they leave in the rooms and whatever coffee packets I don't use during my stay. I'm afraid I can't even be certain how long I've had these, much less where from. I keep them standard in my luggage."

"I see. And you and Ms. Yarnok used to work together in the police, but have since both turned to private detective work?"

"Correct."

"All right then, please call if you think of anything else," the officer said, handing Dave his card. "I suggest you stay in the vicinity but change your lodging. We'll be back to question your friends later."

Dave sighed and went to find his phone. Then he dialed Mrs. Martinson. After hanging up with her, he saw that Shane had left him a message.

Then he checked on Soren, verified that he would be okay, and called Magdeline. He also sent a message to Saville, who promised to send out a watch to the border crossings. Then he went to check on Lidia.

"She's still not conscious," the doctor told him.

"She's going to be all right though?"

"She's stable, but honestly, until we figure out what they were given, I can't say. She's smaller, so if they gave her the same dose, it will take longer for the effects to wear off. I have an IV going, but it's really just wait and see when she wakes up."

"Can I sit with her?"

The doctor nodded and stepped aside for Dave to enter. He'd never seen Lidia look weak before. She was nearly as pale as Victoria. He sat in the chair beside her bed, but he couldn't think of anything to say. So, he just took her hand and held it.

***

Shane was relieved to see the Carabinieri arrive. Pietro got out with his partner, Sasha, and they all introduced themselves while Shane tried to explain, without saying too much. Fortunately, Pietro's English was excellent, and he didn't ask too many questions, as he assumed it was a part of the already ongoing investigation with Saville.

As soon as the front door was open, he started work on the doors from the stairwells onto the upper floors. They would go together, floor by floor, as neither Shane nor Margot could be certain if it was the second, third or fourth floor the sound had come from.

Shane could hear his heart pounding in his ears, as they raced up to the third floor.

Suzanna heard them coming. She had been watching as the Carabinieri pulled up and was waiting when they arrived.

As soon as Shane saw her, his heart sank.

"Oh, thank God! Shane!" Suzanna said, going to them. "I was scared to death you would leave. How did you find me?"

"Is this the person you believed was smuggled in?" Pietro asked, an aura of surprise in his voice.

"She is just one of the people missing."

"Usually it is, pardon madam, but usually it is younger people that are taken," Pietro said. "Are there others with you?" he asked Suzanna.

Suzanna paused and looked at Shane. "I'm sorry, but I don't believe Patricia is here."

Pietro looked out the window, as Saville pulled up. Then he looked back to Shane.

"Patricia is my wife,"

"Ah, now I see more clearly your concern. Come," he said to Sasha, then turning back he said, "I will send Saville up."

A minute later, Henri Saville joined them in the hallway. Shane introduced him to Suzanna and Margot.

"I asked them to search the rest of the premises," Saville said.

"We can sit in here," Suzanna said, motioning to the room she had been in.

***

Larry and Nick had followed the man for hours, praying they wouldn't need to stop for fuel again. He led them up into the Alps, where he turned up a road marked as closed. They waited until he rounded a bend and then headed up themselves.

They were surprised to see the man speed back down past them a few minutes later, followed by a police car.

Larry was even more surprised when he saw Margot with Saville.

Saville pulled his weapon, then lowered it as the car slowed and he recognized Larry.

"What's going on? Margot, are you all right?" Larry asked, hurrying to her.

"Everything is fine. Was that the man you were following?"

"It was," Larry said, turning to Saville, who was staring at Nick. "Nick, meet Henri Saville. Henri, meet Nick Rafferty. Where is Shane?"

"Upstairs with a Mrs. Morgan," Saville said. "I don't suppose you know what happened this morning yet?"

"What happened? Are my wife and son all right?" Nick asked.

"As far as I know," Saville said and turned to Larry. "I think we all need to talk together and get on the same page. It's been a busy morning. Can you tell me who that was you were following up here?" Saville asked, as they made their way back inside the building and up to where Shane and Suzanna were.

"We think he may be involved in Jack's kidnapping."

"And this somehow all connects back to that crazy man that Dave and I were after in Canada?" Saville asked.

"It does," Larry said, "but why was he chased by Carabinieri?"

"When he saw us, he did a U-turn and sped off. That was suspicious, and I had called the Carabinieri. I'm working with them on the border case, and Shane needed to get inside. We're on the Italian border, so they came thinking this was part of the same case. People coming into Switzerland using stolen ID's," Saville said to Nick. "The biggest concern is that a lot of them are crossing against their will as modern-day sex slaves."

"I think they were a little surprised when they found Mrs. Morgan," Margot said.

When they joined Shane and Suzanna, everybody updated everybody else, including Saville, who at this point they needed to bring almost all in. They left out Victoria and human-animal genetic engineering, which wasn't something that Larry or Shane could even begin to explain.

Next, they decided that Nick would take Mrs. Morgan back into town to the motel, while Larry, Margot, Shane, and Henri, continued searching the complex.

Scotland

Anne knew that the house couldn't be too far from the trail if the girls had taken it to meet Sophie. So, she and Ben continued past the fork where they had stopped before and turned down in the direction they believed the house to be. Ben stopped at a patch to the side of the trail that looked like it had been recently traveled.

"It could just be animals," he said, "but let's try it. Give me your hand and watch your step Anne,"

They made their way down the narrow path, through a group of pine trees, and soon found themselves on an open vista, looking down on a large old brick home.

"That must be it," Anne said, "Maybe I should call Sheila and see if she knows who owns it."

"Ruff, ruff!"

Startled, Anne jumped, and Ben caught her just in time to prevent her from stumbling down the steep hillside.

They both turned and looked back at the trees, as two barking dogs hurried towards them.

"Finn!"

"Feather!"

They heard the voices of two girls, and Anne braced herself to see them, but when they came through the trees behind the dogs, neither girl looked anything like Sophie or Lily.

"Hi," the one girl said. "Are you lost?"

"No, are you…?" Anne started.

"We are definitely not lost. We live up the other fork of the trail," one of the girls said.

The dogs were now sniffing Anne and Ben's ankles.

"Don't worry, they won't bite. We don't usually see other people, at least not off the main trail. Where are you from?"

"Canada," Ben said, reaching down to pet one of the dogs. "A friend told us there was some good hiking and we like to explore, so we saw an opening off the trail and decided to check it out. I'm Ben."

"Callie," said the one girl. "And this is my sister, Tabetha."

"I'm Anne. I think you may know my niece, Sophie."

The girls stared at Anne for a few seconds, before Tabetha broke the silence. "They're gone," she said.

"Why are you here?" Callie asked, as she patted her leg to bring the dogs back over to them.

"We would never hurt Pollina or Amber. Sophie knew that. She's been worried because she hasn't heard from them, and you must have a different phone number," Anne said.

"Why are you here?" Callie asked again.

"Our son, Jack, is missing," Ben said, "and we think that Amber and Polina's parents have something to do with it. Have you seen anything odd here?"

Tabetha and Callie exchanged looks.

"The only one there is the man they called Simon," Tabetha said, "They didn't consider him their father."

"So, their mother took them somewhere?" Anne prodded.

"All we can say is that they're gone. Is Sophie with you?"

"No, she wasn't able to come."

"How do we know you are who you say?" Callie asked.

"Would you like to talk to Sophie. I could call her."

The girls nodded.

Switzerland

Sophie was so relieved to have Nick back, she put her phone on silent while Jeremy was down for his nap. She and Nick were just curling up on the couch to catch up, when she saw Anne's name on her screen.

"I'd better take this," Sophie said, grudgingly pulling herself from Nick to pick up the call. She was surprised when Anne asked to put the call on video, and she saw Callie and Tabetha.

They all talked and caught each other up until Jeremy woke up. He wanted to see everyone too and let Ben and Anne know he was still helping look for where Uncle Jack went fishing.

"I wish I was there." Sophie said. "I don't like the idea of them confronting Simon, especially with Callie and Tabetha. It's dangerous. I'm sure if he's there, so are others."

"I'm sure you're right, but Ben won't let them put themselves in danger, and hopefully, the search at the spa will be fruitful. Shane, Larry, Margot, and Henri may find Jack and have him back tonight. Then one of them can go to Scotland for Simon."

"You're right. It's a bit ironic that they're going to Sweden. I wonder if Josephine went there too?"

"You mean, you wonder if she'll go to the lab there."

"She must know about it. I'm just still not sure I trust her," Sophie said. "It sounds like she helped them get away, but what if we're wrong and it's Josephine who is in control. She sends them to Sweden away from Simon, only to follow them and take them herself?"

"After everything we know about Simon, you don't really think that?"

"I don't know what I think sometimes, Nick. No, I don't trust Simon. What if Josephine finds Alice and Jonathan?"

"I think Jonathan can probably handle her."

"Probably. My mind is going on tangents. I'm concerned about Lidia. Soren called Magdeline, and Lidia's still unconscious. And what does that painting mean? Who is she?"

"Why don't you and I take Jeremy for some I-C-E-C-R-E-A-M? All we can do right now is wait and pray."

"Okay," Sophie conceded. "Jeremy, let daddy get your shoes on. We're going for a walk. I'll meet you out front. I want to tell the others where we're going and see if they want anything."

Rosie and Daniel joined them, while Claire went to sit with Magdeline and Victoria. Suzanna was also in their room, as it seemed the most neutral place to put her. Claire had been waiting for the right time to talk to Suzanna and didn't think that waiting longer would be any better. She also felt more comfortable with Magdeline there.

Suzanna looked up, as Magdeline opened the door to Claire.

"Hello, Suzanna," Claire said, walking over to sit in a chair across a table from her sister.

"I'm sorry, Claire. I don't even know where to start, but I am so very sorry for what we put you through."

"Sorry is a good place to start," Claire replied. "I'm glad you're okay. Believe it or not, I was worried when you disappeared."

Suzanna couldn't even look at Claire, as her eyes teared up.

The room was silent for several minutes. Claire had never seen Suzanna vulnerable. Even as children, Suzanna had been in charge. She realized Suzanna didn't know how to handle this, and eventually she stood and went to her sister. Claire put her hand on Suzanna's shoulder and said, "I forgive you."

***

Dave looked up anxiously, as the doctor entered and checked Lidia's vitals.

"We still aren't certain what it is they were given. Soren gave several blood samples and hopefully we'll find a match soon. It's hard to know how to counteract something when you don't know what it is."

"Shouldn't she be waking up on her own, like Soren?"

"Hopefully, but it depends on what it was and how much she received relative to body weight, and what affects it may have had on her organs. I'm going to draw more samples from her now to compare with Soren's. If you don't mind stepping out for a bit. Why don't you go down to our cafeteria? Soren has technically been released, and I sent him there to get something as well. Ask at the nurse's desk, and they'll give you a voucher."

***

Shane, Larry, and Margot joined the others at the motel a few hours later. They had not been able to search much of the complex, as they only had access codes and keys for the main doors and stairwells. The private wings, they hoped to have access to the next day.

They all figured out who would be in whose room. Then Larry went with Magdeline to pick up Dave and Soren.

Victoria was still unconscious, and Margot took Magdeline's place to watch over her.

Suzanna wanted to go to the hospital as well, but given everything else, she would wait. There was a lot of awkwardness between her and Claire, and Rosie pointedly avoided her, as did Sophie. Shane had more questions for her. So, they spoke privately while Claire, Rosie, Sophie, and Nick took the boys to a nearby park.

Meanwhile, Henri Saville would go with another agent to search the cabin where Rosie saw the Chinese men.

It had been an eventful day, and everyone was tired, but Dave opted to sleep in a chair in Lidia's room. He wanted to post a guard, but with hospital security on alert and a description of the men circulated, the police had not deemed it necessary.

"Come on Yarnok. Wake up. They found Mrs. Morgan and could really use your insight on her. You do realize, you've kept me from meeting with Mrs. Martinson. We've got too much going on here, Yarnok, to have you sleeping on the job," Dave said to Lidia. "I'll tell you what. I'll make you a deal. You wake up and I'll... You wake up and tell me. I need you to harass me into an epiphany. That's why we made such good partners back in Seattle. You needled me until my brain kicked in and came up with a reason for you to stop. Don't get me wrong, Shane and Larry are great, but only you know how to really move me, Yarnok. So, wake up. Pretty please."

Chapter 23

Scotland: June 8th

Callie and Tabetha watched the house and phoned Anne and Ben to let them know that they hadn't seen Simon, but both his and Josephine's cars were still in the drive.

Ben and Anne parked where they could watch the drive and waited. They had to get in today. The girls were leaving for Sweden tomorrow and they needed them as lookouts. They had promised Sophie and Nick not to confront Simon alone, but that didn't mean they would do nothing.

"You know, it's possible that Josephine left when Simon came back, so that she could go to Jack," Ben suggested.

"No, not unless she's going to let him go. I mean, you heard how she helped the girls escape from him," Anne said.

"Well, if that were the case, she's had plenty of time. They said they hadn't seen her since Monday."

"I wonder if she's all right." Anne said. "I mean, her car is there. Maybe when Simon discovered the girls were gone, he decided to get rid of her too."

"Too many maybes," Ben said. "I say we just go in. It could be another day before they finish searching the spa."

"What do you suppose he was doing at that house by the lake? I still can't figure out where I've seen it before."

"All of this is enough to make anyone crazy. Now I know what Nick goes through," Ben said, starting the engine.

"What are you doing, Ben?"

"I'm taking you back to the inn, and I'm going to throttle the truth out of Simon."

"You..."

"No! Don't try to stop me. For all I know, he was the one who almost killed you! I have the advantage of surprise, and he may not even recognize me. So, unless you have a better plan..."

"I do. I go with you!"

"I'm not risking that, Anne."

"No, you're not. I am! If you take me back, I'll just call a taxi and come right back behind you!"

Ben saw the resolve on Anne's face and turned up the drive.

Anne called the girls to let them know they were heading in.

Tabetha and Callie had a good view of the main hall, sitting rooms, and what Pollina and Amber told them was Josephine and Simon's bedroom. Callie held the phone and Tabetha took the binoculars.

They watched anxiously as Ben both rang the doorbell and pounded on the door. They waited for what felt like forever, but they saw no signs of movement in the house.

Ben picked up a stone to break a window.

"Wait!" Anne said. "Remember, Callie said that the girls came and went with a spare key. It's probably still here."

"Maybe I feel like breaking the window," Ben said.

"Maybe I do too, but we don't want to risk setting off an alarm. So, let's use this instead," she said, as she pulled a key out from under a potted plant.

They opened the door and cautiously moved inside. Then they heard the voice.

"Josephine! Josephine! I hear you! You won't get away with this!"

They followed the voice up the stairs and opened the door to a bedroom. They both covered their faces at the smell and the sight, as they stared at an outraged Simon, handcuffed, naked, on the bed in his own waste. They stared for a moment more, then went out to the hall and stared at each other.

"I guess we don't have to worry about Simon," Anne said, and for a moment they both burst into laughter.

"Let's search the house," Ben said, and Anne called Callie to fill them in on the situation, then she called Sophie to do the same.

They checked every room, then went back to the bedroom to interrogate Simon. It really was disgusting! Ben threw a quilt over him, while Simon raved like a rabid dog at them.

"You know, I think *we* have the upper hand here," Ben said. "So, tell me, where is our son?"

"Your son," Simon laughed "If you ever want to see your son again, I suggest you let me go."

"Where is he!" Anne demanded and glanced to a whip, hanging on the back of the door.

"You wouldn't dare! You'll never find him without me. So, what's more important," Simon attempted to reason.

Anne took the whip from the door and hit it hard against the bed frame.

"I never knew you were so sadistic. Maybe you have more of the genes than I thought. Perhaps I chose the wrong cousin."

Anne lashed the whip at the bed, and Simon wet the bed.

"Where is Jack!" Anne demanded and raised the whip again.

"Leave him, Anne," Ben said. "He's not worth it. We'll go to Switzerland and find Jack on our own. They can't be keeping him far from the lake."

Simon gaped at them. Could they really know? If so, why were they here? They couldn't know.

"If you thought he was in Switzerland, you wouldn't be here," Simon laughed.

"Come on Anne, we should be there when they find him."

"You can't leave me here!" Simon spit.

"Can't we? What if we were never here?" asked Anne.

"If you leave, you're murderers. At least I never killed anyone."

"Really?" asked Anne, "I've seen the files. The files you thought burned at the clinic in Quebec. All those innocent babies! You killed them! How many? Hundreds? Thousands? What for, so you could try to become immortal? Well, I hope you do live. I hope you live a long, long life, so that you can suffer the way they did, the way Sophie did, the way..." Anne turned away, tears streaming down her face as she remembered the images in the files, and all the surgeries Sophie went through, and all she was going through now.

Lily and Nigel had gone because of the evil Simon was part of, and no matter how much she knew she should, she felt no sympathy for him. She wondered what hell he had put Josephine and the children they raised through.

In the end, it was Ben who gave Simon a bottle of water. After all, he was no good to them dead.

Shane was looking for a solution as to what to do with Simon. The solution came in the form of the man Nick and Larry had followed and the Italian Carabinieri had caught. It turned out he was wanted for more than a few misdemeanors throughout Europe, and two felonies, and they were questioning him on the stolen passports and human smuggling.

After twenty-four hours in an Italian jail cell, he was ready to cut a deal, which included telling them everything he knew about Simon. Unfortunately, his knowledge, though more than sufficient to have Simon locked up, was far less than they had hoped.

Anne and Ben continued searching the house. Anne photographed, while Ben was on video with Larry, who told them to check specific things as he saw them. They took several files, but were surprised to not find a laptop, but there was a desktop. Larry called a computer expert from INTERPOL, who helped them get in. Once the computer was unlocked, Larry hacked in and copied all the files to his own computer.

Ben and Anne finished photographing and took another box of files to the car as the authorities arrived and arrested Simon on kidnapping charges. They hauled him out wrapped in the quilt Ben had thrown over him. He seemed almost possessed as he spit profanities at the police as well as Ben and Anne.

They would go to the police the next morning to make a brief statement, which Larry had prepared for them. Before they left the house though, they needed to delete any camera recording that would show when they had arrived. Larry directed them through this and then updated them on the search for Jack.

As it turned out, or at least according to his testimony, the man working for Simon didn't know Jack's actual location. He did tell them how to access the video footage of Jack from the lake house. He said that his responsibility was simply to monitor and supply. He took food and other items to the spa, but someone else was in charge of picking them up and delivering them to where Jack was being held.

Somewhere

The odor hit Jack almost at once, as it came through the vents. He put a towel over his face and turning the temperature down, went into the sauna.

He almost did pass out, but as it cooled, he revived and waited. About an hour later, they came for him. He listened as they looked for what they expected to be his inert body. Guessing that the air was likely safe now, he made his way out of the sauna and grabbed an arm from one of the gym machines he had dismantled in his radio building attempt.

There were two men, but with the element of surprise on his side, Jack was able to swing his weapon and neatly knocked one out, then the other. He tied them with the electrical cords of the machines and searched them, taking everything, minus a gum wrapper, from their pockets.

Then he walked out. The elevator doors were open, and he pushed the button for the ground floor. He kept his weapon at the ready, but when they opened, all he was greeted with was the fresh summer day. He saw a lone SUV parked nearby and sorted through what he had taken off the men, until he found the vehicle's keyless remote. "Fancy," he said to himself, as he got in, adjusted the seats and mirrors, and pulled away.

He didn't know where he was going, but it didn't matter. He was free. After he had gone a few miles, he saw a convenience store and pulled into the parking lot. Then he took out the phones he had taken off the men. Unfortunately, they were locked with a fingerprint requirement.

"Oh well," he said, as he opened one of the wallets. He went into the store, bought a cold drink, a sandwich, and a map. He also bought a cheap phone, SIM, and prepaid time, from a selection behind the counter.

He thought about asking where he was, but as he was driving a stolen vehicle and using a stolen credit card, he felt it best to not pull any unnecessary attention to himself. Fortunately, the woman behind the counter spoke English and simply took Jack for a tourist.

Back in the SUV, he plugged the phone into the USB and dialed one of the few numbers he actually had memorized, his mother.

Switzerland

The evening before, Henri had photographed everything at the cabin, but they hadn't left much behind. He considered calling a forensics team, but this wasn't really part of his official case. He had just led his superiors to believe it could be. He also knew Larry didn't want more people involved. Henri could understand that. He knew they had withheld information from him during the original investigation. He only knew what he did from going though files with Dave when they guarded Richter.

Richter's escape had haunted Henri, and even though he was limited, due to his official capacity and assignment, he wanted to do all he could to help.

He knew that they had a genetic scientist with them. So, Henri pocketed some hair samples. He would drop them off to Larry when they met at the spa.

Even with video footage of the men's faces from the hospital, there was no match in the INTERPOL database. It was likely they had used putty and implants to alter their appearance.

The registration office only had the name of a company that the cabin was registered under. They said it was part of the ten percent of accommodations leased year around, and anyone from the company could use it at any time.

Henri then got the email and a phone number that had been used for the company contact.

Now, he, Larry, and the two officers from before were back at the spa. They went through the entire complex with no sign of anyone else. The two separate annexes, they would drive to.

Though they were accessible by the tunnels, they wanted to be parked nearby. The one annex was up the hill. The two Carabinieri officers would go there, while Larry and

Henri went to the Presidential annex. It spanned a narrow area where the lake flowed from Switzerland into Italy.

They noted recent tire marks in the parking area and were surprised to discover the private elevator unlocked. What they discovered in the gym was even more of a surprise. Leaving the men tied up, they searched and tried to decide what to do with them. It was clear that someone had been there, but was it Jack, or someone else? Again, Henri took hair samples for DNA testing. Then, he put actual cuffs on the men, and Larry began the questioning.

According to the men, they were much like the man the Carabinieri arrested before. They were only there to restock and knew nothing about who was staying there.

"You see," Larry started. "There's a problem with that story. Where are the items you're supposedly restocking?"

"We come up and check first, then bring items up."

"From where?"

"They were in an SUV. He must have taken it, like he took our wallets and keys."

"So, you did see him?" Henri asked.

"No, I mean, I figure it was a man from the force of the blow. It takes a lot to knock me out."

"Yeah," the other agreed. "Look, we're the victims here. We're just doing our job and, wham! We get knocked out and robbed!"

"Who do you work for?" Larry asked.

"I don't have a name. We get instructions. We carry them out and the money shows up in our accounts."

"And it never crossed your minds that it may be something illegal? Or did it just not matter?"

"Look, I have a family to feed."

"Me too," the other said."

"Someone asks me to bring up supplies to a big wig who wants to remain anonymous. This is a big fancy place. I don't ask questions."

"You don't have anything on us."

"Well, we have you in the presidential annex, and from the looks of it, I'd say we could book you for burglary and destruction of property, to start," Henri said.

"We were the ones robbed!"

"What do you think Larry?"

"They're lying."

"I think so too," Henri agreed. "I say we leave them here to reconsider their statements and get these samples to the lab."

"Sophie was smart to think of bringing a DNA sample for us to compare. I'm pretty sure we'll have the results today, and then we'd have them on kidnapping too," Larry said.

"Let's head out then," Henri said, and they walked away.

"Wait! Wait! You can't leave us here!"

They kept walking.

"Okay, okay," the one said, "We weren't here just to restock. We were supposed to take someone."

"Not kidnapping!" the other hurried to say. "We were just supposed to take him somewhere else."

"Who?"

"We weren't told."

"Where were you taking him?"

"They were going to send directions after we had him."

"Sounds an awful lot like a kidnapping to me," Larry said.

"What make and model is the SUV? License plate number?" Henri asked. Then he called the Carabinieri.

"Where are you going?" the men called, as they turned to leave.

"Relax, they'll come for you shortly," Henri said.

They met the Carabinieri back at the main spa entry, where they traded keys and cuffs, and then they headed down the hill.

"If it was Jack, then he probably drove right past us this morning," Larry said, as his phone rang.

It was Sophie. After the initial emotion of the call to his parents, Anne had told Jack that Sophie and Nick were in Switzerland. He had just called her, and they were meeting him at a restaurant about ten miles away.

As soon as Jeremy saw Jack, he ran straight at him. Jack picked him up and held him. Then Sophie and Nick joined in the reuniting group hug.

"Where were you Uncle Jack?" Jeremy asked.

"Well," Jack began, "there was a lake and…"

"I knew it! I knew it!" Jeremy burst. "I told everyone you went fishing."

Jack burst out laughing.

"What's so funny?" Jeremy asked.

"Nothing, I'm just really glad to see you all! What made you decide to come here? My mom said she and my dad were in Scotland and something about Josephine and Simon."

"She received a postcard from Switzerland, supposedly from Josephine, and I knew that Josephine had been in Scotland. We just assumed they were the ones most likely behind your disappearance. Nick and I came here, and your parents went to Scotland. They found Simon. Apparently, Aunt Josephine left him, and she left him in a rather compromising position, handcuffed to the bed where your parents found him."

"He had also been here," Nick said. "Larry and I followed him to a lake house outside of Bern. He left from there in a helicopter, but we followed his lacky up to a spa connected with where you were. Larry Marquet was already there based on another lead and so were some Italian police, who managed to chase him down and… Ah, man, I'm just glad to see you!"

"Ditto!" Jack said.

"Ditto!" Jeremy echoed.

"Why was Larry there? Is Dave with him?"

"You wouldn't believe who all is here and everything going on!" Sophie said.

She realized what Jack was wondering by the look in his eyes and bit her lip. "She's not here. I'm sorry," Sophie whispered as she hugged him.

"I wouldn't have expected that," Jack replied. "So, what do you say we order? What do you want Jeremy?"

During the night, Victoria began to come around. She was still extremely weak and suffering residual numbness in her limbs. Her biggest dilemma was what to do next.

Victoria, for her family's sake, needed the Chinese to believe she was dead, which also meant that all the people she was supposed to play with and for on Saturday needed to think her dead as well.

"So, does that mean you're all done here, and you and Margot will be heading home?" Henri asked Larry, after finding out about Jack.

"Hardly. You wouldn't believe the number of loose ends. I'd like to tell you more, but I'd have to discuss it with others first."

"Did you ever get any leads on Richter Meschner?"

"Unfortunately, no. Can I show you some pictures? Nick and I took these at the lake house we followed the man arrested by the Carabinieri from."

"Okay," Henri said.

"Does this mean anything to you?" Larry asked, pulling up one of the star charts that had been hanging in the house. "At first, I thought it was a map of constellations, but I can't make any out. I don't even see the dippers."

"Actually, it looks like something I saw once when I did a college trip to China. It was either at the Beijing Observatory or the Shanghai Astronomical Museum, I think Shanghai. Anyway, they had maps of overlaid astrological charts from different time periods. May I?" Henri asked, and Larry handed him the phone. Henri zoomed in on a section of the chart. "Yeah, see here, here, here, and here? This is all the same constellation."

"What does it mean?"

"You've got me on that. I know it's a calendar, but I didn't understand it then and I still don't. Were there others?"

"There's more. That house was creepy, to say the least. Here are the bookshelves. We tried to get all of the titles, but half, I don't even know what language they're in."

"Interesting. The reason I asked if there were other star charts is because the other chart I remember showed the same place in the sky at different times over one year, so that the constellations all overlapped each other, versus only overlapping themselves, like that one. You'd probably need a Chinese astronomer to tell you more."

"Thanks Henri. Thank you for everything. I'll be in touch," Larry said. "Do you mind dropping me at the restaurant?"

"Sure. Shouldn't I come in too?"

"Would you mind not? I promise to fill you in and send over anything you need, like the ID's he took off those two."

"Okay. I'll run by the hospital and chat with Dave. Then I'll be at this hotel over the weekend," he said, handing Larry a card.

***

"Are you sure?" Margot asked Victoria.

Margot had stayed with Victoria while Magdeline went with Soren to check on Lidia.

"How do you know your family is still alive? If it's the information you have that was protecting them, wouldn't that protection become void if they think you're dead?"

"I don't know. I panicked. They wanted me to drug everyone so they could take you. Not you specifically, but Magdeline, Rosie, Sophie, and the boys. They didn't believe I hadn't shared the information with you, but they would accept them as insurance. They could use them like they intended to use me. It was Rosie they were most interested in. I don't know why. Maybe because they observed her growing up. She said there were numerous Chinese doctors who visited the children's home. They examined her and gave her injections. Maybe she had the same injections I did. Only they didn't use her because of her deformities."

"Then why inject her at all?"

"Because they could. Have you noticed how young Rosie looks? She's the same age as Sophie. She's been through several reconstructive surgeries, but you can't even see the scars. She said that's because of Magdeline's treatments, but those wouldn't make her look younger. The injections would.

"In fact, the Chinese may have considered her perfect for their experiments. If you're mixing human and animal genes, it doesn't matter what the human looks like."

"I think we should try to contact your family again before we proclaim you dead," Margot said. "Also, I know that as a mother, I would gladly give my life to save my daughters. Even though you wouldn't physically die, you'd be giving up a life that you worked hard to create. If they've been killed, then it's a waste of the life you've built. If they're alive, I'm positive they wouldn't want you to give up everything for them."

"I'm more concerned that they'll be tortured than killed."

"Think about it though. If you're the doctors, and concerned about information leaks, then thinking that even more people have the ability to expose you is a huge hold. I think that if they think you leaked information to us, it gives them a bigger incentive to not harm your family. It's a psychological game they're playing. Don't let them win."

"I'll think about it. I don't know how long the numbness will last. I won't be able to play if doesn't go away by tomorrow. We have rehearsal Friday morning. I'm supposed to be in Geneva tomorrow, and my violin is still at the chalet."

"No, it's not. Larry thought to have it picked up by the agent who went to check out the cabin. It's in our room."

"Thank you, Margot. You've been so kind to me, and I know I've just been in the way."

"Not true. Yes, there is a lot happening, but none of it is any more your fault than it is Magdeline, Sophie, Rosie, or..."

"Or Alice's?"

"Or any of their victims. I don't know if I will ever understand the scope of what all this is about, but I do know that what they're doing is evil. Purely and simply, evil."

"Do you believe in God, Margot?"

"Most definitely!"

"Why? I mean, how can you with all of this evil going on?"

"For one, I've had too many prayers answered to not believe."

"But how many have been unanswered?"

"None. They may not have always been answered in the way I wanted, but they were always answered in the way, I realized later, was best for me.

"For example, when I graduated from high school, I wanted to go to University in America. I prayed every day to be accepted to just one of the five schools I applied to. I had the grades. Money wasn't an issue for my family, and yet, I was rejected by all of them. Not rejected really. It was more that they were experiencing curriculum changes that meant the major I wanted had fewer spots, or in one school, was being dropped altogether. I did have Universities in both Paris and Lyon practically wooing me. I grew up near Lyon. So, I chose Paris, and I got my first ever driving violation."

"This doesn't sound good."

"The rookie officer who gave me the ticket, was Larry. It was another year before I realized how glad I was that I wound up in Paris. If my prayers to go to university in America had been answered, I probably never would have met Larry, and I wouldn't have my daughters."

"Why would God allow the doctors to do what they do? Why is there evil?"

"Maybe so we can tell them apart. If there's no dark, how would we recognize light? If evil didn't exist, how would we see good? In the scheme of things, no one is in this world very long. Our lives are a small fraction of the world's history. I believe we are here not only to learn the difference between good and evil, but to make a decision between them. It's that decision that affects our eternity after this life."

"So, does not believing in God make me evil? Is everyone who does believe good?"

"No and no. The devil believes in God and there are good people who simply haven't had the chance to get to know God. Once you come to know Him, the choice is yours. We have free will. We can choose to believe in God, or not to.

"I don't know how it all works, but I believe everyone, somehow, will have the chance to make that choice. I choose to believe, and that belief brings me a great deal of comfort. If I didn't believe, I think I would have had multiple nervous breakdowns worrying if Larry was going to come home or not.

"I lost my mother a year ago, yet I didn't. Even though I will miss her for the rest of this life. I look forward to being reunited with her in Heaven. No matter what happens. I feel peace."

"I don't think I've ever felt at peace," Victoria said, as the door opened and Magdeline returned.

"How are you feeling?" Magdeline asked.

"Better. How's Lidia?"

"We still haven't figured out what they injected her with. The concentration in her blood was almost five times higher than it was in Soren's. Her vitals are stable, and they did a brain scan, which came back surprisingly active. They just can't seem to wake her up. They have her on a drip and did a transfusion to try and clear it out of her system. Hopefully she'll come around and, like Soren, not have any residual effects."

"Larry is talking with Jack. They had a hit on the sketch Mrs. Morgan made of the woman she saw at the spa. According to INTERPOL, she's a nurse, who disappeared five years ago from the same University hospital Meschner worked at in Quebec."

"Meschner? When I met the Chinese doctors at the cabin, I heard them mention sending something for Meschner," Victoria said.

"It could be one of the sons. Do you remember anything else?"

"No, I'm sorry."

"Are you okay to talk with Larry when he gets back?"

"Sure, if you'll stay too."

"I'll stay," Margot said.

Scotland

Anne and Ben checked out of the Inn and ordered a taxi to the airport. Jack was staying in Switzerland to go over everything with the others. So, Anne and Ben decided to be there too.

"I wonder where Josephine went." Anne said.

"Would she go to any of your family here in Scotland?"

"No, I don't think so. She definitely wouldn't go back to France, Switzerland, or Canada either. She might go to Sweden. If her girls are there, maybe she decided to follow."

"Maybe," Ben agreed, "but I'm sorry to say, I'm not too concerned about her."

"Fair enough, but if she knew Simon was behind bars, maybe she could help Lily and Nigel come home."

"I'm sure she'll find out."

"You're right, but ..."

"What?"

"I don't know. She's not who's important right now. It was so good to hear Jack's voice. I can't wait to see him!"

Chapter 24

Sweden: Thursday, June 9th

Carl was out for a morning walk when he saw her. He hadn't seen her since he was a little boy, but he knew who she was. He carefully followed her along the river to a boat that was used as a hotel. He watched her board and go down to the staterooms. She appeared to be alone. He wanted to talk to her, but how?

He couldn't imagine why she would be staying there, but she must be here for the conference. That meant he would see her there. He reminded himself that he was well disguised. He only hoped that it was her, not her husband, who would be there.

The week had proved interesting from the start. On the first day, Carl met a surgeon, Dr. Malachi Zendavev, he believed could perform the surgery on Alice. But could he be trusted at the lab? He wasn't involved with the family, and Carl would need an explanation of how Alice's condition came to be. Dr. Zendavev was far more experienced than any other surgeon Carl had met. The man had performed delicate neurosurgeries on premature infants and was familiar with the technology. He even gave a speech on how implants, similar to Alice's, could be used to restore sight to the blind.

As they were staying in the same hotel, Carl arranged to meet with him over breakfast. He wanted to perform the surgery as soon as he returned. To bring in an outsider was a huge risk. He considered the viability of bringing Alice to him. It would all still need to be kept secret, and they'd need an adequate facility.

Crossing the footbridge, he made his way back through the park to his hotel. Zendavev waved from the dining room. Carl waved back and went through the buffet before joining him.

Switzerland

Larry and Jack drove into Geneva. Fortunately, Victoria was feeling better and had even been able to play a bit on her violin. She had also decided not to play dead, and Larry couldn't thank Margot enough for having helped her come to that decision.

Now everyone, well almost everyone, would be coming to Geneva tonight. Mrs. Morgan had graciously taken care of all the accommodations. Dave would stay behind with Lidia, and for now, Shane and Daniel, would stay at the Morgan Chalet.

Today, Soren had also arranged to meet with Mrs. Martinson.

When they arrived at the hotel, both Jack's parents and Henri were in the lobby. It was a happy reunion. Larry and Henri wanted to give Jack and his parents a few hours alone, while they met together. After lunch they would meet for further discussions with Jack.

France

Tony took the electrical kit, borrowed from a friend, down to the wine cellar. He scanned the walls for wires and other objects. Laura had gotten a full plan of the house. So, it should be easy to spot something where it shouldn't be.

It didn't take long to realize something was going on behind the wall Laura said was warmer and that she heard sounds behind. The scanner lit up like crazy! There must be an entrance here, Tony thought, prodding the wine racks.

He looked at the house plans. The electric was connected to the front of the building more than eighty-two years ago. The date on the plans showed the original wiring put in in

April 1940, just a month before the Nazi invasion. The
updated plans showed additional circuits added in 1955.
That was supposedly the year Laura's great grandfather
bought it.

None of the plans showed anything located where the
scanner was picking up electrical activity now.

He went over each of the slots in the racks. Nothing. He
shown a flashlight along the wall. He still saw nothing. The
seams looked tight. It was when he shown the light over
some still empty slots, that he spotted something. The
racks all appeared to be bolted into the walls, but behind
one column of slots, he spotted an odd seam in the wall.

Tony reached through the slot and prodded the wall.
There was light condensation along the seam. Removing a
few bottles from the column, he beamed a flashlight at the
floor. There was an odd indent at the bottom of the racks. It
looked as if someone had made their fingerprint in the
concrete. He bent and put his thumb in the indent. When he
pressed, something shifted, and that section of wall and
racks swung inwards.

Slowly, Tony inched his way inside. Nothing in his wildest
dreams could have prepared him for what he saw. He
stared in shock at the man who lay enclosed under a glass
casing. It was a face he knew. Mathias father, Dr. Meschner.
It looked as though he were in a space age coffin, and next
to that were four others. Tony steadied his nerves and
looked inside the others. The next held another elderly
man. The next three were empty.

Beaming his light around, he noted two passageways. He
didn't dare go farther alone, but hurried out, pulling the
wall closed until he heard a mechanism lock it back in
place, then he hurried up the stairs, almost bumping into
Laura.

"What is it, Tony? You look like you just saw a ghost."

"I think I did. You were right in thinking there is something to the tales of your great-grandfather's friend."

Southern France

Adam was unusually flustered. While not made public, word had come to him of Simon's arrest and Josephine's supposed defection. So be it. He had used Nigel and Lily as far as he needed. The children were nearly ready for the next stage. Without Josephine, in a few days, there would no longer be any need for them. He wondered if Josephine considered her sister before disappearing with the girls.

He didn't think Simon would talk, but the man had let that woman get the best of him. He couldn't be trusted. Even more than that, he wondered just what Josephine had in mind. They both knew about the tunnels that lead between the house and vineyard. He needed to get there, to move all the machines again, but where? He had to be certain the police didn't discover them. Meschner and Morgan, he could do without, but the woman. She was an intricate part of the plan. He would need to bring her here. There was nowhere else. He would also have to be extra cautious to keep her concealed from the boy.

On the bright side, he would no longer have to worry about that pesky woman who lived there. He would go out through the western tunnel and through the woods. The safest way would be to take the early bus into Paris, where he could pick up a van and a couple of strong thugs that had no choice but to be faithful to him. They would take her out through the pool, and just to be safe, he would shift the others to the center and somehow block off the cellar and fermentation room tunnels.

Sweden

Carl was happy that a solution seemed to have been found for Alice's surgery. He started the morning's conversation by asking Dr. Zendavev if there had been any trials of the surgery.

Zendavev had looked at him oddly and asked if he meant legal or illegal. He said that there were rumors of illegal operations being performed in China, but since the virus, much of what little knowledge had been shared from China, was silenced. Only rumors escaped. He asked Carl what he'd heard, and Carl made up a story about a colleague who had gone to China to study certain genetic traits. While there, she had been abducted, and something had been done to her. She managed to escape, but she became very ill. Carl said that the tests he ran to try and determine the cause of her illness all pointed towards a surgery similar to what Zendavev had described in his talk.

It was agreed that Alice would be transported to Arlanda, where there was a private clinic near the airport. Dr. Zendavev would examine her there and hopefully agree to perform the surgery on Monday.

During the lunch break, he had contacted Jonathan to let him know the plans and help with the transport arrangements.

Switzerland

Dave was at loose ends. He hated feeling helpless. He should have caught the men, but no, he let them get away. He should have been more cautious about the whole charade in the first place and made sure that Lidia was never left alone. Yes, she was a trained detective, but this wasn't her case. She was just here accompanying Mrs. Morgan. Dave was responsible.

He looked up as Suzanna Morgan entered the room.

"How is she?" Suzanna asked.

"No change."

"You look exhausted. I brought a bag of clothes and toiletries for her, and I'll be here. You need to take a break."

Dave sighed and looked from Suzanna to Lidia and back. "Yeah, thanks. I won't be long."

"You know, you're a lucky girl" Suzanna said to Lidia after Dave left. "I can see a bright future ahead for the two of you. So, you might really want to think about waking up. Anyway, you think on it while I update you.

"Of course, one of the first things I did when I got back was call Kathleen, the woman I left the party with. She swears that all she did was deliver the note to me. She had no idea that I had been kidnapped.

"The woman who showed up at the resort to take samples from me, she popped up in a missing persons database. They're not telling me much, but it turns out that Jack was being kept in a separate section of the same resort. So, we know it's connected to the projects. I wonder how many nut cases like Meschner are out there.

"I'm sorry, that's a morbid thought. We already know his sons all escaped. That's why I was really surprised it was a woman who came to me. She was just as sadistic as Richter. Sorry. I'm being morbid again. So, now, I will tell you some good news!

"I've been spending time with Claire. She said she forgave me. Can you believe it? I don't know if I can ever forgive myself, but we're talking for the first time in thirty years.

"Rosie is another case, and I don't blame her.

"Anyway, tonight most of us are heading into Geneva. Victoria has recovered enough to play her concert there. Shane and Daniel will be staying behind, and of course Dave. He won't go anywhere until you wake up.

"Come on Lidia. Don't tell him I told you this, but Dave needs you. No matter what he may say to the contrary, that man is crazy about you, and I know you feel the same. So, stop torturing him. He needs you to wake up and help him."

***

Dave paced the corridor between the chapel and the coffee machine. Then he downed his third espresso and entered the chapel. If ever there was a time to pray, it was now. He tried to remember some of the prayers he had learned as a boy, but he gave up. The traditional holiday dinner prayer his dad had said wouldn't cut it, and now I lay me down to sleep, was the opposite of what he wanted. He managed to remember the Lord's prayer and then simply added, "Help Lidia to be okay." He sat in silence for a few minutes, then went to the cafeteria and grabbed a sandwich, chips, and a water to counteract the number the espresso was doing on his empty stomach.

On the way back up to her room, he stopped in the gift shop and bought a bouquet of wildflowers and a box of chocolates.

Sweden

The last session of the day ended, and Carl waited across the street, looking for Josephine. Then he walked back through town and followed the trail along the river, through the park, and over the footbridge to where he saw her earlier. She was on deck, chatting with another woman.

Out of curiosity, Carl went aboard the boat. The woman who had been talking with Josephine set a small dog from her lap and stood, asking him if he needed a room.

He decided to play along. Why not? There was nothing special going on at his hotel tonight, and the price for a night was pennies in comparison. Plus, as a fellow lodger, he would have an excuse to talk to Josephine and find out what was going on.

After he signed in and was offered iced tea, he joined them back out on deck. The day was lovely and the light breeze off the water, refreshing.

To explain his missing luggage, he told them that his hotel reservation had been confused, which is why he needed a room for tonight. He would walk over later to pick up his luggage that was being held at the other hotel.

"What brings you to Uppsala?" asked Amelia, the boat's owner.

"I'm here for the genetics convention at the university this week," he said, glancing to Josephine, to gage her reaction and noted her looking out across the park.

"That sounds very interesting. Are you a doctor? Scientist?"

"More of a student and a researcher," he replied.

"Excuse me," Josephine said to Amelia, "Do you have any recommendations for curry in town? I'm suddenly starving."

"Yes, yes, there is one place guests have told me is very good. It's quite a walk. I can call you a taxi."

"No, I need the walk, and it's such a nice evening."

"Okay, very well. The easiest way will be to follow down this street, past the third bridge, then turn right toward the big square. When you get to the main street, across from the train station, stay on this side and go down, I think, three blocks. It will be on your left. You will be able to smell it when you are near. Shall I look up the name?"

"No, don't bother. I'm sure that I'll find it. Thank you."

Carl considered trying to join her, but he didn't want to push his luck. The mere mention of the convention had made her obviously uncomfortable. For a minute he was surprised she would risk walking through town, but then he realized, as she would have, that those at the convention would be highly unlikely to leave the area around their hotels.

He wondered why she would come here now, of all times, and seemingly alone.

He spent a few more minutes making small talk with his hostess and then went to walk back to his hotel and pack an overnight bag. He also was feeling hungry and would find someplace for dinner. He asked Amelia what was close, and she gave him two recommendations. He decided on another boat, that doubled as a restaurant. That way, he could take a seat on deck and watch for Josephine's return.

He had just finished his meal and was being served coffee when he saw her walking back. He decided to enjoy his coffee and talk to her in the morning.

France

After hours of discussion, Tony and Laura decided against calling the police.

At first, Laura considered that Mathias may have been a part of it all. "He easily could have broken all the bottles and disappeared," she said.

"He would never do that to you," Tony replied.

"Not even to protect his father?"

"Least of all that. You know he's been working the past three years trying to bring his father and those who worked with him down."

"Are you positive about that?"

"I am. Mathias is the polar opposite of his father and brothers. At least Richter," he clarified. "Meschner didn't think much of Mathias. Even though Mathias was the first born, it was Richter he groomed to take over. I know. I saw it when they came to the vineyard for a meeting with Josephine and Simon. Mathias would never hurt anyone. My fear is, if we bring in the police, they may hurt Mathias."

"You really think he's been kidnapped by his own family?"

"I think he was down there trying to figure out what was wrong. He either found the door, or someone came from the other side while he was there. Either way, they couldn't have him sharing what he discovered. If we involve the police, what reason do they have not to kill him? His father won't help him, even if he wanted to, he's a popsicle."

"So, what do we do? If, like you said earlier, the moving and breaking of the wine was an attempt to drive me away, they won't stop."

"They will if they can't get into the cellar and believe you can't get into their secret tunnels."

"And how do we do that?"

"I have an idea. It'll be a pain in the backside, but I think it will work."

Switzerland

The afternoon talking with Mrs. Martinson had been quite enlightening.

As soon as Soren showed her the photo and explained the situation under which it was taken, she told him that she had already doubted the truth of Professor Crabben's death. They were sitting in the restaurant where Ana was working, and it was just the two of them on that side of the dining hall.

"How much do you remember about the CDC program?" Soren asked.

"Too much, but no one can know that I know. If the wrong people found out what I remember... I can't risk it."

I told you that the shipment Crabben was seen with was from China, but I didn't tell you what we think it may have been. Care to have a guess?"

"No."

"Did you ever see a film called "The Fly"?"

"Unfortunately."

"Would the CDC program have involved something similar?"

"I somehow think you know more than I do now, and that's not safe."

"I'll take that as a yes, in which case, I'm curious if you remember seeing any of these men," Soren said, showing her the images of the Chinese men.

Sarah Martinson's intake of breath told him she had.

"They were at the meetings in Paris, as well as some of the private meeting we had. I remember them because they didn't say anything. They just stood in the room, listening, and watching. Why are you asking me about them though? They wouldn't have had anything to do with Ana or my abduction."

"Are you sure?"

Sarah sighed, "I'm not sure of anything. I thought you were trying to link our genealogy to our abduction, because the testing we underwent seemed connected to another case."

"We are, but these men are also connected to that other case now. It's all connected."

"I can promise you that I don't have one drop of Chinese blood in my genealogy."

"And Ana?"

"Seriously?"

"No, not really. We think the Chinese factor is tied in only when experiments with animal DNA was added. We believe that on some level all these projects, The CDC and the Paris project, for example, are working together.

"To get to whoever is behind them, we need to trace what links all the known victims. We have enough reliable information now to be one hundred percent certain, that in some way, somewhere in history, there is a family tie."

"You probably know that Stephen isn't Ana's biological father."

"I do."

"What would you say if I told you that Ana has more than one biological father?"

"I'd tell you she's not alone."

Sarah Martinson looked surprised. "You don't think I'm crazy?"

"Hardly. I realize that it was different before your abduction, but the way genetic manipulation has advanced is crazy. I've learned that many things that are just now coming to light, were being practiced for decades in the dark. It wouldn't have been accepted. It still isn't by most. What happened Sarah?"

"It was Crabben who introduced me to him in Paris. It was at one of the meetings those two Chinese men attended. There were people there from all around the world to discuss cooperation between scientists working in each country on curating the genetic samples. It was mentioned, I don't remember by who, about eventually expanding the program to include animal DNA, but there was never a suggestion of mixing. Well, not at any of the official meetings.

"Anyway, I had already figured out by this time that I wouldn't get pregnant by Stephan. His count was extremely low. I never told him, and the tests were all done at Scangentech. Please don't tell him."

Soren nodded.

"So, I had an affair with the man Crabben introduced me to. He even bought a house not far away when he found out I was pregnant. He never asked me to leave Stephan. He didn't even have a problem with Stephan believing Ana was his. I thought that was weird, but he said he loved us. He also said that he wasn't in a position to be a husband and father.

"My knee jerk reaction was that he must be married, but he swore it was due to his job and Crabben vouched for him. I had worked with Crabben for a few years at this point. I had no reason not to trust him.

"It was after the first ultrasound, when he discovered it was girl that things got stranger. I agreed to be part of a special monitoring program and be injected with supplements. During some of the appointments, I felt like I had been drugged. I remember hearing other men in the room, but not being able to make out what they were saying. At one appointment, I turned my head to see Ana on the monitor. I saw a needle being inserted into me, but then it kept going into her.

"I mentioned it to Crabben once, as he was head of that program at the time. He said they must have been drawing a few cells for genetic testing. I let it go. I trusted him and I trusted Charles. I doubt that was his real name though."

"Ana's father?"

"Yes."

"I discovered later that Crabben was going to ask me to head up the CDC. I wanted to review some files, and when I inserted one of the memory sticks, I discovered files on it from the monitoring program. I was curious and opened it to my file. Ana and I were the only mother and daughter listed, but there were three fathers listed. I thought it was a typo, until I opened another subfile that told me that it wasn't."

"You know who they are then."

"No. It didn't list names. It was all coded."

"Then how did you know it was your file?"

"My initials were there, and the dates on the listed injections matched my appointments."

"Did you confront Crabben about this?"

"No. I didn't want to risk anything happening to Ana. I did turn down his offer to head the CDC though."

"He had already asked?"

"Two days before the abduction."

"You didn't think you could tell anyone? Even Trudie?"

"I couldn't be sure she would even believe me, and if she did, it could put her at risk."

"Can I ask what happened with Charles?"

"He wanted to see Ana, and I would meet him at church. I told Stephan I was going to a women's Bible study. He offered to keep Ana, but I told him they had daycare, and it was good for her to play with other children. So, we went and parked next to the other women's cars. We always arrived late so no one saw us, and Charles would unlock a door to either the basement, where the Sunday school rooms were, or sometimes the chapel. When Anna was about three, Charles started asking to see her alone. Please understand. I love Stephan. Charles was charming, and I wanted a child."

"I understand."

"Ana started to become more withdrawn after these visits alone with Charles. She would sometimes say odd things, and I began to wonder if he was molesting her. I confronted him and he became like a different man. He was enraged that I could even suggest it. He then explained that he had simply been examining her.

"That was when I realized he never loved either of us. We were just another science project. I asked him why he chose me. He made an offhanded comment about me having good genes. I didn't realize how much that comment really meant until I was abducted, and the doctors who raped me said something similar, but they never explained."

"You remember being raped now?"

Sarah nodded.

"Would you recognize those men?"

Sarah shook her head. "Maybe, I was so drugged up. I think there were two, but there could have been two hundred. I have flashes sometimes, but only of two."

"Will you be okay if I show you some more pictures?" Soren asked.

"I guess."

"Most of these are sketches. Tell me if anyone looks familiar."

Sarah took the images.

"That's Charles," she said when she reached the third sketch.

"Ana's father?"

"One of them. I can't even say if he was the primary sperm donor. As I understood it later, they used multiple donor injections of sperm as well as other DNA sources to guarantee the conception and later tests to see whose DNA they needed to supplement."

She flipped through more of the sketches.

"Oh Lord!" she exclaimed in a whisper and pulled on a smile when Ana looked over.

"Are you okay?" Soren asked.

"He's one of the men who raped me," she said, staring at the mug shot of Simon.

"That man was recently arrested for kidnapping," Soren said,

"Are you sure he's locked up?"

"Positive. I'm sorry to have put you through all this, Sarah."

"I understand."

"I really appreciate your time and trust in telling me."

"Well, you seemed to have already known most of it," Sarah replied, as Ana came over.

"I'm on my break now," Ana said.

"Hi Ana," Soren said, stretching out his hand.

"Hello," Ana replied, not taking his hand.

"Ana," Sarah said. "This is Soren. He's helping Dave."

"Okay," Ana replied, now blatantly looking him over.

"He and his wife used to work at Scangentech when I was there, and they're good friends of Trudie as well."

"We're done now. So, you and your mom can spend some time together," Soren said. "Tell Stephan hello," he added.

"I will," Sarah replied, and they walked out of the restaurant.

Soren raised his coffee cup to catch Aida's attention. It was past the lunch rush, and he hoped for a few minutes to talk.

"Can you join me for a couple of minutes?" he asked as she brought the coffee over.

Aida looked around at the two other people still finishing their lunches and sat down across from Soren. "How can I help you?" she asked.

"Ana's father told me that the two of you are good friends. I was wondering if you could give me some tips on how you managed that. I'm sorry, that probably didn't sound very tactful. It's just that..."

"She's hard to talk to, and you're helping on the investigation of her and her mother's abduction?"

"Exactly."

"Well, I don't think I can really help you. It's not that I don't think Ana should try being more open, I do. I've even tried to help her relationship with her father. Look, Mr...?"

"Anglistan, but just call me Soren."

"Soren, I've always been lucky. I have a close relationship with my family. They own this lodge. My relationship with Ana is based on a mutual understanding of loss though. We both lost the men we loved. Ana is so young that I feel a kind of responsibility to help her get past it and move on. I know she went through a lot, and I don't fully understand their relationship, but I can empathize with it."

"I see," Soren said.

"Can I ask you a question?" Aida asked.

"Go ahead."

"Why is their abduction being looked at so closely now when it happened so long ago, and Ana was returned three years ago. Is there something new going on? I mean something that, maybe people should be aware of? Ana mentioned something about someone else having gone missing, but she didn't seem to know much about it, except that the same investigators were involved and seemed even more interested in her mother."

Soren thought for a moment. He knew that one of the Meschner brothers had been caught on the parking garage cameras around the time of the abduction. It couldn't hurt to show it to Aida. He had a few of the facial sketches made of Jonathan on his phone.

"I don't think it's anything that you need to worry about, but I can show you some sketches of one of the men we believe was behind their abduction. I should also tell you, that this sketch is of his brother, but they look nearly identical," Soren said, as he pulled up the images and handed the phone to Aida.

Her reaction was unexpected. She stared at the images, and for a moment she looked like she might cry.

It was the last face Aida expected to see. It was different, yet not. She had seen him briefly without the facial implants on that last night before he vanished. "Kristor," she whispered.

"You recognize him?"

Aida nodded and wiped at her eyes.

"You called him Kristor."

She nodded. "He was a guest here, three and a half years ago."

"Is he the man you fell in love with?"

She nodded again.

"If it makes you feel any better, he's the good brother. I know. I've met him."

Aida looked up at Soren. "You met him? When?"

"Three and a half years ago. He helped on the case. I probably shouldn't be telling you this, but his real name is Jonathan. Jonathan Meschner. He would have been going under another name for safety reasons."

"He mentioned that he was hiding from his family, but he wouldn't explain. He said that he couldn't explain. Can you?"

"I'm afraid I can't. I'm sorry."

"You don't know where he is then?"

"Again, I'm sorry, but no. I'd appreciate it if you didn't mention this to Ana."

"Of course. Of course not."

"Well, how much do I owe you?" Soren asked, standing, and indicating the table.

"Nothing. It's on the house."

"Are you sure?"

"I'm sure, but I'd like to ask you a favor. If you do see Kristor, or Jonathan again. Please tell him I'll never forget him and ask him to call me. This is my new number," she said, pulling a pen and pad from her apron. She handed him the number.

"I will," Soren promised.

"Thank you."

***

Suzanna was looking at the book she won from the auction.

"What are you reading?" asked Claire.

"It's an antique book of Russian fairy tales, the fourth volume. I have the other three back in Seattle. You look surprised."

"I am. I never saw you read fairy tales, even as a child."

"I didn't really buy them for me. I got them when Edgar and I first started trying to have children. I'd seen them in an antique store and thought that the colorfully painted pictures would appeal to a child. I'm thinking of giving them to Sophie. She was close to Alice for a while, and I think Jeremy or any other children they have might like them. Or do you think Rosie would like them?"

"I think it's a nice thought to give them to Sophie," Claire said, sitting opposite Suzanna on the bed. "I wanted to ask you something, about Edgar."

"Yes?"

"What made you think he was in Switzerland?"

"It was just a guess. We had a lot of business dealings here before, but I didn't just come here for him."

"Alice?"

"Yes, and... Would you believe I was matchmaking?"

"Matchmaking?"

"Dave and Lidia."

"But he was in Austria."

"True, but I was thinking of finding Edgar or Alice too. Also, I like it here and wanted to show Lidia around. I was trying to think of a reason to go to Austria or get Dave to come here. You know how that worked out. I felt like it was meant to be when he showed up right next door."

"Wasn't Lidia keeping tabs on you the past three years?"

"She was. I got to know her pretty well during that time, and I like to think we became friends. I don't know if I will ever find Alice, much less be able to ever have a relationship with her. So, I guess Lidia turned into a surrogate. I'm just praying she pulls through this. It's clear that I was right about her and Dave. I felt so bad for him when I went to the hospital."

"You have no idea about these Chinese doctors?"

"No more than what Shane, Larry and Dave already know. When Edgar and I were kidnapped, there was a Chinese shipping company that had been related to one of our acquisitions and delivered supplies to Meschner. It seems they also have been delivering to Quebec, and I imagine other places where the projects are connected."

"Shane and Larry tried to track the company and come up with something viable to launch an investigation. They're very talented at covering their tracks though. Shane is looking into a shipment recently delivered to the university hospital in Quebec City. From what I understand, it seems like Victoria is the one with the links to China."

Claire gave a half smile. "Rosie had some experiences too with Chinese doctors at the children's home examining her."

"I'm sorry."

Claire shook her head. "Everything and everyone are genetically connected. Everyone that is, except us. It doesn't make sense."

"Edgar and I were the main purse strings."

"That would have made sense before, but some of the genetic connections already known go back to before we were born. This was underway before Morgan Acquisitions even existed. And why your company?"

"As you know, Edgar and I were active about a solution for having a child."

"Okay, but even if they just helped you have Alice for the money, why did they keep experimenting with me, and why was Alice so important to them? More importantly, why does Victoria exist? Her birthday matches the date of a supposed still birth I had. There must be a genetic link to us, or it just doesn't make sense. Also, when Nick and Larry were looking for Jack outside of Bern, they searched a house and found a painting of a woman who looked just like Rosie, Alice, Sophie, Victoria and Magdeline.

"Can we talk about our parents, Suzanna? I think we should try to remember. There must be something in our genealogy they missed. I was going to talk to Dave about this, but he and everyone else have their hands full. You and I are really the only ones with the time to research this, and it is our family."

"Okay. Of course, I'll help. I'm just not sure where to start."

"Let's start with going down memory lane."

Chapter 25

France: Friday, June 10th

At five in the morning, Tony had called in every favor he could think of and bartered for a few more.

Boris arrived first with the bricks. Followed by Tobias with the concrete.

"This is insane!" Boris said, when Tony showed him where they would be building the wall. "What on earth do you want a wall for down here anyway? The one you have looks perfectly fine."

"It's a health issue. You can't see it now, because it's been scrubbed, but when it rains, there's a leak that forms from somewhere. I thought about just patching up the seam, but we decided better safe than sorry. So, I took down the racks last night. I figure if we do a daisy chain, we can have the wall built by noon. What do you think?"

"I think I still don't understand. It's a wine cellar. Who cares if there's an occasional leak?"

"The health inspectors. It's a new place and they're coming tomorrow. That leak was causing some nasty looking mold."

"The health inspector is coming on a Saturday?"

"Maybe. You know they like to surprise you, but Laura said that she was told June 11th."

"Sure, we can get it done. It's not a huge section, but why start so early?"

"Laura has to set up for customers tonight, and we need to have all this done and cleaned up."

"Okay. I don't suppose this wine bar has any coffee."

"Oh, but we do. We're even offering fruit and croissants. Lunch is included too."

"So, tell me, what is it with you and Laura? I thought you were still trying to make it work with Diana."

Tony laughed. "Laura's a business associate. She gives the vineyard a lot of business between here and her family's restaurant. She is also kind of involved with a friend of mine, just in case you had any ideas."

"Kind of involved is still up for grabs in my book," Boris said, as they headed back upstairs.

"Come on, I don't want two of my friends fighting over the same woman. Just behave, Boris."

"All right. Just remember, you owe us big time!" Boris said, as Tobias and five other men entered.

"Help yourselves," Tony said, motioning them to the kitchen.

"Laura arrived a few hours later with more food and drinks to prepare for lunch, and by two the wall was up, and the trucks were moved out. A couple of the guys stuck around to help Tony replace the wine racks, and Laura tried not to think about what, or who, was hidden underneath her home.

Sweden

Carl came up from his berth for breakfast. He was surprised at how well he had slept, considering this was hardly the five-star hotel with pillow top mattresses he was accustomed to. The gentle lapping of the waves against the hull had lulled him to sleep though, and the smell of coffee was welcoming his senses, as he climbed to the upper deck.

The only thing that he was really uncomfortable with, was the not so private shower areas. He would have to leave time for a shower at the other hotel on his way up for the final lectures.

For now, he waited for the breakfast he had ordered the night before and enjoyed the coffee. He had hoped to be alone with Josephine or at least share a table, but it seemed that everyone else was up ahead of her, and he wound up sharing his table with an elderly woman and her two daughters, who were clearly flirting with him.

Flattering as it was, when he finished his food, he excused himself to refill his coffee and sit on the couch across the small lobby. The owner's dog joined him. Dogs had never liked him before, but for some reason this one seemed to have developed a crush on him and insisted on laying her furry head on his clean lap. He tentatively reached down to pet the pooch, at which point it began to lick his pants leg as well.

Oh well, he thought. I need to shower still anyway.

"Good morning," came a voice from beside him. "Do you mind if I sit here? Everything else looks full," Josephine continued.

"Certainly," he smiled.

"I hope you didn't think me rude yesterday. It's just that my ex-husband was a doctor slash scientist and I..."

"Not at all," he replied as her breakfast arrived. So, she was calling Simon her ex-husband. That was interesting.

"I'm Liliana, by the way. What was your name again?"

"Fenton," he replied, giving her the name he registered with.

"Irish?"

"Yes, but I live in Sweden now. You?"

"French, but I've been living in Scotland."

"What brings you to Uppsala."

"My daughters are in Sweden."

"I see," he said, not sure if that were true or just part of her story line. He knew from Richter that they had fostered several girls, most as part of the projects.

"They're staying with friends. That's why I have my room here," she added.

Josephine reminded herself to relax. This man was not a threat.

"How was your dinner last night?"

"It was good, thank you."

Carl realized that this conversation wasn't going anywhere. He finished his coffee and said, "I should probably head out. I want to meet up with some colleagues before the first lecture. Perhaps I'll see you tonight?"

"Yes, have a good day."

As Carl made his way back to the other hotel, he thought about what she said and wondered what she was planning. If she really was trying to free herself from the projects, he wished her luck. Hopefully, this evening they could talk more. At least he had already managed a casual rapport.

Switzerland

Dave was snoring like a bulldozer when he suddenly jolted awake. He turned to look at Lidia. Her eyes were open. At first, he just stared, scared from his dream where she was staring at him in a similar manner. In the dream, he was sure she was dead. As he looked at her now, he saw her eyelids flutter.

"Lidia, can you hear me?"

Her eyes focused on him. "I could have heard you from Seattle, Asher. Have you ever tried those nose strips?"

He smiled at her. "It's good to see you too."

France

Adam was not happy that he had been made to wait, but when he heard the raucous going on behind the wall, he knew he couldn't risk moving them until they were gone. The woman, who really mattered most, was in another section. He could go ahead and load her, make sure she was securely connected in the van and come back.

When he did come back, he could still hear men, but they sounded further away than they had before. He listened carefully. Had he heard correctly?

After all the sounds faded, he tried the door. It wouldn't budge. He laughed. They had done the work for him.

"I think I'll just leave you where you are," he said to the inert faces of Dr. Meschner and Mr. Morgan.

He would still need to block off the other tunnel just in case Simon suddenly developed a loose tongue.

It would be late when he got back, but it was better to get to the tunnel in the cover of night.

Switzerland

When Shane and Daniel came to see Lidia, she and Dave were finishing up the box of chocolates Dave had bought.

"It looks like you two don't need these," Shane said, sitting down the box he brought along with a tray of Lattes.

"The chocolates, not now, but the coffee, oh yeah! Thank you!" Lidia said.

"This is from me," Daniel said, pulling a stuffed bear from behind his back.

"Thank you, Daniel. He is just what I need," Lidia said, smiling as Daniel brought the bear to her.

"I think he looks a little like Mr. Dave," Daniel said.

"Thanks," Dave replied.

"It's the tired eyes and ruffled fur, but he's cute anyway," Lidia said.

"So, when are they letting you out of here?" Shane asked.

"If the tests come back clear, I'll be free by the morning. I'd kind of like to make it to the concert tomorrow night."

"I think we can fit you in. The last seats were bought out by us to help prevent any last minute, unwelcome guests. I guess you know we found Mrs. Morgan and Jack."

"Dave gave me the update, and I know Suzanna was here yesterday. I wasn't unconscious. I could hear everything around me. I just couldn't open my eyes or talk. They think it was an herb, like Victoria took, some kind of neurotoxin."

"What's a neurotoxin?" asked Daniel.

"It's a type of poison," Shane said.

"Have you ever seen the movie, 'Snow White'?" Dave asked.

Daniel nodded.

"It's like that, like the poison apple that made Snow White sleep," Dave explained.

"And did you wake miss Lidia with a kiss?"

Dave and Lidia both blushed

"Actually, it was his snoring," Lidia said. "He snores like a bear too."

"All right, I'm leaving now. A man can only take so much," Dave said.

"Good," Lidia said. "Shane, will you please take him?"

"I will, and I won't bring him back until he's slept, eaten some real food and showered."

"Thank you!" Lidia said, smiling.

Dave yawned.

"Come on Dave," Shane said.

"Just one question. Could you really hear everything Lidia?"

She just smiled in reply.

They went back to the chalet, and after Dave was rested, Shane filled him in on everything Soren had discovered from both Mrs. Martinson and Aida.

"Talk about a small world," Dave said. "You know, it's strange how the brothers, who were all raised by that same mad scientist, turned out so different."

"It is," Shane agreed, "It makes me wonder, I never treated Kenneth any different from Daniel, and yet, even as infants, there was a clear difference between them. Mr. Morgan said it was their genes, but I'm not sure."

"They seem to really believe that if they get the right combinations, they can raise an army to take over the world."

"Who's in control of that army though? I mean, unless you are the only one on Earth, you'll always have competition."

"Unless you are the only one with the right genetic combination and the rest of the world has been genetically manipulated to be inferior," Dave said.

"So, I'm looking at the big picture. Everyone is related. That means that this notion of superior genes comes from the idea that there are superior ancestors. However, how do you define superior? Judging from the genetic samples that Soren sent, supposedly to P2P, they consider genetic superiority to be... to be evil. I mean, samples from Nazis and serial killers? Then they add those known for mental and intellectual superiority, heads of states, Noble prize winners, etc.," Dave continued

"They also somehow inject, what Jonathan called a trigger. He said that the trigger could either cause him to kill others or himself. Which makes me wonder. Is there some way that they are keeping the violent genes dormant, then triggering them when it suits their purpose? Then there's Richter. Of course, he and the others we know of were born over thirty years ago. They may not have perfected it. They wouldn't have had the technology or the samples at the ready as they do now. I don't think they've reached their goal yet, but I think they're close."

"I think, if you ever give up investigating, you could become a philosophy instructor. So, professor," Shane joked, "what are your theories about the hybrid human, animal experiments?"

"I'm glad you asked. We know that there is more than one project and likely more than one goal. However, these could be working together. If the idea is to create, let's call it a new world order, where we have the genetically superior here at the top," Dave said, as he began to sketch it out, "Then we have levels. They would need levels. Let's say they breed one level to be smart enough to run the day-to-day necessities, finance, medical, information technology, etc. Then maybe another level would be skilled mechanic, electricians, architects. Another level could be laborers. I don't know how they'll rank them, but I think that's the idea. It's actually fairly basic. The military has ranks and society has always had classes, but these would be created, genetically by the projects."

"And the hybrid animal human?"

"Is needed to help with elimination. There are billions of people on the planet now. They'll have to thin that out, and what better way than to populate the world with killers that no one would recognize, yet those who created them can control? If it looks like, I don't know, a baboon or a kangaroo, no one is going to expect a kangaroo to turn psycho and pull an automatic weapon from its pouch. If they really have mixed human and animal genes, they could be planning a war where not only would you not be able to recognize the enemy, but the concept would be too mindboggling for many to conceive of."

"On second thought, maybe you should write books," Shane said. "I'm one of those, that warring baboons and kangaroos is still too mindboggling for. I'm still trying to wrap my mind around the human side of this, and that's in front of me every day. Okay, let me try to stretch my mind beyond. Maybe if I picture "Planet of The Apes" I can get a picture of what you're suggesting. Why then are they still keeping everyone alive?"

"Are they? We only know what the plans were in the past. That being said, until they achieve their goal, they still need people to experiment with. Autism and other birth defects are something they would want to know how to cure and prevent. Like with Magdeline's work. She healed herself with genetics. They would need to figure these things out in order to maintain the order. Until you either know for certain what causes a defect or how to heal it, you can't have that control."

"And we already know, one thing they have learned to control, is the aging process."

"Exactly! They learn to control aging first, because they want to be around to control the rest."

Daniel came out of the room where he had been playing and asked if they could have lunch yet.

"Yes, you're right. I'm sorry Daniel. I didn't realize how late it was getting. We'll fix something now."

Shane had just opened the refrigerator, when his phone rang with a call from Ralph.

"Hi Ralph. What's up? Uh huh... I think I'm going to hand you over to Dave," Shane said and handed the phone to Daniel to pass to Dave, as he looked through the refrigerator for something edible. He eventually gave up and went next door.

When Shane returned, Dave was still on the phone. He handed Daniel an apple he'd found and told him that when Dave was done on the phone, they would go out to eat.

The waitress had just brought their meals when Dave passed a picture Ralph sent him to Shane.

"He saw it?"

"That's what he said," Dave confirmed. "The sketch is from memory, but he felt it was pretty accurate."

"Dear God," Shane said, as he took it in, "What is it?"

"After delivering to the hospital he had some time. He decided to park his rig and go inside, when he did, he saw a crash cart being taken down to the lab. He followed, and there was some chaos. He said three men wearing hazmat suits took over with the crash cart. Then, everyone else hurried out the emergency exit. He waited behind a corner until the men came out of the lab and overheard them saying that they needed to keep the floor blocked off until *it* could be removed. Then they went out the emergency exit too. Ralph didn't go inside because he didn't know what the hazmat suits were about. He was able to see through the window though, and that is what he saw. He said that it looked like there was blood on the floor around it too. He tried to snap some pictures, but the reflection from the glass kept distorting them, so he drew a sketch."

"Well, I guess this settles it. Your theories are becoming more and more realistic Dave."

Chapter 26

Switzerland: June 11ᵗʰ

Dave, Shane, and Daniel picked Lidia up from the hospital and headed toward Geneva.

When they arrived, Anne and Ben took the boys so that the others could all meet together. Henri Saville was included now.

 Dave had gotten a white board from the hotel, and they were going over the connections Philip discovered, regarding Josephine's family.

"Josephine's grandmother, Lilianna had twin sons, born in Brazil. They immigrated to the United States to live with an uncle in New Orleans. One, Ulf, moved to San Francisco. Ulf changed his name to Maxum Cloverfield, and he was last known to be working at a bank in San Francisco."

Suzanna and Claire exchanged looks.

"What an odd name to choose?" Rosie said.

"Not if you know why he chose it," Claire said.

All heads turned to her.

"We knew Maxum Cloverfield."

"I remember when he came to live with his uncle Fritz in San Francisco." Suzanna continued.

 "He came to America with his brother, who still lived with their uncle Samuel in New Orleans." Claire said. "He chose that name because he believed names meant something. Maxum, was because he wanted to maximize his potential and Cloverfield was to bring luck. Even in the sixties, he didn't feel, Fourleafclover, as a last name would help him in business. So, he went with Cloverfield, figuring there would be a few four leafed clovers in the field. At least that's the story he told us," Claire added. "He and his uncle both loved to tell stories."

"Do you happen to know what happened to him?" Larry asked.

"He was run over by a trolly in April 1980," Suzanna said.

"How did it happen?" Larry asked.

"Our mother always thought he'd been pushed," Claire said. "I still remember the funeral."

"I wonder why Philip didn't find that. That would have been newsworthy, but he didn't even find an obit."

"His brother took the body to New Orleans," Claire said.

"You said you were at the funeral?"

"I was. Our mother knew their uncle Samuel, which is why we came to know Maxum. His uncle Fritz was widowed, and I think Samuel must have asked our mother to help look out for him. She and I both went to the funeral."

"I was already living in Seattle. It was around the same time Edgar and I started looking at fertility options," Suzanna added.

"Your mother was close to the uncle?" Dave asked.

"She spent summers with her cousins in New Orleans. In a way, they grew up together. Samuel was Jewish. He came to America after World War one. His brother was the boy's father."

"Their father was Jewish?"

"Yes, their father's father was Jewish, but his mother was German, and Samuel said his brother took her name after their father was killed."

"Has anyone else thought what I'm thinking?" Dave asked.

"That maybe my father wasn't my father?" Suzanna asked.

"Do *you* think it could be possible?"

"It could be. I'd just never considered it."

"They did seem awfully close, even at the funeral," Claire added. "It could also be that our father isn't my father."

"That would go against it always being the mother's side," Shane put in.

"That was never a definite," Dave said.

"Genes are carried from both parents," Magdeline added. "Though, they may prefer the female genetic line. It depends on the trait. There are some things that are passed only from the mother, others from the father. I can do a DNA test. It would be more accurate with samples from the men, but I'll still be able to tell if you have the same father."

"There is also Marta's daughters and other son, one of whom is Simon" Dave said.

"Josephine's Simon?" Sophie asked.

"It looks that way. Simon had two sisters and another brother as well. The one sister, Natalie, Cora told me married Dr. Nadier and is Adam Hisdak's mother. She's dead. The other sister, we lost track of after she married, but her married name was Meschner, and we will definitely continue digging on that. The other brother, we have nothing on yet."

Sweden

Carl hadn't been able to make much progress. Josephine had agreed to have dinner with a couple of other single women and Carl went to the same restaurant. He had been half invited, meaning they welcomed him to walk with them, but it was definitely a girl's night.

His train to Stockholm this morning was leaving in two hours, and he had to retrieve the rest of his luggage. Josephine was having breakfast with the same women she'd had dinner with. So, he decided to have his breakfast at the other hotel. It wasn't as though she had been in his plans. It was interesting to discover she had left Simon, and he wished her well in that.

He did wish he could learn what she knew, and that Jonathan could have met with her, but he couldn't accomplish that without giving himself away, which would probably only scare her off. Maybe after the surgery, they could come back.

On his way to the train, he saw her again. He also saw the man following her.

Carl watched as Josephine went into a book shop. When she came out, the man was waiting for her. He grabbed her arm and dragged her along into a parking garage. Carl left his luggage and hurried to them. He took the man by surprise, grabbing and twisting his arm until he heard it pop.

Josephine stared at him in disbelief, as he threw the man against the wall.

"Thank you," Josephine said, clearly shaken.

"Come with me," Carl said, holding out his hand.

"I don't want to go to the police."

"We're not, but I think you need a new place to hide, and I can help. We need to go."

They hurried back to where he had left his luggage, and he was thankful to find it still there.

"I need my luggage. I have important information in it that I can't leave behind."

They went back to the boat, and Carl stood guard, while she collected her belonging and stopped at the desk to explain that she was leaving.

Josephine was scared. She hadn't expected to be traced here, but she had been. The man had made it very clear. He didn't care about her. He wanted the files. She hated to bring a stranger into this. The man probably thought it was someone her husband had sent for her, and that much was likely true. She didn't know what else to do though, so she would go with him until she could figure out her next move. They took a taxi to the train station and just made the train to Stockholm.

"Josephine," Carl chanced, knowing she had nowhere to go.

Her eyes went wide. "Who are you?"

"I won't hurt you. I'm on your side, not Simon's."

"Who are you?"

"I haven't seen you since I was a little boy. I'm Carl, and I'm just as much in hiding as you are."

Josephine tried to absorb what he was saying. "You don't look like… "she began, then took in the shape of his hands. They had all had similar hands. "Facial implants?" she whispered.

"They work wonders. Do you know who he was?"

"No, but as you know the network is huge. I didn't think they would look for me here. I was stupid. They must be looking for me everywhere. For all I know, you're one of them."

"I'm working my own project. I'll tell you all about it later. It's not something I can discuss publicly," he said, looking around at the nearly full train.

After they arrived, Carl left Josephine in his hotel suite, while he headed to the A.I. show. He had plans to meet Dr. Zendavev for lunch and discuss preparations for Monday. Jonathan had sent images of Alice's scans, for Dr. Zendavev to look over, and Carl was anxious to hear his thoughts.

Switzerland

Larry and Dave did a final sweep of the concert hall, and Henri sent a watch notice to security, with images of the Chinese men.

The evening went smoothly, and everyone breathed a sigh of relief when they got back to their hotel.

"What do you say to a nightcap on the terrace," Dave asked Lidia. "It's a nice night. Moonlight over the Alps."

"I'll bring the chocolates Shane bought and meet you there. I'll take a merlot."

"I'll be waiting. So, don't take too long, Yarnok."

They were enjoying their drinks when the tremor hit. It was only a light vibration, but it lasted over a minute. The news reported it as a 5.7, shallow quake with the epicenter in the La Thuile valley, near the borders of France, Switzerland, and Italy. No injuries were reported.

Chapter 27

Sweden: June 12th

Carl sent Chantel back up to the lab to assist Ivan. She didn't need to be any more involved in this than she already was, and Jonathan was going to be joining them in Arlanda with Alice later in the evening. Josephine had also agreed to assist.

Saturday evening had been quite a revelation. It turned out that the files Josephine absconded with included the triggers, for him, his brothers, Alice, and others that he had not even been aware of. He wished he knew how to contact Mathias. Chantel said that he was not around when she dropped by the wine bar before leaving. He and Jonathan would take care of themselves, then look for Mathias.

They knew the triggers were sensory but wondered how they could be certain of not having them accidentally activated. The files showed that the triggers had to be paired and delivered simultaneously. All contained scent, the sense most connected to memory. These were paired with audio or visual triggers, which were anything from a pattern of speech, like poetry or a tone of a whistle. Some were also stimulated with an implant, but all had been set by subliminal suggestion, which meant they should be able to unset them the same way.

Switzerland

It may have been Sunday, but that was perfect for Magdeline to use Heather's lab privately to conduct the genetic testing on Suzanna and Claire.

Jack was having a reality hit mentally, just being around people again. The sight of Sophie, Magdeline, Rosie and Victoria together was making his head spin.

"I think we all need to just take a day to relax," Ben said.

They wound up talking to the concierge, who recommended they go to Old Town and the Ancient Arsenal.

Nick, Sophie, and Jeremy joined them.

"Maybe Shane and Daniel can come too!" Jeremy said.

Shane agreed, and after letting everyone else know, they headed out.

Victoria, Rosie, and Margot were going to play it safe and stay around the hotel, as would Soren, who would later escort Suzanna and Claire back to the hotel, while Magdeline caught up with Heather. Larry and Henri took an early flight up to Innsbruck to see if they could locate where Claire and Cora had been held, and Dave and Lidia were going chocolate tasting and sightseeing.

Austria

Henri had a decent lead on where they might be going. They knew it was near the border and Cora and Claire had left on foot. That was enough for INTERPOL to come up with a possible list of three hospitals.

"There can't be that many with a deserted wing. Cora gave us a good sketch to go by too," Larry said.

The first location on the list didn't fit, but the second had the road up to it gated off, which in Larry's mind was a sure sign they were in the right place.

"I don't suppose you thought to pack bolt cutters?" Henri asked.

"No, but after some of the experiences I've had, I should have. How far up is it?"

"About three miles. I have an idea though."

"Please share," Larry said.

"As we are back on the border, I can ask the local patrol to send in a drone to get a closer look."

"I like that a whole lot better than hiking up with no plan of escape, should the worst-case scenario occur."

"I'll make the call then and let you find a place for lunch."

By the time they finished eating, the drone was on location. It was definitely the right place. The Federal Police would send a team in as inspectors.

"There's no way that set up is legal," Henri said. "Just the fact that it's blocked off and I didn't see any other access. They'll be shut down on that basis alone as a safety issue."

Sweden

Richter listened and waited, willing himself to wake up. Mind over matter. He had to get out of there. He couldn't let them get away with this. Both his baby brothers had taken over the project that was rightfully his, and now they were taking Alice away as well. He focused his mind. He knew the lab. He had already planned the best route out. He just had to wake up.

Monday, June 13th

It was one in the morning, and Berna was sitting with Oscar when it happened. She had nodded off while reading. At first, she thought it was a dream when she saw Richter standing in front of her. When she realized she was awake, her heart was pounding in her throat, and she closed her eyes trying to maintain her breathing. Then she felt his breath in her ear, as he warned her not to fight. He took her phone and lifted her to her feet. He knew he could bypass the codes, but this would be so much easier.

He used her fingerprint at each door and elevator, easily making his way to the garage. He stopped, turned, and winked at the camera. Then slowly mouthed. "I'll be back." He climbed aboard one of the medical vans. Once he was outside the complex, he simply pushed Berna out the door and continued on. He knew the codes for his father's crypto accounts, and he could use Berna's phone to access whatever he needed.

Berna moaned and looked up at the moon, not quite full, as it glowed amongst the stars in the clear night. She tried to stand, but she couldn't. She would have to wait until someone found her. Fortunately, night didn't get too dark here in June, she thought, as a wolf howled in the distance, and she passed out.

At seven, Ivan came to check on his parents and have breakfast with his mother before leaving to pick up Chantel. What he discovered chilled him to the bone. He needed to find his mother and contact Carl and Jonathan, but they would be in surgery. He hurried to check the cameras and then headed to the garage, where he took a vehicle to go search for his mother.

Fortunately, it didn't take long to find her. Her pulse was erratic, and he could tell she was in shock. Her leg was swollen, and she moaned as he lifted her into the vehicle.

He called Chantel to let her know what happened and asked her to be on the lookout. He would send someone else to pick her up, and then he would need her immediately in the lab.

He checked his father's vitals. Without Richter, he would grow weaker. Now may be the last chance, while he still had recent stem cells from Richter circulating. He called the surgical team and told them to prep.

***

Jonathan handled the Inner Eye scope, which allowed them to view the surgery via a monitor in magnified, high definition, 3D, while Dr. Zendavev positioned the nano laser.

Josephine watched her vitals while Carl readied for the next phase. They were attempting to enter the optic nerve and sever the nano wire connecting the micro mote. The tissues had completely enclosed the wire, but by going in at the right spot they could greatly minimize the damage.

The tricky part would be when they got to the brain stem. It was still likely that Alice would experience some paralysis, but according to Dr. Zendavev, it could be substantially less than they'd thought. He believed she would retain some sense of feeling, even if only the sense of pressure. Then, with proper attention and therapy, the nerves would heal themselves.

Dr. Zendavev declared success of the first disconnection. One down, three to go, and they had already been at it nearly four hours.

In reality, they were performing four separate mini surgeries. The first three required use of a femtosecond laser to carefully remove a piece of skull, then locate the connection via the Inner Eye scope, followed by precise positioning of the nano laser and careful removal. Even a nanometer off could kill her.

Nine hours in, Dr. Zendavev had Josephine administer more anesthetic. He wanted the brain activity as low as possible for the final surgery. Carl would monitor her brain waves and intravenous drip, while Josephine assisted.

For this one, they were using two lasers. Since it was an intersecting connection near the brainstem, they needed to hit it from two directions, making certain that the lasers would connect and reflect each other precisely in the center of the wire. This would create a deflected beam of lesser intensity to travel down the wire in all directions, shorting out the micro motes. This wire they would not remove.

Carl prepared another injection of stem cells harvested from Richter, along with an anti-rejection serum.

As soon as they finished, Carl went to contact Ivan. When he saw the messages Ivan sent that morning, he went into the recovery room where Jonathan was sitting with Alice.

Dr. Zendavev and Josephine were leaving for the hotel and some, much needed sleep, but Carl asked Josephine to the other room first. She needed to know about Richter.

"I can wait," Dr. Zendavev offered.

"Thank you. I'd really appreciate it. This won't take more than a few minutes," Carl said.

When Josephine read the message, she was hardly surprised.

"I thought you should know. Just in case," Carl said.

"Thank you. I'll ask Dr. Zendavev to walk me to the room."

After she left, they called Ivan to see how the surgery had gone. He felt it went as well as could be expected, but like Alice, it was now a matter of wait and see.

Then Jonathan and Carl had a heart to heart about Josephine's role as their mother in their younger years. They would discuss Richter further with her later.

"We should contact Nick and Sophie," Jonathan said. "He could go after her."

"He could, but it will take him some time to get papers and a flight. I have no doubt he can access funds to do it, but it's more likely to be us he'll come after first. Fortunately, there's no way for him to know this location. My concern is that Alice can't stay here. We have to find a safe place for her."

"Can you help me get her back to Greece? We were safe there for three years. I also think we could find the person we need there to help us deactivate our triggers. You could come too. Then once we're free from that, we could become really free."

"I never knew you were such an optimist Jonathan."

"I need to hope."

"We can contact Sophie and Nick from the hotel tomorrow."

Switzerland

That evening they needed to make some decisions. Claire and Rosie needed a new safehouse, Nick, Sophie, Jeremy, Jack, Anne, and Ben needed to head back to Nova Scotia. Magdeline and Soren needed to get back to their boys and Shane needed to decide what he and Daniel would do next.

Suzanna wanted to develop her relationship with Claire, and Victoria had her next concert scheduled in Lyon. It only made sense for Larry and Margot to go with her and have her stay with them. Hopefully, they would be able contact her family.

The Chinese doctors were still out there and so was whoever took Claire and the woman Suzanna described from the spa.

Jack was probably the most anxious to get home.

"We're still not sure what the point was in abducting you, Jack. Any ideas?" Larry asked.

"No. One minute I was fishing, the next I woke up where you found me. There were no messages. I never saw anyone until the men I escaped from."

"Are you sure there wasn't some new piece of information in what you had on your computer?" Nick asked.

"Not that I'm aware of. I had been going back through everything, but..."

"The picture," Sophie said. "The picture of the girl at the parade. She would be about Magdeline's age. We still don't know who she is or the children at my eighth birthday party."

Claire looked at Sophie.

Sophie had considered getting to know her, but she hadn't because she felt guilty not telling her about Alice.

Nick read her mind and reached over to take her hand.

"What about all the children Josephine and Simon fostered and the girls you met, Sophie?" Larry asked.

"One looked like me and one looked like my adopted mother."

"How old were they?" asked Claire.

"They would have just turned eighteen."

Anne and Ben didn't say anything.

"So, I wasn't the only woman to give birth to daughters of the same features?" Claire asked.

"It would seem not," Larry said, looking at Claire.

"That leads to another question about the painting we discovered in Simon's lake house," Nick said.

"How old do you think that portrait is?" Larry asked, "Based on the clothes and hairstyle."

Margot took the phone from Larry to study the picture. "I would guess, around the time of the Roman empire and the time of Christ."

"I think that we need to find out who she is," Dave said.

"Did they ask Simon's man they arrested?" Nick asked.

"I doubt it," Henri said. "I'll make it a point to inquire. I'm fairly sure that Simon won't say. I got word today that he went completely bonkers. They had to put him in a padded cell."

"There's also the question of Charles," Soren added. "I'm positive that he's still active in this, and Ana is likely still at risk. And what about the girls I saw in Paris?"

"I think if we can find Josephine, we'll get a lot more answers. I still think the phone number she sent has to mean something," Anne said.

"Dave, do you want to check out the restaurant that number went to?" Larry asked.

Dave looked to Lidia.

Lidia looked to Suzanna.

"Go ahead," Suzanna said.

Chapter 28

Southern France: June 14th

The quake had done more damage than Svend anticipated. It had taken him nearly two days to dig himself out. He was just thankful that he didn't discover anyone else under the rubble he dug through.

They had decided on releasing pressure at two different points. Then all chaos broke loose. He wasn't even sure which way Nigel had gone. They were both too busy dodging the falling Stalactites and the cracks opening beneath them. The last thing he saw before ducking into the passage was Adam Hisdak. Apparently, he had been coming to take a midnight soak in the pools. If he'd been in them, he would have been boiled. As it was, he may have been skewered. Svend didn't know and he didn't care. He just hoped that Lily, Nigel, and the children had gotten out.

Sweden

Dr. Zendavev came with Josephine to check on Alice.

Carl and Jonathan were surprised that she had come back with him, but she said she felt safer there than at the hotel. She had told Dr. Zendavev the same, basically true story about leaving her husband and being scared he would find her.

Jonathan contacted Nick. Since he hadn't ever told Nick about Richter being at the lab, he now told him that he had it on good authority that Richter was in Sweden. Then he told them that they had performed an operation. They wouldn't know the results until she woke up, and they could perform more tests. Because of Richter they would need to move her again, Jonathan said he would stay with her and call again when he safely could. He mentioned the possibility of going back to Greece and wanted to be certain that Nick had been able to mail the package.

Nick confirmed that he had. Then he asked Jonathan if he knew about the painting. He didn't, but he asked Nick to describe it and said he would keep it in mind. Then they ended the call, and Nick went to update Sophie.

When they returned to the clinic, Josephine and Dr. Zendavev had a solution for them, at least for Josephine and Alice.

"I'm going with him to Russia as his assistant," Josephine said. "We could also take Alice with us."

"It will make things go much faster as far as getting the visa if she is not only my assistant, but a personal nurse to my patient. Josephine tells me that you are also in search of a good hypnotist. Something about reversing subliminal suggestions? If that is the case, then I suggest you apply to join us. There are three, in Saint Petersburg alone, that I can recommend."

"You could say that we are trying to test the reversal theory of a Pavlov's dog experiment," Carl said.

"On dogs?"

"On ourselves."

"I see. Well, Pavlov was himself my fellow Russian. You would be welcome to stay with me and follow Alice's progress. I'm a confirmed bachelor with a house big enough for a small city."

"Thank you! That is an amazing offer, and I believe that would be best for Alice right now," Carl said. "As far as myself, I'll consider it. First, I have things to tie up at home. Jonathan?"

"I agree. That is an amazing offer. Thank you."

"To be honest, I feel I get much more from it than you. Once in Russia, I can document Alice's case. I see it giving us great insight as far as the physical issues of the future. For example, I told you about the rumors of the Chinese operations. I would imagine many people in the future, like Alice, will want to have the tracking devices removed as well as the enhancers upgraded or replaced. Neurosurgery and artificial, or partially artificial intelligence, is the future. I also get a very talented and beautiful assistant. I have always wanted to play the prince and rescue a damsel in distress. Consider me at your disposal."

Switzerland

"What do you think you'll do after France?" Dave asked Lidia.

"Well, Suzanna wants to stay close to Claire. She doesn't have any other family, and I did come here under her employ. We've talked about continuing to look for Alice and sharing an apartment in France, at least for a while," Lidia replied.

"Maybe somewhere not too far from Lyon?" Dave suggested.

"Maybe," she smiled.

The full moon shown bright over the Alps, as they stood together in silence. She shivered in the night breeze. Dave put his arm around her. She turned to look up at him, warmed by his closeness, and he bent to kiss her.

Larry and Margot walked out on the Terrace and saw them.

"Now that looks like a good idea," Larry said, and Margot smiled up at him.

Part III

Chapter 29

Italian/French Border

The children smiled, as the border patrol met them. At first the guards thought they must be seeing things, but they both seemed to be having the same hallucination.

The children were dressed in simple pajamas and appeared to be dancing under the light of the full moon. There were three of them, somewhat dirty, but beautiful children, holding hands and humming a tune the guards recognized as a lullaby.

They were doing additional patrols along isolated areas of the border and could only assume these children had escaped from a smuggler. They tried to talk to them, but the children only moved further away and closer together.

One guard radioed in, and half an hour later a woman arrived. The children kept out of reach but didn't run. They gave an occasional smile, yet they seemed confused.

"They can't be more than three or four. Are there any towns near here?" the social worker, Linette, asked.

"Not walking distance. The only life you usually find out here is wildlife, and maybe a criminal. That's why we're guessing they must have escaped from smugglers. They're good-looking children. You'd be surprised what they would go for," one of the guards said.

"Unfortunately, I wouldn't be surprised," she replied and went to her car for some chocolate bars to offer them.

The children watched her a few seconds, then they went back to performing their dance.

"That's a first. Three children refusing chocolate." She tried water, thinking perhaps they were too thirsty for the chocolate. Then she tried juice and chips.

"Here," she said, handing a chocolate bar to each of the guards. "Let's try example."

The children laughed, as they watched them eat.

Then Linette went back to her car, dug around, and smiled. She came back to where the children were still dancing and pulled a stuffed bear from a bag. She reached out with it and smiled. The children drew together and backed away.

Then she pulled out a doll. The little girl lit up. They crept closer, holding hands.

The woman could tell they wanted the doll, but they wouldn't come close enough to be touched.

"They've obviously been traumatized by something. I don't want to traumatize them more, but they're in pajamas in the middle of nowhere in the middle of the night."

"Maybe another child," a guard suggested, "I mean, they were clearly tempted by the doll. So, maybe they would come to a real child."

"You may well be right, but I don't have one of those in my trunk. If we try to grab them, they'll just be more traumatized. This is one of those nights," she added, staring up at the full moon.

The children continued to dance and hum, hand in hand, until they grew weary. Then they moved back toward the trees.

"They're on the French side now," the patrol said.

"Have you notified the French patrol?" Linette asked.

"It wouldn't do any good. There are no roads for them to come in on near here."

They waited and listened for another half an hour, then she walked toward the woods. The moon gave off good light, and she saw them a minute later, snuggled up together, under a tree. She walked back and asked the guards to join her. Each one picked up a child, who awoke and stared, startled, but they didn't fight.

When she got them to the children's center, they were sound asleep again, holding hands.

Nova Scotia: Friday, June 24th

Jack had taken Jeremy fishing. They didn't go alone though. Both Tom and Shannon joined them.

Sophie helped go through the boxes of files Anne and Ben had confiscated and mailed to themselves before going to Switzerland. It would take forever to decipher it all. Much of it was not in the English or the French they were fluent in, but German and much of it was coded.

Nick was working next to them, on his computer and was excitedly looking through an article on a woman he thought could be a match for the woman represented in the portrait from Simon's house in Switzerland.

"Soph?"

"Uhuh," she replied.

"I think I found you."

"I didn't know you lost me," Sophie answered, coming over to join him. "Who is she?" she asked, looking over his shoulder.

Nick scrolled back up so she could see the heading.

"There's still no exact hit on the portrait image, but what do you think?"

"Well, I could do worse than a Celtic warrior queen. Boudicca? If I do have her genes, at least I don't have her name."

Anne and Ben both came over to look.

"I've read about her," Ben said. "I can definitely see the resemblance."

"Royalty and a warrior, that sounds like exactly what they're looking for too," Nick added.

"You forgot my beauty," Sophie pouted.

"Never," Nick said. "I wish I could decipher the signature. I've run it through several art sights, but no match."

"It's me," Sophie said, decidedly. "I think we should call Soren. He may have a source to compare it with. Remember the vault he told us about in Switzerland."

"Yeah, but first, he doesn't work there anymore, and second, I don't think it's like a library where you can just go in and pick one out on a whim."

"Maybe not, but I still think we should send it to them. This is just as much about Magdeline as it is any of us," Sophie said, as she scrolled down the article.

"From what I recall, Boudicca, wasn't exactly a nice warrior queen," Ben said.

"Not nice is mild, but definitely a warrior" Sophie said, as she continued reading about the woman whose image, she now believed to be representative of.

Sweden

Richter had left the vehicle in a Riksgransen, ICA grocery parking lot. From there he made his way on foot across the border to the port of Narvik, in Norway.

He was lucky, he ran into one of the men he had worked with before, when he made his way from Nova Scotia. He had just needed someone to take him as far as Gothenburg. Then it was an easy matter to acquire a new identity.

It had been even easier than he hoped. He looked at the passport. He would still need to dye his hair. For now, he was on his way to acquire the tinted contacts. Then he would take a ferry out to the archipelagos where he could take some time to recover physically.

He had rented a nice little beach cottage from the brother of one of the fishermen he came down the coast with. The sea air and hiking trails would be a perfect place to recover and plan.

***

For the first time in decades, Oscar Noostrom opened his eyes. Now they would begin the long road of recovery. His vitals were good, but he was clearly confused when he looked at Berna. He had recognized her, saying her name, but nothing more. He must have noticed the age difference. Even though she had been on treatments to delay aging, she was obviously not the young woman he had last seen.

Now, he was sleeping, as they monitored his brain waves.

"I've thought about this a million times," Berna said, "but I've never figured out how to explain the passage of so many years."

"We'll figure it out together, mom," Ivan said.

"I'm concerned about Richter. I'm thinking that maybe we should evacuate," Carl suggested.

Berna shook her head. "No. I won't run scared. It's not that I don't want to leave, but there are so many people here who depend on you. You and Ivan can make a real difference in the world. With your work, you have a chance to make up for the evils committed by your father. Tell me you won't run from that responsibility."

Carl looked from his mother to his brother and back.

"I need to go to Saint Petersburg, but I promise to return as soon as the trigger is deactivated."

Berna smiled at him. "Thank you. I know you need to do that. I want you to do that, to be free. When do you leave?"

"As soon as I hear from Jonathan and Josephine. I know you're in good hands with Ivan, and Chantel. I just wish that I knew where Richter was."

"We've implemented added security," Ivan said, "and it's a lot harder to get in than out of here."

"Actually," Berna said, "You're the one who needs to be careful. If he was after me, I'd have far worse than a sprained ankle. It's you and Jonathan he wants revenge on."

France

Svend found Nigel at the second rendezvous site, and together, they went in search of Lily and the children. They found Lily two days later. She had been trapped between two separate tunnel collapses and survived by drinking what water she could as it came through the cracks in the ground, from springs below.

She told them what happened with Kenneth and how she told the children to run.

"At least we know they made it out," Nigel said, as he helped Lily to the truck they'd bought from a local farmer.

They checked into a nearby hotel in hopes of seeing a news report on the children and to decide what to do next.

It had been ten days. Nigel and Svend had searched the surrounding woods to no avail.

"Perhaps they were on the news before we found you and came here," Nigel said.

"It's not like we can publicly look for them," Svend said. "There's nothing to prove you have any relation to them, and..."

"And they don't know us as anything other than their caregivers. They don't know anything except the project. They must be so confused. If they were asked, they wouldn't even understand the concept of parents, much less grandparents. We should have found a way to tell them," Lily said.

"They were three and being indoctrinated by Mel. How? If we'd tried, they may have separated us from them," Nigel said.

"We should have found a way," Lily said, wiping the tears from her eyes. "What if no one found them? Even though they made it through the cave doesn't mean..."

"There's no way to know," Nigel said.

"What if Kenneth hurt them?" Lily went on.

"I wouldn't worry about that," Svend said. "My guess is that he would have been looking for his mother. He may be mean, but he cried for days when they first brought him."

"That's true," Lily admitted. "I wonder where they took him from. His accent was American. More important though, what do we do next? We don't know who is and who isn't still out there. It's even possible that Adam or Mel found them."

"I doubt that." Svend said. "If they made it out, they would have had to go through either the tunnel into Spain, which is a good hundred kilometers, or Italy. They'd also have no way of knowing the children escaped, much less by which tunnel. Honestly, I don't see how either of them, especially Adam, could have survived. He was right by the pools."

"They may have made it out through the garden, assuming it wasn't buried," Nigel added.

"This speculation isn't getting us anywhere. We need to contact our families," Svend said. "You said your daughter had contact with agents from the states and INTERPOL."

"Yes," Lily said. "We'll call her tomorrow. I can't face it right now. It all seems too surreal. I don't want to mess up her life with Nick. We need to find out what's happening in Paris. They would know if Adam or Mel made it out. I just feel so, so... I don't even know what I feel anymore."

Nigel sat beside her and put his arm around her shoulders. "I'm thinking that maybe we shouldn't call her at all. I remember the name of the man we spoke to before, and I don't want to risk Sophie coming here and putting herself in danger. You know how she is. Let's go directly to him through INTERPOL. Nigel said, as he turned to Svend.

Svend nodded. "If we go that route, then I should be on the call too, and we need to go over what to tell him."

"Agreed," Nigel said, and Lily nodded.

Austria

Soren and Magdeline looked over the information that Sophie sent them on Boudicca, and then Soren called Trudie, just to see if they even had a sample in the vault.

"You do. Well, is it something that could be requested from Magdeline's lab? Yes, yes, I see the email. We'll fill out the request now. Thank you!"

"Well, that was easier than I thought. It seems that simply because your lab is affiliated with the university, you qualify to request samples."

"You know," Magdeline said, looking at the information from Sophie again, "For the first time since I found out about all this, I'm kind of excited. It is possible that only the mitochondrial DNA was used, but from the bio on her, I have a feeling there is a deeper genetic relationship."

"I don't doubt it," Soren said, "I've always known you were a warrior princess."

"Just promise, if this comes back positive, you won't start calling me Xena."

"How about madame X?"

Magdeline shot him the raised eyebrow look, and they both broke into laughter.

Lyon, France

Larry found an apartment for Claire and Rosie two blocks from him and Margot.

Suzanna Morgan was also setting up house in Lyon and had gotten Lidia a neighboring apartment. and Shane also decided to stay on with Daniel for the time being.

With a little helpful financing from Mrs. Morgan, they were all now living within walking distance, in lodgings, otherwise far outside their budgets.

Lidia and Dave were shopping for her apartment after returning from an extended break where they met with Laura at her wine bar.

Neither Laura or Dave and Lidia felt at liberty to share what they really knew. Laura wouldn't risk Mathias life or having her home excavated. And Dave and Lidia could have no idea that she would believe a single thing they said, even if they had felt able to be open.

As far as Laura knew, they had been hired by Anne and Sophie to find Josephine, and Josephine's whereabouts was something Laura had no idea of.

Dave and Lidia also went by the vineyard and questioned the workers. Then they informed Tony and his father of Simon's arrest. This was another reason that they gave for being concerned about and looking for Josephine.

If Josephine were not found and Simon was declared incompetent, then legally, Tony and his father would be able to petition for ownership of the vineyard. There were no other heirs listed, and as they were already legally in charge, and Tony had title to the plot his house was on, their odds were good.

Victoria had gone to rehearsal and been shocked to find her younger brother waiting for her in the lobby.

"How? When? Are mom and dad…"

"They're the ones who told me to come. They insisted I get away. They covered for me and said they would try to follow if they could. They don't feel life is worth living if they have to live it there any longer. I would have come to you sooner, but I thought they would be watching for that."

"They were. I wondered why I was suddenly being watched, but they never mentioned you. They just showed me a tape of mom and dad. I thought they had already killed you," she said, setting her violin aside and embracing him. She pulled back to look at him and ask again, "How?"

"You aren't the only smart one in the family," he smiled.

"I'm not the only of more than that," she said, turning away.

"We know there are others. I think mom and dad always knew," he said, putting a hand on her shoulder.

She turned. "Please, Cody, tell me everything, and I'll tell you everything that I've found out. The last few weeks have been crazy, and you need to know. I have to rehearse now, but please stay, and we can have the rest of the day."

They talked until nearly midnight, before Victoria made the decision.

"I have a list, a list of phone numbers," she said. I've used one already and I still don't know who the person is, but they have connections to the project in China. They gave me the file on myself, and the same day they did, someone tried to trigger me."

"We should make the call from the phone in my hotel room," Cody said.

Victoria had already left a message with Margot, that she would be late, and possibly spending the night with two of her fellow musicians.

As they road in the taxi to Cody's hotel, she noticed a message from Rosie. It was too late to reply now. They would see each other at the concert tomorrow. Before she shared anything more, she wanted to try and find out if their parent's lives were still at stake. She thought about what Margot said to her before, when she had been deciding whether to go on living herself. She rolled it over in her mind. If they killed her parents, there was nothing to prevent her from working fully with the others, nothing to stop her or Cody from sharing their combined knowledge.

At his hotel, she dialed one of the numbers, and the phone rang the prescribed four times before she hung up. Then she dialed again. The voice answered on the twelfth ring. She believed it was a man, but the voice distortion made it impossible to know for certain.

The first thing she was told was not to say anything to her brother.

"Excuse me?"

"It is good that you called me. He's not who you think he is. The situation with your parents is still unknown, but I now believe that they tried to escape before our previous call."

"I was shown a tape of them," Victoria said.

"It was prerecorded. I cannot say if their escape was successful, but I do know that no bodies have been returned to the compound. The man you think is your brother, isn't. If he is with you, which I am guessing he is, due to your call, you'll need to disarm him. Your brother, your real brother left with your parents. This may seem hard to believe, but the one with you now is not human. You must deactivate him. You can do this by simply pressing the indentation on the nape of his neck.

"After it is disarmed, you should also dismantle, but not without protective gear. Do you understand?"

"I think so," Victoria replied, confused as she watched Cody, and he watched her.

"If you don't, not only you, but all of your new friends will be in mortal danger. I should go now."

"Please, wait. Can't you explain more?"

"Trust me, please."

"I received a letter…"

"Stop! If it is about the ballad, I should have found a way to tell you before. It is safe to read. The melody was changed to make it safe. In fact, you need to read it. It may give you and others many answers. I don't know what it means myself, but

I know the source, and I believe it is trustworthy. Remember, one firm push to the indent on the back of its neck. Just one. Two could cause a dangerous mess that you won't want to deal with. Good luck to you."

Victoria stared at the phone in her hand before slowly lowering it back into the cradle.

"What did they say?" Cody asked.

"They said that they didn't know any more about our parents."

"And?"

"They confirmed that they had mixed human and animal genes successfully and told me not to trust Larry," she lied.

"Did they say why?"

"They said that he had a connection to one of the doctors in the project," she said, trying to make up a convincing scenario. "It looks like you truly are the only one I can trust. Oh, Cody, I'm so scared," she cried, throwing her arms around him and pushing her fingers into the back of his neck.

The body fell slack in her arms. She backed away and let it slump against the foot of the bed. For a moment, she stared, dazed, and then she called Larry.

Chapter 30

June 25th

Larry tried to block out the ringing breaking into his dream. His hand batted the phone off the bedside table. It stopped momentarily, and he cuddled closer to Margot. Then it began again, and he realized it was the emergency ring. Suddenly alert, he dove for the phone and Margot bolted awake.

Margot clicked the lamp on and watched as Larry, holding his phone between ear and neck, tried to pull his pants on.

"Just put it on speaker," she said, getting up to switch the overhead light on.

He did, and they both listened and dressed.

Twenty minutes later they were at the hotel room.

Larry picked up the body in a fireman's carry, and they went down the back stairs together.

"My niece's boyfriend," Margot said in explanation as a group passed them. Those who passed seemed almost as in need of being carried themselves and gave a friendly chuckle in reply.

After they got it into the car, Margot drove while Larry tried to figure out where to find a hazmat suit to perform the dismantling.

Later that morning, Margot stared at the inanimate body that lay on the floor of Larry's office. They had taken turns watching it, just in case. Dave, Lidia, and Suzanna were on their way over, and Shane was taking Daniel over to Rosie and Claire.

Larry had just put in a call to a contact who said they could supply two hazmat suits and was on his way out the door.

Victoria tried to sleep, but she couldn't. Fortunately, she knew the music for tonight's line up so well that she could probably play it in her sleep. She only had five hours before she was due at the concert hall, and Margot insisted she eat something while she studied the previously feared ballad.

The ballad wasn't the only thing on her mind though. She couldn't stop wondering about her family, and that included Suzanna Morgan and her sister, Claire.

The tests that Magdeline did showed that Claire and Suzanna were most definitely the product of different fathers, however, without a sample from the father they grew up with, there was no way to determine which was which.

There were too many unknowns. Was Claire or Suzanna Victoria's biological mother? She knew it would have been Claire who gave birth, but she understood that Suzanna's eggs had also been harvested. Could that be because she was the daughter of the man in New Orleans? Why would they choose someone of Jewish decent? Then again, why not? Even if some of those involved seemed to be former Nazi's, it didn't mean that the project held Nazi convictions.

She wished her mind would settle. She wished she could talk to Claire. Perhaps it was because of Rosie, but she felt much more comfortable around Claire than Suzanna. Suzanna Morgan, though deeply involved, somehow seemed out of place. There was just something about her that didn't connect, even though she was putting in an obvious effort to do so.

Not that Victoria should judge. She'd been the misfit too, unable to connect, until she got to know Rosie and Margot.

She accepted the hot tea and one of the rolls that Margot brought from the kitchen and continued rereading the ballad. She couldn't shake the feeling that answers were staring her in the face, but it made no sense to her. Something, some key was missing. Could the words themselves be in code? She began again, this time marking repeating words.

The musician in her started to put it to the tune. Maybe if she memorized it musically, something would come to her.

The ballad was similar to an old ballad of war, but certain words were changed pointing to a modern meaning. She began again. *"Whispers of technology, fingers tapping at your soul. Warriors come and warriors go, this is never meant for you to know. At the place where whispers spark, treading circles in the dark, here the warrior finds their path, integrated in the math. Futures past no disk can hold. This is the fate of warriors bold."*

Alexandria, Egypt

Leona smiled. Things had turned out better than she expected. The boy was well placed and had passed the word about the collapse, literally, of Adam's project. She had been there once before and had hoped to take over the location herself, but she could adapt. At least Adam was out of the way. The only thing that disappointed her was that she would miss out on delivering his triggers. Oh well, the herbs and spices would last and may still be useful later.

She knew there were many others, and as she browsed the shelves of the rare books section at the Bibliotheca Alexandria, she was learning more and more about their origins. She was learning more about herself as well.

Eventually she would have to go to Paris and later, Berlin, but not until she was well prepared.

She browsed the book on star charts and took it, as well as the books on transmutation and alchemy, to a nearby table.

These were the sources of power she had been led to study. The sources that when combined, and used by people well trained in them, could change the world. They must be used only by the right people, those well-disciplined and intelligent enough to understand and responsibly use the power.

In the wrong hands, the same disciplines Leona hoped to use to improve life and the ways we interact in this world, could be used to destroy the world.

There would still be destruction, but it would be only for the overall benefit.

Leona had become a strong believer in eradication of those who would stand in the way of benefiting the many.

Lyon, France

Larry had been stuck in a traffic jam along the Boulevard De Clichy, and he returned just an hour before Victoria had to leave for her concert.

It was decided that Margot and Shane would accompany her, while the others stayed behind. Henri Seville, on his own time, had already done a thorough security check and would meet them there. Larry would join them later with Suzanna. Dave and Lidia would keep watch over the AI version of Victoria's brother.

"I keep expecting his eyes to fly open," Lidia said to Dave, as she made some popcorn, and he scanned a list of films.

"I guess I shouldn't choose a horror flick then," he replied.

"Nothing sci-fi either, please. He doesn't give you the creeps?"

"More than you know. I keep flashing back to when Saville and I were guarding Richter in Nova Scotia. He was hooked up to all kinds of machines and almost comatose, then, boom! He overpowered a doctor and escaped. Victoria told us how she turned him off, but who knows what might turn him on."

"Thanks for the comforting thought," Lidia replied, bringing over the popcorn and some lemonade.

"Thank you," he replied, smiling up at her. "That smells wonderful. I wasn't expecting dinner with the show," he added with a wink.

Lidia wasn't sure what she wanted to do more, smack him or kiss him. She decided on the latter, and then she chose a chick flick she'd been wanting to see.

When the movie ended, Lidia decided to call Charice and check on her cats. If she was going to stay in France, she would have to make a decision about them coming as well.

While she did that, Dave made some real food.

"What's that smell?" Lidia asked when she hung up the phone.

"Meatballs and a Cesar dressing for the salad."

"No, it isn't," she said, wrinkling her nose. "I think it's coming from him," she added, leaving Larry's office to join Dave in the kitchen.

Dave went to the office door, sniffed the air, and closed the door.

"I think we should put those hazmat suits on," Dave said. "Actually, you go outside and call Larry. I'll get suited up and take a closer look."

"Be careful."

He kissed her, and she grabbed her phone.

After she was out, he hurried into the suit. The smell was becoming stronger and seeping under the doorway now.

***

The concert was in its final encore, when Larry felt his phone vibrate and made his way to the lobby. He went back into the auditorium and told Saville to not let them come home. He would be in touch soon. Then he and Shane hurried out.

When they arrived, Lidia was pacing the sidewalk in front. Shane stayed with her while Larry hurried inside. The odor was horrible, even though he had covered his face with his sport coat. He grabbed the second hazmat suit, pulled it on, and opened the door to his office.

He was relieved when he saw Dave seemed to be unharmed. He couldn't say the same for the body that lay beside him. It looked like a corpse that had been left to rot for a week in the elements. Not a pretty sight.

"It seems to be omitting some kind of gas, and the secretions of whatever they used for blood, is soaking through the tissue and causing an acidic like deterioration. However, I got these out, and they appear to be undamaged," Dave said, pointing to a tissue, where he had laid several small chips as well as what appeared to be bone and sinew and a hand. "I took a chance that his hand would be chipped and possibly readable. It's hard to tell. I was just trying to separate as much of him from the corrosion of whatever this thing is bleeding."

"Good job, Dave. I wish I had bigger hazmat bags. Though, there doesn't seem to be that much of him left," Larry said.

"What's really odd is that nothing under the body seems to be affected. I mean the carpet is stained, but it's not deteriorated. It's almost like, the body is evaporating," Dave continued. "I'm thinking he must have had some kind of self-destruct timer."

Larry scooped the pieces Dave had set aside into a hazmat bag. "I'm thinking we probably don't want to stay here tonight," Larry said. "I'm also thinking we should just leave it here until we analyze the substances. It's clearly not going anywhere now."

"I want to try and get inside the head before the skull is completely gone. Can you take the one side while I take the other? I think if we pull it will separate above the nose. I couldn't do it on my own without it dripping inside."

"Sure," Larry said, looking at the red and white slime soaking its way through the... bone? He gently grasped behind the ear, which began to deteriorate at his touch, as if it was leprosy ridden. He was glad he hadn't had time for dinner, or they would have had a bigger mess.

They had to gently jiggle to pull it apart, and once they did, they were left with a gelatinous mass, that looked much like a human brain.

Larry put it in another hazmat bag, and they left, exiting onto the back portico, where they took off the suits and took in deep breaths of fresh air.

"I did get some good photos of it as it went, which was fairly fast after it started," Dave said.

"Good, I'll look at them later. Right now, I need to call Margot, and you should update Lidia. She's out front with Shane."

"Right, and that?" Dave asked, looking at the hazmat bags.

"Maybe Henri will have an idea. Go on," Larry said, and Dave made his way around to the front.

Shane was trying to comfort Lidia, who was in tears, certain that something awful had happened to Dave.

"Hey," Shane said to Lidia when he saw Dave come around the corner.

"Don't tell me you were worried Yarnok," Dave said.

Lidia ran to him. She looked him straight in the eyes, then gave him a resonating slap. "That was just to wipe the cocky look off your face. I was scared to death," she cried.

"It's okay, I'm fine."

"What happened in there?"

"This," he said, handing her his phone. "Larry put the, uhm, parts I was able to get aside into some hazmat bags. He's working on what to do with those now. We want to have them analyzed before we go back in and clean up. That one there is all that was left when we left."

"Let me see," Shane said, coming to join them.

Larry came around at the same time, and they all looked.

"It reminds me of what Ralph described," Shane said.

"Well, we won't find out more until Monday. For now, I locked the bags inside. It looks like we'll all have to bunk with you and Lidia tonight. Boys with Dave, girls with Lidia, if you can spare the space," Larry said.

"I called Claire and Rosie," Shane said. "Daniel is already asleep there. So, I'm good to go."

Larry yawned, "Sorry. That *thing* had me up since two this morning. Anyway, everyone will be meeting us at Suzanna's."

Paris

It was Sunday, the perfect day to move out of the Institute. After hearing about Simon and now Adam and the majority of operations collapsing in the earthquake, Katerina breathed a sigh of relief. While she loved the science, she had long ago stopped trusting the men behind it.

She wondered just how involved Aaron was. He certainly seemed to have all the information, and she wondered how a historian, working in a basement of a DNA vault in Switzerland, managed to be so well informed about the heads of P2P.

She had known his father and wondered at the truth surrounding his death. No, back up. She wondered if he was dead. He had asked her and others to be part of the CDC several years ago, then after the abduction of his pick for director, the program had disappeared, or had it?

She tried to ask Adam about it once, but he had brushed off the question in the overly nice way he had of treating everyone like ants in his own private ant farm.

She felt bad for the children, who had certainly been killed or trapped in the collapse. No emergency workers would come to rescue them because they didn't exist anywhere on record. The location itself was considered toxic by those not in the know.

She walked down the hallway, looking in the empty labs. The only one there was Oliveria. As head of P2P security, she not only lived on site, but was the one working with Aaron on what to do with the samples stored there.

Was there someone else in the projects who could take over from Adam and Mel? Erickson, maybe? Would they restart here? If Meschner's sons had stuck around, she was certain they would, but all four seemed to have vanished. She knew it wasn't over, but her part was. She just needed to clear her computer and gain access to her funds and identity that had been stored in the systems block chain.

To truly leave the project, she had to erase all signs that she had ever been part of it and start again as someone else. She was too high level to simply walk away.

Chapter 31

Italy: July 2ⁿᵈ

"They still won't talk, but they appear to be triplets. They would be worth a small fortune on the black market," Linette told her supervisor, Deara Brusio. "They're inseparable. They even go to the toilet together. I think separating them would be too much for them to handle emotionally. Is there anyone you can think of who may be willing to foster all three?"

"Not locally. I wish we knew their origin. They could have a family out there somewhere looking for them, but so far INTERPOL has no child knapping reports that match their description, and it's been nearly three weeks. The odds are that their parents are either dead or sold them, whether willingly or out of desperation," Deara said, as she scanned her computer screen and pursed her lips.

"What are you thinking?"

"You said they seem to understand instructions in Italian?"

"They seem to," Linette answered. "They also seem to understand French, German and English, which suggests an educated western European family. That's why I find it so odd they haven't been reported missing. Even if their parents were dead, I would have expected a relative to be looking for them."

"True, but since they won't speak, could they just be following in line with the other children?"

"Not likely. They tend to avoid other children and have had instruction independent of the groups. For example, during the medical examination. They seemed to understand everything."

"I know a family in Milan that used to take in siblings. I'll give them a call," Deara said, as she checked the database for the number and dialed.

Austria: July 5th

Magdeline and Soren were just getting back into a routine with the boys when her parents called to tell them the news. They were taking in three new foster children. They were thought to be triplets, two boys and one girl, escaped from a smuggling operation. They were about the same age as the boys, but they were traumatized and non-verbal. They wondered if Magdeline and Soren would come visit. They hoped that the boys might help pull them out of their communal shell.

"Technically, we both still have time off, and maybe if the boys are busy with other children, we could even pull off some of that second honeymoon," Magdeline suggested.

"I think that sounds like a great idea."

Saint Petersburg, Russia: July 20th

Josephine couldn't remember the last time she had laughed like she had this evening. A part of her said she shouldn't be happy. She had no right to happiness, not after what she had allowed Simon to do to her family. She tried to remember that it wasn't all her fault. If she hadn't married Simon, they would have found another way. There was no escaping the family, and they had been family even before they married. No, this started before her, maybe even before her grandmother and aunt left with the soldiers.

As the story was related to her by a cousin, her aunt Marta, whose husband was injured and had a young son, moved back in with Josephine's grandmother, Lilianna after her grandfather, Peter Fontaine, was killed. Nazis then took over the family Chateau where they lived. Eventually, they killed Marta's husband, son and possibly her brother, but accounts varied, and they would likely never know the full truth.

Both Josephine's grandmother and aunt had also, reportedly, been raped and were known to be pregnant before disappearing with the same men who raped them. It made no sense. All she could think was that they didn't have a choice.

She later learned that her grandmother had given birth to twin boys and her aunt, Marta, had a daughter who married Dr. Hans Meschner, who then tracked his wife's family back to Josephine's mother, Emma, in Ireland.

His cousin, Alexander, had gone to medical school in Paris and came to Ireland at Hans request. Alexander was charming and handsome. He had flattered and encouraged Josephine in ways that gave her confidence she had never felt before. She gave herself to him freely, never exposing the father of her baby. Meschner worked at the hospital where she gave birth, and he promised to find their son a good home.

In her defense, she hadn't known that Simon was her cousin until after the wedding. She felt a sudden connection with her aunt Marta. Marta not only went to Brazil with, but later married and had even more children with a Nazi, who may have killed her husband, son, and brother. Of course, it may not have been the same soldier, but still, he had been one of the Nazi's who took over their home.

Josephine tried to tell herself that by staying married to Simon, she was protecting her family, but she hadn't. If she had, Lily and Nigel wouldn't have needed to work for P2P in order to protect Sophie.

The truth was, she had still felt charmed by, and to be honest, even attracted to Alexander. She had no idea who his boy's biological mother, or mothers were, but she had loved them as her own. To be completely honest, she wanted to stay close to the projects, and helped as much as she could, to keep the connection to Alexander. No, she had no right to be happy.

She let her lust for Alexander Meschner, and the confidence he had continued to nurture in her, cloud her judgement to the extreme.

What could she do now? She had learned that Simon was locked up, at least for now. Still, as far as she knew, Adam, and his father, Dr. Nadier, were still in charge of P2P. That meant that the threat was still as big as ever.

She wanted Lily and Nigel to be free. She wanted Amber and Polina to be free. Yet, after all she had done, she was the freest of them all and once again being wooed by a charming doctor.

Malachi Zendavev had given her not only a new job, but an entire wing of his mansion, complete with a personal maid. To top it off, he was taking her out on the town almost every night, and he helped both Carl and Jonathan find doctors able to release them from their triggers.

They would have a couple more weeks of therapy and tests to be certain, but then they would be leaving. She hated to see them go, but she needed to let them go, like she needed to let go of their father. She knew he wasn't a good man, but he had still been better to her than any other man had, until now.

She would do what she could to help Alice. That was the only person she could help now, and she hoped that somehow, Jonathan, and maybe Mathias, could help Lily and Nigel. Carl had already been given the information on Polina and Amber, and he promised to do what he could to keep them safe.

She rolled over and turned out the light. When she fell
asleep, she saw the face of the man who accosted her in
Uppsala. He seemed to stare into her very soul, and she
woke with a start, wondering who he was and why his face
kept haunting her.

Alice was dreaming too. Or was it a dream? Lately she
had been having a hard time differentiating between
dreams and memories. Her mind felt constantly half asleep.
Jonathan and Carl told her there would be side effects.
She still couldn't see clearly, but doctor Zendavev assured
her that was temporary. She had feeling in her limbs, but
both her arms and legs were experiencing consistent
numbness and tingling, along with occasional painful
spasms. The nerves had been traumatized by the surgery,
but tests showed that there was no serious damage. They
said, it was a bit like stubbing your toe. When you hit it, it
hurts, maybe tingles and spasms, and you may have to hop
on one foot for a while before you walk on it again. In
Alice's case, it would be some time before she could use her
whole body again, and likely months of therapy before she
could walk normally, but she would.
She had so many questions, but some she knew they
couldn't answer. She wanted to know who it was in her
dreams, her dreams that she wasn't certain were dreams.
Before she went to New York and met Sophie and Jack,
there were things in her life that weren't her life, things she
only remembered in pieces.
Ever since she had hit puberty, she had been unable to
sleep for more than a couple of hours. Then when she went
to New York and stopped taking the vitamins, she had
started sleeping like a normal person again. Before that,
she had led two, almost completely separate lives, and she
couldn't help but wonder what had happened to that
second life, or why she could only remember splinters of it.

Had she really owned a cabin? Had she had a boyfriend? She remembered dancing, taking photos, and playing the violin, but in each situation, there had been different men. She also had flashbacks about her time up in Canada with Richter. How could the man, who had continued the evil of Dr. Meschner, also be the same man she had nursed and lugged through the snow to save? Who was the woman who came to take them?

For three years, she had pushed all this aside and made a life in Greece. Jonathan and Carl were now her closest friends, and she trusted them like brothers.

According to Jonathan, he was her brother, in a way. She still didn't understand all the genealogy, the genetics behind her or their existence. She just wanted a normal life, like she had in Greece... like she had for those few days with Jack.

She wanted to rewind time, to go back to that little town where they were stranded in Canada. What if she and Sophie hadn't run, if they had stayed in Nova Scotia and just forgotten what they had learned? Maybe they would have been left to live normal lives.

Jonathan told her she could still have a normal life after she recovered, but how? She knew he needed to encourage himself that it was possible as much as her, so she had only smiled up at him. She knew he felt the same about Aida as she did about Jack. The fact was that no matter how much they wanted to be normal, they weren't. Then again, Sophie and Nick had married and had a son.

If only she could shut off her mind.

A spasm ran through her nerves, and she panted, waiting for the pain to pass. She could feel her body perspiring, and then the pain eased, and once again she was left with only the ache in her heart.

Nova Scotia

Sophie and Jeremy watched as Nick coached Jack, who was preparing for an international skating competition. His first event was at the end of October in Quebec. If he ranked high enough there, he would go on to Helsinki, and then Saint Petersburg for the championship.

Sophie was glad to see him back on the ice. He loved skating, but for nearly a month, he had moped around, doing nothing except fishing day in and day out. He was upset with both Sophie and his parents. He knew they were hiding something from him, and while they had told him about what happened in Scotland, they had not told him about the files they confiscated. Nick knew they had some, and had told him as much, but said it was nothing more than what he had already seen. She knew Jack didn't believe it any more than he had believed she left Greece early because of a birthday surprise.

Nick finally managed to break through to Jack. Even though he went behind his back to register him for the competition, the excitement of being back on the ice won Jack over.

Jonathan, as Sherman, had contacted them to say Alice was recovering well, but at Alice's request, he would not tell them where she now was.

The files Anne and Ben had taken were overwhelming, and many hours were spent on conference calls between Sophie, Nick and Jack's parents and Larry, Margot, Dave, Lidia, and Shane, who had decided to sell his house and stay in France.

Sophie wasn't sure if they would ever get through it all, but she needed to know as much as possible, now more than ever, as she and Nick were expecting a daughter early next year. Jeremy was thrilled at the idea of being a big brother, as well as a cousin to the baby Nick's brother, Matt and wife, Mindy, were expecting around the same time.

Jack and Nick finished the sequence and skated over to them.

"That spin was so cool, Uncle Jack!" Jeremy exclaimed. Even though he had seen Nick do the same spin a hundred times, Jeremy was always eager to help cheer Jack on.

"Thanks buddy," Jack replied.

Jeremy definitely had a way with people, Sophie thought, smiling at her son.

When they got home and Jeremy was down for a nap, she pulled Nick aside.

"I was talking to Magdeline, and I know you are going to be crazy busy in October, so..."

"So, you're planning to go see her?"

"And take Jeremy to meet her boys. "

"And?"

"By that time, there are tests she can do to help us find out what to expect."

"Jeremy is normal, why wouldn't our daughter be?" Nick asked, pulling her to him.

"Because she's a daughter," Sophie answered, pulling back just enough to look up at him. "You know as well as I do that the girls are the focus of the projects."

"I know, and I understand, but I don't like the idea of you going without me."

"I don't like that part either, but it makes sense. You know that Jeremy would love to meet the triplets, and I think it would be good for me too. We sent Magdeline copies of the files, and I'd like a chance to go through them with her."

"You know what? I am not even going to waste time trying to argue you out of it."

"That's because you know I'm right, and you'll be too busy with Jack to even miss us."

"I am never that busy," he replied.

Italy

Magdeline was at a loss. They had been at her parent's home in Milan for over a week, watching the children interact. They had even invited over a neighbor's daughter, so that the little girl wouldn't feel so outnumbered.

The children seemed kind and intelligent. They even smiled a lot, yet they couldn't seem to connect with others, and the only words they muttered were "Thank you" and each other's names, which they had finally told to the triplets on day three. Until that point, they had been referred to by the first three letters of the alphabet.

They played okay but didn't seem to really know how. The boys had, of course, brought a football to play with, and they picked up the game quickly. They seemed to enjoy dancing and humming a tune that Magdeline recognized as an English lullaby.

What had really been surprising was their ability to write. They wrote in English and French, yet clearly understood both Italian and German as well. They had most definitely not come from an uneducated home.

Magdeline had even called Larry to ask if he could try and give his friends at INTERPOL a push to find their parents and possibly look into it himself.

They were still hunting for all the "Family" connections, but there seemed to be nothing urgent at the moment. Victoria was still staying with Larry and Margot, and no one new had gone missing. So, Larry promised he would check into it.

Paris, France

Dave took Lidia into Paris to show her the sites and also to do some more research.

Today, they were enjoying the Louvre'. It was a perfect day to spend indoors, as the heat outside was a dangerously hot 123 degrees Fahrenheit.

"So, this is where you discovered culture," Lidia teased.

"Some. Tell me, what do you think of that?" Dave asked, pointing to an oil of Saint Sebastian.

"I haven't met him,"

"What?"

"Sebastian. Don't tell me you are really thinking about art," Lidia said, almost reading his mind.

"Okay. So, what do you think about him?"

"I think I'd like to meet him and Cora too," Lidia said, looking at the painting. "I'm wondering what you're thinking though, Dave?"

"I'm thinking about all the arrows he's taken and trying to get my head around how he wound up in seminary. He made me start thinking about faith, where it comes from and how you find it."

"That sounds pretty deep."

"Do you ever think about it, Lidia? Faith." Dave asked, as they came to a painting of Jesus in "The Pilgrims at Emmaus".

"I went to Sunday school, but no, not really. I guess I've gotten a little jaded after so many years on the job. I think the last time I was in a church was Alice's memorial," She replied.

"I wonder where she is. Is she still alive?"

"I hope so," Lidia said. "For Suzanna's sake, although, I sometimes hope she's never found, for the same reason. I think it may be easier on Suzanna not to know, so that she can hope for the best."

"Understandable. I worry how it might affect the others too, especially Rosie and Sophie, if Alice was back in their lives. Maybe she was right to disappear, for the sake of everyone. Still," Dave continued, as he looked up at a painting of Sandro Botticelli's "Venus and the Graces", "If she is alive, I can't help but wonder if she escaped the projects. They're quite adept at tracking people. Then there's Jack's abduction. Yes, he's technically related, but not directly, and he's a man."

"What are you thinking?"

"I'm not sure. We know he had a brief relationship with Alice. So, what if? No. That doesn't make sense. Never mind. Why don't we go get some lunch?"

"Okay, but first, tell me what doesn't make sense, because there is an awful lot that doesn't and yet is. So, please share."

"It was just a fleeting idea that if the projects don't know where Alice is, then maybe they would use Jack to try and lure her out. It doesn't make sense though because she would have no way to know he was missing. It wasn't ever publicized."

"True, but whoever took him wouldn't know that it wouldn't be. And maybe they think that one of us does know where she is and that she would find out. Or..." Lidia said, as another thought came to her mind.

"What?"

"Buy me lunch and I'll tell you. I think better when I'm fed," she smiled, and they headed to the café.

After a few bites of her Panini, Lidia said, "I was thinking that if the projects had found Alice, that maybe they took Jack with the idea of mating them."

Dave stared at her over his lemonade.

"It's hardly farfetched. He already had the family tie, but without a direct genetic relation. Mating them could have the potential to pull more family closer together," she continued.

"I wish we could question Simon," Dave gave a half laugh. "We finally get someone who could answer, possibly everything, and he goes off the deep end. According to Cora, he was never sane. The things did to her, it's a miracle she is."

"Her sister sounds like another one who could answer a lot of questions, and what happened to Adam? We know he's still working on the P2P program somewhere."

"He and his father are just two more missing people. I wonder, if we find one, would we find the others? I'm sorry, Lidia. I didn't bring you here to talk shop all day."

"Please," Lidia said, rolling her eyes. "I'm just as into this as you are. Face it, being detectives is in our blood."

Dave smiled, "I guess that's why we're so good together," he said, taking her hand.

Lidia smiled back.

Lyon, France

Victoria looked out the window at the sideways smile of the crescent moon. She smiled back, thinking that fifty-three years before, man had first set foot on it. Now they wanted to mine it, to chip away at its smile, all in the name of advancing technology.

She stopped smiling and just stared out at the sky over the city lights. She couldn't even tell the difference between a star or a satellite anymore. When she was in the Russian countryside, she used to love staring up at the sky. The nights were so beautiful, so clear, devoid of the city light pollution.

She thought of the peasants who had been so kind to her, and she looked at her violin.

She didn't need the money from the big concerts anymore. She had invested well, and she certainly didn't need the publicity. She also knew that she couldn't stay with Larry and Margot forever.

She looked back to the moon. She had made her decision, and the moon's smile suddenly seemed brighter.

Chapter 32

Switzerland: July 21ˢᵗ

Aida cleared the last table. The couple who had eaten there were on their honeymoon from Italy. She couldn't help remembering her time there with Kristor, or Jonathan. It had been short, far too short, but last night she had dreamed of it. In fact, she had dreamed of him many nights since speaking with Soren. It was as though it had been a sign, a sign that it was right for her to still hope, regardless of how hopeless the reality looked.

She glanced over to the kitchen, where Ana was helping with the dishes.

Ana was spending more and more time alone and even seemed to be avoiding Aida.

Ana needed to know what was going on. Her mother had told her some of it, but Ana could tell she was holding back.

Ana remembered the strange times spent with the man her mother met at the church. The man who supposedly was her real father. Ana didn't think he was though. He didn't act like a father, and the more she thought about it, the more certain she was that he had been responsible for their abduction.

After ten years in Brazil, she had forgotten the man's face, until recently, when she had driven by the church, after buying her new scooter.

It felt so freeing to finally have her own transportation, and after Sebastian left, all she wanted was to be alone. She had driven down through town and out towards a riverfront park. The church had been down the road leading to the park. It was deserted and appeared to have been so since it had closed years before. She pulled into the parking lot, which was overgrown with weeds, and stared.

She walked over to the chapel, which was padlocked, and wiped away dirt and cobwebs from the window.

That was when she had the flashback, when she first really remembered his face. She wanted to race back and draw it to show Sebastian, but he was gone.

Later, as she sat by the water, she wondered if the man had ever been in Brazil with her. He and Leona must have known each other, and so many people had come through the estate. Was it possible that Sebastian would have known who he was?

She had since made several sketches, both of him and the other people she remembered.

She considered showing them to Dave, but he was back in France now.

Ana wondered about Soren and his wife. Were they safe? Her mother seemed to think so, but she didn't even trust her mother completely. After all, her mother was the one who had the affair with the man in the first place.

Now that she was eighteen, Ana had been considering various ways to solve the mystery of who she really was and why she had been taken.

It was today that she made the decision. It scared her, but she had a plan.

Ana took the last plate from the washer and put it on the shelf. After the weekend, she would ask for some vacation time. Then she would mail copies of the sketches to Sebastian along with her plan. That way, if anything went wrong, he would know who to contact and how to find her.

August 10th

It was strange being back in Brazil, and Ana was glad that she had converted all of her last pay into the local digital currency. Though she didn't know how to get back to the estate herself, she knew about the raid on it after she left, and that Philip Katz would know the way. Sebastian had trusted him, and so would she.

She knew that he had married that psychologist and now worked at the embassy, which was where she was now headed.

Philip had continued working from home, playing mister mom, and digging into genealogy records. He had just gotten Alexandria to sleep when he heard her pull up.

He'd been expecting her since his uncle-in-law called about an hour before, but it was still hard to believe.

When he'd first met Ana, over three years ago, after she and Sebastian escaped the estate, he hadn't trusted her. She had seemed far too in control. And as he went out to greet her, his first impression was of that same control.

The only emotion he had ever seen her display was toward Sebastian.

"Hello, Ana," he greeted.

"Agent Katz."

"Philip, please. I'm not technically an agent anymore."

"You are still working with them though, aren't you?"

"Why do I have the feeling you already know the answer to that?"

"Because I do."

Philip nodded. Her expression was just as intense as he remembered, and he wished Monica was home.

"Why don't we go in and have some lemonade or tea, and you can tell me what brings you back to Brazil."

"I know you've been helping Dave and Larry with the genealogy research, and I want you to help me too."

Philip paused, as he poured a lemonade, and turned to look at her.

"You want to know why I would come to you on my own, when you're already looking into it for Dave and Larry," she stated, before he could ask.

"Why are you?" he asked, handing her a glass, and sitting across from her.

"There are things I've remembered that my mother won't tell you and that even Sebastian doesn't know about," she said, as she pulled a sketch book from her bag. She flipped through a few pages and pointed. "This is the man who is supposed to be my real father."

"I know. I already have a similar sketch of him."

"He's not my father. At least I don't think he is. I believe there is someone else. And how did you get a sketch of him?"

Philip didn't answer, knowing that Cora was to remain a secret. Fortunately, Ana came up with an answer to her own question.

"I guess the only answer to that would be my mother. Please, I need you to tell me what my mother won't. I know there must be more, or they wouldn't keep asking her questions. They even brought some other people to talk to us. They had supposedly worked at the same lab we were abducted from and are friends of my mom's friend, Trudie."

Philip wasn't quite sure what to say. He had wanted to call Dave or Larry before she arrived, but had been too busy feeding, changing, and getting Alexandria down.

"I'm eighteen, Philip. I'm not a child. I have a right to know the truth of who I am and why I was taken. We can help each other, but I need to go back to the estate to test my memories and see if I can remember more. I came to you, because Sebastian trusts you, and you know how to get there. I'd also prefer it if we could keep this just between us."

"I'm not sure that I can do that," Philip sighed. "This is far bigger than you can imagine."

"I doubt that. I can imagine quite a lot. I know it reaches worldwide, but no one will tell me what "It" even is. All I know is that it has something to do with making perfect children. I've been thinking about the tests they put me through and doing my own research. I really think we can help each other. I need to know the truth of who I am, both for my own sake and for the sake of my mother. She's still scared."

"Does she know you're here?"

"Of course not. She thinks I'm apartment hunting in Zurich. That's what I told her anyway. I doubt she believes it, but she didn't push, and she knows I'm due back at work next week."

"Are you planning to go back?"

"That depends on if you'll help me. If you don't, I'll have to stay longer to figure things out on my own."

She does know how to manipulate, Philip thought.

"Where are you staying?" he asked.

"Here," she said, handing him a card with the name of her hotel and her mobile number, as she rose from her seat.

He recognized the name and was relieved to see that she had chosen one of the safer neighborhoods.

"Won't you stay for dinner?" he invited. He really wanted Monica's take on her.

"No, thank you. I have plans. I hope to hear from you soon. I won't wait."

"I'll call tomorrow, say nine?"

"I'll be expecting your call," she said and headed to the door and back to her rental car.

He had just watched her go and was thinking about what time it was in France, when he heard Alexandria wake up.

As he looked at his daughter, he thought about Ana's request. She was an adult, and she'd spent ten years living under Leona. She had been subjected to medical tests and doubtlessly observed much, which she had to this point not shared. She was right. She could be a great asset to the investigation. She was also an excellent sketch artist. He immediately recognized the man whom her mother finally admitted the affair with. Ana's sketch showed even better detail than Cora's. But how could he help her without at least informing Larry?

It was Monica who gave him the solution, that evening, after Alexandria was down, and they were cleaning up from dinner.

"Just let uncle tell them," she said. "That way, you can make an honest promise to Ana. It's possible he may have already contacted them. I'll talk to him tomorrow. I would like to meet with her before you get too involved."

"You do realize how involved I already am?"

"Research is different than going off, with a possibly unstable girl, to a deserted estate, in the middle of the jungle," she replied, hanging a cleaned spatula on a hook next to the stove.

He smiled at her concern, and Monica looked up at him. They kissed, then looked in on Alexandria, who was sleeping soundly, before making their way to their own bed.

Chapter 33

Saint Petersburg: August 11ᵗʰ

Jonathan was both excited and leery of leaving. He had called Alphi in Greece and was assured that he still had a job waiting whenever he could make it back. Carl had left back to Sweden the day before, and Alice, uncertain of her life and herself, decided to stay and assist Professor Zendavev and Josephine.

Jonathan considered going back to Switzerland, but that was too risky, and it wouldn't be fair to Aida to just reappear. He had already hurt her enough and prayed that by now she had found happiness with someone else.

He went to Alice's rooms and was glad to learn that she was up and had gone out to the gardens.

He found her by the koi pond.

"You're looking good this morning. Alphi says to give you his best. He's glad your surgery went well, but he's sorry it didn't work out between us, and if you ever come back to Greece, you have a job waiting."

"Please give him my best as well."

"Are you certain about staying here?"

"I think it's for the best. At least for now. When is your flight?"

"Zendavev's driver is taking me to the airport after lunch."

"What do you think Richter is up to?"

"Revenge of some sort. I imagine he'll either turn up back at the lab in Sweden or eventually make his way to Paris. I wish I knew how to get in touch with Mathias."

"The brother I never met. And what about Aida? I think you should at least write to her."

"Are you planning to write to Jack?"

"No, he's better off without me, and after so long... If he

wanted to see me, Sophie or Nick would have said something. I'm sure he's with someone else by now."

"Ditto with Aida," Jonathan replied.

"Take a walk with me?" Alice asked.

"Of course."

They walked slowly through the gardens of Zendavev's estate, Alice now using only a cane for support. They spoke little, both just trying to find peace in a time where peace was at a premium. They both knew that a new kind of war was coming to the world, one only a few could even begin to understand.

It would be a war spawned by the revelations of science and the repression of faith. The masses only heard of the wars between political powers. These same power struggles had plagued the world from the beginning of time, and while the basis of good versus evil was still the same, the contrast was about to become much starker.

Lyon, France

Larry hung up the phone. Antonio Spara had called him from Brazil to inform him of what Ana was up to. Larry sure didn't envy Philip and hoped he wasn't planning to go to the estate alone with her. Like Victoria, Larry had never been certain how far he could trust Ana.

Victoria had left back to Russia, just two days before. They were still unsure what had become of her parents and brother, but in the scheme of things, it was low on his priority list.

Victoria had made contact with the family she lived with in a small village between Moscow and Saint Petersburg. And she would stay with them again for a time.

She had also shared that she made contact again with the man who sent her the files and warned her about the artificial intelligence, used to pose as her brother. He had learned that *it* had been shut down before the information *it* recorded could be stored, but he feared they still had snippets from the conversation. He knew nothing more of her family, and he also believed it in everyone's best interest for her to lay low again.

Larry was most relieved she was gone, so that his daughters could come for a visit. Chelle, his youngest had been staying between her older sisters since her classes let out for summer break, and he and Margot would have only a couple of weeks before she headed back to Paris.

Dave and Lidia returned from Paris, just before Victoria left with some interesting news.

While Dave went digging through archives, Lidia made a doctor's appointment at the hospital where the P2P project had been located. She was there ostensibly for a consultation on having artificial insemination. Arriving early and keeping her ears open, she picked up on some interesting rumors, and Dave had traced some interesting history of the hospital itself.

Margot knocked on the door of his office.

"Yes?"

She smiled as she entered. "It's beautiful outside. Why don't you take a break and come with me, while we still have some time to ourselves? I just took some hot scones out of the oven. I was thinking, maybe we could take a picnic out to the lake."

"Just the two of us? Really?"

"Really. Everyone else is helping Shane and Daniel set up their new apartment."

"How did we get out of that?"

"I said we needed time to prepare for the girl's arrival."

"A picnic it is then."

"Wonderful! Does this mean that call wasn't more work?"

"Yes and no, but I'll tell you about it over lunch," he said, following her to the kitchen, where the fresh scones sat next to a picnic basket on the counter.

Outside Paris

When Lily and Nigel tried to contact Larry, via INTERPOL, they were disappointed to discover that he no longer worked there, and the person they spoke with was new and either could not or would not tell them how to contact him. They had offered to take a message and pass it on. What could they say though? They could hardly risk talking to someone else.

After a bit of internet research, Svend discovered that Larry was now working as an independent, private detective. They had tried to call the number on the website, but only received a message that he was currently unavailable. To be honest, Lily was relieved. It had already been three years.

They had gone with Svend to the house where his sister, Louisa, lived and were relieved to find her safe. In fact, she even had a boyfriend, and Svend seemed to think she had improved cognitively. Nigel conducted an exam and both he and Svend were surprised by the results.

"I started taking these about a year ago," Louisa said. "A package arrived in the mail claiming to be a free sample of vitamins for a survey. I still have the letter that came with it," she said, going through a file and handing it to Svend.

There was no return address on the letter, but after inspecting a capsule, Svend and Nigel agreed that they were a mix of Asian herbs along with a genetic compound of unknown origin.

After a month with his sister, they decided to take a chance and all three of them went in disguise to visit the institute in Paris, hoping to discover something about the fate of P2P.

It had felt somewhat surreal going back, and if they hadn't known better, they never would have suspected that it was anything more than a general hospital.

Lily had made an appointment with a fertility specialist, claiming she wanted to help her son and daughter-in-law, who was able to conceive, but unable to carry to term.

She knew other women her age had done this, and with what they knew of the fertility specialists there, who were not part of P2P, or at least not knowingly, they were certain they could at least discover what was known of Adam's fate.

They found it interesting that another woman in the waiting room, also seemed to be interested in Adam, and they overheard her ask about him specifically in regard to having artificial insemination.

Chapter 34

Brazil: August 12th

Ana met Philip at the embassy. Monica had arranged to stay home with Alexandria, and Philip had managed to get Ana to agree to Monica's cousin, Lorenzo, accompanying them to the estate.

Lorenzo was a helicopter pilot and knew only that Ana had been held at the estate and wanted to return in hopes of remembering some things that she had blocked out before. Since the estate was so isolated, a helicopter was by far the best way to reach it, and it gave Philip the excuse for Lorenzo's presence.

After they landed, it took Ana a few minutes to step out of the copter. She stared at the overgrown walls that had held her captive for more than half her life.

Philip followed her through the house, while Lorenzo waited outside. Ana went first to what had been her bedroom.

Everything in the house had been gone through by investigators and left in quite a disarray.

Ana went to the closet and looked through the clothes that were still inside. Much of the contents had been tossed on the bed. She seemed to be looking for something.

"What is it?" Philip asked.

"The clothes I was wearing when I was taken. Most of them were thrown away, but I had this sweater, with a reindeer on it. My grandpa Ulf gave it to me, and I remember crying when I woke up and couldn't find it. I threw such a fit that they gave it back to calm me down. I kept it hidden under another shirt. I meant to take it when we left. Now, I can't find it."

"Since you had it when you were taken, it may have been taken into evidence when they searched."

Ana turned and looked through the clothes on the bed, then she knelt and looked underneath. Then she stood and asked Philip to help her move the bed aside. After it was moved away from the wall, she went through the items that had slipped down the side and made her way to the corner by the headboard. Reaching down, she pulled a board loose and pulled out a notebook. She handed it to Philip.

"I remembered that I liked to draw a lot when I was little. There were more, but they found them and took them from me. I had this one under the covers and then made this hiding place for it. I don't even remember what's in it."

For the first time since he'd met her, Ana seemed human to him. She had always acted so cold and emotionless. Now, he was almost sure she was about to cry.

"I know it's stupid," she said wiping her eyes, "but I really wanted to find that reindeer sweater."

"It's not stupid. It was special to you."

Philip watched as she composed herself, then she moved into the bath area.

"I used to try to hide in here before they took me to the doctors. I remember squeezing myself under the sink. I was so scared." She started to tremble, and Philip cautiously moved toward her.

"I'll be okay. I want to go to her room."

"Okay," Philip said and followed her through to the other side of the main house.

Ana entered the room that was Leona's. She went directly to the dresser, and even though all the drawers were on the floor, she began to feel inside the spaces they had been.

"She used to keep a key hidden here. I remember watching her once. She didn't notice I was there, and I saw her reach up inside of a drawer and take out a key. I followed her outside to one of the guest houses. There was a man, a doctor or scientist, staying there, and I remember she didn't come back to the house that night. I remember sneaking back in for breakfast and Poppie, our housekeeper, pulled a piece of straw out of my hair just before Leona came in. I'd slept in the stables. Leona left later that day and was gone for a few weeks. She did that sometimes," Ana said, moving from the dresser into the closet. Then she left the room and moved through the house to the room that had been Sebastian's.

Ana frowned as she looked at his books, scattered mostly on the floor. She sat on the floor and looked through them. "I'd like to take some, if that's okay. He used to read this to me," she said, holding up a copy of "Pushkin's Fairy Tales".

"I don't see why not," Philip answered.

"Thank you," Ana said, rising from the floor and going to the bed, where she snagged a sweatshirt and two more books, before heading outside.

"It was that house over there, where she spent the night with the man. What happened to the horses?" she asked, as they passed the stables.

"I don't know, but I could ask. I imagine they were sold at auction."

"I just hope they found good homes."

Ana continued walking past the tennis courts, several outbuildings, through a garden, and up cement steps to another large stone building.

Philip was in awe. He knew the estate was large, but had never actually been there, because he was on a plane escorting Ana to Switzerland when it had been raided, and he hadn't figured he'd find anything later.

"This building is where we had school lessons, and the rooms upstairs were used as offices and sometimes examination rooms. Physical examinations, not school," she clarified, as she made her way up the stairs.

Entering one of the rooms, she looked around. The room had been almost entirely stripped, but a lab jacket and a stethoscope still hung neatly on the back of the door and the room was clean.

"Someone has been here, recently," Philip said. "We should leave."

Ana was rummaging in an apparently empty drawer.

"What are you looking for?"

"This," she said, as she pulled out the drawer and then a notebook from behind it.

"What is that?"

"I don't know. I just remembered. I saw one of the doctors put it away once. He referenced it during my exams," she said, tucking it in her bag with Sebastian's shirt and other books. She stood silently, gazing around the room and to the lab coat.

"We should leave," Philip repeated.

"We should take it. It could have DNA on it," Ana said.

Philip thought for a moment. She was right, but odds were, it wasn't DNA that would match anything in the system, and he didn't want whoever it was to know they knew about them. He wondered if the person was there now and felt an overwhelming urge to race back to the helicopter.

"No, I'll report it. They may want to monitor the estate to catch whoever it is or send in forensics. Hopefully, whoever it is, isn't here now and won't know we were."

"They'll know when they see the book gone."

She had a point.

"Okay," he said, grabbing the jacket and stethoscope in the middle, so as not to disturb the most likely areas of DNA traces. "Now let's get the heck out of here."

Ana nodded, and they hurried out, across the property to the helicopter where, thankfully, Lorenzo was still waiting.

The first thing Philip did was take out his phone.

"I need to report this," he told Ana.

"To Spara, or Larry and Dave?"

"All of them. I'll ask them not to say anything about you to your mother. You're an adult now, but I have to report this."

"Okay. I understand."

"Can I see the book?" Philip asked.

"Only if you promise to let me see it too."

"Fair enough," Philip replied. "We can make a copy when we get back."

Ana pulled out the notebook and handed it to Philip, who browsed the pages, as he put in a call to his uncle-in-law.

Lyon, France

Dave finished setting the table, checked the oven and the wine. He adjusted the lighting on the balcony. It was still warm out, but there was a nice breeze, and he wanted the romantic effect of the night's full moon.

He put some relaxing jazz on for background and was triple checking himself in the mirror when he heard a knock at the door.

"Welcome to Petit Chateau, Asher," he said, opening the door to Lidia.

"Petit, definitely," she smiled, as she glanced around his apartment. She was impressed by how well he had arranged the small space.

"Entre,'" he said, ushering her inside.

"It smells wonderful!" she exclaimed, passing the oven. "Who helped?"

"Well, I suppose my mother and grandmother taught me a thing or two, but tonight I'm cooking solo."

"Impressive," Lidia said, as Dave turned off the oven and took the wine from the cooler.

"Should we start with red or white?"

"Start? Are you hoping to get me drunk?" she smiled, "What's on the menu?"

Dave opened the warming drawer of the oven and pulled out a tray of various canapes.

"All of these include one of your favorite cheeses. This one has Gouda, this one Feta and I used Munster on those two. For the main course, we have lamb shank, with mint sauce, Heirloom potatoes and baby asparagus with garlic butter."

"Yum! In that case, let's start with the white and move to the red with the lamb."

Dave smiled and popped the cork. He handed her a plate for the canapes and a glass of wine, then went back to the kitchen.

"You aren't going to indulge?"

"Not yet, but I'll join you in a minute. I want to marinate the lamb once more and move it to the warming drawer."

Lidia watched him working in the kitchen. She enjoyed the view of his back side. He'd been working out and it showed. She also wondered what he was up to. Normally, she'd hound him until he told her, but tonight she just sipped her wine and savored one of the crusts, topped with mushroom and Gouda.

Switzerland: August 13th

Sebastian looked at the sketches Ana sent him. Then he went to see Cora, and they spent the afternoon going over both her and Ana's sketches, putting aside faces both had sketched. Nadier was one, as was Meschner and Charles.

Sebastian didn't recognize many of the people from Ana's sketches, but both he and Cora recognized the man who was supposedly Ana's biological father. The strange thing was where they recognized him from.

"It's not possible," Cora said. "I mean, one of the goals is to stop aging, but he'd be older than me now. I suppose it could be his son or grandson."

"I suppose," Sebastian said. "It would explain why she was brought to Brazil. I only saw him the one time, but it's not something I'll ever forget."

"I can understand why," Cora replied.

"At first, I thought he was my dad, but my dad was dead," Sebastian said, recalling the night, while trying to block the image of his mother in that compromising position.

"I think we need to call Dave," Cora said.

Sebastian nodded.

Rhodope Mountains, Greece & Bulgaria.

Leona climbed the steep hillside. She was in better shape than ever. A small herd of deer grazed off to her right, and down the other side of this ridge was the small compound where she would meet her new colleagues.

This land was sacred and contained mysteries few had ever imagined, but she would soon have a part in not only studying, but in becoming part of them. She wondered if the skeletons had been part of a similar project or if they were really alien. That was one of the things she hoped to discover in her studies. She had already viewed x-rays of the skulls, along with DNA findings from previous excavations, but the site she was going to now was different. The findings had not yet become known outside of the few researchers who discovered them.

Two of the researchers on site were part of the projects, and there were only three other well vetted workers with them, and a cook.

When she first visited her contact in Greece, Leona had not expected this. She only became aware of the project's goals a few days ago, and while it terrified her, it also intrigued her and drove her to discover more.

She could see the building now, as it had been described to her, sitting amongst a small grove of olive trees, with a few contented looking goats and chickens milling about.

After an introduction to her two colleagues, Dr. Ilichad and Professor Komff, as well as her new quarters, Dr Ilichad guided her to where the new projects were beginning to live alongside the ancient mysteries. He rotated a large flat stone slab and revealed a chamber, about six feet down, containing one of the first five bodies they had hidden here.

"How does the chamber work?" she asked.

"Similar to the other cryogenic pods, only we use a special fluid made from a recipe of herbs. It works much like an embalming fluid, and we paint the body with it. See how his face is slightly glossy. There is also a spring that we ran piping from underneath to circulate a cooling flow. At dark we will also give him a friend. One of the skeletons will be reburied on top of him and the stone replaced.

"Seeing as how we are on the border, it is likely that Greece would claim the top half and Bulgaria the lower of the body," he said with a laugh. "Either way, we aren't on any maps and are far enough from the hiking trails that they are not likely to be disturbed. That's one of the reasons those who are buried here must be brought before they are put under. Only a few can make it. Many of them wait too long. Can you imagine, a ninety-year-old billionaire hiking up here to be rejuvenated?"

"Are they all part of the projects?" Leona asked.

"Not willingly. You know we have ways of luring them here. That one over there, came all the way from the Congo. He's a special specimen, a doctor. He came here on the pretext of helping babies suffering with unknown immunology issues.

"Old Hank here though, he knew," Ilichad said, pointing. "He was one who helped us set this whole project up. He found the area back in nineteen ninety-five while working at one of the known sites in Bulgaria. He got to know some of the locals and arranged for the building and donkeys to hull up the supplies."

"Do they know he's here?" Leona asked, looking down at the chamber.

"Yes and no. They think he had a heart attack and was taken to a town in Greece to be buried normally. I hope you'll join us for the official funeral service tonight," he continued. "The help leaves at dusk to go back to their village. Maria will have made us plenty for dinner. She and her husband, who is one of the workers, along with their two sons, live about an hours walk away and come just three days a week. We won't lack anything though. There is a fully stocked in ground cooler, a pump for spring water and the chickens lay quite prolifically."

"What about the births?"

"All in good time. Both of the sons have pregnant wives that we provide medical care for, and there are a few other women in the village, but we need to be careful. We need to discover just what we're dealing with before we start new breeding. I understand you're interested in participating?"

"I'm willing."

"Good," Ilichad replied, looking her up and down. She hoped her new colleague would not prove to be another Nadier.

Lyon, France

Margot brought out the hor d'oeurves and Larry popped the champagne while Lidia showed off her ring and Dave grinned.

"Congratulations!" Shane said, slapping Dave on the back.

"How are you holding up?" Dave asked.

"Better, but I want to focus on you two. It's good to have

something to really celebrate," Shane smiled. "And I'm glad I stayed to see it."

"How's Daniel with the move?"

"He's good. He makes friends fast. He already has two play dates and a possible girlfriend across the hall," Shane laughed.

"Are you really doing okay though?" Dave asked.

"I'm taking my cues from Daniel. Even he's stopped asking about mommy. I think he just believes that she chose Kenneth over us, which she did. And if a three-and-a-half-year-old can move on, so can I. So, about your bachelor party..." Shane started, as his phone rang.

"Hi Philip. Let me hand you to Dave for a moment. He has some good news to share."

"I'm getting married... I'm not sure I believe it myself... Thanks... What's up on your side of the world?... Yeah, hold on, Larry is here too. We'll duck in his office, and you can tell us all."

Shane grabbed Larry and Margot and Lidia followed.

"We promise to fill you in later. Now get back to the party," Larry said to them.

"What's going on?" Suzanna asked.

"Man stuff," Margot told her.

"I think I heard them mention a bachelor party," Lidia added.

"Well then, maybe we should take this time to plan a bridal shower too," Suzanna suggested, and Clair agreed.

Rosie was the only one who didn't seem excited about the impending nuptials.

"I'll go look in on Daniel," Rosie said, and walked toward the spare room where she found him wide awake, reading.

"Hi," Daniel said.

"Hi. Can't sleep?"

"I want to know how this story ends."

"What is it?"

"It's called, 'The Baker and The Mouse'. The baker is famous for breads he makes from the different cheeses mysteriously left in his kitchen by the mouse. The baker doesn't know it's a mouse though, and he leaves a fresh piece of bread out for whoever is bringing him the cheese. The mouse is feeding his whole family with this bread. But now the baker has seen a mouse in his house, which is next door to his bakery, and he set traps for the mice. That's where I am now," Daniel said. "Do you want me to read you the rest?" he asked Rosie.

"Sure," she said, smiling.

When Daniel finished the book, he yawned and said, "The end."

"That was a good story. Thank you, Daniel. I think I should say good night now and let you get some sleep."

"You'd be a good mother," Daniel said as he snuggled under the blankets, and Rosie kissed his forehead.

"Thank you," she said, turning out the lamp and wiping away a tear, before going back out to join the others.

Greece

Jonathan, who was again going by the name, Sherman, was pleased when he entered his apartment in Kalampaka. Alphi's daughter, Daria, had done an excellent job maintaining it and even restocking his refrigerator. He would have to be sure to get her a thank you gift.

Walking outside to his balcony, he sighed as he lounged back in a canvas chair and stared up at the ancient monasteries that clung to the huge outcroppings of stone overlooking the town.

It was good to be back, more than good. When he left, he had never dreamed he could feel at peace again. Yet here he was. He would start leading tours again on Wednesday, but for now, he wanted nothing more than to just sit on his balcony, free. For the first time in his life, he was free. The only person out to get him, as far as he knew, was Richter.

He worried briefly for Carl on that, but Carl wasn't alone, and with the added security at the lab, he felt assured about his baby brother's safety. They were both safer than they had ever been before.

He wondered about Mathias, but he knew that Chantel had seen him in France, and he was also surrounded with friends. Carl decided to try and get a message to him via Chantel, about his trigger and the doctor in Saint Petersburg who helped successfully remove theirs.

He could only imagine one thing, one person, that could make his life any better. At least he had the memories, and who knew what the future could bring.

He got up, feeling suddenly restless, and went to the fridge for a Mythos. He popped the cap and took a long swig. Instead of the relaxation that engulfed him minutes before, he felt a combination of guilt and anxiety. Thinking about the future, when he knew the secret evils that were at work around the world, was like a slap in his own face. He should be helping Mathias, not lounging on a balcony, basking in a beautiful day, and looking forward to meeting his next tour group.

He took another swig of the Mythos and went back outside. His thoughts weren't new, but at least before, he had Alice to protect. He wondered what Brother Archibald would say and decided that he would go up tomorrow, after church, to talk to the man who had been a true friend to both him and Alice.

A gray and white cat appeared on the balcony railing and Sherman smiled. "Did you miss me Talos?" he asked the feline, who made his way onto the table and was sniffing the beer.

"Meow."

"Okay, but just a sip, and don't tell your mistress or she'll never sell me a good baklava again," Sherman dripped some Mythos on the table, which Talos eagerly lapped up. "I missed you too."

After thoroughly cleaning the section of table, Talos made his way onto Sherman's lap. Sherman stroked the cat, who lolled as though he had far more than just a tablespoon worth of beer, and Sherman threw back the rest of the bottle, closed his eyes, and fell sound asleep under the setting sun and a purring Talos.

Chapter 35

Switzerland: August 14th

Aida didn't want to wake up from her dream. She could feel his breath on her cheek, smell his scent, and taste his lips. She moaned as a car horn sounded outside. She squeezed her eyes tight, longing to go back to the dream, but the light shown too brightly through her window, and she could no longer find him.

She pulled herself up and dressed, trying to hold the memory. She went to the window and looked down on the tour bus below. Then she made her way downstairs to help her parents in the kitchen.

She was surprised when she found all three of her brothers in aprons. It wasn't unusual for Fredrick to come up for the occasional weekend, but to see either of their elder brothers, Graham and Hal, much less together, was a real rarity.

"There's the sleepy baby," Graham teased, as she entered the kitchen and donned her own apron.

"What brings you up here, especially at 7:00 in the morning? Is Lada here too?"

"We got in late last night after I picked Hal up from the airport. Lada's getting the kids dressed."

"So, what's the occasion?"

They looked at each other. "Make her wait," Hal said, with a mischievous grin.

"Fredrick?" she tried.

"I'm afraid I'm sworn to secrecy."

"Come on everyone, the sooner we get through this morning's rush, the sooner we can all celebrate," their mother said, with a wink to Aida.

"Celebrate?" Aida asked.

"Why don't you go out and help your father and Mave," her mother, Ellen, responded, smiling.

Hal came and gave Aida a nudge toward the door. "It's what you get for sleeping in, baby sis."

Aida rolled her eyes. She both hated and loved the teasing her oldest brothers gave her at any chance.

As soon as the crowd cleared to the last few lodgers, that Mave could handle on her own, they gathered in the kitchen and their father popped a bottle of champagne.

"I know it's awfully early for champagne, but how often does my eldest son get married," he said.

"Only once. I hope!" Hal said.

"Oh, Congratulations!" Aida said, hugging him. "Who is she? Where is she?"

"Her name is Elke. I met her when my firm did security for an event at the German embassy in Paris, where she works. She grew up in Zurich and is being transferred to Bern at the end of the year, where we'll live. She has two weeks leave she needs to use before the transfer. So, we were thinking of having the wedding in the fall before ski season, and we're hoping you all will be able to take extra time. We're getting married in Greece, on Santorini. Her parents have a huge vacation villa there and said you are all welcome to stay."

"They'll have room for all of us?" asked their father.

"It's eight bedrooms and Elke is an only child. She and I plan to explore the rest of Greece for our honeymoon. She loves rock climbing as much as I do, and there are lots of great sites for it there."

Malcolm, their dad, was going through the booking calendar on his phone.

"I guess I'd better clear these empty dates while I can. I can clear us from October 27th until November 4th."

"That works," Hal said. "I'll just let Elke know. Then we can start making our bookings."

France, outside of Paris

Lily and Nigel made a decision. They would contact Anne.

Lily had come back from her follow up appointment and was deemed fit enough to carry a child. The next appointment would have to be with the non-existent daughter-in-law.

She discovered, from a nurse, after casually mentioning the name Hisdak, that he was presumed dead.

"Oh no, what happened?" Lily asked. The nurse wasn't certain, but she had heard rumors about him and his wife being caught in a landslide.

"One more reason for me to stay a city girl," the nurse said. "If you like, I can schedule a consultation with Dr. Jorden. He works in immunology, but he specializes in children. He's studying surrogates, to understand how they affect the embryo, and vice versa. I didn't think of him before, as he usually works with non-related surrogates. Shall I make you an appointment?"

"No, no. I was just curious. Thank you for your time. My daughter-in-law will arrange the next appointment," Lily said. Dr. Jordan was the last person she wanted to run into.

That evening, Lily and Nigel wrote a long letter to Anne.

France: August 16th

Dave and Larry filled in Margot and Lidia, while Dave went to work on researching the name of the general that Cora gave him to see if he had any descendants. He discovered that a General Heisenberg had been killed when the allied forces liberated Paris. But Cora had met him some twenty years later. He was one of the doctors who tested her as a child. She also said he had been a young man, maybe in his early thirties. That wasn't possible, yet the sketch she had drawn matched the face of the general

Dave found the death record for. Could the doctor who examined her have been his son? There were no records of him having children, but that didn't mean much. There was also no record of his burial.

"I know it must have been chaos, but if there's a death record, it only makes sense that there would be a burial record too, unless…" Dave started.

"He wasn't buried, in which case the death record is probably fake," Lidia said.

"That doesn't explain how he shows up in the 1960's, unaged and then again, forty years later, looking the same. Even with the projects, there wasn't much success with slowing the ageing process until the 1990's. He would have already been in his eighties then. We know they had the ability to affect appearance by the mid 1980's, which was a good ten years before Dolly the sheep was cloned in 1996," Dave said. "Did you know that Dolly was just the first clone from mature cells though? Sheep were cloned, using embryonic cells, in 1984."

"Interesting, but we're not talking about sheep," Lidia replied.

"True, and I think if the Nazi's could clone people, we would have known. They would have made a dozen or so clones of Hitler, and the world would be a hell of a lot different."

"The projects aren't cloning though," Lidia said. "Alice, Sophie, Magdeline, Rosie, and Victoria are all very different, and I didn't even get to know them that well. There are even subtle differences in their appearance. We know that the Nazi's were interested in multiple births and studied twins, but even if they learned how to create a look alike of the general, there's still the process of birth and growing up. It is also possible, and more likely, that he did happen to have a son who took after him. In the long run, I don't see that it really matters how this man, and this man," Lidia said, picking up the pictures, "came to exist, only that they did and are clearly tied to the general. I would go back and check birth records for the 1930's, which is when the man Cora remembers would have been born."

"You make a good point, as always Lidia, but I can't shake the feeling that... but I know it's not possible, yet..."

"You're actually entertaining the possibility that they are the same man?"

"Why would the doctor examining Cora lie about who he was. It's not like he told her either, she overheard."

"Maybe she misheard. He could have introduced himself as the general's son."

"Maybe," Dave said, shaking his head, "But, Cryogenics has been around a lot longer. I mean, even in the 1800's they were using refrigeration to preserve foods. And look at the Egyptians, they were embalming people before Christ."

"So, you think this guy is either a mummy or a thawed human popsicle?"

"We've heard crazier stories. Let's just say, I've become more able to stretch my imagination over the past few years. I wish Philip could come up with some photos to go with the names he found in the Brazilian genealogy records."

"Suzanna and Claire may be able to help with that. They have some old family photos stored in San Francisco," Lidia said. "There could be pictures of the brothers and their uncle from the funeral and even before."

"The problem is that they're in San Francisco."

"Maybe not. Suzanna thought she'd call the storage company and see if they could send all of the contents."

"All of the contents?" Dave asked.

"I have no idea, but her apartment is much larger than yours, so I'm sure it won't be an issue."

"Speaking of apartments, maybe we should start looking for one big enough for both our stuff."

"I'm ahead of you on that."

"You usually are," he smiled. "We make a great team Yarnok."

"We sure do, but just remember, when we're married, I'll be an Asher too."

"You're not planning a more modern hyphenated last name?"

"Are you kidding? I'm looking forward to a good old-fashion style marriage."

Dave almost bit his tongue laughing at that, "Right. So, you'll learn to cook, and I'll be in charge, maybe give you an allowance if you behave, and..."

"Not that old-fashioned!" she said, slugging him in the shoulder. "But I will take your name."

He smiled. "And I give it gladly."

Nova Scotia: August 17th

Ben picked up the mail and headed inside for a break from the heat. Now that he didn't have so much farm to tend to, he'd been working on a special project, a crib for Sophie and Nick's daughter to be.

Most of the mail was junk, lots of ads. There was a flyer from Sheila, in Scotland, with real estate listings and a rather fat letter from an address in France he didn't recognize, for Anne.

"Anything interesting?" Anne asked, as he came inside. She had iced tea and sandwiches on the counter, and the dining table was set up like a police crime board, with pictures and names, and arrows pointing. The table itself wasn't big enough and Nick would be bringing over a whiteboard, when he dropped off Sophie today on his way to the rink.

"I have a feeling that this may be something to add to the table," Ben replied, handing the letter to Anne.

"That's Lily's handwriting," Anne said, taking a deep breath, as she studied the envelope. "I should wait for Sophie. She'll be here soon."

As if on cue, Nick and Sophie pulled into the drive with Jeremy, who jumped out to greet the two sheep and three goats Ben and Anne had kept, while Nick unloaded the white board along with a cork board they'd found.

"I should be done around five. Do you want me to pick up anything for dinner Soph?" Nick asked, after unloading.

"Yes, but I don't know what I want. One minute I'm craving red meat and the next, a shrimp salad and strawberry Sunday."

"I'll get both, and whatever you don't want, I'll eat."

"I may want both."

"I think we need to make sure you're not having twins," Nick said.

"Ha, ha," Sophie replied and kissed him and Jeremy goodbye.

Anne poured them all some tea before she said, "I've just had a letter," and she handed the envelope to Sophie.

Sophie stared at her mother's handwriting, then handed the letter back to Anne. "You read it. It's addressed to you."

"Shall I read it aloud?"

Sophie thought for a moment and sipped her tea. "I don't know. You decide. It's just that it's been so long, I..."

"How about I read through it and give you the highlights, then you decide if you want to read it yourself?"

Sophie nodded.

"Shall I stay or go?" Ben asked.

"Stay, Ben," Sophie said. "Help me set up the boards and tack up that pile," she added, pointing to a stack of pictures and notes they had separated out the day before.

Anne opened the letter and began to read. It started out with apologies then went on about Josephine and Simon, P2P and Dr. Hisdak. Nothing she read was surprising, until she got to the eighth page, where they wrote about the children. She looked at Sophie, who stayed turned toward the cork board, as Ben handed her items to add.

Nigel had written this part on separate pages, and explained how they had manipulated the genes, so that the children from Sophie's eggs were not a true part of the project. Then the letter went on to explain how they had escaped and that the children were all missing.

They wanted her opinion on whether it was best to come home or stay gone. They wanted to do what was best for Sophie, but after so long, they had no way of knowing where her life with Nick had gone. Did they have children? Was she safe? Happy? Had she been able to move on? How was she dealing with their disappearance? Would she want them back in her life?

Anne was feeling overwhelmed as she read on. They told her they were all right and who they were with and asked that she please just tell Sophie they loved her, but they understood if she didn't want them back. Then they gave a different address from the return, for Anne to reply to. They also said they would understand if she didn't reply.

Anne separated the section that Nigel had written about the children and hid it in her pocket, then folded the rest of the letter and put it back in the envelope on the table.

"Well?" Ben asked.

"There are a lot of apologies to Sophie, and they explained how they left to keep you safe," she said. "The majority of it is what we already knew and suspected. There may be a few names in what they say about the P2P project that can help us connect what we already have. To be honest, I think we know more than they do now. They also asked if you wanted them back in your life, Sophie. They want what's best for you. I don't think they know what happened to Simon and they don't seem to know anything more about Josephine than we do. They gave an address to reply to. You can read it, but I think that pretty much sums it up."

"Are you okay Sophie?" Ben asked, taking her hands.

"I'll be okay. I just need to think about what they asked. It's what I wanted for so long, but now... I'll read it later. Let's get back to work," she said, going back to the boards.

Uppsala, Sweden

Pollina and Amber had been accepted to the International University in Uppsala, along with one University they submitted to in Italy. They also had applied to, and been accepted to, California State, but opted out after the separation. Things in both America and Canada were too unstable right now. There was always on-line, but they had already spent far too much of their lives isolated and longed for some kind of normalcy.

They had used Callie and Tabetha's address to send the applications, along with a few falsified records, which they created using a program on Simon's computer. Technically they weren't false. All the information was true. It was just that they had never gone to a registered school. They took entrance exams on-line and passed with high scores, so the records were just a technicality.

Tabetha was starting at Uppsala, so that is where Pollina and Amber decided they would go as well. They had already made several friends, via Callie and Tabetha's cousins, who lived nearby and offered to let them continue staying with Tabetha at the family home. It would be a little crowded, but it would give them a dorm like experience, and they were all excited as they went to the campus for a pre-semester tour.

Richter climbed the steps to the University library. There was a conference focusing on gene editing the weekend before classes began. He was curious to see if his brothers would attend and who they might make contact with.

He had let his hair grow chin length and dyed it a light shade of brown. With the contacts, his eyes were brown now. He decided not to bother with implants, but to simply grow a few whiskers. He was going for a casual look that would fit in better with the students. He knew his brothers would recognize him regardless, just as he would them.

He was just inquiring about a reading room when he saw them. He had to be careful not to stare too long, trying to be certain it was them. There could be no mistake. One was basically a teenage version of Alice, and the other, well, Amber intrigued him. Could one of them be a replacement for Alice that he could mate with?

He noted that they were with a student orientation group and wondered how or why they were allowed to be here.

He wished he could contact Simon or Josephine, but he would have to wait until he went to France. He hoped to go with both Carl and Jonathan at his mercy, but that was contingent on their attendance. Either way, he intended to be in Paris next week. Now, however, he may reconsider.

If his brothers didn't make a showing, perhaps he should focus on watching Pollina and Amber. It might even give him something to use against Simon, who he was certain, along with Hisdak, had taken control of P2P.

There was someone else on his list to deal with too. His father. He flashed back to the night at the University in Quebec and felt his pulse quicken with rage. He had as much rage over Meschner as he did his brothers. He knew he wasn't dead, and that somewhere within P2P was most likely where he was being kept. Switzerland was another possibility, but everyone there, were primarily resources.

Actual facilities were limited, and those that he knew could facilitate his goals of immortality were based in France.

France was also the most likely place to find Mathias.

At one point, he had thought Jonathan and Carl could work for him. They would never be his equals, but they could do his bidding. Carl used to be particularly good for that. They would have gotten Mathias out of the way. Instead, they had turned to agreement with Mathias. They made the decision to give up their birth rights, and in his mind, they had not just given up their right to immortality, but the right to live at all. They were inferior, too inferior for Richter to allow their survival.

The idea that it was three against one now, made no difference. Richter was a god, and he was determined to eliminate his adversaries and take his place as such.

France

Tony was collecting the wine to take to Laura when he noted an odd footprint. What was odd was that it was only a partial print, a heel print, and it was up against the old stone chimney from the original building. It looked as if someone had entered from the storeroom and stepped into the chimney.

He opened the door to the storeroom. The wood flooring showed no other prints, but the heel print was clear as day against the chimney. It made no sense. Where were the toes? The chimney was solid stone, but then again, so had the walls in Laura's wine cellar been.

Tony took the bottles up to load and then came back with a flashlight. He searched all the way around the base of the chimney for any abnormality. He found nothing and decided to go ahead and take the bottles to Laura. Then he would come back and set up a camera. The print had to be fairly fresh, and he wondered if what they had buried behind the new wall in Laura's cellar was still there.

He wondered if he should tell Laura about this, but he knew she would want to come back with him to look herself, and he was supposed to pick up his children to stay with him until school started. With any luck, Diana, his wife might come as well, and he didn't think having Laura on site would be wise.

Chapter 36

Rio de Janeiro, Brazil: August 22nd

Ana was in her third day at the National Archives of Brazil. She started her search with the genealogy records gained from Philip and was now moving backwards. The archives were created in 1838 and she was studying the family lineage of those, like Meschner's family, who had arrived in Brazil long before either of the world wars.

She was surprised to discover a flood of immigration had occurred during the mid-1800's, due to issues in the German states at the time. And she had traced Meschner's family line all the way back to 1850. It showed an Axel and Marianna Meschner arriving from Berlin, but only Axel was listed as German. Marianna was listed as Prussian.

Ana took copious notes, as these particular documents had not yet been added to the online database. It seems they added more well-known entities first, and Meschner's family had remained fairly inconspicuous during their time in Brazil. This explained why Philip had been unable to trace back any further on the family line.

Ana decided to take her last few days off and go to Berlin to see if she could trace back further for Marianna and Axel. Maybe it was the mystery of, the now extinct, Prussia, but something told her to focus on Marianna.

She had just emailed Philip her notes and was waiting for her car when she saw him. He was staring straight at her from across the street. Then he was in the crosswalk, headed directly toward her. She could see her car was waiting at the light, just yards away from her, and she pushed her way through the crowded street, darting into the intersection and trying to open the door of the silver 'Flexi Ride' car. She held her phone reservation up to the window. The light changed, and the cars behind him honked, as he unlocked the door and she hopped in.

"What do you think you are doing?" he asked, clearly annoyed.

"That man," she said, pointing, "he's after me."

"After you?"

"Just get me to the airport, please. Quickly! He's getting into a taxi to follow."

The Flexi Car driver looked in his rearview mirror and spun the car into an illegal U-turn, then sped down an ally. He did a few more covert maneuvers and then, feeling certain he had lost the taxi, slowed to a normal speed, but stayed to side roads.

"Where is your luggage?"

"Room 202 of the New Plaza Hotel," she said, "But if he found me here, he may be there, and I have everything important with me."

"Care to tell me who this *he* is?"

"I wish I knew myself."

"Well, my name is Carlos."

"I know. It says on the app. I'm Ana."

"I knew that too," he said with a wink and pulled onto the main road to the airport. "Do you have your hotel key?"

"Yes."

"I can go get your luggage and be back here in half an hour. It will save you a hotel fine as well," he added.

"Are you sure?"

"Absolutely. I work for myself in this job," he said, smiling at her.

"Okay, I'll watch for you from there" she said, as he pulled up to the terminal and let her out.

Hurrying into the terminal, she found a lady's room and ducked inside, while she used her phone to book the next available flight. Then she called Philip.

It took Carlos forty-five minutes, and Ana had almost given up and headed for her flight gate, when he appeared and called her name from the entry.

"Thank you so much!" she said. "How much do I owe you?"

"Your phone number, perhaps?"

"What?"

"It is always my pleasure to assist a damsel in distress," he said, smiling at her.

"Oh, I uhm…" She looked at him. He was handsome. "Why not," she said, half to herself, unable to not smile back at him. She looked for a pen.

"Here, just send it to my phone," he said, handing her a card. "Then, if I can be of further service, you can call me."

"Thank you, again," she said, and hurried off to check her bag.

He waved to her as she headed to security. She waved back, feeling a weird sense of something she hadn't felt since she had said her goodbyes to Sebastian.

***

Charles was getting impatient. He had been watching her hotel for three hours with no sign of her. He was just getting out to have a coffee in the hotel restaurant when he was approached by a police officer.

"Excuse me, sir?"

"Yes?" Charles asked.

"I need you to come with me."

"What on earth for?"

"We've had a complaint about you, from a young woman. She says you've been stalking her."

"That's ridiculous!"

"Really? Then, can you explain why you've been parked for so long outside of her hotel?"

"I was waiting for a friend, but it doesn't look like they are going to make it."

"So, you are going inside now, because?"

"I was just going to get a coffee! Is that illegal?" Charles was fighting a losing battle with his patience. "I'll have you reported for harassment!"

"As you like, but first, you must come with us," the officer said, throwing a look to his partner, who was heading toward them. "We need you to answer a few questions."

"I've already answered a few of your ridiculous questions!" he spat at the officer.

"I'd watch my tone," the other officer said, "or we can add resisting arrest and assaulting a police officer to the charges."

"Bloody hell! What about my car?"

"Evidence." The officer smiled, as his partner took Charles by the arm to escort him to their car.

Charles wrenched away, and they both tackled him to the ground and cuffed him.

Antonio Spara smiled when he got the call from his cousin, Juan, who was head of police in Rio de Janeiro. This was going to be interesting. With the resisting arrest and assaulting an officer charge added, they should be able to hold him long enough to keep Ana safe and, hopefully, learn a few things.

Philip called Spara as soon as Ana hung up with him, and it only took a few minutes to put in the call to have the man arrested on stalking and whatever else they could come up with. It was the wee hours of the morning in Europe, but Philip couldn't wait to let Larry and the others know they had one of the project's mystery men in custody.

They were even happier when they contacted Carlos, who agreed to be a witness of Charles attempt at following Ana.

The more they looked, after bringing him in, the more they found, including, fake ID's and suspicious connections in his phone logs. Searching his apartment proved even more fruitful when they discovered a large stash of cocaine and fentanyl.

This was one lead, that no matter what, they were determined to not let go of.

Philip hung up his phone and went out on the veranda, where Monica waited for him.

"I sure am glad I married you," he said, sitting beside her and reaching an arm around her.

She laughed, "Right now, I think you're happier about my uncle's connections."

"Added benefit," he confessed and leaned over to kiss her.

A whimper came from the baby monitor, and they both froze for a second to listen.

"I think we're safe," Monica said, reaching to open a bottle of wine. "Now that I'm not nursing anymore, I think we should toast."

"And then?" Philip asked, taking the bottle from her to pour.

"Once I'm nice and relaxed, I expect you to take full advantage of me."

"Cheers," Philip replied, raising his glass.

Berlin, Germany: August 23rd

Ana finished a call with Larry and Dave. After her experiences back in Brazil, she decided to become more trusting of them. Somewhere in her mind, she had always known they had her best interests at heart, but she was so used to only trusting Sebastian, that she found it difficult to trust anyone else. Her mother and Aida were exceptions, to a degree, but even with them she remained cautious.

Now she felt even more uncertain about her mother and welcomed the advanced DNA testing that she had refused before. As soon as she was back in Switzerland, she would take samples of her mother's hair and go meet with Magdeline. The police in Rio de Janeiro had also taken samples from the man they arrested, and those were already on their way.

Once she found the marriage record for Axel and Marianna, she found Marianna easy to trace. She even found a newspaper clipping with her likeness.

Ana stared at the picture for a long time before she went on to read.

Marianna had quite a story to tell. She was a niece of the Prussian king, Fredrick William IV, but upon her marriage to Axel, a commoner, who was known to practice mysticism, she was shunned by her family. The March Revolution was just winding down when they boarded the ship bound for Brazil.

Going back in Axel's history, she found that he came from a modest family of farmers and soldiers. No doubt, the military participation only increased Marianna's family dislike of Axel. He had also done a stent in the military during the rebellion.

Even though Marianna was not in the direct royal line, after seeing her portrait, Ana was certain the connection meant something. It was as if she was looking at a drawing of herself. She also realized that if she was descended from Marianna, she was also descended from Meschner.

The thought made her shudder.

Milan, Italy

Marie and Omar, Magdeline's parents, looked in on the children. They had managed to push their beds together again, right after Magdeline, Soren and the boys left, and they were all lying side by side, holding hands. It was as though they were afraid of being separated. They had thought that the boys' visit had at least started to bring them out of their shells, but now they seemed to be going almost backwards.

At least they didn't insist on going to the toilet and bathing together anymore. Still, they only spoke to each other, and Marie couldn't take one out without the others. They took them to parks to meet other children, and they played with other children, as they had the boys, but never without each other.

They were never bad. In fact, they seemed almost too well behaved, and they were obviously very mentally advanced. Marie had considered having them tested for some type of autism, thinking that maybe they were savants, but she was told their characteristics didn't fit, and the idea that all three would have the same symptoms, especially not being identical, was low. The only diagnosis was separation anxiety due to a shared trauma. If only they could get them to talk about how they had been separated from their parents and wound up alone in the woods.

Austria

Magdeline looked in on the boys, then went to join Soren, who was playing with the telescope, a present from the boy's grandparents before they left.

"It's a beautiful night, Maggie. Come look," Soren said, and she moved to his side to look up into the clear night sky.

"It is beautiful. Soren?"

"Yes?"

"I need to tell you something."

"What is it?" he asked, concerned by her tone. "Are you all right?"

"I'm pregnant."

"Maggie, that's... Wow!"

"Yeah."

"Do you know how far along?"

"Well, I would guess, no more than three weeks."

"Do you feel okay?"

"Physically, I feel fine. It's just that now that we know..."

"We already have the three. What's one, or two, or three more? We may have to get a bigger house, but..."

"What if it's a girl?"

"She'll have three wonderful big brothers."

"And she's a more likely target for the projects. What if they kidnap her for some weird breeding program?"

"First, we don't even know it's a girl yet, unless you performed some new test?"

"No, I know you're right, but..."

"Worry won't help. You're one of the people who taught me that. Look at me Maggie. There is nothing we, nothing you can't handle. Remember, you have warrior queen, DNA in you. I found a documentary on Tube-Vision about her, and she was widowed with two daughters. All of them are commemorated in a statue, near the parliament buildings, in London. There is nothing you can't handle."

"Nothing *we* can't handle. I can only deal with all of this because I have you."

"I'm not going anywhere," he said, leaning down to kiss her forehead.

"I keep thinking about how they took Jack, and we don't even know why. Did I tell you that Claire is sure that they killed her husband?"

"No one is taking me anywhere."

"What about when they held you in France?"

"I promise that I will not leave town without you, not under any circumstances. I do think it may be wise to keep the pregnancy secret for as long as possible though. And if it makes you feel better, we can even go away somewhere once you start showing."

Magdeline smiled up at him. "You always have a solution."

"Come sit with me under the stars," Soren said, sitting on a lounge chair and pulling her down on his lap.

Magdeline felt something wet, suddenly touch her arm. "What was that?" she asked, jerking herself up.

Soren stood and started laughing.

Magdeline followed his gaze under the lounge chair and laughed at herself when she saw Trek and Rubix looking up at her. She fell into Soren's arms.

He whispered, "I hope you won't be this jumpy for nine months."

She laughed and took a deep breath. "I hope not too."

"Maybe you should tell Sophie not to come."

"No," Magdeline said, shaking her head. "If anything, I think it will be better with her here. Nick is going to be gone a lot then, and you can't stay by my side twenty-four-seven. There is safety in numbers."

"Maybe we could send them to police dog training," Soren said, as Trek made his way out from under them and Rubix chased after a firefly.

"Great Idea. Who would suspect a three-legged, firefly chasing spaniel as a guard dog?"

"I imagine Trek *could* look vicious," Soren said, and they both broke into laughter at the Husky, who now rolled around in the grass, only to be startled when Rubix pounced on him.

Chapter 37

Austria: August 27th

Magdeline looked at the DNA samples Ana brought her against the sample she received from Brazil and the one on file for Stephan. She was more than a little surprised by what she saw. Medical records showed that Stephan had only a point zero two percent chance of being able to father a child, yet, according to what she was looking at, he and Anna were closely related. She was, however, just as closely related to Charles.

Knowing what she did of the projects, it wouldn't have been so odd, except there was a signature DNA, produced only in sperm, that matched closely to Stephan and not Charles. This would have made sense if Ana's father was Stephan's brother, but Stephan didn't have a brother.

After running the sequencing for a fifth time, she called Larry.

Lyon, France

"You're going to love this one," Larry told Dave. "Magdeline called me this afternoon. She ran Stephan's DNA along with Charles next to Ana's, and as Sarah claimed, Charles would appear to be Ana's father, however..."

"Stephan is too?" Dave guessed.

"No and yes. Ana shows signature DNA from sperm, that is closely related to Stephan, and not Charles, but would most likely come from a brother."

"What?"

"That's what I said. She ran it five times."

"Doesn't that just mean they used other DNA from him then?"

"Not in this case," Larry said. "She assumed that at first too, which is why she ran it five times. Apparently, there is unique signature that comes from the DNA of sperm."

"Has she told Ana?"

"No. Soren is thinking about going to go talk to Sarah again first. She did say they injected her with other sperm."

"I think Ana should be there too. Alienating her when she's finally become cooperative doesn't seem wise," Dave said.

"You make a good point. In fact, since Stephan knows about Charles, I think all three of them should hear this together, and I'd really appreciate it if you would be there as well. I'd go myself, but the girls leave in just a few days."

"I may as well call Soren myself then," Dave said. "Lidia is busy plotting something with Suzanna, so she may not even miss me. You and Margot, enjoy your family."

"Thanks Dave."

Uppsala, Sweden

Richter made his way down the hallway to the auditorium, keeping his head down, as he recognized a few of the participants, namely Dr. Jordan and Dr. Erikson. He considered speaking to them, but he wanted his arrival in Paris to be a surprise.

The next speaker in the lineup was a professor of animal behaviors. She was to speak on how they were learning to predict nearly any personality trait by studying the genetic codes and how these same studies could be applied to humans in order to prevent criminal or other unwanted character traits from having negative effects on the future of humanity.

In her talk, she spoke on how to reprogram, add to, or eliminate certain genetic components to create a more desirable personality. Some of these studies had even involved using genes from animals of other species to mediate violent tendencies.

"For example," said Dr. Cai. "If you take a wild leopard, you could perhaps, add genetic components of an animal like a zebra, who is vegetarian, and create a leopard with little to no interest in killing."

"Yes?" she said to a raised hand.

"Wouldn't that mean that it was no longer a leopard, but some type of highbred, zepard or leobra, if you will?"

A few chuckles were heard.

Then, Dr. Cai answered. "No. In fact, the genetic variance would be so small that only the animal's desire for meat would be affected. At this point we are only able to safely alter a maximum of point zero seven of the genome. It is fascinating to see how different species genomes can work together, and in the future, a leobra could be a possibility. Our goals, however, are not to create new species, but to understand, help, and in some cases, improve an individual's life. Once we learn and have enough success, we hope to be able to make a significant contribution to improve human society."

At the break, Richter followed Jordan and Erikson, who seemed to be deep in conversation. He followed them to the University canteen, which was primarily students. Most of the other participants would be headed to one of the nearby restaurants, and he had a feeling that meant they were talking about something they would not want overheard. He grabbed a sandwich and a sparkling water from the self-serve area and was able to get a seat at a table where he could easily listen in.

They were speaking freely, because none of the students, which they likely assumed he was, would have a clue what they were saying meant. Richter understood it very well though, and he was very interested when they began to discuss Professor Crabben and the new connections between the China project and P2P.

He also learned that Erikson and Jordan were now leading P2P after Simon was arrested and Hisdak was presumed dead. Little did they know how limited their time was.

Richter's adrenaline pulsed with excitement over these developments. He could hardly wait to get to Paris and take his rightful place. He needed to act fast. He now understood that the girls were at the University because Simon was out of the picture. He wondered about Josephine. He knew Simon had always been the one in charge. This meant they were likely unprotected enough to be easily abducted.

France

Tony checked the cameras, but there was nothing. He had searched the vat room and the storeroom beside the old chimney in vain for some secret latch or button, pushing and prodding each stone. He had even gotten a ladder to check the upper stones, but nothing. Still, he knew there had to be something. It would be physically impossible for someone to leave just a heal print in that position. Clearly, the toe of the shoe had to be inside the chimney.

"Right! A shoe stepping into a solid stone chimney," he said aloud to himself. If he hadn't photographed it and known about the entry in Laura's wine cellar, he would have thought himself crazy. He really wished he could talk to Mathias. Where had he disappeared to?

A terrible thought hit Tony. What if Mathias was trapped in the tunnel? What if he was lying dead right inside this chimney? Tony slapped himself. Mathias could handle himself and he was prone to vanishing, but what if? Tony suddenly felt the overwhelming need to find the entrance he knew must exist.

He tried for the umpteenth time to position his own foot in the same way that the heel print had been. Then he simply leaned into the stones. Nothing.

He had just walked into the storeroom when his watch beeped. He was due to meet his wife and kids for a picnic. He hurried out, grabbing a bottle of Diana's favorite rose on the way. He needed to focus on his family. Mathias was fine, he told himself and hurried to his jeep.

It was his wife, Diana, who gave him the idea, as they sipped the rose and watched the children playing.

She asked him about the wine's origins, and he was explaining the grapes and the process used for that particular vintage, when he remembered the old vat. They had gotten new vats about ten years ago. He remembered helping to change them out, except for one. It was impossible to move, as concrete, supposedly from when they poured the floor years before, had been pushed against it, effectively gluing it to the floor. They didn't want to risk damaging the floor and decided to simply leave the one original vat.

When they got back that evening, it was late. They put the already sleeping children to bed, and he said that he needed to check one of the wine gages.

"Can't your dad do that?" Diana asked.

"He could, but then I'd have to call him and explain which one and why. It's just easier if I run out and do it really quick. I'll take my phone and if there's any issue, I'll text."

"It was fine while you were gone with us this afternoon."

"I'd forgotten about it. I was completely distracted by you."

"I could tell you were distracted, but..."

"I was thinking about getting you home, just like this, but I really do need to check the gage. Then I'm all yours."

Tony hurried to the vat room and flipped on the lights. Then he went over to the old vat. It was the closest to the chimney. He didn't recall anything strange about the vat, aside from it being cemented to the floor. He twisted the spout. Nothing happened.

"What were you expecting from an old empty vat?" he said. Talking aloud to himself, somehow made him feel safer, just in case heel print returned. He walked around to the rear of the vat, remembering the handles they had used to carry the others out. He had pulled on this handle before though when they tried to move it. Or had he? He thought back to that day and remembered that Simon had been in the vat room, which was unusual. Only Josephine had ever shown interest in the production. Simon had been a paperwork and banking guy. Yet, that day, it was Simon in the vat room giving instructions. It was Simon who had pointed out that it could damage the floor to move it, and so they had left that one vat alone.

Tony stared at the handle and beamed his flashlight on it. He blinked to be sure he wasn't imagining the fingerprints. He'd come back in the morning and try to lift them.

Feeling certain that he had discovered the secret, he hurried back to spend the rest of the night with Diana.

Chapter 38

Switzerland: August 28ᵗʰ

Ana was somewhat nervous when Dave called and asked that not just, she, but her mother and Stephan all be there to meet with not only him, but Magdeline and Soren as well. She knew that meant there had to be something irregular in the tests Magdeline had run.

She no longer cared if her mother discovered her trip to Brazil. Ana was an adult, and it was her life. She needed to know who she really was and why she had been taken, why the doctors performed experiments on her. She had developed some theories of her own after seeing the image of Marianna and carefully going through the copy of the notebook she had taken from the estate in Brazil.

The initial discussion was awkward, to say the least. It was Stephan who had the hardest time, not just with wrapping his mind around the idea of Ana having more than one father, but how it was possible for him to be so closely related to Ana, yet not be her father?

Ana's theories and work in the archives brought to light that Stephan's side of the family was indeed crucial to why Ana had been taken.

"It's very possible, from this new genealogy information, that both you and Sarah's DNA play a part. But from what we can definitively trace, we can safely say that you, Stephan, are a family line they would choose," Dave said.

"Who are *they?*" Stephen asked.

"Like we've talked about before, we are aware of multiple projects now, worldwide, and most likely connected, who conduct various types of genetic experiments," Dave said.

"I get that, but to what end? And don't these tests mean that I could be Ana's biological father too?"

"Unfortunately, not," Magdeline said. "While the percentage of genetic match, would in theory, make it an unlikely possibility, when I ran sequencing on more specific gene pairs, there are certain pairs that are missing important matches from your genome. It's really difficult to explain, even to another geneticist. Then there is the fact that the genes would have had to be injected invitro, which Sarah said she saw happen. The specific DNA I looked at had to have come from sperm, but that means that they would have needed not only a viable sample from you, but it would have been an altered sample..."

"I wouldn't have a viable sample," Stephan said, as he stared at the floor. Then he took a deep breath and said, "I guess that settles it. She has to be my sister."

Everyone was silent, as they looked at Stephan.

"My dad had some sperm stored. It was a long time ago, before he met my mom. He said he did it because he thought it was cool. It was still a fairly new process at the time. He told me about it, years later, when Sarah and I were trying to conceive. He even asked me if I wanted to use his. I said it would be too weird, and I never even mentioned it to Sarah. I mean, that would have made my daughter my sister." He chuckled, but he had a pained look on his face. "Whoever this Charles is, must have known somehow. It's funny, even though Sarah didn't tell me my true results, I knew. Still, I convinced myself I was Ana's father. I'm sorry," he said, looking at Ana, and then he stood and left the room.

"Maybe I should go check on him," Dave said.

"No, I'm the one who needs to go," Sarah said, and left the room in the direction Stephan had gone.

"Who is Charles? I mean, what else have you found out about him, genetically?" Ana asked, looking at Magdeline.

"From what I could tell, he's healthy. There's not really much more I can give you. There are some studies which are trying to isolate genes that seem to present higher in certain personality traits, that's not something I've studied, nor do I trust the theory. It is just theory."

"But certain mental and emotional conditions can be passed down," Ana said.

"A propensity for them can, but there is still a lot of influence outside of genetics. So, even if you had those genes, there would likely need to be some kind of external trigger for them. With so many external contributors, it's not an exact science."

"Now I understand why I always felt closer to my grandfather, or rather my...donor? It seems that genes mattered there."

"Not necessarily," Soren said. "I was always closer to my aunt and uncle than my parents, when I was growing up."

Ana gave him a half smile, then turned to Dave. "Will you continue working on my ancestry?"

"Definitely," Dave said. "And I promise to keep you up to date with anything I find regarding Charles."

"Thank you. Philip has been good about that too. Do you think they'll come after me again?"

"I don't know."

Ana nodded and excused herself.

Dave, Magdeline and Soren looked at each other.

"Well, this is awkward," Dave said. "It feels odd to just leave."

"I'm wondering if Stephan and Sarah..." Soren started, when the door opened.

Sarah looked at them and asked, "Where's Ana?"

"She went outside a few minutes ago," Dave said. "How's Stephan?"

"Trying to absorb it. I really think I should go try and find Ana. If you don't mind showing yourselves out."

"Not a problem. I'll be in touch," Dave said, as Sarah left.

Their respective flights home left later in the evening, so they stopped for a late lunch on the way to the airport, and Soren and Magdeline gave Dave the news of a new baby on the way.

"We thought you should know, and you can tell Larry and Margot, but aside from that, we want to keep it quiet," Soren said.

"What about Shane?"

"Not yet," Magdeline said. "He's dealing with enough, and I guess I feel a little awkward about it, because of Patricia."

"Okay. It's entirely your choice, and congratulations."

"Thanks," Magdeline said.

***

Ana walked down past the tennis courts then up towards the back of the property, through the garden, towards the guest house. She saw Stephan sitting on a bench in the garden. A part of her wanted to turn around, but she needed to talk to him.

"May I?" she asked, indicating the bench.

His face was tear streaked when he looked up at her and they held each other's gaze.

"Of course," he said.

"You apologized to me, but I'm the one who should really be apologizing to you," Ana said.

"Why?"

"I treated you terribly. I know that none of this was your fault and I'm sorry."

"Apology accepted, but none of this was your fault either. You were just a child."

Sarah overheard them talking and stopped before they saw her. She turned around. Then she went back in the house, wrote a note, took her purse, and drove away.

France

Tony was surprised to see his sister when they went to have dinner with his father.

"Hey sis! What brings you out our way?"

"I was talking to dad and heard everyone was here together. How could I not come?"

"Aunt Emilie!" Gabriel, Tony and Diana's eight-year-old son called, running toward her.

"Auntie," echoed Amy and Chloe, hurrying up behind their brother.

Emilie somehow managed to hug them all at once and Chloe, the youngest, insisted on being picked up.

"Well, now that we're all here, Emilie helped me put together a much better dinner than the hot dogs I was planning, so let's go enjoy!" said Tony Senior.

"I wanted hotdogs though," Gabriel complained.

"And we knew you would," Emilie said, "so we made those too."

"You're the best!"

"You better at least try your aunt's cooking," Diana told him.

"I will. I can eat both. I just really wanted a hotdog."

"I think he gets his tastebuds from you," Diana said, rolling her eyes at Tony.

After dinner, Tony went to talk to Emilie.

"Did you ever hear about the tunnels running under the town?" he asked.

"Of course. Why?" she asked.

"I think there may be one under the vineyard."

She laughed. "I know there is."

"You do?"

"Yep. It was the one secret I had from you. What makes you ask about it now?"

"I saw this when I was in the vat room, and it's been driving me nuts. I even set up cameras," he said showing her the picture. "I think I know where the lever is, but I've been busy with Diana and the kids, and I didn't want..."

"Didn't want to go alone? Fraidy cat!" she teased.

"Hey, I don't know whose heel print that is, but it doesn't look like a kid's."

"Did you ask the workers or dad?"

"No. Do you think he knows about it?"

"Probably not, though I think he suspects there's one somewhere."

"Will you go with me to check it out?"

"When did you see this print?"

"Ten days ago."

"That means they probably exited out another tunnel."

"How familiar are you with these tunnels?"

"Not very. I used to hide down there sometimes, but it was always so dark. I could see other passages, but..."

"Oh, now I see. Who's the fraidy cat?"

"All right, all right, when do you want to go?"

"Diana will be reading bedtime stories for at least another hour. So, how about now? Plus, she knows I'm with you, so she won't be upset if I get back late."

"You better have some really good flashlights!"

Ten minutes later, they were in the vat room and Emilie cranked the handle at the back of the vat. A lower section of the stone chimney moved inward and revealed a steep stairway.

"The false flue here, opens and closes it from this side," Emilie said, pulling on it and closing them in.

"Did you need to do that?"

"Yes. At least now, if someone else tries to enter, we'll probably hear them. This place is like an echo chamber," she whispered. "It really is creepy."

"How did you find it?"

"Meschner. I saw him use it once. I was also afraid to give away his secret. He always gave me the creeps."

Tony laughed and jumped at his own echo.

"I told you," Emilie said. "Do you ever wonder where they all went? I know Meschner finally croaked, but Josephine and Simon? The kids?"

"I do know what happened to Simon. I'm surprised dad didn't tell you. Simon was arrested, and now he's in the nut house."

"Really?" Emilie smiled.

"Really. A couple of private detectives came by and told us. They were looking for leads on Josephine."

"Is she wanted too?"

"I don't think so. It was her family who hired them. She is missing though."

"What does that mean for the vineyard?"

"If she stays missing, there's a possibility Dad and I could have a legal claim to own it."

"And no one was going to tell me this?"

"I assumed dad would, but you know, he can be a pessimist. Don't tell him I told you. He's probably afraid to get his hopes up. It could take years. And the girls they adopted could show up and stake a claim too."

"While I hope Josephine and the girls are okay, for your sake, I hope they don't show up. This sounds like a perfect chance for you and Diana," Emilie said, as Tony examined the area. "So, which way do you want to go?"

He needed to make sure they didn't go in the direction of Laura's, where Meschner lay. He hadn't really thought enough about this, he realized, as he shifted the high beam flashlight side to side. He hoped there weren't any more bodies lying about. An image of Mathias came to mind.

"Actually, I think I'm good. I mean, these could all go on for miles. I just wanted to solve the footprint mystery. I think I'll just leave the camera's up for that though."

"I think that sounds like a good plan," Emilie agreed, and they made their way back up, but when she pulled on the handle, nothing happened.

"What now?" Tony asked.

"You're asking me?"

"Okay, let me think. If Meschner was using the tunnels, it would make sense for one to lead to his chateau. That would be the tunnel to the right and not that far away."

Twenty minutes later, they came to another split in the tunnel system and began searching for an exit.

Emilie said a silent prayer, as she felt around a section of stone that looked newer than the rest.

As it turned out, they were in luck. The wall opened, and they found themselves in a swimming pool.

"Thank God it's been drained!" Emilie exclaimed. "Is this the chateau?"

"It is," Tony said, as they walked up and onto the surrounding lawn. "We're only a short walk back to the vineyard entrance."

"I broke up with Dennis," Emilie blurted out.

"Aha, I thought there was something more."

"Why? You didn't think I'd ever just come for a visit?"

"Not without Dennis or at least talking about him. Your silence speaks volumes. Is it over for good?"

"I think so. He keeps putting off planning the wedding. I don't think he really wants to be married."

"Did you tell dad?"

"Not yet. He did ask, and I said Dennis was working, which he always is."

"Are you okay?"

"I will be. To be honest, I'm a little relieved. I'm not sure I was as in love with him, as I was comfortable with him. We've been together so long."

"You've been engaged for three years. I think you did the right thing."

"Thanks," she said.

"Does this mean you might stick around here awhile?"

"I gave up my fiancée, not my job."

"I thought you could work from anywhere."

"Technically, but I do need to go into the office on occasion."

"The same office Dennis works at."

"True. It's not like we had a major fight. I was just tired of waiting for someone that I wasn't even sure I wanted anymore. I just need some time to figure out my next move. You know I gave up my apartment, but I can't stay with dad in my old bedroom forever. I'm not a little girl anymore. I was thinking, maybe a week or so, maybe I'll look up some old friends in Calais."

"You remember Laura Sartre?"

"Yeah, I saw on social media that she opened a wine bar. Do you help supply it?"

"I do. That's why I asked. The wine bar is in a section of a large house she inherited. If you decided to stick around longer, you might check with her about a room. She could use some help at the wine bar as well. It's only open for a few nights week because she's still working at the restaurant too, and she's been getting good business."

"I would like to go by, but don't expect me to give up life in Lille."

"City girl," he teased, as they entered the drive to the vineyard.

"Goodnight, big bro," she said, giving him a peck on the cheek, before heading back to their dad's.

"Night, my city sis," he replied, waving after her.

Chapter 39

Uppsala, Sweden: Sept. 3rd.

It was the last Saturday before classes started, and the girls were all excited. Callie had gone back to Scotland the day before to finish her final year, but she hoped to finish early and join them all in the spring. She had already passed her entrance exams and talked to counselors about studying to become a veterinarian. Some of her prerequisites were already covered by work she had done on local farms in Scotland.

Today, Tabetha, Pollina and Amber were going hiking with Tabetha's cousins Sara and Jonas and his friends Fredrick and Lars. Pollina had developed a bit of a crush on Lars and Amber on Jonas. They also knew that Tabetha was crushing on Fredrick and Sara, who was recently graduated and already engaged, had agreed to play matchmaker.

They were all laughing and having a great time as they made their way up a trail at Kungshamn Morga nature reserve. None of them realized that they were being followed.

Richter was stealth, staying a good distance behind them and blending in well with his walking stick in hand. He followed them to a lake, where they all readied to go swimming. The day was warm, and the lake crowded. Richter took a water bottle from his pack and climbed to sit on a tree branch, where he had a perfect viewpoint.

Twenty minutes later, the girls laid out a picnic, and the guys came running, dripping water all over. The girls scolded them while laughing at the same time.

Richter was quite enjoying the show and thinking that watching them could be a great help in choosing which one he wanted for his own. He hoped to get them both to France but had to be certain to at least get his future mate.

He was leaning toward Amber now. He liked the idea that she didn't look so much like Alice. He knew she was still part of the same line, but her mitochondrial DNA had not been edited, which is why she looked so much like her aunt. It was a natural trick the genes played, something he would find interesting to study. He also liked that he wouldn't risk running into any duplicates, she would be his. His original, yet with all the abilities of someone bred of the project. He liked the way her mouth curled as she teased the boys. Yes. It was Amber who would be his queen. He could spare one more week to watch them and get to know their schedules and patterns.

He knew they weren't staying on campus, and that should make it easier. He just needed to get them alone. They always seemed to be around far too many people. It wasn't that crowds were an issue, quite the contrary, it was often easier to take someone with a crowd to serve for cover. The problem here was, they were nearly always with Tabetha and her friends and family. He hoped none of them would get in his way. He really didn't want to be a killer. Yes, some would have to be eliminated, but these were young, healthy specimens who could prove useful to the new order he planned to procreate.

Quebec City, Canada: Sept. 6th

Ralph recognized the name on the cargo list and called Shane. He had also borrowed his wife and one of his daughter's smart phones and set up two of them up to record and hopefully get video. He had one on each side of the trailer. One was hidden in some insulation, so he doubted he would be able to hear any audio, but the camera lenes was perfectly disguised. The other, he had tucked inside a wheel well and probably wouldn't catch much in the way of video, but it should cover the audio. His eldest daughter's phone, he kept with him. If anything happened to it, she's the one who would give him the hardest time, that and he might need the other two longer in order to transfer the data if Shane had any issues with the live feed. He had been told in no uncertain terms, that his daughter needed her phone back in her room before she was home from school.

Ralph had arrived early to slip the second phone, unseen, behind the wheel, then he went inside to see if there were any doughnuts. He was pleasantly surprised to find not only doughnuts but homemade coffee cake, a bowl of fruit, and bagels with cream cheese. They also had a new coffee maker, one of those where you can choose your individual brew.

"This looks great, Carol! What's the occasion?" Ralph asked the receptionist.

"The old coffee pot gave up the ghost. So, I thought we should celebrate the new one. Help yourself. Two of the guys called in sick, so there's plenty. You'll have a bit of a wait for the cargo."

"I know. I came straight here from dropping the kids for their first day of school. Thanks Carol," Ralph said, as he filled a paper plate and a large coffee.

An hour later, the plane had finally landed, and Dane came in to join him.

"Hey Ralph! How's it going?" Dane greeted.

"Good, thanks. You?"

"Same ole, same ole. I see they're back," Dane said, looking out the window.

They watched as the plane pulled up alongside the open trailer and five men disembarked. Ralph recognized the one as the man Shane told him was supposed to be dead. When the cargo door to the plane opened, three of the other men came inside, and one spoke to Carol. Dane went over to see if they needed anything, but Ralph stayed, watching. The dead man went inside the cargo hold with the other.

The men who had come in were now helping themselves to coffee and doughnuts. Then they sat and started jabbering away, in what, Ralph guessed, was Chinese.

Ralph hit record on his daughter's phone and refilled his coffee. Then he did a double take, as he looked out the window. He could have sworn he saw a monkey bounding across the tarmac. Then he saw the two men follow in the same direction.

It crossed his mind that he should alert the guys who were still jabbering away, but he didn't. He just let it play out. He turned away from the window and sat down with his coffee and a maple bar. Dane was doing some paperwork, so he just sat there, eating and recording. He also turned the camera on selfie mode to continue watching through the window. He then saw what looked like two more people. He could only see feet and lower legs, hurrying away. What he saw next was clearly a monkey of some sort, and it was heading toward the lounge.

One of the Chinese looked up and saw the monkey and alerted the others.

The one who spoke to Carol, said, "We need your help!"

"What's happened?" Ralph asked, biting his tongue.

"Look behind you! Come! Hurry! Both of you!" he said, turning to Dane.

Ralph looked and saw a menagerie scurrying all over the tarmac now.

"This should be interesting," Ralph said to Dane, as they followed the men outside.

While the men were hurrying around, trying to corral the

birds, monkeys and a few reptiles, Ralph removed and pocketed the mobile phones. He then looked inside the plane's cargo hold. The only thing inside was a bunch of open cages. He hopped down and sidestepped a snake.

"Over here!" Ralph yelled, hopping onto his trailer. He had what he considered a healthy fear of snakes.

One of the Chinese men ran over and caught it up into a bag. The only animals they were able to catch were the reptiles, two baby monkeys, and a bird who seemed to take a shine to Dane and had perched on his shoulder. Dane wasn't thrilled when they put the net over him as well as the bird in order to trap it. After they re-caged what they could, they loaded the trailer and gave Ralph orders to take it to the University Lab.

Ralph was just pulling out of the gate when animal control pulled in. He laughed and wondered about who all he had seen running away and why? He could hardly wait to offload and call Shane.

Lyon, France

Shane watched the video in disbelief, as Professor Crabben uncovered a large cage, and two people stepped out, followed by a monkey. Then Crabben and the young man who had gotten off the plane with him darted away, while a middle-aged man and woman finished unlocking the other cages, then hurried off in the same direction as Crabben and the other man. A few more monkeys jumped down from the plane, followed by a few birds and several lizards and snakes.

"What is that dad?" Daniel asked, coming over to Shane.

"A video a friend sent of animals escaping their cages."

"Why were they in cages? Are they going to the doctor or a zoo?"

"I don't know. Right now, they're trying to go free."

The sound of frantic Chinese began to sound in the background.

"I hope they get to be free," Daniel said, "except the snakes. They're creepy!"

"I agree."

"Why are they speaking Chinese?"

"How would you recognize Chinese?" Shane asked.

"I was watching a documentary on Chinese Pandas. It had sub-titles, but that's what the people talking sounded like."

"You may be right. You have a better ear for languages than I do. So, was there something you came in for? I thought you were playing with the neighbors on the playground. Is everything okay?"

"I was, but look," Daniel said, pulling back the curtain to reveal the sheets of rain falling outdoors. "The others all went home, so I did too. Plus, it's lunch time."

"You're right, and I'm suddenly hungry," Shane said. "I just need to make a quick call to Larry, and I'll make us some lunch."

***

Emilie was torn. She enjoyed the week, and Laura had offered her both a room and a job. She could still work online and drive up to Lille when needed. The biggest factor was that she didn't have her own apartment anymore. They had talked, and Dennis told her she could still stay at his place, but that would be too strange, and she didn't want to risk him trying to get back together. They would be better off as friends.

She walked past the Meschner chateau and turned around. That footprint Tony showed her worried her. She had tried to brush it off, but it niggled at the back of her mind. She had already broken the outer mechanism, so that no one could go into the tunnels through the vat room, and she was glad the inner was broken as well. That made her feel safer for her family. Even though she didn't know where the other passages led, she didn't like this one so close. She didn't like the idea of any Meschner being able to sneak around the neighborhood.

The chateau appeared to be deserted. Tony did say that Mathias had been there and even stayed with Tony for a while. She didn't understand how Tony could still trust a man that was Meschner's son. So, they'd been childhood friends? Emilie still didn't trust him. It was too long ago, and they had left to live with their father, who to her, had the stench of evil.

Going into the pool, she felt around the area of the entrance until it opened, then she disabled both the inner and outer mechanisms.

"There!" she said, feeling like she had helped trap some evil spirit in its grave. She told Tony that evening, and all he could think, was that it was a good thing he hadn't told her what was behind the wall in Laura's cellar.

Uppsala, Sweden: Sept. 7th

The opportunity was too good, Amber was walking through the cemetery alone, after a late night in the library. She had insisted that Pollina go on for dinner with Lars.

She was gazing up at the stars, thinking this would be an interesting place to do some night photography when she felt something hit her shoulder.

"Excuse me," she heard a man's voice say. Something about the voice seemed familiar. She looked to her left and saw him jogging away. Her vision of him seemed blurred and she stumbled, suddenly feeling dizzy. She had to sit down. She had just gotten to her knees when she passed out completely.

Richter was back in seconds, picking her up, and less than a minute later, he had her in the back seat of his rental car and they were on the way to a private airfield.

Switzerland: Sept. 8th

Stephan was still in a bit of a daze. A part of him still hoped Sarah would change her mind and come back. Ana was at work, and he almost didn't open the door when the bell rang. Thinking it could be about Ana or Sarah, he made himself get up and answer.

It was a large, certified package addressed to Sarah. He signed for it and then stared at it, wondering what it could be. Should he open it?

After everything that had happened, he decided it could be too important to ignore. He was right. He scanned through it and the horrific images it contained, along with several USB sticks, then called Dave.

Canada

He had done all he could, Victor Crabben thought, as he sipped his coffee. They were safe, for now, and he hoped that the information he sent to Sarah would be enough to expose everything and keep them and many others safe. The thing that had been most difficult for him was exposing his son as the security leak at Scangentech.

He had thought long and hard about who to send the information to. He knew that Sarah would have the understanding and ability to get it to the right people. He also felt that she had the right to know the whole truth of what had happened to her.

In the files, Crabben exposed the work happening in Quebec, as well as France, China, and other locations he had contact with. He had seen it all. He smiled at the woman, Roberta, who was cooking in the kitchen.

"It smells wonderful! Do you need any help?"

"You have helped us all more than we could ever repay," she said. "You gave up your life to save us."

"It wasn't a life I could live with anymore. You haven't had your life for years. Hopefully, you'll be able to get it back soon."

"Are you sure she's safe?"

"She'll be fine, and once everything is out, you'll be able to call, and she can join you here or you can join her in Russia."

"Chinese was hard enough. I don't know if we could learn Russian too. Remember, we're normal humans."

"So is Victoria. Lots of people have special abilities and she got away before they could do any real damage. Now, let me do something besides sit here sipping coffee. I need to be active."

"You can tell Cody breakfast is ready. He's fishing by the lake." she said, as her husband, Kent, came in with more eggs.

France

Richter would need to prepare things at P2P before taking Amber there. For now, he had her safely stashed at the old Fontaine estate.

***

Larry, Margot, Dave, and Lidia, watched as the pages printed. There were over five thousand of them and Larry had to go to the office supply store to buy more reams of paper and ink, but they wanted this in hard copy, photos and all.

It had taken over an hour just to download all the files Stephan sent. They were organized by countries and cities and included Canada, Brazil, Argentina, Australia, UK, France, Germany, Spain, Switzerland, Egypt, and China. The cover letter claimed that there were likely more, but these were the known locations, goals and names associated with them.

Shane joined them after Daniel was in bed. They didn't want to alert Claire, Rosie, or Suzanna, by asking them to babysit.

They divided the countries between them and were still reading when Daniel woke up the next morning. He wasn't enrolled in a school there yet, so Shane spent Friday taking him to Doctor Merieux's museum of biological sciences and hoping he might learn something himself. It was definitely intriguing.

Fortunately, Daniel was already supposed to spend Saturday at a water park for his new friend, Bastian's, birthday. Then, Shane had arranged for him to stay with Claire and Rosie overnight, on the pretext of planning Dave's bachelor party.

It was Sunday before they felt they had a decent grasp on what they were seeing, and Larry decided the best contacts in the various locations to send what information to, while being careful not to expose the victims of the projects.

Chapter 40

France/Denmark: September 11th - 19th

Richter had been parked near the institute in Paris when he spotted the surveillance. He waited, patiently watching, until he saw both Erikson and Jordan brought out in handcuffs. That was his queue to get back to Amber and move her to a non-known location until he figured out what was going on.

Professor Crabben was careful to present enough evidence, before sending the reports, of illegal activity per each jurisdiction's laws. And over the next week raids were conducted, in all countries indicated, of medical facilities and other properties linked to the projects in the reports. He had even named himself and his son as complicit in illegal activity.

Richter had needed to leave Amber in a vacation rental, while he searched for a permanent location. He noted that no raids had taken place in Sweden, and while it was risky, the other possible countries would be too difficult to sneak into with her in tow. There were already accommodations he could use in Malmo, and that was a far enough distance from the lab in Northern Sweden, that he felt it the best solution. He was wrong. Fortunately, he realized his mistake before they left Denmark, when he saw a missing persons bulletin at the port with Amber's face on it.

Damn it! He had not considered the issues that came with her being a normally enrolled student. When the project had been in control, the products of it, like Amber and her sister, had also been under their control. Now, everything seemed to be falling apart. He pulled out of the port and back onto the main road. He hated this uncertainty. He had no place to go now. He pulled over to study a map and think. That's when it happened.

Amber had begun to come around a few minutes before. She could feel the car moving, feel the seatbelt hooked around her, and she waited in silence hoping for a chance of escape. She felt the car slow. She listened, trying to understand where they were and hoping he hadn't pulled over to dose her into oblivion again.

He didn't seem to be doing anything but sitting beside her. She heard the beeping of the GPS and then the sound of the paper map being unfolded. She could also hear other people. She recognized that they were speaking Dutch, which at least gave her a clue as to where she was.

The voices seemed to be coming closer. Carefully moving her left hand toward the seatbelt buckle, and her right to the door handle, she suddenly sprang into action, unlocking the belt and jumping out of the car. She nearly ran into the couple who had been returning to their own car, parked nearby.

Richter bolted toward the passenger seat, but he was too late, she wasn't alone anymore. He spun the car out of the parking lot. Had they seen him? Did they have the license number? He didn't have much time. He pulled down a quiet residential side street and parallel parked between two SUV's. Then he grabbed his luggage and casually walked toward a busier main street, where he boarded a bus toward Kastrup Airport. It was the only thing that made sense. A man walking around, wheeling two suitcases, stood out too much. From there he could catch a cab to a hotel without it registering to anyone.

He needed to get somewhere safe to regroup and come up with a plan.

Greece: Sept. 20th

Sherman, AKA Jonathan or Kristor, felt a huge sense of relief as he watched the news of the raids. He also noted, with relief, that none had been conducted in Sweden. He had been in contact with Carl and they both suspected that it must have been Mathias who was responsible, as the public reports listed the source of the information as anonymous, and aside from Richter, Mathias would have been the only one privy to that many locations. Their only thoughts on why Sweden had not been exposed was that Mathias would have known about Oscar Noostrom, and correctly assumed that no danger was posed by the projects of regeneration at that location.

They wished they could find Mathias. Chantel had returned to France, only to discover he had gone. She had waited a week without gaining further information, then returned to Sweden.

Sherman went to Maria's bakery to pick up some pastries and then meet with Brother Archibald at the monastery. He had been invited to a special tea and fundraiser for the monastery and was helping put together a flyer. Despite a good tourist season, the monasteries were still playing catch up after the 2020/21 closures and there were many repairs to be made.

Sherman also wanted to talk to his friend about the raids, Sandra, and his thoughts on some other personal matters. He had found the friar to be a great confidant, and after all the help he gave them before, knew that he could be trusted. Aside from Carl, Archibald, and Maria's cat, Talos, were the only ones he could speak freely with.

Archibald also voiced some concerns to Sherman, regarding rumors he heard of something odd happening in the mountains between Greece and Bulgaria. While they were only strange stories to most, Sherman recognized the seriousness of their possible truth.

Lyon, France

Suzanna hung up the phone and went over to Claire's apartment. Rosie had already left for her new job, helping at a local daycare, and they would be able to talk freely. The boxes from the old storage unit in San Francisco were on their way and Charice assured her that all was going well with the business. In fact, the city had recently begun a clean-up program, that was pulling the homeless population out from the center of Seattle and housing them in makeshift housing, using old industrial buildings that had been deserted. Even Boeing had donated hangers to be used.

Claire and Suzanna had become closer over the past couple of months than they ever had been. They were even discussing Claire moving in with Suzanna and letting Rosie have a place of her own. It was clear that Dave's engagement to Lidia had been hard on her, and Claire hadn't realized until she noted Rosie's avoidance of all wedding planning, that her daughter had developed a crush on Dave.

Both Suzanna and Claire, along with the others, watched the news of the medical facility raids very closely, and they both wondered if there were more locations. The fact that there were none mentioned in the United States seemed odd to Suzanna, who suspected that Mathias must have been the one behind it.

Claire was also hoping to discover what may have happened to her other babies she'd been told didn't survive.

"Perhaps it's just a mother's instinct, but ever since I met Magdeline, I've wondered about the twins. It was the only time I had been pregnant with a boy. I wish there were some way to get in touch with Doctor Marshall."

"How long has it been since anyone has heard from him?" Suzanna asked, as she poured them coffee.

"Three years is what Sophie said. His son has tried to contact the medical team he was supposed to be with, but there doesn't seem to be any record of that team being in the Congo after 2020."

"I know that's a volatile region, but if we can find the right people, I'd be willing to pay for a search team," Suzanna offered.

"I'll pass that along to his son, via Sophie," Claire said. "But let's focus on happier things today. I have a funny feeling that we may be in the calm before the next storm."

"I do too," Suzanna agreed. I know Edgar is out there somewhere and eventually those not caught in these raids will regroup. So, before the next storm, let's plan this bridal shower!"

***

Laura and Emilie found that they worked well together, and with Emilie's help, Laura would now be able to expand the café's opening hours.

Emilie had a degree in interior design, and today they were working on adding new accents to the café. Emilie ordered new cushions through the company she worked for, and they were getting ready to put up some new art on the walls.

"Who did this one?" Emilie asked, pointing to the painting of Laura. "It looks like the Chateau around from the winery."

"It is," Laura answered. "His name was Jonathan, or rather, Carl, as I found out later."

"As in Carl Meschner?" Emilie asked, feeling suddenly tense.

"Yes, but he's not his father," Laura said, noting Emilie's unease.

"I only knew Carl as a child, and he was mean then, but I know my brother was friends with Mathias. The whole family scares me though," Emilie said. "Why did you think his name was Jonathan?"

"I found out later that he was trying to get away from his family. I think he wanted to start over. He's a talented painter. He did several others that are still at the chateau."

"Where did he go?"

"He may be in Switzerland, but we don't really know."

"Did you have feelings for him?" Emilie questioned when she saw the look on Laura's face.

"Yes, and it was mutual. We had an argument before he left. He sent this painting as an apology. I'd really rather not talk about it if that's okay."

"Okay," Emilie said, thinking she was going to have a long talk with her brother about this. Surely, he knew.

Emilie thought about the tunnels and wondered if Laura knew about them. How much did she know about the family? Had she met Richter? She realized she shouldn't judge all the boys based on memories of them as kids, and Carl had been the youngest. She, like her father, just hoped they would never have to see any of them again. Even though Meschner had died a few years back, she couldn't get over the prevailing sense of evil she felt just at the thought of him. She also squirmed internally at the memory of how he looked at her. Simon had given her the creeps too, but he was secondary to Meschner, and it was difficult to believe his sons could be so different.

Uppsala, Sweden

Amber was back in class for the first day since her abduction. The couple she met in the parking lot had driven her to the police, where she made a report and was then escorted back to Sweden, where she gave yet another report to authorities.

The problem was that she didn't dare to fully explain who Richter was. She wanted to go on living like a normal person, and to explain him, would mean exposing both herself and Pollina. Besides, who would believe it anyway? So, she had simply given a description of Richter and told them as much as she could remember from her short periods of consciousness.

She and Pollina had later spoken at length about their memories of Richter.

They were relieved about the news of the raids. Even Tabetha didn't understand their interest, but as soon as Pollina saw that Dr. Erikson had been arrested, she knew exactly what it was all about. She had half expected Amber to be found that day. In the end, she was glad Amber's escape would not connect them.

They only hoped that the descriptions Amber gave the police would match a file to show he was Meschner's son. Amber claimed he used various disguises as they moved. Since she knew his true appearance as well as a few she had seen him use, Amber helped give police three sketches.

The police had looked for DNA but found none on her clothes and Amber hadn't been alert enough to fight or scratch him at any time to get some under her nails.

"Why do you think he took you?" Pollina asked. "We always thought they would come after me first, because I look like Sophie and the other woman she mentioned. Did he say what he wanted?"

"I think he was taking me to P2P. Then the raids happened, and he couldn't. I'm not sure where he was planning to take me. He started acting desperate when he saw the raids spreading. Do you think they're done now?"

"The raids, probably. But we didn't see any of the sons arrested or even hear Meschner's name mentioned. Even Simon's name was kept out of it. It's only because I recognized the institute and Erikson that I knew it was connected to us."

"I wonder where mom is."

"Me too. I hope she gets away. I really think it was Simon who controlled her."

"To an extent, but why didn't she take us somewhere away from him sooner, especially if she really is our mother? You know we can't be sure that she didn't take us from…"

"From the project? It's true. We could have been test tube babies," Pollina said.

"Or we could have been taken like Sophie was, and our real mother or mothers think we're dead," Amber said.

"I don't think so. Remember, you look like Sophie's mom, who is our aunt, and Sophie thinks that Josephine is our mother."

"True. I think what's so hard is that I was just starting to feel safe and normal. I think he wanted to mate with me," Amber said. "He was talking to himself a lot. I was half asleep, so I thought most of it was a dream, but now I'm remembering more. I think he wanted to take over P2P and use me to start a new generation. It's all jumbled in my head, the things he said."

"Maybe we should change our appearance," Pollina suggested, "Just in case someone else comes after us."

"Do you think it would matter?"

"It can't hurt, and it would be fun. We can totally remake ourselves. Josephine left us enough money. We could even experiment and try different looks to see which one the guys like the most," Pollina said, trying to cheer her sister and allay her own fears.

"I don't really have a guy. You do."

"Jonas was really worried about you."

"More than anyone else?"

"You've seen how protective he's been since you got back. Take advantage of it."

"I don't know if I can," Amber said.

"Did Richter touch you? I mean…"

"I don't know. I was too out of it. I don't think so. I don't think they do it like normal men. I mean, I don't know, but even the thought of him touching me… I do remember him stroking my face once, but it was more like he was examining me. It was just weird. Maybe he examined the rest of me when I was out. The police asked me a lot about that too. They wanted me to have an exam, but you know why I refused."

"I know. I would have been the same. You never know which doctor may be connected, or if a normal doctor might find something odd and want to examine us more."

"I just want to focus on studying for now," Amber said. "I'm going to try and add a class to my schedule. The counselor thinks I'm trying to distract myself from what happened and that it will be too big of a load. She's only half right. All these first term classes are way too easy. I spend half my study time doing personal research."

"I get it, Amber. You know I do."

"I know you get it better than anyone else can, but…"

"It'll be okay," Pollina said, putting her arm around her sister.

"Do you ever wonder about what Sophie told us? I mean, about God?"

"I did, but not a lot. Tabetha and Callie don't go to church, except on holidays, and you never mentioned it after we talked with Sophie."

"I didn't really think about it either again, until now. One of the things I remember Richter saying was that he would be a god and I would be his goddess. Then, I just thought about what Sophie said, and I wondered."

"Do you want to go to church? I mean, we could always walk to the cathedral."

"Maybe some time, but I think I want to go alone, when I feel safe again. Of course. I'm probably safer now, while they're still actively looking for him."

Pollina looked at Amber with concern, but she didn't say anything more. They both had classes to get to. She'd talk to Jonas later and ask him to keep an extra close watch on Amber. She also considered calling Sophie, but she decided it was best to stay as far removed from any connection to the projects as possible.

Nova Scotia

Sophie stared at the paper in front of her. Until three years ago, she had always felt close to her parents. She had believed they were safe and that she could trust them with anything. Now, she couldn't even get down the first sentence to them. It had been over a month since Anne received their letter. Larry had asked if she wanted him to find them, but she said no. They were free now. It was up to them, or up to her to contact them. It bothered Sophie that they didn't write directly to her.

The biggest surprise in the information they gave to forward to Larry, was the location where Adam had moved the main sections of P2P. Larry had asked Henry Saville if he could have someone check out the area, but due to the danger status of the site, whether falsified or not, he couldn't get authorization to take a team in. He had done a drone fly over and noted there had been a major displacement of rock in the area compared to previous arial photos, but otherwise his hands were tied.

Henri later risked a hike in by himself, but he hadn't discovered anything. At a later date, they might take out some newer equipment to try and have the site declared safe to examine, but if anyone was there, they were well buried.

Sophie wondered if her parents had gotten news of all the raids. Surely, they must have. Would that change anything? Were they still staying with the sister of the man, Svend, they had worked with? Did she dare to tell them about Jeremy or about the daughter she carried now?

"I shouldn't even have to ask myself these questions," she said to Nick, as he came in from putting Jeremy to bed. "Why is this so hard?"

"What do you have so far?"

"Nothing," she said. "I've been thinking on it for a month, and I have nothing. I just feel numb. In four weeks, I'll be in Switzerland and then meet up with you in Russia."

"If we make it that far," Nick said, sitting beside her.

"You will. Jack looks better at every practice."

Nick smiled. "He's still not himself though."

"That makes two of us, and we still don't know why they took him."

"Maybe that's how you should start your letter then," Nick suggested. "Tell them what happened to Jack and ask them why they think he was taken."

"You're right. I wonder why Anne didn't suggest that?"

"Because this isn't about her, and Jack is home."

"It's about all of us," she said, rubbing her growing abdomen. "All of us."

"You know, it's okay to be angry at them," Nick said.

"The problem is, I don't feel anything, and that scares me."

"I imagine they're scared too. They've probably assumed by now that you don't want to see them."

"I do though, I think. I want back the life I had with them before I knew about their involvement, but that isn't possible."

"No one can change the past, only the future."

"Oh, thank you, wise husband, for that bit of knowledge."

"You're quite welcome, wise warrior queen," Nick responded, and Sophie crumpled up the paper in front of her and threw it at him. She was unsure how she felt about her genetic relative, Boudicca, but Nick seemed fascinated with her.

"Have you mentioned Suzanna's offer to Tom?" she asked, changing the subject.

"Not yet. That's something that needs the right moment. I did invite him to lunch after practice tomorrow, if you don't mind taking Jeremy with you."

"No problem. Ben likes having him around. He can't get as into the files as Anne and me. I don't think he's really grasped the scope of it."

"Who has?" Nick countered, as he started to make some herbal tea.

"Since when did you start drinking herbal tea?" Sophie asked, when she saw him preparing two cups.

"Since my pregnant wife started craving it. It's a male sympathy symptom," he replied, smiling.

Sophie smiled back and pulled out a new piece of paper. She decided to take Nick's suggestion. He was right. It would be easier if she didn't write about herself. An hour later she had finished, by telling them when she and Nick would be out of town, and if they wanted to come back, they should do it then. It was their house. If they wanted to come home, she would ask only that they stay in the guest house out back, where she had lived, before they left. They could work out who would move where after Christmas.

"What do you think?" she asked Nick when he finished reading it.

"I think that whatever you're comfortable with is best. It would be nice for Jeremy to meet his other grandparents, and Christmas is a good time to reconcile," he said, smiling. "And it gives you time to adjust. I notice that you didn't mention Jeremy."

"I felt like the less I said, the better. You're okay with it if they come here?"

"We were looking at other places before anyway. So yes, whatever you want is fine."

"I was thinking that if we find out they came back, we could even look online at places again, before we come back."

"I'm thinking we should just start looking again, regardless. We've saved enough. Then if they come back, fine. If not, we put this house on the market. They did put it in your name before they disappeared last time."

"You're right. I'll add that to the letter. Thank you."

"Anything I can do, I'm all yours."

Chapter 41

Canada: October 19th

Jack finished the triple twist with a perfect landing and Alice smiled at him as he skated to her. The crowd was cheering as his numbers came in for a perfect score. He turned as the cameras and reporters gathered around him. Then he turned back to Alice, but she was gone. He pushed away from the reporters and fans, who crowded around him and ran up the aisles, looking down each row, searching for Alice. He turned to call for help, but everyone had vanished. He had to find her. Her name echoed through the empty stadium as he called out.

A phone was ringing in the distance. No, it wasn't distant. It was right by his head. His eyes opened and Jack's hand reached for the phone on the nightstand. It wasn't a call though. It was his alarm. It was five in the morning, and he needed to get down and have breakfast. It was always best if he ate at least two hours prior to practice, which started at 8:00.

He forced himself out of bed and into the shower. Normally he would wait until after practice, but he needed to wash away the remnants of the dream. He had thought the nightmares were over. He needed to focus on his skating. He didn't even want to think about anything else now. He wasn't a kid anymore, and this could be his last hurrah. He was determined to make it all the way. Why did she insist on haunting him?

Austria

Sophie and Jeremy made their way through customs and out to baggage claim, where Soren was waiting for them.

Jeremy was excited to see Soren again and couldn't wait to meet the boys.

While Jeremy was a ball of energy, Sophie hadn't slept in eighteen hours and was more than thankful when Soren lugged her luggage off the belt and kept Jeremy occupied during the drive to the house, so that she could nap.

It wasn't a long drive, but just the half hour or so had been refreshing, and it was already evening. She just had to make it through dinner and get Jeremy to sleep.

Soren woke her, after taking Jeremy and their bags inside, and Jeremy was already playing in the back yard with Spencer, Thadeus, and Hamilton. Magdeline greeted her with a hug, and Sophie smiled when Magdeline smoothed her sweater, revealing her own pregnancy.

"We're keeping it a secret. Even the boys and my parents don't know yet."

"Congratulations!" Sophie said. "Do you know if…"

"It's girls," Magdeline said.

"As in twins or…?"

"Just twins, thankfully. You?"

"Still just one, as far as I can tell," Sophie said.

"I have dinner on the grill for the boys," Soren said. "I'll eat with them, but yours is right here," he said, pulling two plates from the oven and heading outside.

"Is he for real?" Sophie asked, "Or am I still dreaming?"

"I trained him well on the first three," Magdeline said, smiling. "Nick seems like a good guy too."

"He is, and I wouldn't trade him for the world, but as I remember, Soren is a much better cook."

Over dinner, they discussed which tests they wanted to run, and watched the boys play. When Sophie started to nod off again, Magdeline insisted she go lie down in the guest room. They would wake her up if Jeremy needed her.

October 20th

Sophie could hardly believe it when she woke up and looked at the clock. She had slept ten hours straight. She got up and found Magdeline in the kitchen and the boys outside.

"You were exhausted. Have you been having trouble sleeping?" Magdeline asked, "or been tired a lot?"

"Only on the plane. I've been fine otherwise, except..."

"What is it?"

"Anne had a letter from my parents. I sent the information to Larry, but it wasn't much we didn't know. After the raids... I don't know. A part of me has dreamed of having my family back, but another part... I don't feel like I know them anymore, and now, they may or may not be waiting when we get back."

"That sounds stressful."

"Nick and I did some house hunting before we left, and we're waiting to hear back on two of them, but the market is so competitive now and even though it's in my name, I don't feel right about selling the house until we know, which gives us a lower offering amount."

"Mom! Mom! Come and watch!" Jeremy called.

Sophie hurried over "Good morning to you too," she said.

"Morning," Jeremy smiled and gave her a quick hug. "Watch this!" he said, as he threw a ball, and Sophie watched as a three-legged spaniel did a jump, twist and catch, worthy of a gold medal. She clapped.

Magdeline came to the door. "That poor dog," she said. "Let me formally introduce you to my boys. Spencer, Hamilton, Thadeus, come meet your aunt Sophie," Magdeline called, and they all hurried over, followed by Rubix and Trek.

After introductions, the boys ran back to play and the dogs retired to the patio, while Magdeline and especially

Sophie, who hadn't eaten breakfast yet dug into a plate of pastries and cut fruit.

As soon as Soren was back from work, they would go to Magdeline's lab and take samples from Tessa, which is the name Sophie and Nick had decided on for their daughter.

"The boys didn't even react to me," Sophie said, as she lay on an examining table.

"After their introduction to Victoria, I don't think anything surprises them anymore, though, they have started asking exactly how many aunts they have. They know I was adopted, so that made it a little easier to explain why I wasn't completely sure."

"What about your parents? Have you told them anything?"

"No. So far, there hasn't been any need to, and they are extra busy with the three children they're fostering."

"Are they still not communicating?"

"Not if they don't have to, and we still can't even place their country of origin. What's really odd is that they understand multiple western European languages. It's not that odd for the region in itself, but we just can't imagine how no one seems to be looking for three, clearly intelligent, healthy children.

The only explanation seems to be that their parents were killed, and they didn't have other close relatives. We're guessing that their introversion is due to shock. They don't sulk or cry. It's possible they saw their parents killed and were then taken to be smuggled across the border. They may not even be registering what happened. It would make sense for them to be blocking that kind of trauma out. They must have escaped, somehow. All we can do is hope they adapt and are able to move on. If any parents can accomplish that, mine can." Magdeline said, "And that's the last sample. She looks great."

Sophie turned to look at the monitor, as Tessa stretched. "Oy! I felt that one! I'm just glad she's not wearing ice skates yet!"

Greece: Monday Oct. 31st

The wedding had been on Saturday and was beautiful, along with the reception, which included several lambs, roasted on a spit, fresh farm vegetables and fruits, all sorts of local pastries, wine, and dancing well into the next morning. Aida was very happy for her brother, but as much as she loved Santorini, she was ready for a real break, away from the rest of her family.

They had spent Sunday resting from the festivities, and today she was catching the ferry with her brother and his new wife to the mainland. From there, they were headed to another island, but Aida had booked tours of her own. She would start in Meteora and then come back down to Athens to do some shopping and catch the highlights of the acropolis before her flight back to Geneva on the 12th.

While her parents needed to be back sooner, they had told her to relax for an extra week before their really busy season began in mid-November.

The sun was setting when her train pulled into Kalampaka. When she first made the reservation, she had been uneasy about traveling in a strange country on Halloween, but then she learned that it was not a holiday commonly celebrated in Greece. However, as the taxi took her to her rental apartment, she could have sworn she saw a ghost.

It had happened before when she'd seen a man of similar build and posture. She had even experienced it with a lodge guest after her return from Italy. It only made sense that she would think of him now after watching her brother, new sister-in-law, and other couples, during the wedding and reception.

It took her a second to realize the taxi had stopped, and Soros, the driver, was unloading her bags. Getting out, she thanked and tipped him, then looked up the code for the door on her phone and retrieved the key that had been left for her in another box by the stairwell.

Aida made her way up to the third-floor unit she had rented for the week and collapsed on the bed. She was glad that she grabbed a gyro earlier. She was exhausted and not up to finding anything more tonight. Forcing herself from the bed, she unpacked a few necessities and looked around the unit. There was a decent sized bath and shower, a small sitting room and kitchen with a two-burner stove, a small refrigerator, and a coffee pot. She was pleased to see that some coffee and biscuits were waiting next to it. At least she would have something more for breakfast than the sad looking banana from her purse before having to food shop. She also doubted much, if anything, would be open when she woke up.

The night was warm, and she opened the bedroom windows. Unfortunately, they were not screened, and she had to close them against the mosquitos that loved to buzz in the night. She already had a few itchy red welts. She went to the balcony running across the back from the kitchen to the bedroom, and thankfully discovered a screened door there.

Then, she pulled back the covers and slid into a deep sleep.

Chapter 42

Kalampaka, Greece: Nov. 1st

Aida stretched and blinked against the sunlight streaming through the bedroom window. She rolled out of bed and pulled on capris and a t-shirt before making her way to the kitchen. She was surprised when she saw that it was already 8:30. She eyed the coffee pot. There was a delicious smell of baked bread coming from somewhere nearby, which reminded her of the bakery she and Kristor had gone to in Verona. That wasn't even his name, she told herself, as she rubbed her eyes and went to brush her teeth and take a quick shower.

Twenty minutes later, she was dressed again and heading out to follow her nose. She discovered the bakery just next door and was happy to see sfougatos, an egg dish, similar to a crustless quiche, and ordered two. She also bought some olive bread for later, yogurt, juice, and bottled water from the cooler along with an iced cappuccino to go.

As she left, she spied a fruit stand being set up across the street and made a note to come back later when her hands were not so full. It was all she could do to balance her cappuccino while getting back into her apartment.

Once back, she took the sfougatos, coffee, water, and her sad looking banana out on the balcony. It had been too dark when she arrived to see, but now, she could see the monasteries just to the right, standing high like guardians, looking over the town from their pillars of stone. It was amazing! The purple and pink bougainvillea bushes on either side of the balcony seemed to sparkle in the morning sun.

Aida had just arranged her food on a small table and was taking a sip of her cappuccino when she was surprised by a visitor peaking around the bougainvillea. He gave a short "meow" as if to introduce himself, then boldly came to sniff at the table.

"Hello to you too," she said, picking up her plate. "Do you mind? That's my breakfast, and you look well fed, much better than many of your relatives I've seen here."

She took a bite of banana, and the cat climbed onto the other chair a few feet away and simply stared at her, then began bathing himself.

Finishing her breakfast, she took the plate into the kitchen to rinse, then went back out to finish her coffee and browse through a guidebook.

"So, where do you suggest I start?" she asked the cat, who simply jumped down, walked over to her and began rubbing against her legs. "You sure are friendly. Do you have a name?" she asked, noting the collar he wore. "Can I see?" Aida stroked the cat and looked at the tag on his collar. "Well, hello, Talos. It's nice to meet you," Aida said, holding her hand to him. She was surprised when he put his paw in her hand. "You are a smart kitty," she told him.

Then she heard another door opening to her left, which must have been from the apartment units next door, and Talos jumped up on the wall and darted around the bougainvillea.

She smiled to herself, picked up the guidebook, went inside, and got ready to start exploring.

Aida hiked the trail to the convent first. She was surprised by how busy the trail was and discovered that there were two groups. One was doing a pilgrimage through ancient religious sites of Europe, and another were theology students. There were also several couples. Aida seemed to be the only solo traveler.

Once to the top, she was much relieved to discover a small stand selling, if not cold, at least wet beverages. She had finished the water bottle she brought with her at the midpoint.

For the Monastery, tomorrow, she decided she would take a tour bus. It was much warmer here than it had been on Santorini and there was no sea breeze.

Inside the gift shop, she bought some souvenirs for her family, post cards and another bottle of water for the trek down. The sun was setting by the time she returned. She had stopped to take many pictures along the way and wound up chatting with an American couple, Ivan and Jannie, who invited her to join them and some other friends for dinner.

Now, she was desperate for a shower and anxious for dinner. Slipping on a dress and sandals, she headed out, only to discover the evening had turned chilly and she had to run back up three flights of stairs for a sweater. She definitely would not be gaining weight on this vacation.

The taverna, where they met was one of the oldest in the area. Aida also soon discovered an ulterior motive in being invited; Jannie's younger and recently divorced brother, Matt, who was the only other solo person in the group.

Aida smiled pleasantly through the evening, and for the most part, enjoyed herself. She just needed to find a way to not wind up with Matt, being too interested. His sister was already making suggestions of things he and Aida might enjoy. It wasn't that there was anything wrong with him, she just didn't want to be in an international rebound relationship.

They were all still dancing and drinking when Aida made her excuses to leave. Jannie pulled her aside before she got to the door, and Aida simply told her that she wasn't comfortable vacation dating someone who lived on the other side of the world, and that she had booked this trip for some solitude before the winter rush. Fortunately,

Jannie understood, they exchanged emails and Aida headed back to her apartment.

She had left the balcony doors open, and she shivered against the cold, then put some coffee on, and bundled up. Surprisingly, she wasn't really tired tonight and took her coffee out on the balcony, where she gazed up at the clear night sky. A shooting star suddenly flashed by. She closed her eyes and made a wish. When she opened her eyes, Talos was staring at her from behind the bougainvillea, just as he had that morning, only this time he didn't come to join her, but turned back at the sound of a man's voice.

Aida froze and listened. He was speaking Greek, but the tone, the rhythm of his speech made her heart jump. A part of her wanted to sneak a peek through the bougainvillea, but reason stopped her. Maybe she should go back to the taverna and see if Matt was still there. At least he would distract her from her imagination. That would be selfish though, and the last thing she wanted to do was hurt him. So, she sat there, taking deep breaths between sips of coffee, as the man's voice continued on. He must have been on a phone call, she thought. If she was going to be here a week, she needed to get used to it. Looking back up at the sky, she saw two more shooting stars. She'd have to look and see if there was a meteor shower in the area. A meteor shower over Meteora, she thought and smiled.

The next morning, she discovered who Talos belonged to, when she saw him sitting outside her landlady, Maria's, bakery.

She hadn't made the connection before, as Maria had been gone when she arrived. As they chatted over coffees. Aida's curiosity got the best of her, and she asked about her neighbor.

"I noticed that Talos went over to his balcony whenever he heard him there."

"Ah, that is Sherman. He's a good friend, and he keeps an eye on this character," she said, looking at Talos, who yawned in reply. "If you are taking the tour of the Monasteries today, you may meet him. He's one of their top guides. He's also single and since he shaved, quite handsome," she added, with a smile at Aida.

"Thank you, Maria. Speaking of the tour, I should probably be heading out."

"Okay, just let me give you something. I'll be right back."

"Here," Maria said, returning with a bakery box. "You may have a different guide, but I know he will be there, and I want to give him these baklavas. I'd appreciate it. I twisted my ankle and can't do the three flights right now." she said.

"What if I don't see him?"

"You will, but if not, just ask. Everyone who works up there knows him."

"Relax," Aida told herself, as she walked to the center of town. "His name is Sherman, not Kristor, not Jonathan, Sherman. He's a Greek tour guide. And I need to stop talking to myself."

When she arrived at the ticket office, she was told that she would be with a guide named, Angela.

As they got off the bus at the Monastery, Aida asked Angela about Sherman.

"Oh, no problem. I'll be happy to give those to him or point him out to you, when we break for the gift shop," Angela said. "I believe his group is just ahead of ours."

"Thank you. I'd really rather not carry them around during the tour."

"Not to worry. I'll hand them straight off to Brother Archibald. They always meet up. He'll be sure to get them."

"Thank you," Aida said, handing off the baklava. For a minute, her heart sunk. A part of her needed to know who Sherman was. She shook the feeling off. She could still see him, even if she didn't see him here, he would still be her neighbor for five more days.

As they entered, she saw Angela hand over the baklava to a friar, she assumed was Brother Archibald. The friar then vanished through a side door. She could hear the tour finishing up in the chapel ahead, and she recognized the voice as Sherman. He seemed to be effortlessly changing between multiple languages. She tried to get to the front of her group to sneak a peek at him. She needed to put Kristor's ghost to rest.

By the time she made her way close enough, all she could see was his back, as he ushered his group to the next part of the tour. She took a deep breath, then turned to try and focus on what Angela was saying, but all she could hear was Kristor. It couldn't be him, she tried to convince herself, but something inside refused to be convinced.

When the tour finished, Aida looked around, hoping to spot him, but he seemed to have vanished.

Parcel Islands, South China Sea

The fishing vessel pulled into a small port and several men, in hazmat suits, offloaded the caskets. They had been told that they contained the bodies of those killed by a new virus, and that the bodies were being brought to the isolated island for study.

The building they were taken to didn't look like much. It was nestled between a dense grove of palm trees, their fronds waving over the roof that was lined with reflective solar panels. Between the reflection and the palms, they were nearly invisible from above, and the outside looked like no more than another navel storage facility.

Inside, both the building and the caskets were a completely different story.

The half-moon was shining brightly among the stars, and the night was clear, as the hazmat suits were stripped off the men, and their bodies were set adrift.

Then the doctors returned to the building and opened each casket, carefully, and hooked up the intravenous tubes and heart monitors.

Kalampaka, Greece

Most of Sherman's group had decided to hike down to the town, and the few who didn't returned with Angela's group. He opened the box of baklava and Archibald brought espressos.

Back in town, Aida looked up at the neighboring building. She noted that it also had a front door code pad, so she wouldn't be able to just go knock on his door. What would she say if she could? She had thought about it a million times, but nothing seemed right. And what if it wasn't him?

Regardless, she could hardly stand around all day, staring at the door. Maria had closed the bakery, bringing in her tables and chairs for the day, and there were no other outdoor seats on the block. The fruit market was still open, and she took the opportunity to buy some oranges and figs.

The late afternoon brought breezes and light, but steady, rain. It also brought Talos, meowing at her door.

"Oh no. You can stay out there. The balcony is covered. I'll even come join you. Maybe you can tell me more about our neighbor," she laughed at herself and was glad that no one else was around to hear her.

Talos just stared at her until she sat, then he hopped up to make himself comfortable on her lap.

"So, what do you do here when it rains?" she asked, stroking him.

In answer, he yawned, turned in a circle and settled back down for a nap.

"I see," she said, petting him as he purred, and Aida bit into a fig. Then, she took out her notebook, hoping that writing about her day would help her think. She wound up with a page full of doodles.

Talos had moved under the table, to continue his nap, when she went inside to make more coffee. And Aida eventually dozed off too. When she woke up, it was after 17:30. The rain had stopped, so she decided to take a walk and explore more of the town.

As she walked down the street, she saw a poster for a coral concert at a local orthodox church. She located the church and heard what she guessed was rehearsal. It was beautiful. There was also a café next door to it. She looked at the menu. They didn't open for dinner until 20:30. The concert began at 20:00, in just another twenty minutes. Ducking into a small market, she bought a marzipan and nut cake to hold her over.

She pulled her sweater close against a chill breeze as she waited in line. From the sound of conversations, she may have been the only tourist in attendance. That was good. It meant she would see and hear more of the real Greece. She didn't need to be able to understand Greek to enjoy the music.

After walking home from returning the tour bus, Sherman was completely soaked. He was getting his clothes out of the dryer when he heard a plaintive meowing at his balcony door.

"What's up?" he asked Talos as he opened the door to go out.

Talos raced inside.

"What do you think you're doing? It's not raining now, and I don't have any food for you," he said, trying to shoo the cat back out. Talos was stubborn though, so Sherman reached to grab him, but Talos slipped through his arms and hid himself under the shoe rack by the front door.

"What is going on with you? Did you run away from home to live with me? I hope not, because you can't stay," Sherman said as he pulled on a clean shirt from the dryer.

"Come on now, out with you. I need to go find myself some dinner."

Talos seemed to be ignoring him, as he swatted at the lanyard from Sherman's guide badge, that hung from the small table next to the shoe rack.

Sherman had just put on his jacket and opened the door, when Talos darted out with the badge in his mouth.

"I don't believe this," Sherman sighed, half laughing and half annoyed. He knew Talos would be stuck at the bottom of the stairs, or so he thought, until his neighbor came in and Talos made his escape.

Sherman hurried after him. He had known the cat since Maria got him as a kitten, and while he had always been mischievous, this was a new trick.

Every time he caught up with Talos, the cat would look back at him and dart off again. At this point, they were nearing the city center, and he was worried Talos might be hit by one of the many mopeds zooming around at this time of the evening. The streets were getting busy with everyone coming out for dinner. Then he noticed that Talos had stopped and made himself comfortable on the ledge of a fountain, where he also decided to drop Sherman's badge.

Hurrying over, he fished out the badge, gave Talos a look and grabbed him by the scruff of the neck, while he called Maria to tell her of her furry son's adventure.

A few minutes later, Maria pulled up on her moped, apologized to Sherman, and he thanked her for the baklava.

"Come by and get some more, anytime, on the house."

"Thank you, but don't worry. I saved the badge, and it looks like he led me to dinner," Sherman said, glancing at the café.

"I was wondering," Maria asked, "What did you think of your neighbor?"

"Who?"

"I gave her the baklava to take to you."

"I didn't meet anyone. She must have been in Angela's group. I got the baklava from Brother Archibald, who said it was from Angela."

"No, no, no. It was from Aida."

"Aida?"

"Yes, the pretty girl renting the apartment next door. Ah, there, that's her there, coming out of the church," Maria pointed. "I told you she was pretty, but you look like you just saw a ghost," she said. "What's wrong?"

"Nothing. Nothing's wrong, Maria. Thanks again for the baklava."

"You are welcome, now go introduce yourself. It looks like she's heading to the same café as you," Maria said, with a wink and sped off with Talos stuffed in a large purse draped over the handlebars.

Sherman stared. Was she really here alone? Maria didn't mention her family. What would he say to her? He thought about just leaving and hoping to avoid her until she left. He didn't want to avoid her though. He wanted to see her more than anything, but it had been so long. She could hate him now.

Even though he had explained the best he could that they couldn't be together, he had still sneaked out on her. Could he be with her now? His trigger was gone. He didn't think anyone was looking for him, aside from Richter, and maybe Mathias. Only one of his main reasons still existed. He didn't know if he could grow old with her.

He was just about to turn away when she looked up from her menu and straight at him. Their eyes locked and he knew he had to go to her. He walked slowly toward her table.

"Kristor," Aida said, when he reached her table.

"Sherman, please. May I?" he asked, motioning toward the empty chair across from her.

She nodded and wiped at her eyes. She didn't want to cry. She reached across the table toward him, and he took her hand.

"It's really you," she said, as she stroked her thumb along his finger. She could feel the pulse of their hands beating together.

"Aida. I'm so sorry."

The waiter came then with her order and asked if Sherman wanted anything. He simply asked for the special, anxious to give his full attention back to Aida.

"How would you like that cooked?" the waiter asked.

"Medium,"

"And did you want the pasta or the garden salad?"

"Garden," Sherman answered, barely glancing at the waiter.

"Red, white or rose?"

"Excuse me?"

"The wine, sir. Would you like…"

"Her choice," Sherman replied, motioning to Aida.

"Uhm, rose," she answered.

"Will there be anything else?" the waiter asked.

"No, thank you," they replied in unison, as they looked at the waiter with tense smiles.

When they looked back at each other, they suddenly broke into laughter.

"Oh, Aida. I don't know where to start."

"Are you safe now?" she asked.

"I think so. I wanted to… I dreamed of seeing you again, but until just a couple months ago, I didn't even dare think about it, and it's been so long, I thought you wouldn't want to see me."

"I dreamed about you too. When I first arrived, then at the monastery today, and when I heard your voice, I thought my mind was playing tricks on me. I only saw you from behind, but…"

The waiter returned with the wine, and they waited patiently while he uncorked the bottle and poured. He barely turned away before returning with a cheese platter.

When he left again, Sherman said, "I'm not even sure what I ordered. I just thought asking for the special would be the fastest way to get him to leave. I was obviously wrong," he said, as the waiter returned with his salad and a basket of breads.

Aida smiled and held her glass for a toast. "To reunions,"

"To reunions."

Chapter 43

Saint Petersburg, Russia: Nov. 11th

This was Jack's first day in Russia, and he was anxious to check out the ice. Helsinki had been stiff competition, but he had just pulled it off.

He was now walking down Nevsky Prospekt. He stopped to look up as he came to the Kazan Cathedral and took several photos. The architecture here was amazing. In many ways it was like Europe, but he hadn't been able to think about sightseeing when he'd been in Paris, and even in Geneva, he had been hopelessly distracted. Now he was going to enjoy himself!

He still didn't have all the answers he wanted, but he was content to focus on skating again, and this time it was all for himself. He wasn't worrying about his parents, or Sophie, or anyone else. He was simply fulfilling his own life goals, and he felt a sense of freedom that he had been missing for four years.

He clicked a shot of a dove descending onto a cross atop the dome of the cathedral, then checked his watch and hurried on to the metro station.

***

Josephine looked at the ring on her finger as it glinted in the sunlight over the garden. It was a deep red ruby, pear cut, and surrounded with five small diamonds on either side, in an antique platinum band.

She couldn't legally marry him without going through the legalities of divorcing Simon and exposing herself. Still, he had friends among the priests, and they had not asked questions, but performed a simple private ceremony with Alice and the gardener, Josiah, as witnesses. She could hardly believe she was a polygamist. She laughed out loud.

Carl had gotten word to her about Pollina and Amber. Thankfully, by the time she heard about Amber's abduction, she was already safely back at the university, and they doubted that even Richter would try again. At least for now, he would be in hiding, and they would be safe. Her only concern was what he might be plotting while he was hiding.

Even after all the raids, she knew that there were other projects, aside from Sweden. She had taken copies of what files she could before leaving and given everything to Carl, but there was much that Simon hadn't kept in Scotland. She had also given Carl, Simon's laptop, but they were still trying to find a way to bypass the retina scan without erasing the hard drive.

She walked through the rose garden and onto the enclosed sunroom off the back terrace, where Tatiana, one of the staff, was serving tea.

Malachi was there, reading and waiting for her. She bent to kiss him before she sat, and he excused Tatiana, preferring to pour his own tea. He poured one for Josephine as well.

"I was thinking," Malachi said. "We never had a proper honeymoon. Alice is doing well, and she already assured me that she would be fine if you and I were to take a week and go down to the Caspian Sea. I have a small dacha not far from the beach. What do you say?"

"Da, I say da," Josephine smiled at him.

"Then why don't I drop you and Alice to do some shopping along Nevsky Prospekt? It will be a good test for her. I'd hate to think of her staying alone in this big house for a week."

"I think Josiah has a crush on her," Josephine said.

"In that case, I want to be certain that she can be comfortable getting out on her own. She'll have full access to my car and driver, but I'm thinking we should take her through the metro. If she's going to stay here and be independent, I think it's time for her to start experiencing how to do so."

"Have you asked her?"

"Yes and no. I mentioned shopping, but not the metro. Her Russian is perfect though. So, aside from anxiety, I think she will do fine, and there is no time like the present to find out."

Alice straightened her, now black, hair. She decided she liked the way the raven shade complemented her eyes. She smiled in the mirror. It was time to start living this new life. She wondered how Sherman was doing back in Greece. Maybe someday she would be able to visit there again.

She smiled in the mirror and smoothed on some lip balm. The Russian air was dryer than she was used to, and she reminded herself to look for some good lotion while they were out.

She checked herself in the mirror again and took a deep breath. She was as ready as she would ever be.

Athens, Greece

Aida and Sherman wound their way up the trail to the acropolis. Her flight was supposed to leave the next day, and she hated the idea of leaving him. They had spent nearly every minute of the past days together, with Sherman taking time off to come down and be her personal travel guide in Athens.

The first two days, they had talked almost non-stop, catching each other up on the past three and a half years. He told her as much as he could and was surprised to find out that she had met with Soren and about the situation with Ana. He even considered coming back with her, but they agreed, it was safer for him to stay in Greece. They would work something out and had been discussing that something for the past few days.

"I don't want to leave," Aida said, as they sat on the steps of the temple of Athena. She laid her head on his shoulder.

"I wish..." Sherman started, "I wish that I was... a normal man from a normal family."

"Is there something more you haven't told me?" Aida asked.

"You know there is, but I couldn't even begin to explain it."

"You could try. Even if it doesn't make sense, just tell me. Trust me, please."

"I do trust you, probably more than anyone. I also couldn't take it if anything hurt you, including me."

"Look," she said, turning to face him directly. "I know that your family was involved in some weird medical experiments. I know that Ana underwent some strange medical tests when she was abducted, and I know that your family is connected to the raids on medical facilities back in September. You've told me that much. I also know about your brothers and that the eldest, Richter, is dangerous. How much more can there be? Nothing will change who you are and the fact that I love you."

"I love you too, Aida, and I want to grow old with you."

"Is that a proposal?"

He smiled and brushed her hair back from her forehead. "It's a simple truth that may not be possible because of some of the experiments my father was doing."

"Are you sick?" she asked, suddenly concerned that he was hiding some terminal illness.

"No. In fact, I don't ever remember being sick. I have a, how should I say, enhanced immune system. I also have genes that have been programmed to slow my aging."

"What do you mean?"

"I mean that when you are eighty, I won't look much

different. There, that's it. I know it sounds crazy, but I literally can't grow old with you. I mean there's a chance that there may be a way to reverse the programing, but..."

"Wait, stop, please," she said, and stood.

For a minute, he wasn't sure if she was going to just leave or laugh at him. She did neither.

"You're basically saying that your father succeeded in slowing the aging process. That is something people have been trying to do, probably from the beginning of time. Is there a way to slow mine down?" she asked, sitting down beside him again.

"I don't know. The genes were manipulated and inserted invitro. You do believe me?"

"Honestly? I don't know. I mean, how old are you?"

"Thirty-eight."

"You do look younger, but not that much. Are you sure those genes are working?"

"We, my brothers and I, were programmed to age normally to a certain point. In a normal life span, I would never look over forty."

"I guess I'll have to save up to afford plastic surgery if I don't want you to have to feel like you're kissing your mother or granny in another twenty years."

He took her hands and kissed them. "I don't care about that. I've met your mother, and she's lovely."

"Wait until I show you a picture of granny."

He smiled.

"You know," she started, "it's possible that in another ten years, science may be able to reverse everyone's aging. It's also possible my plane could crash tomorrow. What I'm saying, is life is an unknown. There's no guarantee either of us will live to see the next day, no matter how our genes are programmed. I believe we should live and try to enjoy each day as it comes."

Sherman took her face in his hands and kissed her.

Saint Petersburg, Russia: Nov. 18th

Josephine and Malachi left earlier that morning and Alice was feeling restless already. She spent a couple of hours helping Josiah rake leaves in the garden before lunch. He was nice, but she wasn't ready to think about a relationship, and she didn't want to hurt him. With that thought, she decided to stay inside the rest of the day. She spent some time after lunch browsing and reading in the library, but she couldn't seem to focus. She could go into the city, but was she ready to do that on her own? There was only one way to find out, she thought, and called the driver to bring the car around.

As they were driving towards the center, they passed a skating rink, and Alice decided she would buy some skates and go to the rink herself. She hadn't skated, except for the one time in New York, but she remembered how free she felt in those moments. She wanted that feeling again.

***

Sophie made her way through customs with Jeremy, who ran to Nick when he saw him. Nick picked him up as Sophie pulled their carryon through and fell into Nick's arms.

"I missed you two, I mean three, so much!" Nick said, looking at Sophie. "She's definitely growing."

"You mean I've gotten fatter," she pouted.

"I didn't mean that at all. You're radiant when you're pregnant," Nick defended.

Sophie smiled at him.

"I missed you too!" She said, looking up to kiss him. "And I have gotten fatter. I've been eating too much of Soren's cooking. He taught Jeremy and their boys how to make cookies last week."

"They were good too! Right mom?" Jeremy asked, from his perch, now on Nick's back.

"Too good! From now on, I'll need to play rabbit."

"How do you play rabbit, mom?" Jeremy asked.

"You see who can eat the most vegetables at every meal."

"That doesn't sound like a very fun game."

Nick and Sophie laughed, and she pointed to her first bag coming around the luggage belt.

***

That evening, Alice had the driver, Pioter, take her to the ice rink. At first, she was tentative, but soon she fell in line with some of the other skaters and began to just do simple laps. She didn't want to make a spectacle of herself. She just wanted to be normal and free.

She did laps around the rink until it began to get crowded, then she skated off and walked over to a food truck, where she bought a couple of pirozhki, a vegetable kabob and two hot teas. She gave one of the pirozhki and teas to Pioter.

"Thank you, Madame," Pioter said with a smile.

He was a nice, fatherly type, and Alice was happy to have someone to share a casual dinner with.

"Do you like to watch skating as well?" Pioter enquired.

"I do."

"Well then, perhaps you would enjoy the 'Frost Trophy International'. It is taking place this weekend at Udelny Park, the largest rink in Saint Petersburg. My daughter, Carine, has an extra ticket if you are interested?"

"I am. Thank you Pioter!"

"Not at all. It is good to see you out and smiling," he said as he sent a text to his daughter. "Where would you like to go next?"

"I think I'd like to go back to the house now."

"Very well."

On the way, Carine called, and they made the arrangements. Carine would come to the house so that

Alice could meet her, and then Pioter would drive them to the event, where they would meet up with Carine's friends.

Alice was excited to be meeting knew people. It gave her a sense of fitting in, and if Carine was half as charming as her father, Alice was certain they would be friends.

Once back at the house, Alice thanked Pioter again, chose a book from the library and went to her room. This was all going to work out, she thought to herself, as she walked the ornate hall. She stopped and looked out past the sunroom at the falling snow. In the morning there would be a fresh blanket, covering all that had been before. It would be beautiful and fresh, just the way she needed to believe her life could now be.

***

Victoria received the information of her family's escape and instructions on how to have her triggers deprogrammed. There was a specific hypnotist she was directed to go to in Moscow. It had taken five weeks to feel certain that they had deprogrammed both triggers, and now she felt as if the weight of the world had been lifted.

She clutched the train ticket to Saint Petersburg. She could hardly believe she was going to be with her family again.

Chapter 44

Switzerland: Nov. 19th

Ana was excited for Aida. She knew her friend had met someone in Greece, yet for some reason Aida was being secretive as to his identity.

"I can't believe you don't have a picture of him," Ana said.

"It's awkward," Aida tried to explain. "I knew him before, and I don't know how to tell my family. You see, they were worried that he hurt me before. So, I deleted the photos on my phone, just in case my parents decide to snoop. He has them though."

Ana couldn't quite believe this, but she had overheard them saying that they worried about who he really was. For a minute Ana thought it was Kristor, but Aida said his name was Sherman, and he was a Greek tour guide. That was about all she could get, but Aida had never pushed Ana to reveal her secrets. So, Ana decided to show the same respect in return.

In fact, Ana was distracted by a man herself. Ever since Brazil, she had been messaging with Carlos, the driver who helped her escape Charles. He was coming to visit in a couple of weeks, and Ana was both excited and nervous about introducing him to... Well, technically he was her brother, but for practical purposes, Stephan would continue to be known as her father.

Saint Petersburg, Russia

Alice recognized Sophie immediately, when she saw her in the lady's room at the ice rink. Ducking into a stall, she realized that Sophie being here only meant one thing; Jack was here.

She thought about texting Carine that she was unwell, but that would only cause Carine and her father to worry. So, after she was certain Sophie was gone, she left the stall, washed her hands, pulled her hat down and her hair forward to hide her profile. She would have to tough this out. She had been in far worse situations, but none of them had ever felt like this.

She watched through the entire competition. She watched Jack and cheered as he received his trophy. She zoomed in to take a photo on her phone. He looked so happy.

Alice managed to hide her feelings through it all, until she was back, alone in her room, and then she cried more tears than she had over her entire lifetime. She cried, until she was completely drained, and exhaustion overtook her.

Saint Petersburg, Russia: Nov. 21st

Jack and Nick were both ecstatic as they boarded the flight to Montreal. Sophie, Nick, and Jeremy were in the Center row and Jack thought for a while, that he would have two seats to himself. It was Jeremy who alerted them.

"Mom, look! It's one of my aunts!"

They all looked up at once, and for a minute, Jack felt like he'd been struck by lightning. Then Victoria reintroduced herself and took the seat beside him.

"We only met briefly in Geneva," she said. "What brought you all to Russia?" she asked, turning to Nick and Sophie. They talked for a while and brought each other up to date.

"That's wonderful! I'm so glad they're safe!" Sophie said, when she heard Victoria was going to meet her parents and brother, who had managed to escape prior to the raids.

Sophie didn't mention the possibility of being reunited with her own parents. There had been no messages from them, but she wasn't going to think about that. She had Nick, Jeremy, Tessa, Jack, and his parents. She had a family.

She even had another mother in Claire and sisters in Rosie, Magdeline and Victoria.

Sophie could see that Jack was uneasy, but there wasn't much they could do. The flight was packed.

Nova Scotia, Canada: Dec. 24th

It had been awkward at first, but after nine hours on a plane, they had relaxed, and Jack found himself enjoying Victoria's company.

Now, she and her family were living in the same town, and they were at the Christmas market together picking up last minute gifts for their families, who were spending Christmas day together at Nick and Sophies new house.

Sophie and Nick decided not to sell the other house, but to let Victoria and her family stay there until they could readapt to normal life and find a place of their own.

Christmas was also the date that Dave and Lidia had chosen to be married, and they would all be present to celebrate via video.

Greece: Jan. 7th - 2023

After the holiday guests were gone, Aida's family closed the lodge for a week and headed back to Greece for another wedding.

Her family was not as thrilled about Aida's wedding as Hal's. It wasn't that they disliked Sherman, but that they couldn't quite understand why he was now working as a tour guide in Greece, under a different name. Also, his strange disappearance, four years ago, made them uneasy.

As Kristor, he told them he was a book editor, turned writer. Now he was using another name as a tour guide. He also seemed to have no family, and the idea of their only daughter moving to Greece, to be his wife, set off serious alarm bells.

Aida tried to explain with the best cover they could think of. She told her parents he was under witness protection. But, while that explained the life and name change, it did nothing to quell their unease.

"What had he been witness to?" her parents asked. "Does it mean that you could be in danger?"

Aida explained that for their safety and hers, nothing about his past could be divulged. She wasn't even supposed to know what she did.

Fortunately, his neighbors in Kalampaka and the people he worked with seemed to love Sherman, and seeing the friendships he had, helped calm her parents to a degree.

They had a simple wedding in a small chapel, with only her family, and a few of Sherman's friends as witnesses, and Brother Archibald officiating. It was also the first wedding they had been to with a cat in the wedding party, but Talos could not be left out, and surprisingly, managed to keep his bow tie on through the photos.

They needed to be cautious with the photos too. Aida knew Ana would want to see them, and if she were to recognize Sherman, it could cause big problems. For this reason, he grew back his beard and wore implants.

For their honeymoon, Hal's in-laws offered the use of their house on Santorini. At the train station in Athens, Aida hugged her family farewell and promised she would come back to visit soon.

"I'm not really that far away. Just a short flight," she said, when her mother started to cry.

"As long as you're happy," her father said.

"I am."

"Remember, if anything goes wrong sis," Fredrick said, "You have three big brothers who will hop on that short flight and beat the living daylights out of him."

All three of her brothers threw Sherman a warning look. "Not to worry," Sherman replied, "I'd do the same."

With that, they shook hands, and her family left for the airport, while Aida and Sherman headed for the port.

France

Richter made his way through the tunnel toward the chateau. He had followed the network of tunnels from Berlin and was tired of feeling like a mole. He was ready to come back above ground and ready to find Mathias and eliminate the threat he posed. Then he would go back for Carl and Jonathan.

He was concerned when he discovered the exit via the pool was non-operational. Fortunately, the one into the Chateau opened easily, and he took the elevator up. He wondered who had been down there. Had it been broken on purpose? It would have to have been, he thought. If it was Mathias, wouldn't he have disabled the elevator? Even though, it was the most modern, it was the most well disguised, but his brothers would all have known about it.

Later, he went to inspect the entrance to the winery and the other house. He could fix the one to the winery, but there was really no need for it aside from an alternate escape route. What he discovered when he moved on toward the other house though, gave him confidence that he would not be in need of any escape, because he could simply do as Carl had done and become his brother.

He smiled as he looked down on Mathias, entombed in the cryogenic coffin. He could make it a real coffin. All he would have to do is pull the plug, but then he would have to deal with eliminating a body, and why do that when there was so much potential to use Mathias in his future research. He was even more pleased as he checked the other sections and discovered who else was there.

***

After the holidays, and after Dave and Lidia returned from their honeymoon, everyone got together via video for a round table to discuss the findings from the various files and research.

Philip and Dave started off with the genealogy. "Josephine's grandmother was Lilianna Fontaine. During the war and after Lilianna's husband was killed in 1941, her daughter, Marta, and her family came to live with her and Marta's younger brother, Michael, at the Fontaine chateau. At some point, the Nazi's commandeered the estate. In 1944, Marta's husband, son, and brother were killed. In 1947, both women were declared dead. Rumor had it that both Marta and Lilliana had been raped and were pregnant when last seen. However, I was told that at some point, Lilianna returned and died in 1989," Dave said and passed the story to Philip.

"Further research proves that both women survived and were taken, supposedly with the fathers of their babies, to Brazil, where I found a marriage certificate registered to a Lilianna Fontaine and Hans Joseph Ikeman. She gave birth to twin boys, Ulf, and Peter. Around the same time, I found a marriage record for a Marta Elisabeth Fontaine and Herbert Wilhelm Heisenberg. Marta had four recorded children with Herbert. The first was a daughter, Analina, in 1945.

"I'll start with Analina, and hopefully you can all follow this. In 1970 she married Hans Meschner. Han's father was Rudolf Meschner. Rudolf's brother was Joseph Meschner, father of the infamous Dr. Alexander Meschner. Joseph died in 1952 and Alexander's mother, Mary, remarried in 1955 to a Gavin Marshall. They moved to Canada together and had a son named Thomas, who is father to Shane's wife, Patricia. The rest of this story, I believe you already know.

"Marta also had a daughter named Natalie. Natalie married Franz Nadier. They had two children, a girl and a boy. The boy, Adam, changed his surname, for reasons we can only guess at, to Hisdak. According to Cora, whose connection we will get to eventually, Adam caused the death of both his mother and sister. After that, he and his father came to France.

"So far, I've only been able to follow one of Marta's sons, Simon. Care to pick it up Dave?"

"Simon moved to Paris 1971, where he went to medical school. Then, whether knowingly or unknowingly, married his first cousin, Josephine, who had become a nurse. This however, is not where Josephine's involvement started. Let us back up a little.

"Going back to Lilianna. She was Scotch-Irish and moved to France with her husband, Peter Fontaine. Aside from Marta and Michael, she had two older children, who left to go to University in Scotland. Their names were Emma and Paul. Emma, who married a Gerard Chedaux, was mother to Josephine and Lily. Lily married Nigel O'Hare and they adopted Sophie. Paul is the father of Jack's mother, Anne, and her brother Quill, who now lives in New York.

"We know that Josephine had an unplanned pregnancy at seventeen, and was sent to Paris, to stay with her father's family until after she gave birth. We don't know whether the baby was a boy or a girl. We do now know from a diary discovered by Anne and Ben in Scotland, that the father was none other than Alexander Meschner. No blood relation, but in case you lost track, he is her cousin Analina's husband's first cousin. See how the family is beginning to weave together?" Dave asked. "And now, I'll hand it back to Philip."

"As you know," Philip began, "the original case that tied this all into Brazil, was the kidnapping of Ana Martinson and her mother, Sarah. It took a lot of digging, but we have a couple of connections there as well now. This is in large part due to Professor Crabben, wherever he may be, and the file that he sent to Sarah, who is also MIA. I digress. Going back to Alexander Meschner's father, Joseph, we discovered close working ties with him and a General Walter Heisenberg. We don't yet know the relation to Herbert Wilhelm, but we assume it's there. General Heisenberg and Joseph Meschner worked closely on various Nazi research programs. One of these programs was named; "Operation Infinity Genes". The goal of this program was to enable certain individuals, who were proclaimed worthy, to live into infinity.

"The file we were sent on Ana allows us to see that General Heisenberg and Joseph Meschner succeeded, to a degree. When Joseph died in 1952, Heisenberg enlisted his brother Rudolf.

"General Heisenberg was determined that he and his line live forever. He chose Rudolf and Joseph's sister, Gretta, as the mother. This was likely the first ever case of invitro fertilization, and it succeeded in the birth of three children, two girls and one boy, in November 1951. The girls were named Cora and Lona, AKA, Leona. The boy's name was Wilhelm. Wilhelm was separated from the girls and raised by his father, while the girls were raised by Gretta.

"Wilhelm later raised a son, Charles, who is in fact, his younger brother. The mother is unknown. So as to not weaken the infinity genes, they continued to use the general's sperm and DNA. General Heisenberg did not die as recorded but lived until April 1992. His son Wilhelm disappeared in 1998. Technically, this means that when Leona told Ana she was her aunt, she wasn't lying. The other interesting fact we found is that Charles is a twin. His brother was named Walter, after the general, but as of now, we can't say what happened to him."

"Ana came up with the other tie, when she discovered a mirror image of herself in a book on the Prussian royal family. We can trace Stephen Martinson's family tree back to Prussian royalty as well. This likely explains why they chose Sarah, for Charles to impregnate and why they would still use sperm from the Martinson lineage. My guess is that there is another more direct tie to Sarah as well."

A baby could be heard crying in the background of Philip's computer, and they all took a break, while Philip went to help with his daughter, Alexandria.

When they all returned, it was Claire and Suzanna who picked up the narrative.

Through the family letters and photos Suzanna sent for, they pieced together that their mother did in fact have an affair, but not with Samuel. The letters showed a longstanding romance with a friend of Samuel, Detrik Hoffman, who had yet to be connected to the family. He was now added to the list of people to look into.

In conclusion, Larry and Nick shared what they found out about the books and charts at Simon's lake house.

The books were a combination of royal genealogies, astronomy, astrology, alchemy, and other occult subjects, as well as medical journals.

It was a well-known fact that many high-ranking Nazi's were very much into astrology. Some even maintained personal astrologers. The files that Prof. Crabben sent, as well as those found at the house in Scotland, confirmed that P2P, the Chinese project, and others, were firmly rooted in astrology.

There were records of where certain heavenly bodies had to be at conception. Dates of certain occurrences were listed side by side with lists of procedures. Even the star charts of the genetic doners were included, and certain procedures to add individual genes needed to be in sync with those individual's charts.

"To sum it up," Larry said, "It would take several lifetimes to understand it all, but at least now we know how all of us are connected. There is a lot we may never know. The question is, how much do we need to know?"

"I know some of us, would like to find family members who are still missing," Suzanna started, nodding to Shane.

"While this is true," Shane followed, "at this point, I think we can understand that they had their reasons for leaving, and perhaps they did it for our benefit. At least I'd like to believe that," he concluded and left to check on Daniel.

There was an uncomfortable moment of silence until Lidia cleared her throat and nudged Dave.

"Go ahead," Dave said, smiling. "You tell them."

"We're pregnant!" Lidia burst out.

"I know we're not family, but…"

"Yes, you are! Genetics aren't everything!" Magdeline exclaimed.

Congratulations and agreement were voiced all around.

"Siblings-Regeneration"

Switzerland: July- 2033

Kenneth watched on as the first five returned from their swim across the lake. They were nearly ready for the next phase.

At only eight, Kenneth had gone for training at one of the largest bases in Northern China. He was there for two years before he was advanced to the training in Egypt. That is where he learned the arts of Meta and Quantum physics. After three years, he was sent to the United States and the next year, he was in Beijing, China, testing and receiving accolades for his scores.

Soon he would run his very own project. For now, he was enjoying learning from the great generals and top scientists, like his part brothers and fathers.

The camp was full this year with enough developed students of P2P to keep up the training for the younger children. They were his very own squad, and he was proud of them as well as himself.

He thought back to his summers here. He had been five the first year, and he loved the long swims back and forth to the small island in the middle of the lake where the combat trainings were held.

Wilhelm came through the woods behind him, followed by the woman called Leona. She was always a mystery to Kenneth. She was the one who found and rescued him, placing him safely with her brother Wilhelm. For that, Kenneth was forever grateful. In some ways, he considered her a second mother. The training he received both from her and while he was in Egypt, took him to a level beyond them all. He had developed what he thought of as a third eye, and that eye told him that his real mother was still alive somewhere.

Yes, soon enough he would have his own project to direct, but first, he was determined to discover where they were hiding his mother.

Berlin, Germany: October 22nd - 2033

Alexander walked out of the coffee shop on the north bank of the Spree River in Berlin. He looked at the ledger balance on his Basink app and transferred the remaining JCL coin from his last job into his sister's account and used the tip-bot to send a few more drops for her birthday.

Her response was instant. "Thank you, but it's your birthday too, silly."

"I know," he messaged, "but you have better taste, so I thought I'd let you shop for both our gifts." he added a smiley face and received the same back.

It was a ritual they had, and it worked great. Neither was ever disappointed in their gifts.

Amanda was able to work anonymously, while Alexander made the deals on her behalf.

Their father had set it up for them years before out of determination to maintain their freedom, should he ever be discovered.

They had not known their father's secret until he died five years before, and they were passed the keys to his private database. It took them awhile to absorb the implications, but they now understood why they had been so restricted growing up.

Today they were twenty-five and free, for the most part, but in the back of their minds they knew a day could come when their father's warnings and fears for the world would come to pass. Once that happened, their lives could never be the same. They would have to take on the responsibility of the DNA they inherited.

Nova Scotia: November 19th -2033

Jack skated across the frozen pond, with both his son and twin daughters chasing behind him.

He let them pass him and then followed them over to where their mother, Victoria, and aunt Sophie were grilling the fish. Nick and Jeremy had made a huge bonfire. Cody and Shannon, Matt and Mindy and Tom, with his fiancée, Megan, would be there to join in soon.

Life was pretty amazing, Jack thought. He never could have imagined how the crazy events of years before could have led him to so much happiness.

Sophie and Nick's daughters, Tessa and Abigale, were roasting marshmallows with Matt and Mindy's boys, Olan, and Chris. Shannon and Cody were expecting their third child now, and Tom, after searching unsuccessfully for his father, before having him declared dead, was finally happy.

Over the past ten years, nearly the entire world had seen a calm overtake the chaos. And even though many mysteries, like what had become of Sophie's parents, still remained, Jack couldn't remember a time when he, his family and best friends had ever been happier.

Parcel Islands, South China Sea: Dec. 4th - 2033

Doctor Marks and Professor Chee inspected the occupants of the glass coffins.

"The gills look well developed," Marks said.

"I am not completely satisfied with the oxygen readings," Chee replied. "I say we give them at least two more weeks."

They advanced to the next section, and Chee brightened. "These are my favorite. I do not believe you will have seen these before," Chee said, smiling at Marks.

Marks leaned over to look in the coffin and jumped back when Chee stimulated the nerve to activate the change.

"Godzilla would be proud," Marks stuttered.

Chee laughed. "Where do you think the idea came from?"

"As long as he and our King Kongs over there don't start fighting each other."

"I think not. Amazing how human they look. Is it not?" Chee asked, as he took the readings and they moved to the next section. "As you know, we incorporated both Gibbon and Baboon genes in about half of the subjects and chimpanzee in others. It is wonderful how the modification worked, so that only the behavioral qualities are visible. He could be your son," Chee smiled, looking down on the occupant of another capsule.

"In a way, I feel these are all our children. After all, it is our research that gave them life," Marks replied.

Chee smiled again and nodded.

"So, how much longer until we can start the release?" Marks asked.

"I see no reason we can't do a test run anytime now."

Marks bent over one of the capsules to more carefully examine the occupant and take notes. Chee released the coffin locks, gave the trigger, then stood back and watched.

Beijing, China

Professor Ling was growing more concerned. Since she was first alerted to the missing samples, she had been going through the records of those with access. This morning, she discovered that her own records were being accessed, and her supervisor had advised her not to waste her time. Something in his tone seemed more like a warning than advice.

She thought back to her colleague, Dr. Cai, who first put her on to the possibility that samples logged as going to one location and project, were in fact going elsewhere.

When she looked deeper into the various projects, she realized her colleague was right, but before they had a chance to discuss it, Dr. Cai was killed in a car crash.

Ling trembled, wondering about the odds that the crash was really an accident.

www.ingramcontent.com/pod-product-compliance
Lightning Source LLC
Chambersburg PA
CBHW022232020726
47496CB00004B/868